AKILINA
OUT OF THE WOODS

PATRICIA A. BOWMER

Published in Australia by For Your Inspiration Pty Ltd
E-mail: info@patriciabowmer.com
Website: patriciabowmer.com
First published in Australia 2012
This edition published 2012

ISBN: 978-0-646-56716-7
Copyright © Patricia A. Bowmer 2012
Cover design, typesetting: Chameleon Print Design

National Library of Australia Cataloguing-in-Publication entry
Author: Bowmer, Patricia A.
Title: Akilina out of the woods / Patricia A. Bowmer.
ISBN: 9780646567167 (pbk.)
Dewey Number: A823.4

For Gary, Tin Ko and Jing Jing

Contents

PART 1: DESCENT

CHAPTER 1

One moment, their car was carefully hugging the pavement of the two-lane suspension bridge. The next, it was head-to-head with a yellow and black truck that had swerved directly into its path.

It barreled towards them like a wasp, staring at Halley with its dead headlight-eyes. Its metal crash bar jutted mercilessly, sneering *Hit me, if you dare.* Halley strained to see through the truck's tinted windscreen but all she could see was a mirrored reflection of cloud and sky. She narrowed her eyes. A man's face became visible, his eyes hidden behind a pair of dark sunglasses. The man wasn't moving. His face was devoid of all expression. It was like he was already dead.

Halley went cold all over. She saw it all in a moment, and she saw what would happen. But she didn't move: she couldn't decide what to do. Sean, asleep, was oblivious.

Just before the crash, the truck swerved back into its own lane, avoiding the direct head-on collision. But, in the avoidance, it caused something far, far worse. Halley's car was hit on the left fender – a grazing, scraping, pushing blow – and it was useless, useless, to hold onto the steering wheel so tightly that her knuckles turned white: the car's wheels were no longer in contact with the road.

Staring at her hands, her eyes found her ring finger, where the wedding ring used to be. She'd just removed it that morning, yet it was as if it had never been there at all. Having worn the ring for two years, this surprised her – it should have left an indentation in the skin, at least for a little while. It was painful for her to lift her eyes from her bare finger, from the reality of the choices she had made. When she did, she found she was staring out through the windscreen at the empty blue sky.

For the car was flying, ever so lightly, ever so gracefully through the air, over the crash barrier. They were surrounded by gulls. Cawing and flying, in their natural element. Soaring.

The car rose high in the air. In the rearview mirror, the suspension bridge was etched in the sky behind them. Sorrow engulfed her. Her plan to end their marriage suddenly seemed so insurmountably foolish. She had plenty of time for regret, plenty of time to think about what she and Sean would not be doing together for the rest of their lives. The children they might have had; Sean's birthday party; the trip to Africa. All gone, all in that instant. And it was Friday night. Silly, how sorry she would be to miss the trip to the pub. She willed herself to wake up, to go back to the seconds before the crash, to do something different. But she couldn't. Her entire life had led her here, to this moment of inaction.

The car, buoyant, surfing the air, seemed to realize that this was not its element. With a heave, it turned downwards, nose first, and plunged deep, deep into the cold, dark waters below the bridge. Almost immediately stillness engulfed the scene. But for a few bubbles drifting seamlessly to the surface, the accident might not have happened at all.

Underwater, all was silent, but for the very faint and immensely fragile sound of their heartbeats. They were alive. For how long depended entirely on Halley.

CHAPTER 2

Eden watched from the riverbank. She knew Halley had been planning on telling Sean that afternoon that it was over; that she never should have married him; that, even from the very beginning, it had been a mistake. She felt a lump in her throat. It wasn't the first time she'd watched helplessly as Halley made a disastrous decision, but she didn't judge her. She understood. And she knew she had to be nearby, to help Halley pick up the pieces. That's why she'd been so close.

But without any warning, their car had gone flying off the bridge. The sound of the car striking the water hit her like a blow. She began shaking, the tears flowing freely down her cheeks.

"Oh no oh no oh no...oh, Halley. Don't let this be. You should've just let him love you. Then everything would have been okay..."

Then she remembered something more important than Halley and more important than Sean. More important than everything.

"What about the baby – what will happen to the baby?" Her eyes grew huge. Usually Eden was the first to laugh, and her giggles were a delight to hear. Now it felt to her like she'd never giggle again.

Crouching low, she held onto the gnarled surface of a low-hanging willow tree, and got quiet, watching the skin of the river, observing the slow bubbles surface where the car had gone under. She couldn't help Halley; she was just a little girl, and the current was very strong.

She stared at the river, as if it held the answers. Despite her youth, or perhaps because of it, Eden could think about a problem for as long as it took to figure out the answer. She usually knew right away, but if she didn't, she'd be patient and think about it. Hard. She watched the river. The river: moving fast, with hidden depths, full of all sorts of unknown things. With ups and downs and twists and turns. It knew its way. If only Halley knew her way so well.

"Save the baby, save the baby, save the baby," she chanted to herself, as if, by saying it enough times, she could make it come true. Her sing-song voice filled the air. Because it made her feel better, she continued the mantra for some time. The willow dropped slow-falling leaves into the river's flow as she thought, and she watched their small yellowness swirl away.

She decided. "A new place to begin," she said. With her decision, her ready smile returned.

Standing up, she turned away from the river, and began to walk into the deeper part of the dense, dark forest. A ten-year-old girl she may have been, but in her walk, there was something about her that made her seem older than her years.

PART 2:
FOUR YEARS
EARLIER

CHAPTER 1

Someone was in their bedroom. Standing over her. It was dark. The dead of night. Halley tried to scream. But she was frozen. The girl! It was the girl again. Her face, invisible in the dark. Halley tried in vain to move, to break free. Her heart pounded. *Help*, she screamed in her head, *help, help*!

A moment later the spell broke, and she was flailing her arms and shouting and sitting up in bed in a panic. Fernando reached for her. What's wrong babe? Oh my god oh my god oh my god someone was here what are you talking about take your hands off me what take your hands your hands your hands ok babe ok.

He lay back down and was asleep in seconds.

But it wasn't ok. It was nowhere near ok.

Halley continued sitting up, breathing fast, cold with sweat, with panic. She was alone again. Yet someone had been here. Some vague, terrifying threat that she couldn't place, couldn't get away from.

The rest of the night she was feverish and frightened. She half-slept, too hot, but too afraid to put her arms outside the blankets. When morning came, Fernando remembered nothing. But Halley, well, Halley never forgot.

The other times, it had been a man. The clearest memory she had was of his shoes by her bed. Men's shoes. Not sneakers, but big, dark, men's shoes. His face, like the girl's, had not been visible.

They had breakfast together, and did not speak of the dream. Then they got ready for their hike. It didn't take long for Fernando to grow impatient.

"Aren't you ready yet?" He stood with his hands on his hips, his elbows jutting out from his sides. The bulk of his body took up all the space in the room. "God, you take forever."

Halley lifted her arms overhead to get her backpack down from the hook by the door. The movement changed Fernando's attitude immediately; his eyes roved down the lengthened profile of her body, over her breasts, her waist, her hips. He looked like a cat lapping up warm cream. "Mm," he said to himself, "Even after all this time, you are still so hot..."

She turned quickly. "What did you say?"

"Nothing, baby," he answered. "Just hurry up."

Halley looked at him for a moment, and then focused on her backpack. She slid her plastic-sheathed contour map inside, behind the food, resting it flat against the back of the pack. Fernando was leading today. He would have marked their route on the disposable plastic map cover with indelible red pen, as always. The extra map was just a precaution. The First Aid Kit was there and fully stocked, the small red and black compass was properly magnetized, North showing where she knew North was. She placed it into its special front compartment, and zipped the pack closed. "I'm hurrying...I've just got to find one more thing..."

Halley rushed into the bedroom. Fernando breathed out hard through his nostrils. "Jesus Christ," he murmured after she'd gone, his lust dropping quickly. "It's just a day trip."

Alone in the bedroom, Halley swallowed hard, and rubbed her eyes with the back of her hand. *I won't let him make me cry again. No way.* Her jaw clenched. *I've got to focus, do this right.*

Quickly, she reached for her small pocketknife on the top of the dresser. Her hand stalled halfway: there was that photo of them again. She picked it up, the pewter frame weighty in her hand. It had been taken a couple of years ago, on one of their first hikes together. Halley had set up her camera on a tripod. She wanted to have a picture of them together, to have something permanent of this elusive, handsome man.

In the photo, Fernando had his arm around her shoulders and was staring straight into the camera. He was deeply tanned and darkly Mediterranean; the camera flash had made his black eyes glitter, like they had been embellished with tiny specks of diamonds. He wore his hugest smile; his straight white teeth looked like he was being photographed for a toothpaste ad. *Or like he's hooked the best fish in the pond and is showing it off to his friends,* she thought. *That's what he used to call me back then, the best.*

She frowned; she could hear him pacing in the living room. She didn't want to look at herself in the photo; she knew what she'd see. In contrast to Fernando, her head was turned; she was looking up at him with softened eyes. With admiration. It was as if she'd forgotten there was a camera there at all. A song played in her head as she looked at the photo: *you put me high, upon a pedestal...*

She still felt the same way, even after all that had happened. She still admired him.

"Come on, Sparrow!" Fernando shouted, using the nickname that used to sound so cute. "Get your ass out here. It's time to go!"

She put the photo down, her arm falling heavily to her side. When had it all changed? It had begun so well. The rough grey carpet stared blankly at her and held no answers.

Moving quickly to stem the tide of emotion, she pulled on her combat trousers, buttoning the knife into the pocket. As she pulled her hand out, her old watch caught, pulling the clasp open. She closed it again and made sure it locked. *Focus, Halley. What else? What else are you forgetting?*

On top, she was wearing her simple red sleeveless t-shirt, designed to wick moisture from the skin. She liked its small feminine twist, its picture of a crown sewn on the front in shiny red sequins, outlined with tiny pearls. A Queen's crown. The thought made her smile. Pulling open the closet door, she grabbed her bright orange windbreaker. It was light but very warm. She held it up next to her long-sleeved t-shirt. It was a slightly different shade of orange. She frowned; Fernando didn't like it when her clothing clashed. Still, she stuffed the windbreaker into the top of the pack.

Taking a last look around the bedroom, her eyes lingered on the familiar place she called home, as if she was cataloging it in her memory. Finally, she walked out of the room, closing the door firmly behind her.

Together they left the house.

CHAPTER 2

The music smashed against her as they drove: Metallica's "Enter Sandman". It was Fernando's latest favorite, very trendy. He always favored trendy things. She listened to the music, anticipating: first it was the heavy guitar (he took one hand from the steering wheel and played air guitar) and then the ugliness of the first verse. These, she could handle. But when the music slowed, it was like the singer had slipped inside her head, and was pounding on the soft inner surface of her skull with a hammer. The beat was hypnotizing. She found herself mouthing the familiar words: *Sleep with one eye open...gripping your pillow tight. Exit light...enter night... Take my hand – we're off to never-never land...* The guitar, screaming. The sound of doom. Her heart was pounding. She reached over to turn off the music with a sudden twist of her wrist. There was abrupt silence in the car.

"What? Why'd you do that?" Fernando said. "I was enjoying that."

He looked at her with annoyance and switched it back on, but, seeing her face, he made the small concession of forwarding it to the next song: Savage Garden: *I knew I loved you before I met you...I think I dreamed you into life...* He hummed along; this one was popular too.

She stared out the window. That was better. The lyrics reminded her of the day when they'd first met, of the firm but gentle way he had shaken her hand, of the way he'd held her gaze a moment too long. Scenery flashed by the car window: tree, tree, tree, river, house, tree, the greens and browns calming. He had felt so familiar to her, she thought. Really, it had been like meeting herself, embodied in a man. On their first few dates, even the music he had played had been right – as if by telepathy, he had chosen all her favorites. "Soul music" she called it, and she had felt him a kindred spirit who saw the world the same way she did. She hadn't mentioned it at first, had just held it to her chest like a small treasure. Much later, when she brought up the music in a desperate attempt to prove that indeed they did have common ground, he had looked puzzled. It was a *Top Hits* album, he'd said; he'd never really listened to the *words* of the songs. She had masked her disappointment with a quick kiss.

Now, she stared out the car window and thought of that false kiss, of his thick lips and his ready smile, of his easy laugh, and his goddamned pied-piperish charisma. He had pulled her in, just like that. It had been so easy to hand over control of her life to him, to hand over her power.

The song finished as they pulled into the parking area. She noted the trail head; she'd not been here before. She wished suddenly that she'd paid more attention to the route they'd driven to get here – they could be anywhere. She hadn't noticed how long the drive had taken, and that made her doubly dependent on Fernando, because she couldn't bring herself to ask where they'd come. The question would just inflame him. At least she had her own map.

Fernando went to get their packs from the trunk. She sat in the car and watched him in the rear view mirror; this was how they always did it. He ran his hand through his thick dark brown hair, and she knew he was thinking about the new style, trimmed short at the sides, and subtly teased up on top with sticky gel. He'd had many compliments about it. It did look good. God, he looked like a movie star. It was unusual to be so adept outdoors, and yet to be so immaculately groomed, so caught up in appearance and the latest trends. Sometimes he seemed like he was just playing the part of a wilderness guide for a Hollywood blockbuster, rather than his work being his passion. It was

Halley's passion – she just wished she were as instinctively good at it as he was.

She watched him move, as always, with assurance. Self-absorbed, she corrected herself, that was more the word, as if the whole world should say *'Bless You'* when he sneezed.

When had she first noticed she'd got him wrong? Maybe it was the first time they'd made love: she had touched his strongly muscled chest with two fingertips, running them across his smooth skin. He was so beautiful, golden and chiseled, more like a statue than real flesh-and-blood. And she had felt...*stubble*. It had felt exactly like her legs when she missed a few days of shaving. Confused, she ran her fingers over the spot again, more slowly. He noticed, answering her unspoken question with a shrug of his broad tanned shoulders. "I haven't waxed in a little while." At the time, it had seemed endearingly feminine.

Halley got out of the car and took a quick glance at her watch: ten am. Not so bad; they'd planned to be at the trail head at nine-thirty and she knew Fernando always allowed extra time for her to get ready. It did take her a long time lately, but it wasn't because she was 'disorganized and stupid', as Fernando put it. She glanced at him checking and rearranging the contents of both backpacks, and then looked at the trees.

It was also because of the doors. And the windows. There were so many to check. She couldn't just do it the one time; it needed three times to be absolutely certain. It was a large house so this meant running from room to room while he was in the shower. She couldn't check them when he was around: if he caught her at it, it would ruin it. No, she couldn't let him see her doing it or tell him anything about it.

Now there was the stovetop too, with its four burners. That really slowed things down. But the stovetop helped the ritual: she could shut the kitchen door, and could do the checking even when Fernando was out and about – he rarely ventured in there. She'd thought this addition was a clever idea, but it quickly became essential and time-consuming. Check each knob once, from left to right, then do it again, from right to left. The thin black line in the center of the knob had to be exactly vertical, and sometimes she'd hit one of the knobs with her hand in her haste, and she'd have to start over again. That's what took the time. If Fernando shouted at her through the kitchen door to hurry up, it also meant she had to start over, because she hadn't been fast enough the first time.

Most important, she had to check the basement door. The door, non-descript when they'd first moved in, was now quite striking: she'd succumbed to a compulsion to paint it a high-shine glossy black. It took three coats to get the depth of color just right. That done, she'd decided it needed a new doorknob, and she went from shop to shop to shop until she found the perfect one, a transparent mock crystal with gold fittings.

She could see the door clearly in her mind. Checking that glossy black basement door was always the final check, done just before they left the house. Once, last October, she had discovered it was unlocked. She didn't know how it could be unlocked – no one ever went down there. She could remember the feeling even now, a year later, how her heart had clenched at the discovery, how her hands had gotten so sweaty that the mock crystal knob had slipped in her grasp, and she couldn't get it to lock right away. She thought about the door: had she checked it before they left? She couldn't remember. She simply couldn't remember.

* * *

"What's the matter with you?" Fernando asked, as if he'd been bothered by something for quite a while. "Why are you breathing like that?"

Halley jumped, startled from her reverie. The woods came back into focus.

"What? Sorry…"

Fernando looked at her for a long moment, and then shook his head. He turned his thick arm to check the face of his large silver watch. "Twelve o'clock. Well, at least we've made good time."

Halley couldn't believe two hours had elapsed. Lost in her thoughts, she'd seen nothing of the walk.

Fernando took off his backpack and removed the contour map from its waterproof pouch. With a flick of his wrist, he shook the map open, and pulled out his compass. Halley waited quietly. Fernando studied the surrounding countryside, marking the position of the large peak to the left and the shorter one slightly to its right, and compared this with the map. He confirmed the map's North-South orientation with the compass, and nodded to himself. With precision, he folded the contour map along its original fold lines and stowed it back in the plastic case, and then in his backpack, along with the small red compass. He pulled out a thin white towel from the pack and wiped the perspiration from his bare shoulders and arms. When he offered it to Halley, she shook her head.

"Hot today," he offered.

Halley dropped her pack to the forest floor and quickly removed her long-sleeved t-shirt, which was wet with sweat. She hadn't wanted to stop before to remove it, afraid he'd get angry at her for slowing them down again. She felt him watching her, and fumbled with the zip of her backpack, shoving the shirt in on top of the windbreaker. She was about to put her backpack back on when she felt his gaze shift down towards her chest. Fernando was staring at her. "What? What's the matter?" she said, with a slight hesitation in her voice, as if she were dreading the answer. Her shoulders had hunched in together and her chest sunken, as if she were awaiting a blow.

He seemed to be thinking of just how to put it. The edges of his lips lifted in a mocking smile. "Just wondering where you got

17

that ridiculous shirt. A crown, Jesus, Halley. It's so…" He lifted one eyebrow.

Fuck you, she thought. *Fuck you, you bastard.* She opened her mouth, but closed it again. *Maybe he's right. Maybe it is a stupid shirt.*

He turned around and begun to walk, leaving Halley to put her backpack back on. She jog-trotted to catch up with him, and followed silently, three feet behind.

The sound of her footsteps bothered her. As her green hiking boots struck the path and moved the leaves around, they seemed to be whispering *"weakling, weakling"* at her, with each stride. She was a weakling: she knew she had to leave Fernando, but she couldn't do it.

That's not fair, I'm not a weakling, she thought, as she watched Fernando's swinging stride. *I have tried to leave him. Even though he acts like he hates me sometimes, he always pulls me back. Like that time on High West Mountain…*

She remembered the occasion well; it was the most recent time she'd tried to leave. That time, she'd come really close. It had been a four day hike, and they had planned to swap leadership at the end of each day. But on the second day, when it was Halley's turn, she could feel the distrustful way he watched her with the map, his impatience and his questioning and his doubts about her ability. His attitude made her doubt herself, made her make silly mistakes.

She'd gotten angry and left him. They had climbed separately for days, both aiming for the same base camp. He was there on the mountain with her, but for the first time, she didn't seek him out. She got lost a few times, but that didn't matter so much; she always managed to find her way again, backtracking and using the map and compass.

After two days, she found she could take a few breaths before she thought of him. After three, the light in the forest seemed to change in a subtle way, becoming brighter and less threatening.

It would get better, she knew; in time, she would be all right alone. The fourth night, she slept soundly.

When she woke the next morning, she saw his familiar handwriting on a flat grey rock – he had written her a message with a coal from her own campfire. She had felt a sharp constriction in the center of her chest. The message simply said, "Thinking of you".

He hadn't written "I love you", or "I'm sorry" or even "Goodbye". His intent in writing the message was unclear, and she couldn't be sure why he'd come close again. She hated the message, the way it made her long for more, long for him. *Why can't he just leave me alone!* She knew the reason – it was situated somewhere between her "beautiful body" and the powerless way she admired him; he couldn't bear to let either of these things go. She rubbed the message out with the toe of her boot.

But she kept thinking about it. It twisted and turned and ate away at her resolve. She didn't mean to, but she found herself tracking him and finding him later that day. Quickly forgetting her days alone, her competence, she handed leadership back to him. He didn't seem at all reluctant to take it. She had gone back to him again, and was disgusted with herself.

It happened this way, over and over. It wasn't that he was overtly abusive. She'd never have stayed with him if he'd hit her, or cheated on her, or abused her openly. What he did was far more subtle, she thought, and hard for anyone else to see. Her friends all said he was great, handsome, that she was nuts to even think about leaving him. But she knew. He was undermining her, like the slow erosion of a hillside. Eventually, she would simply collapse.

Coming back to the present, she stared at his strong back. *I've followed him too far. I think this is how drowning must feel.* She had an image of icy waters closing in over her, suffocating her. She coughed; there was a full sensation in her lungs that was disconcerting. She cleared her throat but didn't speak.

After a long while, Fernando broke the silence. "You haven't said a word in hours," he said. "What's on your mind?"

Halley was surprised. Fernando rarely asked her questions like this, questions that invited her to speak openly. "I was thinking about us," she said. They had stopped walking and were facing each other. The sun filtered through the trees.

"What about us?"

She couldn't quite read his tone. "I don't know," she stalled. "I was thinking about that picture of us on the dresser...you know the one?" Her hands moved as if drawing the frame of the picture in front of them. "The one I took with the tripod." It wasn't really a lie – she had thought about that picture earlier.

Fernando's forehead creased. "What, the one out on Cougar Mountain? No...wait, it was in the canyon, that's right. You led that day." He said it like her leading was a liability. "What? What about the photo?" He seemed to see it in his mind, and his eyes softened. "Oh, yeah," he said. "I remember now." His tone had changed. "You were so hot that day, baby..." He took a step towards her.

Halley blinked.

"You know, Halley, you're still hot," he said. "Still so beautiful." His eyes pulled at her. "I love that picture; I love the way you're looking at me in that picture."

Halley felt as if the ground had become soft under her. It was always like this; he always won. "Oh, Fernando," she said, looking up at him. His name felt of satin to her, the name of a Latin lover from some tropical climate. Inviting images overcame her: the taste of mangoes, ripe and in season; the passionate dance of a tango; the color red; the feel of hard muscle against her chest. Her face flushed. She found herself tumbling fast into the depths of his black eyes, which, when he wanted them to, could seem bottomless.

He took another step closer. "I love when you look like that, as if you can't wait for it. Come here..." He nodded his chin at her and crooked the forefinger of his right hand. He smiled his devastating smile.

She started to move towards him, but her body clenched. "But you said…you said we had to hurry, that it got dark earlier now." She couldn't bear to be blamed again for their being late.

"No, baby, there's time for this." He smiled invitingly, and opened his arms. When she stood just a pace away from him, he reached out with one muscular arm and drew her tightly up against him. The feel of his solid body pressing into her was unbearably good. He held her upward gaze; they seemed to breathe as one.

* * *

It was over quickly anyway, she reflected, zipping up her combat trousers. She hadn't even had to take off both boots.

CHAPTER 3

They walked for another hour. She was thinking about the strong outward curve of Fernando's tanned shoulders when the first sharp pain hit her. It took her by surprise, striking her right where her inner eye would be, if she had believed in such a thing as an inner eye. The pain was so sharp and so sudden that she stumbled, inadvertently bumping into Fernando's solid back.

"What the...?" he said, turning around to face her, and at the same time taking a step back from her.

"I'm sorry. My head..." She sunk onto her knees, both hands pressed against her forehead.

"What's the matter with you?" His tone didn't suggest patience. "Do you need some water or something?"

Halley looked up and tried to meet his eyes, but he just slicked his away, like a car skidding on an icy highway. It made her feel like she'd simply disappeared.

Abruptly, she looked up. She could hear a baby crying, in deep distress. The pain in her head grew. The wail and the pain were insistent and pulling, but when she looked at Fernando, he seemed oddly unfazed.

"The baby..." she said.

The sound crowded her head, dragged at her. The crying was pulling at a deep place inside of her. Suddenly, she could hear another voice, that of a young girl. It was saying something over and over again, what was it? *Save the baby, save the baby, save the...*

The pain in her forehead throbbed urgently.

"What baby?" He looked around with aggravation, cocking

his head slightly. "I hear a bird calling, I hear some insects. I hear you…" He took a prickly breath. "Come on," he said, gentling his voice with apparent effort. "Try. Please. For us. I need to get back. We're at the end of the trail anyway." He looked at her, as if unsure whether to continue. "You keep…God, Halley…why do you keep acting so crazy? What's the matter with you?"

Her eyes were closed and she didn't answer. He waited.

"Come on. Get up off the ground. You're acting like a lunatic." He bit the words out. His large hand reached down to help her up.

Her eyes opened and she stared at his hand, overcome by a strong sense of déjà vu.

This scene had played out before, somewhere in her past. The world was suddenly unstable and shifting. Time was no longer a straight line. She had the sensation of falling, of tumbling off the very earth on which she knelt. She closed her eyes and the vividness of the seeming memory swept her away:

She had taken his hand; he had pulled her to her feet. With effort she had forced herself to numb her feelings, to dismiss the cry of the baby. A moment later, she had let him lead her out of the woods.

Her eyes opened, and the feeling of déjà vu vanished.

A new feeling replaced it: utter despair. For she could see her life stretched out before her. Empty; aching. In that other lifetime, she had followed Fernando down a path which was not her own. That path was littered with what-never-would-be's: the centering love of another; a sense of self-assurance; the feel in her hand of the tiny hand of a child; a long life filled with purpose and meaning. All this, she had lost. She had followed Fernando one last time, and that one last time was the point around which the rest of her life pivoted.

She could see it all with great clarity. Their relationship wouldn't work; in the end, he would leave her, and the Halley he would leave would be too damaged to ever love again. In some strange, parallel universe, her whole life had already played out. She had made the wrong choice, and from this choice, disaster had followed.

But it didn't have to be this way.

"A new place to begin," she whispered, looking up.

"*What?*" Fernando said, his forehead wrinkling.

"This is my new place to begin."

Rising without his help, she experienced a sudden clarity. The leaves on the trees were more defined than usual, their individual veins appearing as finely crafted lines; a single bird cried; a musky pine scent permeated the air; even her skin felt more finely tuned.

Fernando, in contrast, had faded. He seemed to have become subtly porous, as if she could feel the slight breeze pass through the infinitesimal spaces between his cells. He was suddenly less relevant.

"I won't follow you. I have to find the baby. I have to save him."

He blew out a hard breath. "You're crazy! There's no baby – I told you – if it's anything, it's a goddamned bird." His impatience got the better of him; he let the word *goddamned* draw itself out long and sinewy, and then snapped it at her like a whip.

But even as he spoke, the keening grew louder, more a wail now than a cry. It couldn't be ignored; it was like the whine of a manual car stuck between gears. The urge to make it stop was unbearable.

He stared at her through his suddenly solid black eyes. "It's the end of the trail. I'm not wasting my time looking for some imaginary baby lost in the woods. I'm going back to the car, Sparrow. You can do what you want." His eyes dared her.

He stepped around Halley, and began walking the path back towards the car.

CHAPTER 4

Halley watched the shape of his back as he walked away. She watched, and she forced herself not to follow. It was strange that even at a great distance he still looked tall, like a leader. He turned the corner and the trail's vast and sudden emptiness made her throat hurt. *Oh My God Oh My God Oh My God.* The force it took to keep herself from following him made her gasp aloud; it was as if he were pulling her innards out along the trail behind him.

He hadn't looked back. She couldn't believe he hadn't looked back.

Time passed. The trail remained empty.

Looking up at the sky with closed eyes, fighting back tears, she pressed her palms together with fingers interleaved as if in prayer. She tried to breathe. The blood pounded in her clenched fingers and the hollow between her palms grew warm. After a long while, she opened her eyes. She turned around, away from the empty trail where Fernando had been.

She stood at the end of the long straight trail, staring hard at the trackless wilderness before her, at the close-knit forest. It was a terrible place for the trail to end. She was alone; afraid to move; with no idea of where she should go next. It was a crossroads-without-a-crossroads.

Shaking slightly, she felt Fernando, felt each step he took away from her pull at her body. She stared straight ahead. Silence; stillness. Even the air hung quiet, the clouds immobile, as if stuck, waiting for her move, her choice.

She couldn't go back; she couldn't follow Fernando any longer. That was not her path. Though the crying had stopped, she knew the baby she had heard was real, that it was alone, that it needed her help. No one else could save it. She didn't know how she knew; she just did. There was no turning back.

In her loneliness and desperation, she asked herself pointed questions aloud. "Where do I go next? How do I find this baby by myself? Out here in this wilderness, full of thorny things and sharp teeth. How do I carve a trail, alone?"

She looked outwards for wisdom. None was forthcoming. To be at the end of a trail, without a crossroads, alone; to discover that she had been heading the wrong way, following the wrong guide, for quite some time; to have an urgent, illogical need to save a baby she heard crying in the woods, and to be unsure how.

The "next" was unclear, but in the "now", the storm clouds broke open, and rain began to fall, pricking her exposed skin mercilessly, chilling her in her stasis. Freezing her to the spot.

"Which way, which way?" she said to herself, urgency in her voice. She willed a leader, other than herself; she willed a hero. A hero would find the way, would take charge, and would save this baby.

The first step off the trail. She took it.

And fell, headlong down a steep hillside, tumbling, rolling, moving. And the thing was, the bruises and thorns didn't hurt as much as the staying over long, as the following the wrong guide. She was off. She was begun.

PART 3:
ALL TIME
AND
NO TIME

CHAPTER 1

The rain stopped as quickly as it had begun. In some more civilized place, the end of rain might have left silence in its wake, but here in the woods it did not: when she stopped falling, the first thing Halley noticed was the incessant, battering noise.

The woods aren't like people think, she reflected, trying to catch her breath. *There's no silence in the woods, no peace.*

All around her were whispers, chattering, the thick rustle of insects burrowing under piles of dried-out leaves. An orange and black millipede moved its legs on a nearby tree – Halley imagined even this tiny movement was adding to the chaotic noise that surrounded her. It strummed itself higher up the tree, its bright skin in sharp contrast to the grey of the tree trunk. Bird calls resounded, high pitched screeching that shocked her senses. Each call was different, as if there were no two birds alike in these entire woods. Water roared over rocks in a hidden riverbed, terrible in its power.

Without warning, a black snake slid out from the surrounding undergrowth, slipping quickly in front of her. It was so fast that she didn't see its head, only the length of its long black back, skimming over the dirt. It didn't pause, and her startled scream lasted exactly as long as it took for the snake to slide its length by her, and move off into the undergrowth.

Her scream had been unearthly – it was not so much a scream as a subtle unraveling of her voice. She felt a cold sweat begin: she had not expected snakes in these woods. There were no snakes anywhere near where they lived. She'd never seen a snake move so fast. To what far away place had Fernando brought her?

She imagined snakes all around her, poised, ready to strike.

Curling her body in, she sat on her haunches and tried to keep her limbs close. A scrambling sound next to her made her jump, made her think snake! but when she focused on the spot where the sound had come from, she saw only a crow, picking its way carefully in the scrub. It was a glossy, cool-looking thing, its eyes piercing as they darted about.

Near the crow, she noticed her pack. It must have been dragged off during the roll down the hillside. She must retrieve it. But she stared at the pack without moving, thinking only of how very far away it seemed. Even this small distance was insurmountable; it was impossible to imagine traversing the whole forest alone. Hardening her belly, she stood up, and took an unsteady step forward. The crow, seeing the movement, let loose a shriek that filled the forest. It took wing.

Halley's hands were trembling as she grabbed the backpack and sat back down quickly, under a tall, thin tree. She hugged the pack into her belly, as the enormity of what she had done began to sink in.

She was alone. She was deep in the woods, possibly lost, and was not even sure why she was here. The baby she'd come to save was completely silent, and this left a strangely filling emptiness. Was Fernando right? Had she just made up the baby? Or was it simply too late to save her? This last thought stunned her. She sensed the loss of an irretrievable treasure, like a fire that burned a lifetime's worth of family photographs.

A sharp crackle of leaves snapped Halley from her reverie – the snake had made a lunge towards the crow! Without thinking, Halley screamed "NO!" and it was only Halley's loud shout that allowed the bird to flutter away, leaving the snake with a mouthful of long, black tail feathers. After she screamed the word she was confused – why would she care whether the snake ate the crow? Why would she care enough to try to prevent it?

A sudden picture formed in Halley's mind, as if in answer. It was a picture of her, stretched out still and motionless – pale as skim milk. She shivered violently. As if it were her own death she had foreseen. As if her shout had been to save herself. Bile rose in her throat, choking her, and she was desperate to get up and move, run away.

She was afraid to get up though, and not just because of the snake; she was afraid of herself. If she got up at this moment, her treacherous limbs would follow Fernando right out of the woods, right back to him. *It's so much easier to follow him, even if it's down the wrong path, even after all the pain.* To stop herself, she made a quick bargain; she would not leave this spot until she was sure she could force herself not to turn back.

In her self-imposed stillness, she sat and fingered the weathered canvas of her backpack, staring at its blackness. Fernando had given her the bag two years ago. "Your bag is the wrong kind," he'd said. Said it kindly enough, this was true, and only after first asking whether he could "tell her something personal". She'd been honoured by the question, had gone warm at the word "personal". She'd had no idea.

Each time she'd picked up this "gift" of Fernando's she'd had a feeling of ineptness. She had carried her old bag for years – had it been "wrong" all that time? Had everyone known but her?

The chill in the air brought her back to the present. Unzipping the backpack, she pulled out her long-sleeved t-shirt. It was still damp with sweat but it would have to do. She shrugged it on, and tied the windbreaker around her waist. The action engaged her mind, and she was able to think about what to do next. She must figure out her whereabouts, she knew, before she moved away from her last known position.

Feeling around inside the pack, she let her fingers explore the familiar objects: food, sealed in plastic bags; water canteen; slim sunglass case; insect spray. She shoved the objects around, growing more and more uneasy. Where was it? Where was the map? She picked the backpack up and peered inside, looking for the familiar green and grey shading. *I'm just panicking. It's got to be there. I put it in myself.* Taking out the objects one by one, she laid them in the space between her knees. When the bag was empty, she sat for a long time, staring at the contents spread before her. No map. She thought of her compass in the small zip compartment in the front of the bag but she knew even before she looked – it too was gone. In her mind's eye, she watched Fernando at the back of their car earlier that day, rearranging the packs. *He took them out. He took out my map and compass.* She imagined what he had said to himself, "Sparrow won't need this. I'm going to lead."

"Goddamn him!"

With a sudden, unexpected fury she threw the black backpack from her, watching it fall in a long arch, hearing the quick crack of leaves and branches when it landed. It was a reckless thing to do, but she was so sick of how the backpack made her feel, sick of the subtle message of her incompetence that it carried. It was the same message signalled by Fernando's removal of her map and compass, and it was infuriating. It was just like him, deciding for her what she needed.

The combat trousers had lots of pockets; they would hold everything she had to carry. The insect spray and sunglass case would fit nicely in the left side pocket, and the canteen could be strapped over her back. She ate the apple and the cheese from the food supply, and tucked the sealed zip-lock bag with energy bars and dried fruit and nuts into her right side pocket. The absence of the backpack on her shoulders was agreeable; it allowed her chest to lift and her shoulders to move down and back. She rolled her shoulders around, enjoying the feeling.

It was when she lifted her gaze again to the broader landscape that the truth came back, and it was like someone had punched her in the stomach. The woods were so vast. The aftertaste of the cheese on her tongue turned rancid. She'd never been here before – she didn't even know where she was. How could she find her way alone, without her map and compass?

She swallowed; there was more to it than that.

How could she go on, without Fernando? Her breath caught in her throat. His going sat there in her belly, and the apple she'd eaten turned to a heavy stone of grief that left room for nothing else. When he'd walked off, he had taken the solidity of her core with him and replaced it with this unbearable, hollowing weight.

She leaned back against the thin tree and dropped her head into her arms. Her grief overflowed, pouring from her in wracking sobs. The pain made her whole body shake and was vast enough to fill the entire forest. It was the pain of letting him go, but it was also the harder to bear pain of taking herself back.

As she sat sobbing, a strange burning sensation began to move through her body. A condemning light was blazing into all her darkest places. Moving inside her; then intruding into her, slipping into crevices she had long closed off, had forgotten were there. Without Fernando to hide behind, she was fully exposed to herself, and she couldn't bear what she saw. Clenching her jaw, she made tight fists of her hands, her fingernails digging her palms.

Goddammit! It hurts, it hurts, it hurts. I want to make it stop and make it better and I want to go back to him and I know I can't because he doesn't even really exist not the way I want him to but it hurts so and I'm so afraid and it's so dark here and so dark inside and so not-quiet and the snake and what do I do next and…

She sucked at the air, and her body shook. The leaves in the smaller branches of the tree shook with her, crackling and rustling, as if absorbing the force of her distress.

The crow hopped back, unnoticed. In its beak, tightly, it held a small scrap of paper. Old, worn, the writing on it faded, but still legible. It dropped the bit of paper next to Halley, and hopped backwards, head cocked to one side.

When Halley finally lifted her head, her neck felt stiff and tight. Her whole body hurt. Inside her felt empty, scoured out. It took a few moments for the forest floor to come back into focus, and when it did, she stared numbly at a single black feather. She picked it up and turned it over and over, running her forefinger along its edge, feeling the soft serrations. It was comforting. She tucked the black feather into an inner pocket, zipping it for safe-keeping.

When she looked back at the forest floor, she noticed a graying piece of paper. She picked it up. It was faded, hard to read. She studied it carefully.

You will be all right

She just had time to decipher it when a sudden wind lifted the bit of paper high into the air, and carried it away.

Getting to her feet, Halley let the words settle into her. You will be all right. In them, she felt a breath of hope. Brushing the leaves off her chest and arms, she took a deep breath, and gently moved her limbs about. While they were stiff and probably bruised from her fall, nothing was broken. That was something anyway.

With courage she did not feel, she began to walk. If the baby was here, she was going to find it. It would be near a trail. That was all she had to go on. But first, she had to find a trail.

Trance fought to stay still. What luck! He could hardly believe it. She had come here to begin again, of all places. Here! He allowed himself a quiet smile. Save the baby; as if she could. She couldn't even save herself.

He pictured the car underwater. All their lives depended on her. And he knew she'd never do it, never save them. She'd not done one heroic thing in her entire life.

Oh, she would die. They would all die. He would see to that. But first, he would have a little fun with her.

CHAPTER 2

F inding the trail was simpler than she expected. After the first few hesitant steps, it became obvious, and she wondered what she'd been worried about. Leaves crunched gently under her feet, dusty brown, vibrant red, orange as warm as a campfire. The different colors were a wonder. Walking with Fernando, they had all been brown. She had never taken the time to look before.

A line of ants moved across the path, and she stopped to watch. They were carrying food over their heads to their nest in a tiny ant convoy. Careful not to crush them under her heavy boots, she stepped over. It was so easy not to do harm. All it required was paying attention.

Soon the going became effortless, and she made quick progress. Without the weight of the backpack, her step had more of a bounce, and her arms swung freely. The air was still, and she felt an unexpected sense of peace. She stopped and slowly removed her long-sleeved t-shirt, breathing deeply, taking her time to tie it around her waist on top of the windbreaker. She smiled to herself and resumed walking.

I like not having to look at Fernando's back all the time. I never realized how much he blocked the view. The trees look like they're lifting their arms to encourage me. It's like walking inside a cathedral.

Near her legs, there was a sudden crackle in the bushes, followed by the appearance of a large bird in full flight. Halley jumped. Through a clearing in the trees, the bird flew to the wide sky above. *That was an eagle.* It weaved in the sky until it disappeared from view. She continued on.

A few moments later, the trail took a sharp turn to the right, and began to track steeply downhill. The gradient made her speed increase, first to a faster walk, and then – as she was reminded of the joy of speed – she increased the speed herself to a spirited run. It was not a fleeing sort of run; it was a run of celebration. The exhilaration of running downhill! There it was, in the sound of her feet on the loose leaves, in the sweat that formed on her brow and arms. The world flew by in a fast-moving blur, and the ground slid effortlessly beneath her. She skirted rocks covered with green moss, not slowing her pace, but moving side to side like a Billy-goat down the steep slope.

The downhill ended abruptly, and she slid to a halt. A set of rough-hewn stone steps led upwards. With the back of her hand, she wiped the sweat from her forehead. The steps were steep and large – she'd have to stretch her legs to climb them. It looked like they carried on to the top of the hill. She began to climb, the muscles in her thighs burning. Fifteen minutes later, she came to a lookout, where she stopped to catch her breath, hands on her knees, panting. Sweat ran down the groove in her back. The view was masked by thick cloud. *On a clear day, I'd be able to see exactly where I am, or at least where the forest ends.* She made her way across the lookout. The trail continued down the other side of the hill. It was steeper, and she loved the bounding down, leaping from one leg to another, keeping her footing, keeping her balance.

When she reached the bottom, she kept running, following the path through the trees. The ground was studded with small rocks, which were the perfect footing for pushing off, and she augmented her run with a few extra leaps and bounds. As well as rocks, underfoot were pine needles. The scent reminded her of Christmas.

Further on, the trail became grooved, as if water flowed down the center of this trail in rainy times. Halley stayed on her toes, one foot on either side of the upraised edges of the groove, adjusting to slight variations in the terrain. It was like dancing at speed with an agile partner, a meditation in motion. Her breath came fast, but she moved with assurance, with an underlying sense of knowing that this sprint through the woods would take her exactly where she needed to go.

The waterfalls that crossed the trail came as a surprise. Gushing down the hillsides, they made the footing more treacherous. She slowed her stride, until finally coming to a halt on a stone bridge with worn wooden railings, where she stopped, breathing hard, to observe one of the more dramatic waterfalls. The outside edges of the falls were bounded by large, black rock, furred with green and yellow lichen. Bushes and small shrubs held on as far as they dared. At the inner face of the waterfall, where the water roared down thickly, only weedy grass could survive, growing tightly in rock crevices, hanging long and lush and rebellious in the abundance of fast-flowing water. Halley imagined climbing up the waterfall, feeling the cool flow of the water against her skin, using the bushes and rock to pull herself up. Her eyes moved downward to explore the river bed at the base of the falls. "Butterflies…" she whispered, in surprise.

Hovering over or resting upon the rocks, were a multitude of butterflies, their wings the blue of sapphire. They were outlined by the finest of black lines, as if drawn in at the last moment with the thinnest brush of a very careful artist. This black edging gave them just the slightest bit of substance, for their blue seemed ethereal and holy. Grouped together as they were, they made the world seem abundantly full of butterflies. Gossamer-winged. The river lent a slight, wispy fog to the air. Halley stood and watched the butterflies, her brow suddenly furrowed with concentration.

"Butterflies! Butterflies!" she was shouting. She was four, and her voice had the enthusiasm and volume of someone new to the wonders of the world. "I've never seen so many butterflies in my whole life!"

Her father smiled as he raised a finger for quiet. "Shhh – you'll scare them off. These are called Ceylon Blue Glassy Tigers." He paused, as if for emphasis. "They're a very special butterfly."

Her daddy knew everything! All about plants and all about some strange place called Asia, and even how to climb the rocks that surrounded their mountain home. She knew this because of the thrilling bedtime stories he told her, all about his adventures.

And now it seemed he knew about butterflies too. He held her small hand tightly in his large one, and she felt very safe, and very, very loved.

Halley – the grown-up Halley – was shaking: her parents were dead. Their memories were carefully tucked away, like a cherished wedding dress preserved in tissue paper. As if they would crumble if taken out and held, turn to dust in her fingers. The memories of how much they had loved her were tucked away so tightly that she could no longer feel the strength of their love. Or, more importantly in her view, the pain of their deaths'.

The butterflies made her miss her father with a sudden, wrenching ache. Grief soared through her, flaming and searing. Her arms wrapped around her of their own accord.

I still don't understand death. I could never really believe I wouldn't see them again. Speak to them again. The finality of that silence between us unfathomable. Unbearable.

She watched the butterflies, and rubbed the wetness from her cheeks with the back of her hand.

I don't want to look. I don't want to think of them.

Nevertheless, the memories came fast: her father riding a bicycle he'd altered so he could sit upright to see more of the world; her mother buying the most useless, most vibrant items at neighbors' garage sales; their Sunday walks; the cluttered home that never got light no matter how many lights they switched on.

So much I miss. So many things I wanted to say, that I'll never get to. She closed her eyes. *So many things in my life they will never get to know. Why did you have to die, damn you!*

When she opened her eyes the butterflies were still there. Her stomach wrenched with the urge to throw something into their midst. She swallowed hard and looked down at her muddy green hiking boots and the rough stone bridge under her feet.

The butterflies flew: they were not concerned with her anger; they were simply butterflies.

"I love you, very, very much." Her mother had written that in a birthday card. Halley had forgotten about the card, until she'd found it years and years after her mother's untimely death, as she searched for herself in a box of mementos.

I love you very, very much, Halley thought. *That doesn't stop, does it, that love? I've got to believe it doesn't stop.*

She raised her eyes to the butterflies, and found her anger was spent, as if it had spread out among the rocks and the water, had lit upon the wings of the butterflies and been lifted away.

But the grief remained.

She watched the butterflies, feeling heavy and unable to move.

Some of them were at rest on the river stones, while others flew gently above. Some landed for only a moment, and others stayed for a long, long time. Like souls, living different length lifetimes. As if earth and heaven were that close, that one could simply alight from a stone and flutter above. And land, and flutter, and land. Could the difference between living and dying be so simple, so free of pain? Could death be nothing but a lifting off, a fluttering above?

Maybe they are right here with me. We love you, very, very much.

Standing on the stone bridge, she slowly un-wrapped her arms, suddenly conscious of the way she had been holding herself together. She placed warm palms onto the cool wooden

41

railing of the bridge. *Here, I leave my grief.* She felt it flow from the cavities of her heart, down the blood vessels in her arms, into her long fingertips, and from there, into the railing of the bridge. From the bridge, it ran into the landscape, which was surely large enough to hold it. She let her hands drop to her sides.

She stood still a long moment, thinking and then rested her hands again on the bridge rail. "And here, I also pick up my joy." This time she closed her eyes, and let joy and life pulse through her.

After a long moment of silence, she opened her eyes. The butterflies were still flying, but they were bluer than before. She allowed herself a small smile.

The pools of water below the butterflies looked cool and inviting, a welcome contrast to the heat of her tears. She took a deep breath, and bent down to the nearest pool. It was invigorating to splash her face and arms with water. The dirt that had caked on her slid off in long white lines. She drank deeply.

She was about to break into a run again, but she paused. *Mom and Dad would have told me to take care of myself out here.* She filled her canteen, capping it carefully. *There, that will get me a little way at least.* She began to run again, feeling stronger and better fueled.

The black edging of the butterflies had soaked up much of her grief; their soothing, ethereal blue wings stayed with her, and lifted her as she ran.

Gradually, the dirt of the path changed from brown to a warm, brick red. It was studded with rocks, perfect for dancing along at a fast pace. When the path turned uphill, she slowed to a jog. Ferns unrolled long fronds into the moist air. Large leaves shaped like elephant ears were abundant. The solitude was uplifting. She'd often wanted to run through the woods alone, but had always been afraid. Once, she'd seen a tall woman on a trail like this, running fast, with an air of confidence, of fearlessness. A golden aura protected that woman, an aura of the woman's own making. Halley's eyes had followed her as she moved off. She longed to be that free.

And now...now she was! She laughed with delight, and continued to run until her need to run was satisfied.

When she finally slowed to a walk, her pulse dropped quickly and her breathing began to quiet. The trail continued. The leaves crunched under her boots like old friends.

I haven't felt this way in so long. It's like I've returned to my body, after being away for a very long time.

The woods now seemed reassuring and welcoming. It was a glorious moment. She breathed deeply of it, drawing it in. The urge to turn back was gone. She stayed with this feeling, feeling its foreignness, embracing it. It had to do with releasing her anger and her grief, with picking up her joy. Finally, she stopped walking. She reached her arms up in the air, stretching her body tall, lifting her eyes to the tree canopy above, lifting her chest, as if praying.

As she lowered her arms, her eyes lit on her left hand, and she felt a sudden jolt of alarm.

I used to have a ring, didn't I?

A strange buzzing filled her ears and gripped her with a sense of panic.

What's happened to it? How come there's not even an indentation to show where it was?

Holding her left hand in her right, she stared hard at the finger where the ring should be. It was hard to see – with dismay, she noticed the fading light. It was getting dark. Fast. She looked around her with rapidly growing unease.

The sun had already moved below the tree line, and the sky was becoming overcast. Suddenly night was here, leaping out at her from the shadows. Even as she let her hand fall back to her side, the trees were fading from green to grey; soon, they would be black. She felt a chill of fear, augmented by the suddenly noticeable coolness in the air. *It must be because I've stopped running. I need to put on more clothes.* Quickly, she pulled her long-sleeved t-shirt over her head, and slipped the orange windbreaker over the top, noting with dismay that the shirt was still damp. The extra layers didn't help; she quickly began to shiver. Trying to generate warmth, she rubbed her hands together. Her fingertips would soon be turning white as her body preserved heat for her core. Steeling herself, she took a deep breath and looked around.

The path had become misty, as if suddenly peopled by strange spirits. It had been straight earlier in the day, but now it appeared winding and rooted. Her pulse lifted. Even the friendly cathedral trees looked threatening, standing tall and emaciated. She shook her head and took her eyes from the tall trees, looking down to the ground. *Got to calm down.*

Her breath caught in her throat – on the forest floor, the tree roots looked like snakes. A bolt of fear shot through her, making her step back fast, breathing out hard, opening her eyes so wide that it hurt and staring hard at the spot where she was certain she'd just seen movement. She waited several moments. It had been an illusion. It was just a tree root.

"It wasn't a snake," she said, experimenting with her voice –it was reassuring to hear a voice, even if it were just her own. She continued to talk aloud, choosing her words carefully. "You're going to be okay. Don't worry. You can do this. You'll find shelter. Stay calm…"

She fought the urge to run, to panic – that would be the worst thing she could do. It would waste valuable time, and only scare her more. And there *would* be snakes out at this time of night. She forced herself to take deeper breaths. It was smarter to move slowly, to give them time to feel the vibrations of her footsteps. They were shy creatures, and would just crawl away. *If* they heard her coming.

She began to walk again, stepping carefully. The forest became thick with night, and, though she moved slowly, she kept stumbling over tree roots and rocks. The shock of it made her heart thud painfully.

"See, Fernando was right," she said sharply. "You're so stupid! You wasted all that time with your running, and now you don't have anywhere to sleep. You don't know how to do this alone. So smug, feeling so free. And now you've failed on your first night, not even finding shelter."

She hated the disgust, the bite of the words, but found it impossible to silence herself. Even when she stopped speaking aloud, the voice continued in her head. *Stupid, stupid, stupid...*

In frustration, she growled aloud, trying to drown out the interior dialog. The growl was frightening. Uncontrolled. She glanced around her quickly, scared at being alone but suddenly even more frightened that she might *not* be alone.

She stopped moving. It was safer to stay right where she was, to curl into a small, hard ball. She closed her eyes and thought of the roly-polys she and her brother used to play with. By touching one of their feathery legs very gently – with care, so they didn't hurt them – they could make a roly-poly form itself into a round, armored ball that sheltered its soft bits. She remembered the feel of their rough skin as she rolled them around the palm of her hand. When put back on the ground, the roly-poly would wait a moment, then open up again and scurry away. It would be good to be that sort of creature, to carry one's own armor. Laying herself down on the hard earth, she hugged her knees into her chest.

The ground was cruel. She had no sleeping bag or blanket. Her backpack, which might have served as a pillow, she'd thrown away. *Stupid.* Quickly, she ate two of her energy bars and half of the pack of dried nuts. She drank some water from the canteen, but it disappeared too quickly, leaving her thirst far from quenched. She forced herself to save some for morning.

Darkness quickly engulfed her. With the coming of night, the woods grew louder. Creatures accustomed to the night shadows began to wake and move about. Their calls were like none she had heard before. They might be insects, birds, or large tree-dwelling animals. Their chorus built in intensity, until she had to cover her ears with her hands. This gesture shut out the ache of the noise, but still the cries crept into her head between tiny gaps in her fingers. It made her picture all manner of awfulness in the coming night.

It became, suddenly, ominously, still. She turned her head and stared up: a slice of sky was just visible between the trees. It had been overcast. Now the sky had turned a heavy black, and as she watched, a yellow hue appeared at the edges. The temperature dropped fast. She knew the warning signs, and her body tightened instinctively just before the first blinding flash of light. It was soon followed by the inevitable boom of thunder.

The first drops of rain tested her gently, as if for resistance. Then they quickened, thudding hard into her, coldly, and without compassion. The forceful rain stripped away the last remaining pleasure of her day. It ran boldly down her face, washing away her slim confidence. The frequent lightning lit the forest with a blinding white glare, its after-image making white ghost trees dance before her eyes. She shut them tightly. She was in terrible danger of being struck by lightning. If it were going to happen anyway, she didn't want to watch. *I've been out in lots of thunderstorms – I've never been struck before.* The thought seemed worse than senseless, and was soon followed by its logical conclusion. *There's always a first time.* She shut her eyes tighter; there was nothing she could do about it. The thunder boomed. She felt the ground rumble under her.

The rain became a deluge of hungry sheets of water plunging across the forest, falling as if too heavy for themselves, as if they were over-full and their thin skins were bursting. The water could not get back to earth fast enough, and it fell with an unexpected and fearsome urgency. It was relentless. It didn't seem possible that it could rain so hard for so long, that thunder could be so loud.

The rain bore down on her, birthing mud, sweeping away the leaves with its rivulets. She didn't move. She knew she was crying but couldn't feel the tears flow down her cheeks; they merged with the rain and washed into the earth. The rain needled arrows of cold into her flesh. It ran into her ears and down her neck, inside her thin shirt. It embraced her with icy fingers, intimate and terrifying. She prayed for someone to appear, to help her, to tell her what to do.

Her violent shivering continued for some time, but eventually, it stopped. This was a bad sign; even her body's will to live was abandoning her. She stared blankly at the space where the canteen lay – she didn't move to open it and let it fill with rainwater.

In the dimmest, coldest, darkest hours of that long night, the rain became alive with murderous intent. Waking in the small hours of the night – the hours that smelt of death – could make even the strongest spirit long to leave this earthly test, to pass onto a calmer, easier place. And she had never felt strong at all. She longed for the freedom the rain offered, longed for it to become a drowning river that would release her from herself.

It was not the rain that made her long for death, not the night alone. It was facing all the moments that had come before. It was facing her past that she could never erase, the shame of the choices she had made. It was facing herself in darkness.

She watched herself from some distance, and knew that, for the woman who lay curled on the cold, wet earth, there seemed not a single point of light in the universe, that the point of it all had become impossibly elusive. She was sure that the baby had perished. How could she save it, when she couldn't even save herself?

When all was black, her exhaustion led her into a troubled sleep. She dreamt of being swept away by unforeseen tidal waves.

Through that long, dark night, the man watched as her confidence ebbed away.

You are right to lose hope. You don't have the power to save yourself. Soon...soon I will come for you.

CHAPTER 3

The sun's warmth on her face woke her, and she immediately longed for the sweet unconsciousness of sleep. She was still here. It hadn't been a bad dream.

She was completely water-logged. Her clothes were flattened against her skin, saturated by the rain. Her vibrant orange windbreaker was covered in mud, and her combat trousers had fared no better. She stood up and removed the two outer layers, shaking the windbreaker to remove some of the mud, and wringing out the long-sleeved t-shirt, watching the muddy water drip onto the earth. She tied them around her waist, and shivered in the one layer remaining, the damp red sleeveless t-shirt with the sequined-on queen's crown.

Hunger growled through her, followed closely and urgently by thirst. She felt in the pocket of her trousers for the last of the energy bars and the nut mix. It was lucky they'd been in plastic bags. She ate them quickly, without tasting them. The canteen water disappeared almost as fast. *That's breakfast over. And lunch and dinner too. That's all of it, gone.*

She folded up the zip-lock bags that had held her scant food supply and tucked them neatly into her pocket. The movement was purely mechanical; it seemed pointless to be saving plastic bags in her hopeless situation.

She stared blankly at the ground, thinking of the confidence she'd felt the day before when she was running, as if searching for it amongst the wet leaves. It was gone. It had been like trying to fill an empty reservoir with one heavy rain. The deluge had only dampened the mud.

She had a sudden uncomfortable sensation of being watched.

Glancing around her for the source of the feeling, she was met by a burst of loud chattering in a nearby tree. It wasn't, as she'd expected, a bird. It was a tiny pair of lion-like monkeys.

Their small faces were black, be-maned by a darker orange of rough fur. In sharp contrast to the black of their faces their fur was a deep gold, the color of the sun in a child's drawing of the seaside. They sat motionless on the tree branch. Their long tails hung down, thin and nearly hairless at the base and down their length, but towards the end, thickened with short, course, darker fur.

Just like the tail of a lion, she thought. *Lion-monkeys, that's what I'll call them.*

As if they'd heard her, the tiny smiling lion faces looked towards her, then back at each other, and then towards her again. They chattered back and forth, taking turns. "*Ch-ch-ch-ch ch.*" "*Ch-ch-ch-ch ch-CH.*" Their voices were loud and resonating. She felt suddenly self-conscious, as if they were discussing how messy she looked. They moved their arms about, as if punctuating particular points with special emphasis. They shook their manes. Then, as if they had come to a concordance, for a moment they were silent. They stared at Halley, long and hard. One of them yawned suddenly, and she imagined a tiny roar. Together they broke into a pleasingly fluid motion, swinging away through the trees, arm by arm, using tails as well. They looked like they were on a mission.

Watching the monkeys move away, Halley's loneliness hit her hard. Even monkeys had friends. The longing she felt for another was so powerful, she felt nauseous. She moved to shoulder her black backpack, and then remembered she'd thrown it away. She moved off; she couldn't bear to be still any longer.

The forest floor was wet and muddy, the leaves soggy underfoot. There was an air of decay, as the leaves crumbled into dirt, providing food for the mature trees. *It's a form of cannibalism,* she thought with a shudder.

Walking was difficult. Where she least expected it the ground deepened with mud, sucking at the edges of her shoes. Water dripped from the trees. When she glanced up, it fell with astounding aim into her eyes, making her blink rapidly. After a short while, she lost the trail, and while she attempted to make progress, she felt she might well be traveling in circles. She had no map and no compass, and even if she had, it wouldn't help. She had no destination. Her only aim was to find the baby she had heard cry.

She felt an urgent need to leave the woods, to see the edge of the horizon again. But first she had to find the baby, she reminded herself. In her head, she could still hear its wail. *As if I could even help it! Why did I ever come here? I should have just stayed with Fernando. Maybe it wouldn't have been so bad, to stay with him. Maybe it wouldn't have been so dark.*

Doubt nibbled at her, a school of small, hungry fish, doubt for her competence, for her ability to make decisions, for her ability to protect herself. The doubt grew sharper teeth with each misstep, with each lost moment.

As Halley traveled, the undergrowth grew drier. *The storm couldn't have been as big here, for it to dry out so fast.* As dry earth reappeared, the topmost layer of leaves began to crisp. The birds cawed and trilled, as if celebrating the sunshine. Her guess at some of their calls was confirmed – a group of Black-faced Laughing-thrushes noisily announced their presence – their black face guards made them look like masked robbers. She liked the song of the Jungle Crow the best. It was always louder than the others, and she liked to imagine its cries as the words "Don't Quit; Don't Quit; Don't Quit".

She needed the encouragement. Her hunger gnawed relentlessly, and her mouth was parched. The vibrant red berries on the bushes mocked her, red demon eyes winking. They looked alluring, but she couldn't be sure they were safe to eat. Reluctantly, she left them. The situation was getting desperate: she'd had a full day with very little food, and just two canteens of water.

Come on Halley, we've been this way already! Get your act together! Think!

The self-criticism reminded her of the way she'd talked to herself the night before. She knew why she didn't like to be alone. Her voice was cruel. She tried to break the pattern by speaking aloud. "When did I start to speak to myself this way?" she said. "I remember a time when I used to believe I could do anything, could be anything." She had no answer. The endless day stretched on and on, and the blisters on her feet burned and then burst.

Hours later, she came upon a dried-out waterfall, its rocky, desiccated riverbed spread long and empty before her. She stopped short. Her hand moved to cover her mouth.

She knew this waterfall. This river.

The surprise of this realization immobilized her completely. *It can't be.*

This was where she and her father had planted wildflower seeds. In the fertile land near the river, the seeds had sent a multitude of shoots skywards. It had been a long-lasting delight of different colors, sizes, shapes, and textures. She would sit and run her fingers along the various leaves, feeling their softness or their roughness, observing how their veins ran along their backs, even tasting the flowers as they bloomed each season.

The summer she turned twelve, the scarlet ibises had come, as if by magic, to sit upon the grey rocks of the waterfall, their red plumage glowing in the sun. That summer, she began to come to the waterfall alone for the first time. She told herself it was to watch them, but it was more than this. It was carving out her first private space. The birds gave her a focus, each tiny move they made, as they dipped their curved black beaks in the water, as they showed off, just a little, with their brilliant color, their self-assurance. The hours she'd spent watching them spread their wings wide to splash in the water were some of her most treasured memories. During that summer with them, she'd transformed slowly and peacefully from girl to woman. The wildflower garden by the waterfall had been her soul-place.

Her head was pounding, and a light sweat broke out on her forehead.

This can't be the same place. I've never been here before. There's been nothing else familiar about this forest...we drove hours to get here... I didn't know the trail head...

The truth stirred and grew large, too large to leave any room for doubt.

She was trembling. Her own words came back to her, the words she'd spoken to Fernando before entering this strange forest: *A new place to begin.*

What had she done!

Somehow, she had unraveled time and space from its usual continuum. *I didn't mean it. I don't want to begin again.* She was breathing fast, her heart pounding hard. A sense of vertigo threatened to overpower her. The world was moving in a way in which it should not. This waterfall belonged in a different country. In a different time.

She stared at the place where the water no longer flowed, and felt herself dry up. Sinking down, she trailed her hand on the dry earth at the edge of the empty river, rubbing marks in the dust. It was as drained of moisture as a thin cotton sheet hung too long in the summer sun. Between her fingers, Halley crushed a small bit of loose dirt, and watched it filter through her fingers.

Her eyes traveled upwards to the trees. *That was our swinging tree.* On long summer afternoons, she and her brother had swung from a rope tied to the largest tree, leaping off in full flight like young gibbons, trying to plumb the depths of the pool at the waterfall's base. The remnants of the rope were still there.

And there...that was my garden, she thought. All that remained were dead, wilted heads of wildflower blossoms. An unseemly smell of rot was in the air. She tried to remember the flowers alive, to see the garden.

The river was empty, the life gone. As if it had been dammed and blocked and would not flow again. She hung her head. She didn't want to look anymore. *It's been so many years. But I never imagined this place could dry out, that the wild flowers could die.* The loss was vast, a desecration.

She sat down on the ground to compose herself, legs crossed, hands on her knees, staring blankly. Abruptly, she collapsed forward, as if she could no longer hold herself upright, and she rested her head in her hands, her face covered. *No. I don't want it to be gone like this, don't let it be. Did I do this? Did my words change things from how they were?*

She closed her eyes tightly, forcing them to remain closed, willing it to be untrue, and willing that when she re-opened her eyes it would be as it was. Her brow was furrowed, a deep tense line.

When she did open her eyes, nothing had changed. It was worse looking again on the devastation, when she had recreated how it used to be behind her closed eyelids.

She picked up one of the flowers and examined it, looking for answers, trying to understand what had happened. Her heart began to pound faster. The stem had been cut straight through. Still holding the flower, she lifted her eyes to the mass of dead flowers; they all had been cut. "Someone's done this on purpose," she said, very quietly. The words, spoken aloud, made the reality sink in.

Halley scrambled up, and moved away fast from the dry riverbed and dead flowers. She was suddenly quite frightened. *Who cut the wildflowers?* If the flowers had been cut purposely, the waterfall might have been blocked intentionally too. Someone had destroyed her soul-place, and they had done it on purpose. It was crazy to think it had been done to destroy *her,* but that's just what she thought.

The daylight was beginning to fade. The ground, littered with dry leaves, crackled and crunched with each footstep. As she moved further into the woods, away from the dry waterfall, the noise made her uneasy. It gave away her position, making her too easy to track.

At a fork in the trail, she stopped to decide which direction to take. The leaves continued crunching for a moment after she had stopped, and then were suddenly silent. She was being followed! Her eyes widened as she swallowed a scream.

"There aren't any large animals in these woods," she said, measuring the depth of her fear by the tone of her voice. Even in the gathering dusk, her soft voice was moderately calm; its sound reassured her. She thought for a moment. "But I didn't know about the snakes..." Randomly, she chose a trail, and rushed forward, trying to outdistance her fear.

The path she chose was difficult. Exposed roots of trees got in the way and slowed her down. At first she tried to step high and move between them in a fast jog. She was quickly exhausted from the effort. Looking back over her shoulder, fear pounding in her, she tripped and landed shockingly hard, scraping the skin off her palms on a rough tree root. The tears that blurred her vision were out of proportion to the pain of scraped palms. She blinked them away, and got to her feet fast, heart racing with imagined terrors. Another loud crackle somewhere behind her made her whole body tighten. *I've got to hurry, got to find somewhere safe. I can't spend tonight outside.*

In the past, Fernando had found their shelters, following thin trails, seeking out hidden caves with his sharp eyes. But he wasn't here to help. Her eyes sought small tracks off the main trail, visible only by a slight discoloration in ground cover. She'd have to be moving slowly to spot them, as they were often unused for weeks or months. The call of an early owl made her heart leap painfully. *I've got to find a place to hide.*

Unwillingly, she slowed her walk even more. Sweat ran down her forehead into her eyes. She rubbed it away impatiently. The hair on the back of her neck lifted: the sound of someone tracking her was suddenly louder, more obvious. She wheeled around, her hands held high in a martial arts guard, steeling herself to face whatever was there.

The empty motionless forest made a mockery of her stance. No one was there. She felt a collapsing inside. Dropping her hands, she turned around, and walked on. She tried to ignore her quickened breathing and the sweat trickling down the back of her neck.

It took longer than she liked, but she finally found a small off-shoot trail. It was just as she'd expected: overgrown, with small flexible branches that snapped back into place after she'd pushed through. In the ebbing daylight, she moved hastily along the path, and after several minutes, came to the edge of a massive tree. She knew this type of tree: it would shelter her. She stood very still.

If she stayed this frightened for long, alone in the woods, she'd go mad. So she didn't enter the shelter straight away, telling herself that the delay would prove the woods were safe, that she wasn't afraid she was being followed. After all, what protection did a tree shelter really provide?

She stood outside the shelter, trying to assuage her fear by telling herself a story about the tree, like a bedtime story one would tell a young child to chase away nightmares.

"Long years ago," she said aloud, "this tree sprouted roots from some of its high branches. It was on a quest similar to the quest that draws you."

She stopped; it wouldn't do for the tale to be told this way, in a hurry, in a voice tensed with fear. With effort, she gentled her voice and slowed her speech, and then she continued. Now her voice reminded her of a river, smooth and flowing.

"This tree – Ballyo, it was called, after an ancient wise man – had grown so tall that it had lost all touch with the earth. With the source. It reached for the ground through its limbs, sending out long aerial roots, aiming to bury them deep in the rich earth.

Ballyo had grown very tall; without the extra strength of a more vast foundation, it would topple in the high winds of winter."

There, that was better.

"Over time, the aerial roots stretched their fingers towards the earth. Some died, alone on their heroic journeys, dwindling away to nothingness. The evidence of their failed attempts hung for all to see, in the shortened hairy strands that hung only half-way to the earth."

She paused, and thought of herself, thought of her journey. Would she be one that made it, or not? She closed her eyes: the crackles she heard would just be birds nesting down for the night. *I won't let myself look around.* She forced herself to continue.

"Some, the strongest aerial roots, made it. These touched down, and felt within the earth for crevices and finger-holds. They found them, and they grew, over the course of many life-times. Those lifetimes were full of the usual mix of joy and sorrow, life and death."

She would not allow herself to think of her own life yet, of what it had cost her to live until now. She breathed deeply, and continued the story.

"Eventually the roots found the quality of earth they sought. It was warm and dark and full of nutrients, and it opened the way for them, and they became deep-rooted. They had found their homes and they grew strong and thick, and were then responsible for the strength of the tree entire."

Halley stopped talking, and assessed her body. It had worked – she had been soothed by her own story, her fear calmed. She was ready to examine the shelter that Ballyo could provide.

Between the main tree and the roots was a sheltering space, roofed by small branches and leaves. She was drawn to the leaves immediately, by the ordinariness of their shape. They were just like leaves should be: no fanciness, the main body just a simple elongated ellipse. The leaf had one central vein from which many lines of veins radiated, each at a thirty-degree angle; this made the little leaf resemble nothing so much as the etching of a tiny Christmas tree, ready to be decorated. She ran her finger along the back of the leaf, letting the central vein slide under her fingernail. She liked the thickness of the vein, the way it filled the space under the nail, the way it stood out from the back of the leaf. The rest of the leaf was soft and smooth, yet nicely thick. Everything about it was re-assuring.

Better still, the space these leaves roofed was almost fully en-circled by long, slender roots that were anchored into the earth. She ran her hand along one of them in memory of her story. *Brave root.* Some of the roots had thickened and were now the size of her forearms. They were like small tree trunks themselves. Between neighboring roots, only tiny gaps existed, so the shelter inside was almost fully enclosed.

A small opening remained that acted as an entrance. This was fringed with more hairy roots that were working their way to-wards the earth below. *Not failures.* She had remembered some-thing else about this tree: the aerial roots absorbed nutrients and water directly from the air. They were of value to the greater tree – it wasn't just the ones that had touched the earth that were worthy. All were worthy.

She peered inside. The shelter was surprisingly spacious, with room for her to stretch out full length if she curled up just slightly, and still have plenty of space around her. It was carpeted with the ordinary-leaf-shaped leaves, which were brown and old. They would make a soft bed.

Just before she entered the shelter, she looked behind her, back into the darkening forest. Standing half in and half out of the entrance, statue-like and silent, she willed whatever it was that had been following her to show itself. Nothing appeared.

She moved inside and lay down. Her exhaustion dragged her into a deep sleep, where she dreamt of all manner of food and drink. Occasionally though, she grunted and fought, as if in the midst of some nightmare from which she could not awaken.

CHAPTER 4

Something startled her awake. Her eyes snapped open. It was dark. There was an acrid tang in the air. It smelled like a match had been struck, but she couldn't see or hear anything. For a long moment, all was still. *Just my imagination, playing tricks on me.* Still, she sat up, intent on slowing the rapid-fire thumping of her heart.

A red spark appeared in the air. She watched wide-eyed as a tiny blue flame moved slowly through the air. It touched something, which burst into sudden flame. The heat of it – a torch – leapt out at her, seeming to scorch the very air.

There was a dark figure sitting in front of her! So close, it could have reached out to touch her. The torch blinded her. She shoved herself back hard. But, mistaking the distance between herself and the tree roots, she slammed the back of her head. Sharp pain shot through her; acid pouring into her stomach. Her breath came in quick gasps, too quick to get enough oxygen. Halley was shocked into silence, and, try as she would, she could not speak, could not scream. Frozen in place, her body began to shake uncontrollably. *It could kill me.* The thought made the blood in her head pound harder, made her dizzy and lightheaded.

Silence filled the space between them. When the dark figure finally spoke, the quiet had lasted far too long to consider it normal.

"Don't be afraid," a man's voice said. "I saw you crying. By the butterflies. I thought you were lost. I wanted to help you, but I lost sight of you." He looked at her closely. "Please stop trembling like that, like I'm some sort of monster – I won't hurt you. I want to help you."

Why then, bring the word "hurt" into it?

Shaking her head, she willed the voice away, trying to block it from her ears. It was too silky, too smooth. She couldn't see him properly in the darkness with the torch light in her eyes. She was acutely aware of his body invading her personal space, violating her sense of safety.

Did he say he'd seen me crying by the butterflies?

She thought about the waterfall that had reminded her of her parents, about the butterflies hovering. *But that was so long ago! Has he been tracking me all this time?* A shudder moved through her again, and she pulled herself closer, making a smaller bundle of her body.

"I don't need your help!" She thrust the words out as if they were weapons, willing power behind her voice. "I'm not lost. I know where I am and I know what I'm doing." Unintentionally, she spoke fast and with a sense of urgency. "Please. Just go away." Her right hand had wrapped itself tightly around the thickened trunk of a nearby tree root.

He didn't move or speak.

Her voice had wavered. It held the truth of the night she'd spent unsheltered in the rain, of the long, devastating days she'd spent wandering lost.

He kept quiet, as if letting her think.

In the darkness, an image played before her eyes: the dried-out waterfall; the decapitated flowers. She wasn't safe. She wasn't safe at all.

After an overlong pause, so long that Halley grew desperate to shift her position and move her rapidly numbing legs, he cocked his head slightly, like a bird of prey.

"I don't believe you," he said.

The words stretched out long, an elastic band that threatened to snap. He considered her. "You're so small," he said, with something like kindness that was not kindness in his voice. "You can't know what you've gotten yourself into – you're a little sparrow, in a large and dangerous wood. I can show you the way out."

"But what about the baby?" she said. She covered her mouth with her hands, but it was too late.

With a wave of his hand, he dismissed it.

"The baby. Its mother ran out of formula. I showed her a shortcut back to the trailhead. They're safe now. And, more importantly, that baby is quiet."

"Oh."

It was a small word to express the heartbreaking sense of loss she suddenly felt.

He seemed to mistake her expression. "Forgive me, I've been terribly impolite. I haven't even introduced myself. I'm Trance. Trance Darkling."

Halley felt she was hearing him from some great distance. The baby was gone. It had had nothing to do with her. She would not be the one to save it. She looked across at the man before her. He could lead her out of the woods, back to her real life. It had not been a new place to begin after all. "Oh God," she whispered aloud.

Immediately she regretted it. The man shifted the torch, and she could almost see his face. In the half-light, his eyes had narrowed. Her despair over the baby was quickly replaced by a renewal of her fear of this stranger. *Trance Darkling?* The air left her lungs. *What kind of name is that?*

She shook her head again, harder this time; his sing-song voice and his words had dulled her senses. She tried to calm herself. Spots of light swam in front of her eyes. The words this stranger had spoken swirled around her. *He said he won't hurt you, Halley. He saved the baby. He knows the way out. You need his help. You're imagining things – it's only the darkness that's making him so scary.*

Letting go of the tree root, she held one of her hands in the other and felt how cold and small her hands were, felt her pulse thudding fast in her veins. *Oh stop it Halley – just let him help you! You don't know what you're doing and you need help!*

She watched as the stranger leaned forward, as if easing himself. The movement narrowed the distance between them. He smiled, and the familiarity of the smile was disconcerting.

Tentatively, she asked, "Can you really show me the way out?"

All her instincts said to run, but she didn't. If he could help her, she could get out of the woods and never come back. To be free of the darkness, to be in the light again, the thought was lovely. Enticing.

The steel in her voice had melted away. She sounded small and weak, as he had described her. Halley shifted uncomfortably on her thin buttocks. The air in the shelter was heavy and close. She stared hard at the man before her, felt the familiarity in his mannerisms with simultaneous attraction and aversion.

As the torch burned lower, Trance stared back. "Of course I can show you the way out," he repeated smoothly. "Please, have some of my water – you must be desperately thirsty."

Invitingly, he held out an old canvas canteen, but though her eyes watched it thirstily she didn't move to take it.

I am so thirsty. Her very cells were crying out for water.

She leaned forward and took hold of the canteen, took his offering. Drinking in long, hungry gulps, some of the water spilled out, dripping down her chin and along her neck and even intrusively down, down below her queen t-shirt and onto her breasts. It reminded her of the rain during her long unsheltered night, of her longing for death. She shivered anew.

Even with her vast thirst, the water was not refreshing. It tasted metallic and foul. Hurriedly, she passed the canteen back.

"Look – you're shaking," he said. "Please, let me help." His voice was gentle, his eyes soft. "At least tell me your name."

"Halley. My name is Halley." Drawing on some strength deep inside her, she spoke with sudden certainly. "I won't decide anything until morning. Not until I can see your face more clearly." In the dark, he was all shadow, only vague hollows where his eyes should have been.

"All right."

She sat still, watching him closely, speaking no more. But inside her head, she belittled herself. *Get a grip Halley – he's just trying to help.* The hairs stood out on her forearms though, and she could not "get a grip" at all.

When the torch burned out, the voice in her head spoke more urgently. *Who are you Trance? Why have you come here? Something about you is deadly to me. I can feel that deep in my bones.* She shifted her seat uncomfortably. *But I don't know where to go, and I've been lost since I fell down the hill into these woods. I'm not strong enough to get back alone.* The blisters on her feet burned and her head throbbed where she'd bashed into the tree roots. She was afraid to put her hand to it, afraid she'd feel the wetness of blood. Her hunger was deepening – she needed food and water, and she didn't know what she was going to do – she couldn't last much longer. She longed to silence her voice, but it hummed on. *Sparrow. I wish I knew what it* meant *to be a sparrow. I want it to mean free and able, quick to maneuver. If only Fernando had been calling me those things when he called me Sparrow...if only this man was...*

On a sudden impulse, she felt in the inner pocket of her jacket. She had an irrational urge to touch the crow's feather, the totem she had carried to remind her of its message at the start of her journey: "You will be all right".

It wasn't there.

Swallowing hard, she began to check the rest of her pockets, already knowing she wouldn't find it.

In time, her exhaustion pulled at her with long boney fingers, dragging her back to sleep. It was the deep sleep of the lost, who dread awakening because they know when they do, they will find they are still powerless.

She slept. He did not. He watched and waited, knowing that when she woke, she would already be tamed. Indeed, she had been tamed the instant she'd allowed him to stay.

Always so easy with you, he thought. *Your weakness is my strength. So many times I have nearly finished you. This, this is my time.*

CHAPTER 5

I n the early morning light, he stepped outside. She followed.

Walking several steps behind him, she noted the broadness of his shoulders. Her eyes worked their way down the back of his body, searching for clues. His jacket hugged the muscles of his upper back tightly, the fabric straining. Where his waist narrowed, it went suddenly limp. His lower body, encased in tight jeans, reminded Halley of a quarter-horse, thickly muscled, designed for short bursts of power and speed. She couldn't see the lines of his arms or shoulders, but the way his body moved suggested strength there as well.

There was more to his walking movement than just strength. He moved with assurance, with power. The canteen slung over his shoulder swung with each stride, back and forth, its movement mesmerizing. His stride was long, as if he were in the habit of moving quickly, perhaps impatiently. She had to half-jog every now and then just to keep up. Taking her eyes back upwards, she noticed his whitish-blond hair. It was cropped close all over, except for a small thin braid that snaked from the base of his skull. She could just see the root of the braid – the rest of it was tucked inside the collar of his shirt.

Her leg stalled half-way down to the ground, and she had to consciously place her foot down to continue walking. The white snake braid didn't fit. As if hearing her thought, he stopped walking and turned to her.

His expression was hard to read, but the make-up of his face was spell-binding. The cleft in his chin cut deep, the square jaw with its promise of strength. She saw with surprise that his face was absolutely and strangely symmetrical. His eyes were a light ice-blue. The white color of his hair contrasted sharply with the deep tan of his skin. The darkness she'd sensed during the night was not there. At least not in his face.

He didn't speak, only nodded slightly as if to acknowledge that she was following him, before turning again to lead the way.

Later, when she had settled into the pattern of his footsteps and was stepping carefully over tree roots, when she was feeling more at ease with him, she happened to look up again at the back of his head. Just at that moment, he'd turned to look to the left. She felt a deep unsettling in her stomach. *His ears.* They were oddly out of proportion, too small for his head. *The ears of a predator,* she thought.

She tried to ignore how she felt. She didn't want to distrust him, didn't want to face the action such distrust would require. It would mean she'd have to leave him. Then she'd be alone again, lost. She just couldn't face it. They were only ears. *And yet they make me feel frightened again…like that white snake braid.*

Trance stopped and turned around again. For the first time, he smiled at her. It was a broad smile, open and warm. But his even, perfectly white teeth made a caricature of his faultless smile, made it seem unreal. His thick lips moved slowly and unhurried as he spoke for the first time that morning.

"We're nearly there," he said. "Soon, we'll be at the river. We can take my boat and we'll be out of the woods in no time."

Was he watching her for a reaction? He seemed to be.

"Don't worry," he added. "I know the way."

She smiled back, but the smile was false, as if she were willing the muscles around her jaw to lift, but not quite succeeding. He didn't seem to notice, and to her, it felt the same as all her smiles; forced from a deep place inside that was not smiling at all.

He turned to lead again, and she followed, carefully avoiding looking at him. It struck her that she had been watching him as she used to watch Fernando – from behind. Following. A surge of anger flowed through her.

"These woods can be dangerous you know," he said ominously, without looking around. "I've heard of people who came here for day hikes, and were never seen again. No one finds their bodies or their bones. It's as if they just disintegrate, out here alone."

She was silent, and he stopped to look back at her.

"Oh – I've frightened you. I'm so sorry," he said gently. "And you're cold too – look, you're shivering. Here, take my jacket."

He slipped the canteen from his shoulder, and placed it carefully on the ground. With the movement, the long white braid slipped free from his collar, and hung loose down his back. It was at least six inches long, braided tightly and with precision. She couldn't take her eyes off it. Removing his jacket, he stepped close to her.

She hadn't noticed before, but the color of the jacket was ambiguous; it might have been green or grey or even black. For some reason, this ambiguity, this un-graspable-ness alarmed her. Cape-like, he swung it over her. She watched it settle down over her body, as if in slow motion. The jacket was on her, over her shoulders, hiding her orange windbreaker completely. Her nostrils filled with a dank, stagnant smell –the smell of him. It was a smell remarkably out of place in someone with such clean, fresh looks, with his blond hair and blue eyes and small white teeth. It was like the jacket had been put away wet, left to grow moldy in a wardrobe without enough airflow.

He rested his hands on her shoulders a moment too long, as if to comfort her, but the weight of him, the weight of his jacket, was oppressive. The pressure of his hands was so great that she imagined herself moving into the earth, towards dampness and darkness.

Instinctively, she took a step backwards, slipping his hands quickly from her shoulders. Her mind worked fast – she still needed his help – she must not offend him. "Thank you," she said. "That's very kind of you. I'll be much warmer now." She shuddered and fought to control it so he wouldn't guess at her revulsion.

Trance slid his canteen back over his shoulder. He did not tuck the braid away again, and it hung whitely down his back against his grey shirt. She thought to question him about it, but instead kept carefully quiet. He led the way again through the woods, she heavy in his jacket, he utterly silent.

As they walked on, she found her eyes fixed on the white braid. It blinded her to everything else around her. She pondered why it was important, what it said of his character. She was frightened of him, but couldn't decide why. *Is it me? He seems so kind, so concerned. So familiar. I really do need his help. He hasn't done anything wrong. And yet...*

She couldn't place her finger on what was wrong, couldn't explain her intuition. The small hairs on the back of her neck stood out alertly; they had done so since she had heard him following her the day before. The wild-flowers on the forest floor were suddenly too bright. They were glaringly bright, their colors jarring. They looked illusory, as if they had been colored unnaturally to add a false brightness to her world. To seduce her into following.

She tried again to discern the source of her unease. The word came suddenly, causing her stomach to lurch: *Evil.* There was nothing to pin the word to, no reason for it to occur to her just then. He was handsome and smiled so well and yet there was a sense of evil about him. As if his ears and the braid he had hidden down his shirt collar were marks of his nature. Even more than anything physical, it had much to do with the way he had entered her life, in the dead of night. His feet crushed the leaves as he led the way. Even that was awful. And he was only walking, tramping along in his heavy black boots. The evil she sensed walked there with her, chilling her. She tried to shade her eyes from the brilliance of the wildflowers. Her heart beat like a wild animal, newly captured. *It's like waking at three-thirty in the morning all alone in the dark, and noticing a light has been left on and thinking, but I remember turning that light off... that's how he makes me feel.* She shuddered.

"Ah, here it is. The river." His words broke the long silence. He turned to face her with his perfect smile. "There's my boat..."

She wasn't listening; she was down on her hands and knees, scooping water into her cupped palms, gulping it down fast, letting its fresh taste wash away the lingering flavor of his water from the night before. Splashing her face, she rubbed her cheeks with the palms of both hands, as if to remove the past two days. She longed to keep her hands over her face and not have to see Trance again. His voice interrupted her thoughts.

"First, we'll eat," he said. "We won't be able to once we're on the river – the current is far too strong."

"I don't have anything left," she admitted quietly.

He lifted his eyebrows in what might have been a mocking expression. With a fast and unexpected movement, he spun towards the river. A knife flashed in the sunlight, and he thrust deep into the water, spearing a large, big-bellied fish. He heaved it out onto the riverbank. It thrashed on his knife, desperately sucking at the unfamiliar air. He smiled as he pulled it off the jagged knife. Holding the fish tightly in both hands, he smashed it on the rocks, smashed the life out of it, slamming it again and again. All the while his lips were raised in that terrible smile.

"What's wrong, Sparrow?" he said sharply, looking up at her only when the fish was finally still. "It's only a common carp, not some fish on the endangered list."

She stared at the blood on the rocks.

He contained himself. "Please, don't look so upset," he said, his voice softer this time. "We have to eat. Out here, we have to hunt to survive."

Halley didn't answer.

He gutted the fish with what seemed unnecessary cruelty,

roughly jerking its insides out onto the ground with his bare hands. She wanted to run away, but she was so hungry her mouth was watering. And anyway, she didn't trust what her intuition was saying about him. What was "evil" anyway? Was hunting evil?

Building a searing fire from loose twigs and dry leaves, he roasted the flesh of the carp. It was a freshwater fish and it should have tasted sweet and of the wilderness; she gagged as she ate.

Trance reached across and rested his hand on the sleeve of his jacket that she wore. His movement had an air of ownership.

"There, that's better," he said. "You were weak with hunger."

His inflection disturbed her. He had put special emphasis on the word "weak".

Trance stood up.

"We must hurry."

CHAPTER 6

Trance held her wrist firmly as he shepherded her towards his boat. He knew the urge to run was growing in her – it was visible in a captured animal tightness about her eyes. He shoved her roughly into the rear seat of the boat, and, leaning his heavy boots hard into the gravel riverbed, he pushed off from shore. Quickly, he hauled himself aboard. The boat shook precariously. Trance seated himself on the middle seat, facing the shore. With three pulls on the oars, they were away and moving fast down the steely river.

Halley's heart beat a staccato pulse. There was a metallic taste in her mouth. The river was swift but the water's surface strangely smooth. Trees flashed by on the edges of her vision. The piercing shrieks of birds split the air. It was all too fast and too loud. Too out of control.

Soon, they entered a gorge with high overhanging walls, and Trance looked directly at Halley for the first time since they'd boarded the boat. She was sitting as far as possible from him, shrunken inside his jacket. He rowed from the middle of the boat, facing Halley, guiding the boat without looking behind him to see the course they should follow.

How can he row without looking? The question became trivial when she saw the coldness of his eyes.

"Beautiful, isn't it?" he began, his tone unexpectedly soft, belying his face. He gazed up at the rock walls, worn perfectly smooth by the passage of water. "Have you traveled this river before?"

"No," she said, in a small voice. *Could I make it to the cliffs if I swam? Even if I could, there'd be no way to climb out. The walls are too smooth.* She moved uneasily on her seat.

"Are you sure?"

She wouldn't meet his eye. Her travels by boat had been curtailed a year ago. The memory of that last trip she knew intuitively not to share with Trance. Still, the memory flooded her, and she turned her eyes to the grey wooden planking of the boat's floor:

She and Fernando were using single-man kayaks to avoid traversing some difficult terrain. By foot, it would have taken hours to reach their campsite. In the approaching darkness, she had decided it was far safer to take the water route across a small bay.

Halfway out the wind rose unexpectedly, blowing them off course, out beyond their planned depth. He waved to her from his kayak, gesturing that she should move closer towards shore. His gesture made her notice the shark net – their kayaks were well outside it. The space inside the net loomed empty. Suddenly she felt disoriented – what were they doing outside the shark net? Wasn't it dangerous to be in the open water? A second later, she laughed aloud – of course they couldn't kayak inside the shark net – it only ran across a small section of the bay beach! She shook her head, glancing across to Fernando's kayak to see if he'd heard her laugh. She'd like to tell him her silly thought.

The smile left her face. There was a vertical fin – moving straight towards his boat.

She acted immediately. She ploughed her paddle deep into the water, pulled left-right-left-right with all the strength in her torso, and gained the lead. On seeing the turbulent wake made by her kayak, the shark veered towards her. She would never outrun it. But she had saved Fernando. That was all that mattered.

A moment later, the shark reared up towards her, its white teeth promising death. She swung her paddle hard, smashing the shark full-on across the nose. Not a killing blow, but enough to disorient it. It dove suddenly, and a few moments later, she saw it hundreds of meters away, headed out to sea. They both dug their paddles in, and made fast for the far shore.

Halley had never forgotten the wonder in Fernando's voice when they were finally safe. "My God, Halley!" he'd said. "I can't believe it – you saved me! That shark...I didn't even see the fin!"

He'd stopped and stared at her as if she were someone he didn't know. "Who would've believed a little Sparrow like you could save me!" Halley could see that in Fernando's eyes, she was admirable, and this meant the world to her.

Trance's voice slammed her from her reverie. "Had you not chosen the shortcut across the water, Fernando's life would not have been at risk. Your heroism!" he scoffed. "It was nothing. It was a desperate act brought about by your own foolish choice of route."

Halley felt his words as a blow. That moment, that moment had been hers! How dare he try to rewrite her history! She felt the bile rise in her throat, felt fury at his misinterpretation. She had been there! She knew she had saved Fernando's life.

She opened her mouth to speak but a terrifying realization silenced her absolutely. *How did he know I was thinking about that day when I didn't say a word? How did he know about that day at all?*

He continued the conversation as if she had replied. "Ah, but I can see the truth in your eyes – in the way you shrink back from me. You see I am right. You know you made a foolish choice that almost killed Fernando. He knew it too."

The words were a hot knife cutting through Halley's mid-section. She recalled again being safely ashore with Fernando, his words, his strange, double-sided compliment: *"Who would've believed a little Sparrow like you could save me!"* At the time, his admiration had made her feel elated. Now, the words took on a different meaning entirely. Fernando had been saying he was surprised she could save him, not that he admired her. He'd not believed in her, not at all. She dropped her eyes.

Trance was quiet – he was leaving her to brood.

CHAPTER 7

The bow of the boat cut a deep channel through the strangely still waters. Halley watched the steep granite walls for an opening, for anywhere she could escape. The terror was deep in her now, flooding her body, fed by the realization that this man knew all about her. He even knew her thoughts.

Trance watched her calmly. Then his eyes narrowed. He'd thought of something new.

"Most women I know wear their hair differently to you," he began. His thick lips curled. "They tie it back tightly. They are neatly groomed. You would do well to follow suit."

She reached up to touch her hair but quickly lowered her hand. The nights in the woods had left her wildish. Her hair was tangled. Parts had weaved together into links like strong hemp rope. Leaves were stuck in these links, dried mud, bits of twig.

"I've known women who brush their hair a hundred times a night, garnish it with oils to keep it lovely." His words hit her like stones. "Women who care for their skin, keeping out of the sun." He smiled, as if reflecting on their beauty. "They are youthful, attractive."

Halley stared back at him from her sun-darkened face. The skin around her eyes radiated soft lines, caused by squinting at the bright light of the sun. Her arms and legs bore scratches and bruises. The "women he knew" would not be damaged this way; they would behave with grace and poise.

She was filled with a deep sense of self-repugnance. Her bruises had earlier made her feel courageous and proud. She had even liked the feel of her hair after several days on the trail. But now she felt dirty and clumsy and unkempt.

From above them came a sharp angry cry. It was an eagle. It flew at Trance, talons exposed, a fury. He ducked; cursed; threatened the bird with his oar. He would have smashed it to pieces, just as he had done the helpless river fish, but it was too swift. It flew off into the trees.

The sight of the eagle made Halley feel a lifting, her spirit rising with it from the cold, bitter seat on the boat. The bird, temporarily thwarted, settled on an overhanging tree at the top of the cliffs, to watch them speed downriver. Its angry shriek echoed after them.

She said it first, as a whisper.

"No."

The word resonated in her belly, growing larger, rumbling like the beginnings of an avalanche.

"NO!" She spoke louder this time.

Trance looked up, all vestige of softness gone.

As if possessed by the eagle, she fought back.

"I won't hear any more! You know nothing about me – you can't judge me. You're wrong! I know who I am and what I have done. And I am not afraid of you!"

The smoothness of the river was gone. The wind had come, and was whipping the wavelets into small grey mountains.

This lack of fear: it was a lie. Her face had a sheen of sweat and she was breathing fast.

He sat, absolutely still and silent. His silence was what finally broke her, his set expression of utter contempt.

It wasn't until she had slumped forward in defeat that he spoke again. "A spoiled child," he hissed, "an ugly, wild, utterly spoiled child. If you are so special, why were you all alone at school? Why did the others not choose you for their teams or as a playmate?" He paused, continuing in an even harsher, bitter voice. "Why always by yourself on your bicycle? Why were you the brunt of all their jokes?"

She sank back onto her seat, deflated.

"What sort of woman would try to kill herself?"

The boat drifted. He had released the oars into the oarlocks, and was caressing the side of the boat with his right hand, gliding it back and forth, back and forth, while gazing up at the sky.

"Would a beautiful woman try to kill herself?"

He let his hand slip gently from the side of the boat into the cool water, allowing the hand to drag along behind the boat, creating a small wake. He sat back, as if pondering a rhetorical question, swishing his hand left and right.

Halley watched the disturbance his hand made in the smooth water. Her body jerked when he added, more loudly this time, "Would a woman who was loved by many try to kill herself, Halley? Someone who had a vital purpose for which to live?"

He answered the question himself, by shaking his head slowly, side to side. The white braid swung silently, over first one shoulder and then the other, negating the statements, rubbing out that beautiful, well-loved woman.

Halley bit her lip; she could taste blood.

More softly, he added, taking his gaze from the sky and staring hard at her with hostile, ice-blue eyes, "Or someone like you, Halley?"

He removed his hand from the water, and shook it hard, splashing cold water into her face. "Or someone like you, Halley? Someone ugly and unloved, incapable of doing anything right?" His voice grated over her, sandpaper rubbing off her flesh. "Do you remember Halley? Do you remember? The knife? The little black knife. You just *sat there* for hours, thinking about how it would feel on your wrists. Holding the knife. How it would feel to do it. Wondered if it would be too dull to cut. Crying. Wailing. Too cowardly to go through with it." He rolled his eyes with contempt, and continued more softly, each word drawn out, long and deadly. "You should have done it, you know. No one would've cared."

She looked away. His words brought it all back, made it real in an unbearable way. She had told no one about that time, not even Fernando. She was crying again, and these tears were not healing. They were the crumbling away of some deepest part of her. Her spirit retreated, and she hugged herself to herself and tried to will his words away. But she couldn't.

She sat, staring into the water, moving his words in her mouth like bits of broken glass, rubbing them off her flesh, tasting their sharpness.

The river narrowed, the rocky outcroppings becoming first small boulders, then large, dangerous ones. The boat picked up speed.

Halley saw herself, deep down at the bottom of a featureless well, with her head sunk on her arms. From this place, she could look inside and know: she had been here before. She had heard the very words Trance had spoken before. She thought carefully, as the answer swooped away from her, and then swooped back into view with greater clarity.

He had known where to strike. How had he known?

The white water began to bubble and froth around the boat, and she pondered the eagle's timely swoop. There was no coincidence here. Trance had seemed familiar because he *was* familiar; he was the darkness she had fought all her life.

From deep within her, from an untouched, undamaged place, she felt herself arise again. Not a roaring or a gushing or even a bubbling. Certainly not visible to Trance as he seemed to luxuriate in the damage he had wrought; she did not stand up or even sit up taller. It was if she had removed his coat, and let the orange glow of her windbreaker show through, though she did not.

The growing roar of the river awoke Trance from his reverie; he glanced up, his ice-blue eyes taking her in.

She looked down. It was she who was facing the course of the river. Listening for the break in the roaring, for the lull, she waited. When she heard it, she glanced up quickly. The river was being split asunder by a smooth, blackened rock in the center of the white water. He glanced over his shoulder. They raced towards it, but Trance was smug, certain he could simply use his oar to steer them around.

At the moment they came alongside the rock, Halley leapt to her feet, throwing all her weight outwards, away from the rock. The boat twisted, its bottom rising up from the river, lifting, flipping, like a salmon turned over going upriver. They were flung overboard, into the deep, frothing, turbulent water.

CHAPTER 8

Underwater, Halley held her breath and began to swim. *Got to stay under. Move towards shore. Let him drift downriver.*

The current was fast, and before she had got her bearings, she was swept unexpectedly into the sharp edge of a rock, scraping the skin off her knee. Her face clenched in pain, but she was careful not to cry out, not to open her mouth underwater and begin the process of drowning. She clenched her teeth and added force to her stroke, making her way cautiously through the swift water.

Trance was all around her, as if he had become the sharp-edged rocks in the river, the water that threatened to drown her. Maybe it was because of his jacket – she noticed the weight of it suddenly – it was like he was still grasping her by the shoulders and pressing her down. She stopped swimming and struggled out of it. Once off, the greedy waters sucked the jacket swiftly away. Without it, her remaining clothes felt powerfully buoyant.

Just a few more moments underwater...a few more strokes. Pulling hard, she drew herself away from the spot where she'd tipped the boat.

Finally, in desperation for a breath, she shot to the surface. She sucked in air hungrily, at the same time searching the river for Trance, her body poised to duck back under. She imagined his face, compressed with fury.

From the corner of her eye, she felt rather than saw the movement. The light of the sun was suddenly blocked, as some shadowy thing hurled towards her, fast. She had no time to react.

Something struck her hard on her right arm, throwing her body sideways. Pain shot through her and she hit the water, her mouth open, making her swallow water, too much water. She began to cough furiously.

Trance! God! Wait…NO!

It wasn't Trance. It was the pointed hull of the boat, rearing up at her. Pulled to by the current, it came at her once more, white and sharp and deadly.

Instinctively, she threw herself back underwater, diving, trying to pull herself deep. Her damaged right arm sent a thrill of agony through her. After the first pull, the arm wouldn't work at all; she could use only her weaker left arm. *Faster, come on Halley! You've got to get down!* She watched for rocks, afraid the current might bash her against them again without warning. She needed the deeper water – that would save her.

Holding her breath, she prayed: *Make it go away, make it go away. I can't hold on much longer.*

It came at her again, dropping down underwater like a bird after a fish. She swung both her legs up and landed a desperate shoving kick on the hull. The boat shifted. It was just enough. It was caught by a downstream current, and pulled away. In a moment, it was gone.

She breathed out hard. Flattening her arms to her sides, she kicked herself upwards, moving like a rocket. When she reached the surface, she was coughing and spitting out river water. Her whole body was shaking. The current grabbed her, and she was dragged downriver.

Her only thought was Trance. Had he been swept downriver too? She scanned the area but didn't see him.

Kicking hard to stay on the surface, she stared at the shoreline, praying for a way out of the river. Ten feet ahead, she saw it – a break in the smooth canyon wall, at a corner in the river where the water looked calm. Just beyond it, the fury of the whitewater increased dramatically. Hurriedly, she scanned the bank. No sign of Trance. Just the green and brown of trees and rocks.

The river was already pulling her towards the rougher whitewater. She made fast for the shallow corner, trying to ignore the sharp pain each time she pulled with her right arm. At first, she made no progress, swimming hard to simply stay in one place. She decided to go diagonal to the current, took a deep breath, and kicked as hard as she could. When she broke free of the river's pull, it was with a sudden sense of popping. She moved into the calmer water of the sheltered area and treaded water, breathing fast.

The shoreline was fronted by large rocks; she scanned them to find a way out of the river. *There, that one.* Her chosen rock sloped into the water at a steep angle. Though slick with black moss, it was her only hope. The rest of the rocks were smooth monoliths, between seven and ten feet tall.

The sloping rock was split in one obvious spot, forming a ridge she could hold onto. Catching the fingers of her left arm in the ridge, she pulled hard, and managed to slide part-way up. Unexpectedly, the weakened rock slab sheered off, and she fell back into the water with a splash, going in over her head. Exhaustion filled her as worked her way back up to the surface. It was hopeless.

Don't give up Halley. Try again.

This time she used her damaged but more sensitive right hand, gritting her teeth, feeling for tiny ridges in the rock that meant her life. The ridges she sought were small, barely visible, but her fingertips could feel them. When she found them, the edges of her fingerprints held on tight. Miraculously, she felt her body pull upwards, until she was sliding up the slanted rock face. Carefully, so carefully, she lifted her left arm, finding another hold, and then another. Inch by inch she moved up the slick rock, away from the river. Finally, she made it to the top.

Warm. The rock is warm. She lay still on its flat surface. In time, the rock's warmth and afternoon sun warmed her. The lesson she'd learned from Trance echoed in her tired head.

Listen to your intuition. What is bad is bad. Do not let it close.

This time, the lesson was learned.

CHAPTER 9

Halley didn't move. Her saturated clothes dried slowly, releasing her skin from their tight, wet grip. The warm afternoon sun gave way to twilight. The insects in the woods resumed their dull humming. The sound was like dozens of musicians that were busy, productive, and happy. A few hours later, the noise built to a deafening, chaotic crescendo, as if the insects were now playing in an orchestra and the conductor had gone slightly mad. Just at the peak of the noise – as if the conductor had angrily called a halt to their music with a sharp downward slice of his baton – the sound came to an abrupt halt. The insects were immediately and entirely silent.

In time, a three-quarter moon rose high above the trees, shining through a gap in the leaf cover. Its elliptical face lit her prone, unmoving form. The moon burnished her to a milky color. It was as if she had picked up a goblet full of deeply nutritious white liquid, and, as she drained it again and again and again, she was colored white from the inside out. Despite the healing light, she still couldn't find the strength to move.

In its own time, the moon crossed the sky, leaving Halley alone once more on her flat river rock. The blackness in its wake seemed darker for the light that the moon had so callously borne away.

Then…then the forest was peopled with the most frightening of wood sprites, who longed to reach out and drag her away, to pull her along by her straggled brown hair to some terrible place. But worse, far worse than the wood sprites, were the other piercing eyes that watched her. Their evil was palpable. Perhaps it was Trance, cursing her under his breath, his white-snake hair and ice-blue eyes shining like death. It was too dark to be certain. Halley only had the sense that she was being watched by some hostile being. Her body felt very small, very vulnerable to all sorts of harm. She kept herself as still as she could.

Indeed, she lay so still, that, to those who watched her from the woods, she seemed dead. Her breathing, if indeed she was still breathing at all, was inaudible. A hand placed gently upon her back would not have been felt to move up and down with the workings of her lungs. A bold man it would have taken to kiss her forehead; her cold skin would be like a foretelling of the grave.

Anxious looks were exchanged, and a little girl's voice whispered urgently that Halley should be checked on, and helped.

"No. She needs to do this alone. Leave her be. And you..." Here, the speaker lifted her chin to nod in the direction of the threatening figure, "...you back off!" If words were visible, the speaker's would have been colored a brilliant orange, framed by a strong border of red.

The threatening figure took a reluctant step back from Halley, but the air remained taught with danger.

CHAPTER 10

With the first touch of the morning sun, Halley rose as if reborn. Pushing up on all fours, and then sinking back on her heels while stretching her torso and arms long in front of her, she lowered her chest to the rock. She was saying grace, thanking the powers that be that had kept her alive, that had protected her alone on the flat rock all night.

Slowly, she lifted her chest and sat up tall. Taking a long, full breath, feeling her breast bone rise, she shoved herself to her feet and gazed around with wonder at her world. The air seemed light and extraordinarily breathable; the trees welcoming; the rock surface firm.

I'm alive! I'm still breathing!

Before, she had not valued the simple, regular joy of breathing. She'd never noticed how pleasurable it felt to have air move in and out of her lungs. *Feeling my breath, I can hardly believe I once tried to kill myself, to stop this breath. It seems unimaginable, to choose to stop breathing.* She let her belly expand on her inhale, and felt her torso and then her chest lift; she mentally followed the reverse of the breath, the compression of her body on the exhale. *I fought so hard to stay alive, to keep this breath. It must mean something.* The new sense of self-preservation was comforting.

Halley stretched herself tall, swinging her arms overhead, and joining her hands together to reach up even taller, filling her lungs more deeply. As she stretched, her right arm throbbed painfully, reminding her of the boat that had smashed into her in the river; the arm hadn't hurt in prayer position on the rock.

She slowly lowered it to examine the damage. The right arm was swollen, but the bleeding had stopped. She moved it carefully, bending it at the elbow and rolling her wrist in a circle. It hurt, but no bones were broken. *I'll have to find something to keep that cut from getting infected. Aloe maybe? If only I had my First Aid kit...*

Halley relaxed her arms to her side, and concentrated on the pulse of her body. The battering on the river had left her sore, but the soreness seemed irrelevant. She was more interested in her choice; how, in traveling the thin knife edge between life and death, she had chosen to grasp life with both hands, and hold on tight.

I'm alive – now I've got to keep me that way.

With a sinking sensation, she realized her canteen was gone, torn from her during her near-drowning. Halley looked down at the river. She couldn't chance a slide back down the rock into the water, not even for a drink.

Suddenly, from behind her she heard a familiar sound: Ch ch ch ch ch. *The lion-monkeys!* Her smile came easily. The corners of her lips lifted slightly and the edges around her eyes softened. It didn't take any effort at all! This simple fact made her eyes fill with sudden tears. With the fingers of her right hand, she touched the small apple in her cheek and moved it upwards to feel the tiny wrinkles around her eyes. This smile was genuine, and, although the muscles in her face were working in an unfamiliar way, this was the way they were supposed to work.

The sound of the lion-monkeys grew louder. *I wonder where they are?*

"Ch-Ch-Ch-Ch..." one called.

"Ch-Ch-Ch-Ch!" came the reply.

The short exchange was followed closely by the sound of something falling to the forest floor.

Turning, she left the flat rock at the river's edge, and walked a short distance into the woods. There they were. It was like running unexpectedly into two long-lost friends, who couldn't wait to embrace her in a tight circle of camaraderie. Surely they wouldn't be the same monkeys, but still…

"Hello, lion-monkeys! It's nice to see you again. What are you up to this beautiful morning?"

They were in a loose-fronded tree. On the ground near the tree, was the yellowish-green of a banana skin. *Bananas! They're eating bananas!* Halley laughed aloud. Here was food, at last. The monkeys looked down at her, cackling and observing, just as she observed them.

"What are you saying, monkeys? Are you wondering why I didn't see the bananas before? I guess I had my eyes closed!"

Not wanting to disturb them, she chose the next tree over, and reached up to pick a banana. She held it with wonder, savoring the moment. When bent back, the banana stem broke with a light snap, and the scent of it made her mouth water. The sudden in-rush of saliva was almost painful. The peel split into three even pieces, and she remembered her school-teacher, Mr. D, once showing her that if you pressed the center of a banana, it would always split into three segments. *The father, the son, and the holy ghost,* she thought, breaking the banana in half, and then splitting one half of the banana lengthwise up the middle, eating one long segment at a time, then licking the banana off her fingers. *Id, ego, superego. Mind, body, spirit.* All sets of three, as in nature.

The banana segments crushed easily between her tongue and the roof of her mouth. She savored the flavor. Renewed strength flowed through her body, and she quickly ate a second, third and fourth banana. She chose some that were greenish to carry away with her.

Her hunger somewhat satisfied, her thirst seemed suddenly worse. She stood still, thinking. A small bird landed nearby, and picked its way carefully through the leaves on the forest floor. It settled down, and began to shake and wriggle, to flap its wings up and down. Drops of water flew from its feathers, and it ducked its head under the leaf cover, scrabbling and splashing. When it finished, it stepped out of the leaves, moved away a short distance and smoothed its feathers with a wet beak.

Halley's mouth hung open.

The monkeys went "Ch-Ch-Ch-Ch" overhead, as if laughing.

When the small bird flew off, she reached a tentative hand down to the loose leaves, shifting them to one side. Underneath was the remains of a banana tree, blackened around the edge as if lightning-struck. A good inch of stump remained, but it was now completely dry. Where had the water for the bird's bath come from? Had it been rain water? Thirst pounded in Halley's head.

Fighting the urge to move, to search elsewhere, she stared hard at the tree stump, as if she could will its hollow to fill with clear water. *Oh my God...* The bird bath *was* slowly re-filling. *The roots...the roots of the tree are still there! It's sending water up to a non-existent tree...*

Eagerly, Halley dropped to her knees and leaned her face into the hollow, sucking up the water. It tasted of dirt but she didn't care.

Standing, she brushed herself off and felt the renewed strength in her body. She ate one more banana as she puzzled over how to carry the rest away with her. *It would be much easier with a backpack. Maybe I can make something.*

Nearby was a tall straight grove of greenery. She knew it to be bamboo. She removed her pocketknife, choosing one of the thinner stalks of bamboo and sawing away at it. *This is going to take forever.* Reaching up high on the stalk, she threw all her weight onto it in one quick thrust. It took a few tries, but the force eventually was enough to push the stalk over, and its roots came loose from the soil around its base. She worked downwards from the top of the stalk, slicing and stripping off thin segments. She paused at the top-most shoots, and lingered a moment to strip off the thicker outer red bark, tasting the bitter but nourishing inner leaf of the bamboo shoot.

When she'd cut enough strips she sat cross-legged and quickly weaved them into a bag. It took most of the morning but there was something healing in the effort of creation, in the making something with her hands.

Halley walked back to the banana trees and saw with delight that the hollow had refilled. Again, she drank it dry. The lion-monkeys were curled up together on one of the branches, sleeping soundly, like an old married couple taking an early afternoon nap.

As she loaded her new pack with the green bananas she'd picked earlier, she swallowed hard. The backpack, even with its rough edges and unevenness, was embellished with beauty.

CHAPTER 11

It was mid-day, and it was getting hot. Reaching down, Halley unzipped the long legs of her combat trousers mid-thigh. The zippers went the full way around each leg, and the final bit of each zip came free with a slight tug. The loose legs of the combat trousers fit nicely in her new bamboo backpack, and gave the bananas some protection. Still hot, she stripped off the windbreaker and long-sleeved t-shirt, and rolled them into small balls. They too squeezed into the top of the bamboo backpack.

A slight breeze dried her sweat, and cooled her body. On impulse, she touched the sequined crown on the front of her red t-shirt. The edge of the sequins fit nicely under her finger-nails, and the sensation of moving them there felt strangely good, a sensation a child would seek in a moment of insecurity or change. Dropping her hands to her side, Halley bid farewell to the banana-and-water site, and made her way back to the river.

She had to decide where to go next. The flat rock where she'd spent the night had a home-like feel to her, and she stood on it wide-stanced to get her bearings. From there, a small, steep gully fed into the river. The main course of the river continued around a bend. *Funny, I didn't notice that gully before – I could have found water there more easily. But maybe not food… And I did so like seeing the lion-monkeys again.*

The gully was the right way to go. But it was steep. White water streamed down the rocks, rushing back towards the river, glinting dangerously in the sunlight. The volume of water flowed with force; if she slipped in those sections, she would be carried back down the slope of the gully towards the river.

Even the drier rocks appeared to have been recently wet, perhaps due to the rain. These were black with moss, slippery. Partway up, there was one spot fronted by rocks as tall as her – and she could see no way over or around. She hoisted her bamboo backpack a little higher onto her back, and looked away from the gully, back towards the face of the wider river.

This looking back was a mistake.

The scene – the turbulent river with its strange grey water; the dark jagged rocks, and their cutting edges; the sharp tree branches being flung around by violent whirlpools – all brought back Trance, and his cutting words. The boat trip was only yesterday.

He had re-opened her wounds, and they hadn't even begun to scab over. *When I was busy finding food and water his words didn't seem to matter so much. I was focused, I had something vital to do, something particular. Now that I've got to go on alone, to find my way in this vast empty place...*

She could hear him everywhere, his words echoing in her mind: "...*ugly and unloved, incapable of doing anything right...*"

She clenched her fists. It wasn't him. It was she who doubted herself; she had always doubted herself. She could see his words in the air in front of her, and the word "incapable" stood out in bold and was underlined twice. What if he was right? She would choose a poor route, be unable to navigate the steep gully. She would die out here alone.

She wanted to hide her face in her hands, to hide here forever. Never have to see another human being ever again. Be a hermit in this forest, grow old here, unobserved and far from judging eyes. Never speak to another person again. Sink into the earth.

"Or maybe you should just jump into the river. Kill yourself," Trance's voice whispered. "Do it, Halley. Do it..."

The hiss of the words terrified her. Wildly, she looked around her but no one was there. Yet the words had been spoken aloud. She went cold all over: she was the only one there. Could she have spoken the words herself? *But it wasn't my voice...or was it?* Her eyes opened wider. She wasn't sure. *I'm going nuts! I've got to move, got to just do something.*

"Come on, Halley," she said aloud. "You know you can do this. You've done steeper sections before."

"But never alone. You've never done this alone."

She didn't move.

Trance was still with her. Or was that Fernando she was thinking of? It didn't matter. They were beginning to seem one and the same: unkind men who encouraged her to doubt her abilities.

She closed her eyes and remembered the joy of breathing on first waking that morning. *Hell with that, kill myself!!* She opened her eyes. The voices would not have their way.

I want to live. I want to keep breathing...

Quickly, she pushed between the twisted vines and entered the start of the steep gully. Immediately she was cocooned in greenery. There was a new density to the air, the humidity trapped in this enclosed spot forcing a sudden sweat onto her back and thighs. The atmosphere sapped her strength, and though she tried to move, it was not easy. Beyond the vines, several plants clustered close together. They looked like overgrown spider plants, but their leaves were thicker and less flexible, colored a dark, flat, forbidding green. They blocked the way entirely.

She started to push through. The first of the plants quickly snagged her shirt. When she tried to pull free, the plant pushed sharp spiky teeth into her, making tiny painful pinholes in her flesh, freckling her with blood. The plants didn't just look threatening: their leaves were armed with tiny protective spikes.

Halley bit her lower lip and tried to work her way carefully, but there was simply no avoiding the plants. Finally, just when she'd thought she'd made it and was about to step out onto the rocks in the sunlight, a long leaf snapped off, lodging itself in the thin muscle at the front of her calf. She dragged it behind her for a stride or two hoping it would fall out. It didn't. She tore at it, pricking her hands several times before she managed to throw it to the ground. Cursing loudly, she stomped on it. "God-dammed stupid horrible rotten plants! I hate these stupid plants!"

She was finally on the slick rocks of the gully. It took only a moment for her to slip on the slimy black moss, coming down hard, scraping her hands and knees. Blood stained the rocks.

Staring at it, Halley felt an uncomfortable foreboding. The red was startlingly bright. She rubbed at it with the toe of her hiking boot, and when this wasn't good enough she splashed it with water until it finally disappeared.

But as she climbed higher up the gully that afternoon, the cuts on her palms and knees continued to bleed, leaving behind small drops of blood, creating an irregular but fairly obvious trail. She was too busy trying to stay upright to notice. The afternoon wore on, and the blood dried to a deep rust, droplets of her left behind.

The color of the rocks gave an indication of their dryness. After a few slips on black rocks, she realized that the lighter-colored rocks weren't really lighter-colored at all – they were just dry. She stayed on these and the going was a little easier, except for the times she risked ducking closer in for a drink of the fresh-flowing water. The treads on her hiking boots gripped the dry rock well, steadying her climb. On the edge of the gully were loose vines and small tree trunks – these were useful as hand grips to pull herself up the steeper sections. After stumbling through a few pools of deep water at the base of waterfalls, she learned it was quicker to stay on the rocky edges of the pools, to skirt around the deep water.

At one tricky spot, she was forced to lean her body backwards out over a sheer drop, facing the cliff, supporting her weight on her feet and holding on tight to the roots of trees which stuck out from the cliff-face. She was careful not to put too much weight on the roots – if they came loose she would fall to the rocks ten feet below. It was intense work, and sweat dripped into her eyes but she couldn't let go of the roots to brush it off. Blinking to clear her vision, she tried not to think about how far she could fall, and what would happen if she did.

Later, the muddy places on the edges of the gully nearly pulled her boots from her feet. Using both hands to hold the boots on, she pulled them out, the ground making a wet sucking sound of rebellion, as if reluctant to let her go.

Towards the top of the gully, one of the deeper waterfall pools had no footing along the edge, and there was no other way around. Halley stepped gradually into the pool, and the bottom slipped away from below her feet. She swam fully clothed across the pool, gasping. The water bit at her with cold teeth, the footing underneath becoming uneven and hidden by the dark greenish water. Her hiking boots skidded on the unseen rocks, hitting her shins hard into their edges.

At the final, steepest section, the one she had seen from far below, she paused. The rocks blocking the gully were indeed taller than her. She took a deep breath, and grasped rough rock with her fingertips, pulling herself upward, keeping her body in a forward lean in case of a slip. Sweat dripped down her face, and her mind and eyes and body focused only on the climb.

Perhaps this was why she didn't see the young girl sitting at the top of the gully, watching her every move.

CHAPTER 12

At the top of the gully, Eden watched. Each time Halley cursed and kept going, she clapped her small hands in silent applause.

She was clapping for herself as much as for Halley. Her plan – the one she had made after watching the car plunge into the river – had worked. Halley had begun again. She waited until Halley had made her way to the top of the gully, scratched and bleeding and dirty, and then she slowly unfolded herself to stand.

At the top of the gully, Halley closed her eyes and rubbed them hard with the heel of her hands. The pressure on her eyeballs felt good, relieving the tension that had built up during the climb. *Ah, that's better.* A heavy surge of fatigue overtook her – that climb had been hard work. She would sit down and rest for a while. Before resting, though, she made a quick assessment of her surroundings.

It was then – with a huge start – that she saw the young girl. She was hidden amongst the trees, her clothing of deep greens and browns blending in with the forest. Halley might have missed her completely, had it not been for the girl's brilliant blue eyes.

The young girl sang merrily, "There you are! I knew you'd make it!" She smiled brightly, staring at Halley in the way of an old friend who's missed the sight of someone for a very long time. Her own confusion must have shown on her face, because the young girl added, "I'm Eden..." with a hint of surprise in her voice, as if Halley should've known her name. "I've been waiting for you. I didn't think you'd take so long. But then I didn't know you'd meet Trance before me!"

The young girl giggled and pointed back down the gully, to the river.

Halley glanced back the way she'd come. For the first time, she could see the full course of the river Trance had led her down. It was steely grey, swift-flowing, marked by dangerous partially-submerged rocks.

She followed its course, remembering the journey, fixing the point where she had flipped the boat. Her eyes moved to the sloping rock where she had climbed out and spent the night. She fingered the rough straps of the backpack. Looking to the base of the river gully, the sight of the spiky green plants made her wince.

As if drawn by some mysterious force, her eyes traveled back to the river. She took a fix on the sheltered spot again, on the sloping rock. A few hundred meters from where she'd climbed out, there, just beyond the shallow, sheltered area, the river ended abruptly, falling off into a sheer, deadly waterfall. At the bottom of the waterfall, the water frothed and boiled with such fury that its foam was visible, even from Halley's great height. The waterfall must be smashing into a rocky bottom. It would crush whatever went over it into tiny, bloody pieces.

The way out...he said he'd show me the way out. He said he'd help me. But he wasn't going to – Trance meant for me to die...

Her eye began to twitch.

But he'd have died too – that doesn't make any sense.

Frowning, she pictured Trance's face as he had looked just before she'd flipped the boat. *So dark – he was so dark ...it was like he was already dead.* The darkness was building around her again, pulling at her, pulling her under.

"Halley, remember..." Eden said quietly, in a voice older than her years, and using words that most young girls wouldn't use, "Remember...you fought him before it was too late. You won the battle against his darkness."

Halley could think of nothing to say, and she was silent for a long time, staring at the river.

"Was it you I heard crying?" Halley asked suddenly. *But I thought it was a baby...*

Eden giggled. "It wasn't me..."

The giggle drew Halley's eyes away from the river and back to Eden. Looking at her again, Halley shook her head like she'd just awoken. What was this young girl doing here anyway, all alone in the wilderness? And who was she? "Your name is...what?... Eden? Eden? Right? Why were you waiting for me? What are you doing here?" *No more of this keeping quiet when I run into strangers in the woods. No more playing nice.* "And how did you know my name?"

"Those are very clear questions. Very clear," Eden answered. As Halley watched, the look in Eden's eyes became immensely old. Her giggle disappeared. "I am to accompany you on the next part of your journey. If you want me to... Or I can just disappear, and you can go on alone."

With a giggle, Eden jumped – suddenly all youth again – and grabbed for an overhanging tree branch with her hands. She caught it, and swung her light body around in a small arc, landing to perch on the branch high above the ground. She was nearly invisible again, as if she'd become part of the tree. Only her blue eyes shone out.

Halley looked upwards. "How old are you?" she asked. "You're so young to be out here alone. But the way you talk seems so... so old..." Halley cocked her head, trying to see her more clearly. "How old are you?" she repeated.

"I am as old as your last memory of confidence," Eden said elusively. She paused, adding, in a softer voice, "Can I go with you?"

The question hung in the air, soft as the touch of a feather.

The sunlight filtered between the leaves, softening the edges of the young girl. Where it lit upon small specks in the air, dust angels appeared. From high in the tree, Eden's eyes shone blue, a blue that suddenly reminded Halley of the butterflies, the Ceylon Blue Glassy Tigers.

Not knowing why, but feeling it to be right deep in her belly, Halley said, "Yes."

CHAPTER 13

Eden swung down from the tree, a huge smile on her face. "Hooray! Let's go then! Let's go!"

She skipped forward – the green of the woods seemed ready to swallow her.

"Wait! I don't know which way to go," Halley called after her. *I've never led anyone else before. I think I know the way, but…*

Eden was just visible on the edge of the trees, waiting.

Halley looked around hesitantly, thinking hard. Trance had lied about leading her out of the woods. She was more lost than before she'd met him. And now there was no baby to pull her forward. Her eyes widened. The baby – maybe he'd lied about the baby too!

She knew it, suddenly, as certainly as she'd known the baby was there at the start of the trail. Her lips lifted in a gentle smile. Her journey was still about the baby – the baby she must find – and she had to choose the path that led towards it. But the baby gave no cry, no indication of where it was. Halley pondered this curious silence. Way back at the crossroads-that-was-not-a-crossroads, at the start of her journey, she had heard the baby cry, but not since. It was one of the many unexplained things about this journey, like realizing she'd been in these woods before, like Eden knowing her name. Like the fact that she wasn't worried about the baby, she suddenly realized.

She should be worried about the baby. She knew now that Trance had been lying about having seen it. The baby was still alone, was still alive, and would wait for Halley until she arrived. It was a certainty. As certain as the fact that Halley was still alive, that she was wearing a bamboo backpack of her own making, and that she had just met a young girl named Eden. It was simple really. She knew because in the spot in the center of her forehead where she'd first felt the pain of the baby's cry, she could feel the baby's life pulsing. This subtle pulsing assured her that the baby was all right. Halley knew it wasn't normal to feel a pulse in this spot – it was normal to feel a pulse at the temples, or in the neck, but not there, not right in the center of the forehead. It meant something – it meant the baby was alive.

She focused her attention again on the immediate issue. *I've got to take the path towards the baby. But I don't know the way.*

"Yes, you do!" Eden said, reading her thoughts. "You know the way. Come on! Let's go!"

Halley found herself walking forward, stepping around Eden, and moving into the woods. It was only after she'd been going a while that she realized she was leading the way. She knew the way. Halley felt a thrill that was, at once, both foreign and very familiar.

Once found, the path was easy to follow. It stretched out in front of them, long, even, and level. Even the tree roots cleared the way, staying obediently under their wide-branched trees. It was the smoothest path Halley had taken in some time. There were no strange rustles from the bushes, nothing to startle or frighten. Perhaps this was because Halley was becoming used to the forest, but it felt to her more like a subtle agreement had been made among all the creatures in the woods to make the way easy, to allow time for her to calm.

The sun through the trees made a patchwork on the forest floor, shading it with shifting, irregular patterns of dark and light. Sometimes a shady place would suddenly become light, as the clouds and sun traded places and opened the way for a sunbeam. Halley was struck by the patterns, and contemplated their meaning. *Without the dark, the light would be invisible; it would have nothing with which to contrast. What do I mean, I wonder? It's like Trance and Eden. They seem so very different, and yet both seem to be of one whole, of a pattern.* She toyed with this idea, visualizing the Chinese symbol of two intertwined and opposing fish, each with a tiny piece of the other, seeing in her mind the counterpoint between mountaintop and valley. Halley was so lost in her thoughts that she bumped right into a stray branch that bisected the smooth path. She stopped short, suddenly aware that she'd been daydreaming. Carefully, she pushed the branch aside to step past, remembering to hold it for Eden so it didn't snap back on her. Eden took a few steps in front of Halley and then stopped to look down in the overgrowth at the side of the trail.

"Look," Eden said with a giggle.

Halley had already begun walking and bumped right into Eden, eliciting another giggle from the young girl. She looked down to see what Eden was pointing at. It was a wildflower, its base buried deep within a bed of leaves, its long stem ending in a spray of purple flowers. She quickly looked away.

"Look closer," Eden said.

Halley looked at the flower reluctantly, and then took her gaze along the edge of the trail. Its border was lined by a multitude of these small, jewel-like flowers. The trail was not simply dusty and leafy; suddenly it was purple and fragrant. The sight triggered the familiar pulse at the center of her forehead, as if the baby's life force were strengthened by Halley's noticing beauty.

"You get so lost in your thoughts, in where you're going, that you forget to look at where you are," Eden said. "Or even notice where you've been…" Eden put a fist to her mouth, as if to silence herself.

Eden hadn't meant to say what she thought aloud, Halley thought. She looked back at the purple wildflower. A small ladybug crawled along its stem. Its polka-dotted back reminded Halley of herself as a ten-year old girl, playing with her brother in their garden. He was gone too, that big brother, or as good as gone, she reminded herself, living in New Zealand for many years. They rarely talked anymore. Halley missed him but found it hard to talk to him by telephone. She found it hard to talk to everyone. In her memory, at least, they were as they had been:

They were wild things, young savages covered in mud. Their adventure that day had been bold: they'd run the garden hose softly for over an hour – 'Without Permission' – and they'd built a thin river down the edge of the garden. Now they were floating tiny twigs and leaves down the river – ships, they called them, headed for China. On one of the twigs, a red polka-dotted ladybug landed. They both cried out in delight – the ship had its first passenger!

The purple wildflowers had formed a border for their river. They'd called it a riverbank.

Halley started: these purple wildflowers weren't wildflowers at all – they were once part of the family garden. Or at least, the family garden had contained flowers like these. Halley reached down with one finger; the ladybug crawled gently up. Its legs tickled, stirring the tiny hairs on the back of her forefinger. It traveled down the finger, then into the sensitive arc of skin between her thumb and forefinger, and from there into the center of her palm, forcing her to turn her palm up to the sky. Her hand was a position of supplication, as if she were asking for and receiving something from above.

"It's so trusting. Why does it trust this way?"

"Animals and insects are smart. They know who to trust," Eden answered.

And so do you Halley, when you stop long enough to really look, Eden thought. Eden was frustrated; she wanted to stomp her feet. *You want confidence; it comes from opening your eyes and looking deeply, and then acting on what you see. Open your eyes, Halley.*

The ladybug sat in the palm of Halley's hand, as if waiting.

Eden's thoughts continued. *I have to remind you of how you used to believe in yourself, of your old sense of certainty. Because,* she thought, suddenly giggling aloud at how silly it all seemed, *you are not how we meant to turn out!*

She skipped on ahead.

Eden's giggle awakened Halley; she took a last look at the ladybug before blowing gently on the palm of her hand. The ladybug lifted its wings from its sides, and flew off. Halley mouthed the words from her childhood, words her big brother had taught her:

Ladybug, ladybug
Fly away home
Your house is on fire
And your children are alone

What a scary nursery rhyme to teach children! Still, she liked the words – she always had. They reminded her of a time when she would climb to the highest limb on the maple tree in their garden, unafraid. Sit with a large, heavy book that was far too advanced for her years, reading words she didn't really understand, until the light faded and she had to climb down with great care.

Remembering didn't hurt as much as Halley had thought it would. *So many things I've forgotten, and forgotten on purpose. As if by forgetting, I could deaden the pain of what came later. But I think I've also deadened my wisdom,* she thought solemnly. *I seem to have forgotten much more than I intended.*

Eventually, Eden and Halley walked side by side, slowly, looking around them with care.

It was easy to track them. Distracted by scenery, by memories, they took no steps to camouflage their trail.

Distractions: for him, there were no distractions. There was only his one specific intent. He walked purposely. There was something awful in the way he moved, in the way his arms swung back and forth in a wide arc, the way he planted each foot down on the earth with assertion, with dominance, as if he enjoyed trampling the things in his path. He wore the green jacket she had discarded in the river. The white braid hung freely down his back, and his ice-blue eyes shone.

He allowed himself a smile when he stopped for a leisurely drink. There was no hurry. He had all the time in the world.

She did not.

CHAPTER 14

"Tell me about you," Eden said, much later that day. It was a big, wide-open question.

Halley's eyes played on the unfurled fronds of a tree fern. They were curled up in tight circles, bright green, and lightly fuzzed with short, spiky fur. Like Halley, they had yet to open. She shook her head. "I don't want to talk about myself," she said. Taking her eyes from the tree fern, she turned to look at Eden's small, unthreatening figure. "I mean...I don't...I mean..."

Eden's eyes were gentle, their warm blue reassuring. "It's okay. You can tell me – I won't laugh. Please. Tell me." Eden knew talking would help. It always helped her, even when it was just her stuffed bear she talked to; Fluffy always listened and he never ever talked back. She looked away from Halley to the tree fern.

"I'm lost." Halley bit her lip, and shook her head slowly, looking down at the ground. She hated saying it aloud; she didn't mean she was lost in the woods. Her fingernails dug into the palms of her hands.

"Lost?"

Halley swallowed. "For the longest time, I haven't known why I'm here on this planet, or where I'm meant to go, or what I'm meant to do. I've tried to live some sort of valiant life. That sounds so stupid – a *valiant life*". She watched the sunlight play along the ground, and felt her face grow warm with embarrassment. "But that's what I've tried to do anyway. To be a hero, in some small way. But I haven't..." She paused, deciding to tell the whole truth. "There's a baby...lost here somewhere that needs me." *The whole truth*, she reminded herself. "I still miss

Fernando, still love him…and Trance reminded me of how I once tried to kill myself…and…"

The words ran out. She stared at one particular red leaf on a small bush filled with green ones, and waited as if expecting a blow, waited for Eden's harsh judgment of her weakness.

Eden reached out and placed her small, cool hand lightly on Halley's upper arm. She rubbed up and down, very softly. "You sound just like I did when I found out they'd sold Suntan to that awful man. Remember?"

Halley nodded.

"He had that terrible white truck with all the horses jammed in," Eden continued. "He didn't even take Suntan's saddle…"

The red leaf was so vibrant, like blood. Like a fresh cut, bleeding. Things could bleed for so long.

"They never told me what they did with him, where they'd taken him. I wanted to send him carrots at Christmas, but they wouldn't tell me where to send them," Eden said. "I felt just like you do, then. Like I'd never want to ride a horse again. Like nothing would ever be right."

They were quiet for some time.

"You can tell me more, if you want. I'm a good listener."

Halley hesitated before speaking. "I don't trust myself anymore. I can't hear myself, and when I can, I doubt that my instincts are right." There was an edge to her voice, as if she was walking on a thin ledge and could slip off at any moment.

"I know what you mean." Eden picked the red leaf from the bush that Halley had been studying and handed it to her. "Here," she said, "this is a lucky one."

Halley started.

"Its color reminds me of blood…"

"Well, I suppose, but…Dad used to say it was good when leaves turned red, because the color red symbolizes happiness. That makes it a lucky color." Eden waited a moment until Halley took the leaf. "I think you get to trust yourself by doing things.

It's like…like the first time I jumped a cross rail on Suntan…"
Eden smiled, remembering. "I didn't think I could do it. I was really, really scared. But then I did it, and I knew I could do it. Like that." She looked at Halley until she nodded. "I don't think you're lost. You just didn't know it would be so hard to get where you've got to go. Come on. Let's walk."

Their feet scuffled along in the leaves. Eden kicked some up in the air, and let them fall gently around them. Halley smiled a small smile, and gave the leaves a kick herself. They both stopped short at what she had uncovered. On the ground was a silver bracelet.

CHAPTER 15

Halley tucked the red leaf into her trouser pocket – if red was a lucky color, she would keep it. She could use some luck.

Bending down, she picked up the silver bracelet, which was tarnished almost black around the edges. It must have lain there a long while. The metal was cool to touch, but warmed quickly where she held it. She turned it around. It was heavy, a quarter inch thick, and about two inches wide. There was a small gap in its circumference to allow it to be slipped onto the wearer's wrist. The bracelet was carved with a pattern that rose and fell over its entire length. It resembled a long series of ocean waves. She slipped the bracelet on her right wrist, squeezing it gently to make sure it would stay in place. It made her arm appear stronger.

"It looks nice on you," Eden said. "You should keep it."

They walked on.

Halley fingered the bracelet now and then, liking the sensation of its weight on her wrist. It gave her a sense of melting into, becoming one with, the land. The feeling was linked to the bracelet, but it was more than that. It was due to the sharing of the truth about herself with Eden. Talking so openly had brought the two of them closer, instead of leaving Halley feeling judged and alone. That amazed her. All her life, she had hidden the things about herself that she considered ugly or unattractive. She'd tried to present herself as positive, controlled, together. She'd lied. The lies had left her alone, isolated in a great empty cavern she had unwittingly carved. *I was always afraid to talk to people, afraid they wouldn't like me if I told the truth.*

But today, she had told the truth. Eden hadn't turned away in disgust, hadn't rolled her eyes and told her how stupid she was. She had simply listened and accepted what was. How glorious this felt, this small thing, this being heard. As if she were a tiny, premature, featherless bird shivering in the cold, and Eden had picked her up and held her in warm palms to her heart.

I was so afraid I'd bring people down if I told them how bad I felt. She listened to Eden skipping behind her, humming a tune. *It doesn't seem to have brought Eden down any. Maybe sharing the truth, the painful bits, is really a gift. Maybe it makes the one I share it with feel strong and wise and helpful.*

"You okay?" Eden asked.

"Just fine," Halley replied.

A tree with a large upraised scar in its center caught Halley's eye. The thick tissue of the scar was lighter in color than the rest of the trunk. It looked like the tree had been stabbed with a knife, and the knife dragged down for several inches. Awful; but it had survived. *It's stronger at the scar than any other place.*

Thinking of her own scars, her own wounds, she wondered why she had labeled them "secrets" and "private" and "ugly", why she had sought to erase them from her mind. They were the most instructive things in her life. They were the strong places.

Halley was becoming ready to see the truth, ready to look at the moments of her past she was uncovering. She could think of the blue butterflies and the purple wildflowers, and even the memories that Trance had re-stirred, and not try to blank them out.

A sudden chill ran threw her. She narrowed her eyes. There was more, wasn't there? There was something else she wasn't remembering. In her mind, she could sense its vague outline. Her awareness heightened, she became conscious of an unusual sound. She became painfully alert.

Above her, a cold wind rattled the trees, causing a thousand leaves to rub against their neighbors. The trees were too full, their leaves scraping and shoving each other in a battle for space. The air was overflowing with their whispering, and the sound for which she was listening so intently was masked by the leaf noise cramming the air. The small hairs on Halley's forearms stood to attention. Willing the trees to *Still!* and *Be quiet!*, she listened hard. The other noise was still there, underlying the scraping of the leaves. She couldn't make it out. It was urgent to understand it! It was advancing relentlessly toward her.

"Can you hear that?"

"What?"

"That sound...I'm sure I hear something. Listen..."

"The leaves? Do you mean the leaves, moving in the wind?"

"No. It's not that..."

A small ridge formed between Halley's eyebrows. Her breathing quickened. She glanced behind her. Back the way they'd come.

"Oh no..."

Stretching back in the distance was the long, straight, open path, with its unfurling tree ferns and dinosaur leaves and banana trees. It was midday, and the clouds had gone. The sky was a brilliant, startling blue. The sun, directly overhead, erased the patterns of light and dark. All was illuminated and all was revealed and the sun was painful to behold in its brightness.

For the sun revealed the truth: the path behind them was no longer empty.

CHAPTER 16

Trance! It was Trance moving towards them.

He came at them fast.

She stared at his ice-blue eyes, his fine white teeth. She couldn't move.

He called to her. "Thank God you're okay. I was afraid you'd drowned."

Her pulse throbbed. It was as if he'd arisen from the grave.

"I kept searching for you," he was saying. "Then I saw your blood on the rocks. I followed the trail of your blood..."

My blood. My life, draining away...

Trance was closer now.

Eden grabbed her cold hand, pulling at her urgently. "Come on!" she shouted.

But Halley was mesmerized. He was death, and she was drawn to him.

His sing-song voice droned on. "I see you've met Eden..."

"Let's go!" Eden shouted again.

Eden! She had to protect Eden! She awoke from her reverie, and they began to run.

He pursued.

"Don't look back!" Eden shouted as they tried to outdistance him. "Don't listen. It's his voice paralyzing you!"

"Don't run," Trance called after them. "You know I won't hurt you. I'm the only one who can get you out of these woods. Please, stop."

When they didn't, he quickened his pace, his long stride lengthening into a loping run.

Halley ran, and didn't look back. His footsteps thundered behind her. He had to take only one stride to their three.

"Quick! Down here!" Eden shouted, with a desperate burst of speed. A small, rocky trail led off the wide, smooth path.

They ran recklessly, leaping from rock to rock, their urgent need to escape making them take dangerous risks. When the path became suddenly flat and easy, they ran stretched out long and strong. Then tree roots suddenly strangled the way and they had to pull back quickly or fall over, they had to waste time jumping their feet carefully through the roots at a pace *not-fast-enough-to-get-away.* They fled as if they were soft-skinned animals pursued by a hungry predator; they fled as if their lives were at stake. Halley's forehead throbbed – the wail of the baby echoed in her head. It was a terrifying sound. The baby was at the edge of death.

The path narrowed. With dismay, Halley saw that it led along the high contour line of a steep hill. On one side, the hill fell away sharply, a drop of several hundred feet. On the other was a high rock wall. There was no way off the path with Trance behind them. No way to go but forward. They ran a hundred feet more. It grew narrower.

No safety net, no railings. Nothing to stop us flying off the edge if we take a wrong step.

Her eyes were focused on the drop. She wasn't watching her footing. Landing wrong on an unseen rock, her ankle gave way with a sharp twist. She lost her balance, and her flailing arms beat at the air. For a moment, a stretched out moment where she could feel every cell in her body, she was sure she would fall, would crash to earth hundreds of feet below. Then she threw her weight sideways towards the rock wall and crumpled down onto one knee. She was breathing fast.

It took a second for the terror of the near disaster to settle into the base of her spine. When it did she held herself completely still. A moment later, she looked back – Trance hadn't caught up. Not yet. Cautiously, she gripped the rock wall, pulling herself to her feet while cursing at the slipping of her sweaty fingertips. She took weight onto the ankle gingerly.

"Are you okay?" Eden said.

"I think so..."

Halley let go of the security of the rock wall. "Listen, we've got to slow down – this path is too dangerous." Her voice sounded thin to her ears, like a high cloud.

"No – he's too close," Eden said urgently. "We've got to move!"

Halley hesitated.

"We've got to run!" Eden shouted, looking behind her.

Halley looked where Eden was looking and saw Trance. His voice began echoing in her head, drowning out Eden's words.

"You're right, Halley...slow down...you'll get yourself hurt. Wait for me. Let me talk to you." He sounded as if he were soothing a headstrong child. "You're not strong enough for this. It's too dangerous."

Halley watched him move, as if he were flying over the terrain; she found herself admiring his footwork and his competence. She saw his lips rise in a smile; it looked alluring. Maybe he was right. Maybe she should just wait.

"*No! You've run harder trails than this. Trust yourself, you can do this!*"

Halley wasn't sure whether she or Eden had said the words. She wasn't even sure she'd heard them spoken aloud. But she began to run.

Lengthening their strides, gasping, Halley and Eden turned a sharp corner, and Halley saw with a surge of joy that there was finally a small break in the rock face, where a thin track climbed up the hill to the right. "Come on – he'll think we've gone straight!"

Grabbing onto the trunk of a thin tree, she pulled herself up onto the barely visible dirt track. She extended a hand to Eden, but Eden ignored it and simply leapt up, as light on her feet as a well-toned cat.

They moved quickly up the thin, steep track, into dense woods. Tree branches caught on their clothes and snagged their hair. Low shrubs scratched their shins. They made hard, noisy progress. A few hundred meters up the trail, Halley held up her hand to signal Eden to stop. She raised a finger to her lips. Softly at first, and then more loudly, they heard Trance pounding down the high contour trail they had just left. As he got closer, she could hear him talking.

"Halley…remember that time you ran away on the beach, how you got lost? You were all alone. You were only five years old. Doesn't this feel the same?" His footsteps were getting closer. "You need someone to find you, Halley. You need someone to help you. Let me help you. I want to help you…" The words were enticing, the tone of his voice gentle and warm.

The memory from her childhood, her lost on the beach, became vivid in Halley's mind. She recalled being held protectively in the arms of a strong lifeguard, and how good it felt to be made safe by someone else.

Eden gripped Halley's arm tightly. "No," she whispered. "You don't need him. Remember? You found your own way back that day. Believe in yourself."

Eden's words reminded Halley of the mantra she used to repeat to herself when she was young and scared: *believe in yourself believe in yourself believe in yourself.*

She focused her mind, repeating the words in her head; they had a humming, warming quality to them, and allowed Halley to block out what Trance was saying. With a thin edge of her mind, she listened to him moving away. Although the distance between them grew, the volume of his voice remained the same.

"You'll only get killed out here," he said. "The animals will attack you in the night, without me to protect you." He paused, as if relishing the thought. "Even if you do find your way out of the woods, you'll never get by the woman on the plains."

His words became muffled, and then died away completely.

CHAPTER 17

Silently, stepping like natives, they worked their way up the thin dirt track. It was narrow and muddy, and the footing was treacherous. The trail must have just been cut back; sharp-edged branches poked out at odd angles, threatening serious injury if they were incautious. Halley's breathing became rough with the exertion. In places it was too steep to climb with legs alone; here, she grabbed onto the trunks of trees and hoisted herself up, her feet scrabbling along behind her. Eden followed closely, using the same trees for purchase.

The trees dwarfed them. Halley couldn't see over, and so tightly were the trees bound by vines and shrubs that she couldn't see between them either. The world narrowed to the slim, steep track, to the slipping and catching of her feet in the dry gravelly earth. The birds were silent, as if they were afraid to give away Halley and Eden's position with their song. There were turn-offs and side-trails; Halley ignored them and stuck to the main track. By some implicit agreement, Halley and Eden didn't speak, moving quickly and carefully up the steep hillside.

So Trance is still alive. Funny. He doesn't seem handsome anymore. Just deadly. She carefully worked herself around the sharp tip of a tree branch. *His voice surrounds me with death.* Her biceps burned as she pulled herself up a steep section. *And he's still with me, even though I've left him behind. I can still hear his voice. It's like he's inside me.* Her right foot slipped backwards and she grabbed hold of a thick tree trunk to arrest the slide. *I can't listen to his voice. I've got to choose not to listen.*

The climb continued. As they rose, wild camellias appeared, their white flowers thickly punctuated by many pin-headed yellow stamens. The flowers were pretty to look at, but the fallen ones were slick when stepped on. Halley and Eden soon learned to avoid them. Vines caught their ankles, tightening and grasping and pulling. Worst of all, the green spiky plants that had plagued Halley on the river gully re-appeared, hooking on clothing and not letting go, tearing at tender skin. Still, Halley and Eden pushed their way through, higher and higher, leaving the lower forest behind.

Finally, the track began to level. They were reaching the apex of the hill. With the leveling, the shrubbery thinned and the going became easier. Sunlight warmed the skin on the tips of Halley's shoulders, and the world became one shade lighter. As the way began to open, Halley could see that the track was coming to an end. She stopped suddenly.

It wasn't just the track that was coming to an end. It was the entire forest.

For the first time, Halley could see far into the distance: grey granite; mountains tipped with ice; blue, blue sky.

"Wow," Eden said.

"Yeah. Let's stop a minute."

She sat down quietly under the tall trees. Cross-legged on the damp earth, she slipped the sweat-darkened straps of the bamboo backpack off her shoulders, and set it at her feet.

This moment of transition was important, this being present atop the mountain they had climbed. It was a time of synthesis; a time of reaping. Halley's chest was high and lifted, her spine straight. A camellia flower fell to the ground next to her, and she watched it fall, and was contented to see it fall, contented by the way that nature knew when it was time to let go, time to move on.

Eden sat down next to Halley, settling as gently as the falling flower.

I feel just like I did when I closed the door of Dad's house for the last time. She had lingered there too, holding the cool brass doorknob in her hand, knowing it to be the last time she'd close that door. *The woods are like that. Once I've closed this door, I can't come back.* She looked out at the blue sky and the mountains. *Even if I do come back, I won't come back as the Halley I am right now. I'm not even who I was a few days ago, when I first came into the woods with Fernando, when I left him to go looking for the baby.* The moment tasted bittersweet. *I wonder if a cicada feels this way when it leaves its old shell hanging on a tree. I don't like leaving behind bits of me, even when they're bits I was truly done with.*

Halley breathed deeply into her belly, feeling it expand against her clothing, feeling her ribcage rise. She tried to breathe in her new self, to let the change simply be. The pungent smell of the earth and the sweetness of camellia pollen filled her senses. Into her awareness swooped bird song, swelling around her. The ground felt solid and sure under her sit bones. She glanced at Eden, and saw that the girl's eyes were fixed on the high mountain peaks in the distance. She wondered if Eden was scared, or if she was looking forward to the next challenge. She looked lost in thought.

"I'm hungry," Eden said suddenly. "Aren't you hungry?"

Halley laughed. "Yeah, I am. I'm famished!"

Could it possibly be the same day she had sat by the river eating bananas with the lion-monkeys, the same day she had climbed the river gully? It seemed so long ago – no wonder she was so hungry. Reaching into the bamboo backpack, she removed the bananas she'd picked earlier in the day. It was lucky they'd been unripe when she'd stowed them, or they'd have been a mess by now. As it was, the day's heat had ripened them nicely. Their scent made her mouth water. "Look what I've got!"

Eden clapped her hands excitedly.

The bananas disappeared fast; they looked at each other.

Eden said, "Wait for me…I'll be right back!"

Halley watched as Eden ran back down the path. *What's she up to?* It didn't take long to find out. A few minutes later Eden returned carrying six small coconuts, struggling not to drop any of them.

"Of course!" Halley said. "I noticed them when we were walking."

"We can eat them, and we can drink them too," Eden said. "Our picnic wouldn't be complete without something to drink." Giggling, she added, "It was such fun climbing the coconut trees."

Halley smiled. "I should've gone with you. I love to climb trees."

Her eyes fixed on the coconuts, and she thought of the long thin trunk of the coconut tree. "How much do you weigh?" she said, as she got her pocketknife out.

"Why?" Eden said.

Halley pried drinking holes in the tough fibrous shells of the coconuts, digging all the way down through the coconut meat to the liquid center. "I was wondering how you got up the coconut tree. I've never been able to climb one myself."

"It is pretty hard, if you don't know how. I read a book about it – you do it like a frog. I'll show you sometime."

Halley nodded and they began on the coconuts.

Through the small holes – they had to purse their lips to stop liquid dribbling down their cheeks and into their ears – they drank the sweet, grainy coconut water.

"It's like kissing a coconut," Eden giggled.

"What do you know about kissing?"

"I know enough. From TV."

When the liquid was gone, Halley sawed a larger circular hole in the coconut hulls, and then reached her hand inside to slice out the thick, moist, white flesh. She laid the bits of coconut on a flat leaf, and when the work of cutting it out was finished, they ate it all. The simple meal was abundantly nourishing.

Halley and Eden sat a few moments longer. Halley memorized the woods around her: their scent; their look; their lessons.

Then, like the camellia flower she'd watched fall, she knew her time had come. She pushed herself up to her full height. Slipping on the now empty bamboo backpack, she gestured to Eden to follow, and she led the way forward, out of the woods.

CHAPTER 18

Halley had only walked a hundred yards when she stopped suddenly. Eden kept going, bumping right into her back with a bounce and a giggle.

"Why are we stopping?" she asked. She stepped forward to stand next to Halley, who put a restraining arm in front of her.

Eden's mouth dropped open.

They faced a nearly vertical scree slope, completely bare of vegetation. But for a few rocky outcroppings and some scattered patches of tall yellow grass, there was nothing that would slow their descent.

The scarred landscape was ugly and lifeless.

Thoughtfully, Halley reached down and picked up a handful of dusty pebbles. *Scree, just scree. I can't remember ever going down a hill this steep with just scree under foot...* She shook the pebbles in the palm of her hand, listening to their almost musical sound. The air was still and the sound stood alone in the silence. Spreading her fingers, she watched the pebbles slip through and cascade to the ground, some rolling further downhill, continuing the motion that she had begun. It was much drier here than in the forest, where the vegetation held moisture in the earth. She rubbed her hands together and felt the graininess left behind by the dust.

Suddenly breaking the stillness, the wind began to whistle. It had an animosity about it, that wind: it snatched leaves off the nearby trees and flung them at Halley and Eden; it threw bits of debris into their eyes; it stirred the loose dust into tiny whirling dervishes that traveled across the face of the hillside, giving the illusion that the barren descent was alive with small, threatening figures.

In the face of the ugly barrenness, the hostile wind, in the face of the dust dervishes, Halley thought how easy it would be to duck back into the woods, to return to the path she knew. Even after she'd said she couldn't go back; even if Trance were still in the woods. At least she'd know what to expect. *Better the devil you know...*

She shook her head. It was time to move on; something was pulling her forward. It was still about saving the baby, but it suddenly was about more than this. *It's about saving me too.* This thought hadn't occurred to her before, but it made perfect sense. The sense of suffocation she'd been feeling for the last few years was lifting. But here, near the woods, it still lingered in the air. *That's open air in front of me. I've got to reach it. But first, we've got to get down this hillside.*

Eden stood by her side, waiting.

It'll be a rough scramble. Best not to stand here too long thinking about it! "Okay," she said, straightening her spine, and breathing in deeply. "I'll go first. Aim for the bigger rocks and the grassy spots. They'll slow you down a bit." She pointed out a few places for Eden to aim for. "You ready?"

Eden nodded.

Halley stepped forward, aiming her feet towards a clump of rock several feet down. She immediately slipped, and began to slide. Fast. Then faster. The pace was dangerous. If she tripped, she'd go into a free tumble down the slope. She dropped onto all fours, sliding on her bottom, grabbing at weeds to slow her pace.

But sliding down on her bottom meant she was immersed at head height in dust. Her eyes filled with grit, and she began to cough. She couldn't see Eden. She shouted for her, but there was no reply. She coughed urgently, trying to clear her throat. Again, she was sliding faster. Her elbows jarred against the earth, her teeth banged together. One by one, her fingernails broke off with sharp bites of pain. After what seemed an eternity, she made it through the dust and could see again. She ground her heels into the earth and came to a skidding stop.

Halley looked behind her, back up the face of the hill. *Where are you Eden?*

Suddenly, she could hear giggling, and Eden's small figure appeared. She was on her back too, sliding down the hillside. She was absolutely covered in dirt. The pebbles she'd dislodged slid down around her like an entourage. From her laughter, Halley gathered that Eden had found a way to make the descent more fun. She skidded to a stop beside Halley.

"You looked so funny," Eden said. "You're doing it this way…"

She dropped her whole back down onto the ground, pretending to slip down the hillside with every muscle, even her jaw, clenched tight. Then she turned around and clambered back up to Halley. "It's like riding horses," she said, sitting back down again. "Or skiing. If you tense everything up, it's a lot harder. Try it this way." She got into position. "Try lifting your bottom up and letting your whole body go soft." Eden lifted her bottom up off the ground, and hovered over the earth a few inches. Her feet were planted in front of her, the palms of her hands hugging the earth behind, her fingers pointing down the hill. She began to move, and then to slide. It looked just like a small child playing at crab-walking on the beach. It worked going down a hillside too: the resulting movement looked effortless. In fact, it looked kind of fun.

Eden dug her heels in to stop, and waited, looking back up the hill, while Halley tried it. Halley was tentative at first, still tense through her legs and arms, and Eden shouted, "Let go! It's much more fun that way."

So Halley did. She started slowly, but then she crabbed her way fast down the hillside like Eden, using her arms and legs, her belly exposed to the sky. She caught up with Eden and then passed her. It took a little while to get used to the speed and the slipping a little bit out of control, but when she did, a giggle built in her belly. It bubbled there, until it spilled out over her edges. To her amazement, she too was laughing aloud. Finally, after much dirt, and scrambling, they reached the bottom.

It didn't much matter that they were both scratched and bleeding from minor scrapes, and that their clothes were torn in several places. Their laughter was what mattered, their doing of this *thing-that-could-not-be-done.*

When they finally stopped laughing and caught their breath, they looked at each other. At the same time, both said, "High Five!", and they broke down into a fit of giggles again. It took a while to rub away the tears of laughter from their eyes.

CHAPTER 19

They were facing a tremendous and very intimidating plain. The openness remained unbroken until, hazy and far in the distance, the grey boundary of mountains could just be made out. It was as if the world had grown larger. Halley's eyes felt like they were stretching to reach to the horizon, and she had to squint to bring the mountains into focus. The plain leading to the mountains was enormous.

It was also almost completely empty. The few scrub bushes that were visible were no taller than Eden's knees. The sky was immense, a huge blue and white canopy over dry yellow earth, its vastness unbroken by a single bird. *It's like standing on the edge of the world. It looks like one of those old sailing maps where the earth is flat and a ship can simply sail off the edge, if it goes too far.*

The view frightened her. But it also left her confused.

Eden voiced her thoughts. "Hey...," she said, cocking her head to the side, "...this isn't right."

"What do you mean?"

"In Mr. D's Earth Science class...we learned all about these things called climate zones. I got an 'A+' on my paper about it." Eden stopped, obviously enjoying the memory of that success, before continuing. "I'm sure the *climate zone* we've been in is called a '*humid sub-tropical climate*'."

She sounded just like Halley remembered herself sounding at Eden's age, using words too big for her mouth.

Eden continued, "I remember Mr. D said it funny, very fast, like it was one big long word *humidsubtropicalclimate* and I had to look it up in my book to make sure I spelled it right on the test. But this…" she said, pointing to the vast plain, "…this is a tundra. And a *humidsubtropicalclimate* zone can't be right next to a tundra!" She stopped, out of breath, and nodded her head once, with authority.

"Still, here we are," Halley said.

"Yes…but…"

Eden looked at the mountains.

"Well, it doesn't make any sense! Not if Mr. D was right about the zones. And I believe him. He's very smart." Eden stared, as if by looking for longer she could force it all to make sense. Then she added, breaking into a giggle, "I feel like I'm dreaming a very silly dream! But I'm glad you're in it, Halley." Then she sobered, finishing quietly, as if to herself, "I've never left the woods before…"

Halley was thinking about the class Eden described. She remembered about climate zones too. Eden was right – what they were experiencing wasn't possible. But, still, like she'd said herself, there they were. Just the two of them, facing this wide, empty tundra. No other way to go.

A new thought occurred to her: once they entered the tundra, there would be no place to hide from predators, animal or human. She knew it was right to be prepared for predators. *Trance is still back there somewhere. He's tracked me twice already – if he tracks me here… I've got to find a way to protect us.*

Halley looked around. There were still a few trees nearby, and below one of them was a staff of white wood, stripped of bark, two inches in diameter, and a few feet long. *I can use this as a weapon.*

The white stick felt rough against her palms. The texture was more noticeable than it should be. It set her fingertips to tingling. She held it thoughtfully, running her fingers over upraised edges where shoots had broken off, and then the smoother areas between the shoots. As she did so, she was stunned to see an image of the baby appear in front of her. She gasped aloud. It was the first time she had ever truly seen it, instead of just hearing it cry.

It was like a movie projector was showing the image against the trees. Around the edges of the vision, the woods were still visible. In the hazy circle where the vision appeared, the baby lay swaddled tightly in a thick white blanket. It was sleeping in a deep pile of brown leaves, under a tree whose branches bore close resemblance to the stick Halley held. Halley looked around quickly. There must be a thousand trees like this one nearby. *The stick must be the link,* Halley thought, gripping it more tightly, afraid to move lest the vision dissipate.

Halley stared at the baby, and a feeling grew in her. It was like watching springtime – from the first tiny green tip pushing through the winter's final snow, to the sudden bursting profusion of color. The feeling was a purple and yellow crocus, glowing, growing, bringing life where there was none before. The feeling was hope.

It soared through her like nothing she had ever known before, like nothing she could have described in the commonplace words of love. Her eyes widened and glistened.

The baby was breathing calmly, and Halley watched it for a long, long time, watched its tiny chest lifting and falling. Each inch of it seemed a miracle, and she cataloged the full curves of its arms and legs under the swaddling, the tiny upturn of its nose, the soft down of its hair.

My angel, she thought.

A leaf swirled gently through the air to alight on the baby's belly, and the baby stirred in its sleep, moving its small mouth in and out of a pucker as if it were dreaming of sucking at its mother's breast. Its lips moved just a little and shaped into the smallest of smiles.

Halley found herself smiling back at the vision as she held the white stick tightly with both hands. It was as if an unaccountably warm and benevolent breeze had stirred her soul all the way to the bottom.

Suddenly she was compelled to touch the baby, to bring this vision into her reality. She removed one hand from the stick, holding tight with the other hand, afraid to lose the link to the vision. She reached slowly for the baby's cheek. The baby's closed eyes relaxed, as if anticipating Halley's warm touch. Or maybe it was dreaming a lovely dream. She reached the baby's cheek, and then Halley saw herself in the vision with the baby. Even as she stood watching, she could also see herself kneeling beside the sleeping infant.

It should have been the strangest sensation imaginable, but Halley didn't notice: she was too caught up in unbelievable softness of the baby's cheek. Gently, she moved two fingertips along the cheek, then over the smooth forehead, around to the other cheek. The down of the baby's head felt like velvet, and she ran her palm over it again and again. It was impossible to get enough of how this baby felt. The baby opened its mouth slightly, utterly relaxed and content. It snuggled into Halley's hand, as if it too longed to be closer than close. Halley could have stayed in that moment forever.

But the vision changed: the baby's eyes flew open, as if startled. The Halley in the image stood up fast – her eyes were fixed on a point that the "real" Halley couldn't see. The image of Halley in the vision stretched taller, broader, more ferocious: she was facing something that was threatening her and the baby, that much was clear, and she would protect the baby. No matter what.

Halley drew her hand back quickly, gripping the stick again with both hands and with a new urgency. The stick could be used as a weapon. But her action had an unanticipated effort – now only the baby appeared in the vision. The image of Halley had disappeared.

The baby began to cry. First, it seemed to be crying at the removal of Halley's hand, as if Halley were the sun and the baby were the earth, and without her touch all was lost. All things would wilt without her. The baby cried with the voice of all the children who had ever been lost in the world, even though it couldn't yet use words: *mama mama mama*, its cry said. *Where are you? Why won't you come back? Mamamamamaaaa.* Halley's eyes filled with tears.

At first the baby's cry held the hope of resolution, as if Halley could get back if she tried hard enough, as if the baby and the mother could be re-united. Urgently, believing it might get her back to the baby, Halley removed one hand from the stick and reached out again, but she found she could no longer touch the image; the baby remained alone. Time passed, and the baby's cry became the desolate sound of the lost, of those who will never be found.

She watched helplessly as the baby's mouth opened wide, as it scrunched its eyes tightly closed, as it wailed like it couldn't bear to be left alone for one moment longer. Halley felt as if her heart was being scraped by a knife; her shoulders pulled up by her ears; she broke out in a cold sweat. She couldn't help the baby and it was maddening, this powerlessness. She couldn't even see what was threatening it. From her throat arose a strange, high-pitched cry, like the scream of a mother eagle, sharp beak open, fierce talons raised. The sound foretold the terrible protective violence of a mother whose offspring is threatened. More than this: the sound was the scraping-open of a heavily barred door that must remain closed.

Until the time is just right for it to be opened, Eden thought, watching all this closely. To Eden, the sound Halley made was very scary. Eden didn't like it. She didn't like it at all. Worse was the way that even Halley's eyes had gone cold.

Eden had to help Halley push back her natural instinct to protect the baby, until later, until it was needed. There was a right time for an eagle to tear out throats with its talons, Eden thought, and that time was coming. But it wasn't now – right now the baby didn't need Halley's protection – the threat was only in her mind.

It was good it was, because it was clear to Eden that the powerful side of Halley – the eagle side – was still too dangerous. It couldn't be released until Halley fully understood its power, its wildness, until she could control and direct it. Otherwise it would overcome her; it might even turn against Halley herself. When she was ready, Halley could use the wildness how *she* wanted to. Then she would be truly powerful.

Eden touched Halley on the hand. "No," she said softly but firmly.

She removed the stick from Halley's hands, and rubbed her small hand across its length, with her eyes closed. She held the white stick out to Halley, who appeared completely unconscious, though her eyes were open.

Halley came back into herself. The stick Eden was holding out to her caught her eye. It was about twelve inches long, polished smooth, and whitened by years in the elements. It looked almost like ivory. Even before Halley touched it, it filled her mind entirely. The force of it made the world shift.

How strange. I…just a moment ago… I felt like I could tear out someone's throat. What was that all about?

Her hands were clenched in white-knuckled fists, and she opened them slowly, staring at them without comprehension. As she reached for the white stick, the violent thoughts and feelings lifted from her conscious mind. She could not for the life of her recall what had upset her – she could only feel that her entire body was tensed, as if for a fight. About her lips, she held the remnant of wildness. She moved her jaw back and forth, feeling her teeth unclench and her lips relax. Whatever this feeling was, it seemed to come from somewhere outside of herself. She disowned it, pushed it away. Even the piercing scream – that unearthly sound she'd made and the only thing that she could remember clearly– she quickly dismissed. It was too scary to have come from inside her.

Halley felt calm and in control again. She held the white stick, moving her finger to touch its sharp-ended point.

Childish to be reminded of a unicorn, a silly imaginary beast! Absolutely ridiculous!

Still, Halley held the stick with reverence, thinking of unicorns. It felt good to think of them, to lose herself in their image of whiteness and light.

She looked at the stick carefully, turning it slowly in her hands, as if trying to recall something important that was just out of reach. *Is what I'm trying to remember about the baby?*

Dismissing the thoughts as unproductive, she hoisted her backpack a bit higher on her shoulders, and looked at Eden. "Are you ready to go?" she said. Eden nodded quickly, and Halley led the way onto the plains.

Halley held the white stick in her left hand as they walked. She relaxed with her innermost knowledge that the baby was safe, was waiting for her. Like before, she could feel its pulse in her forehead. *So beautiful…my angel.* Absently, she rubbed her fingertips together and was perplexed when the word *soft* fell into her mind.

The pull of her mission to save the baby pulsed through her body and pushed her forward onto the yellow tundra.

CHAPTER 20

As they moved into the tundra, what remained of the path disappeared. It didn't matter – they had no need to follow a particular trail anymore. They simply followed their feet towards the tall grey mountains.

The yellow grass tickled their ankles, swaying with the movement of their bodies, but not breaking.

Eden stopped once and looked back.

"Look," she said, pointing.

Halley followed the direction of Eden's gaze. The sea of yellow grass carried no trace of their onward journey. It was as if it had never been parted. That meant they couldn't be followed. But it also meant Halley couldn't follow her own path back to the woods. She felt like crying.

After a few hours walking, Halley stopped and stretched. "The mountains are a long way away," she said. "I think we'd better rest for the night." The blisters on her right foot had burst and were stinging with each step, and her legs throbbed with the burning sensation of overworked muscles. "There, that's a nice spot." She pointed towards a flattened area, where the yellow grass was matted down.

"Or…" Eden turned in a slow circle. "Or…how about under that bush with the pink flowers?" she said, gesturing to a more sheltered spot. "That would be more fun, like a real clubhouse!" She sobered. "And no one could see us there."

Halley agreed. The threat of Trance finding them was also on her mind, even if they were hard to track.

Eden popped her head inside the bush shelter. She was out again in a flash, scooping up several handfuls of fallen pink flower blossoms, and tossing them onto the ground inside the shelter. She popped her head back in and surveyed her work. "There – that's prettier! Look."

Halley looked in. "It's beautiful."

With the onset of evening, it was getting cooler. Halley re-zipped on her trouser legs, and donned the long-sleeved orange t-shirt. "Here, you have this," she said, handing Eden the orange windbreaker from her bamboo backpack. "It's going to be cold tonight."

Eden held it up. "How'd it get so dirty?"

"I slept outside. That was my first night. I left it too late to find shelter – stupid, huh? It bucketed down rain." Halley felt her cheeks grow warm with embarrassment. "Sorry it's so dirty…but it'll keep you warm anyway."

"Oh, I don't care. I think it makes me look like a cheetah! And I think you were very brave to sleep outside in the dark, all alone."

Halley laughed. "Come on, Cheetah, let's get inside."

They curled up in the nest-like hollow inside the bush. Eden's pink blossoms formed a soft bed. Halley took the side closest to the shelter's entrance, to protect Eden from any unexpected night visitors.

As the sun set, they became surrounded by the riotous night cry of cicadas. The sharp, high-pitched chatter took Halley back to the hot summer nights of her childhood. She fingered a flower blossom, turned grey in the dark, and remembered the old army cot with the thin fabric bed ("Don't step on the middle, you'll go right through," her father had warned her a million times). She'd bring that old green cot out onto the porch when it was too hot to sleep inside. It felt like camping out, but she was safe at home. Her bedroom window led to the porch and she left it open so she could climb back in quickly if she got scared. Listening to Eden settle in, hearing her breathing deepen with the onset of sleep, she realized something. She'd never had to climb back inside; she'd never got scared.

She'd been like Eden then. In the nights of her childhood, when she'd slept amongst cicadas, everything was possible and nothing was frightening. She'd been thoughtlessly brave, and she had never, ever pondered the future. She was simply alive, acutely aware of everything, and that was enough. The mulberry tree, with its lush berries that existed for the sole purpose of being *skwooshed* under bare feet, staining the soles of her feet a vibrant wine color; the taste of nectar from the yellow honeysuckle growing on the fence – she would pinch the end off the tiny flowers with her fingernails, and pull the pin-shaped stem through the thin flower to relish its sweetness; the simple pleasure of walking tip-toe along the four-inch width of the neighbor's fence, until the neighbor shouted at her and she had to wait until next time the neighbor was out to try it again; the majesty of leaping from the garage roof, a superhero, rolling into a tumblesault when she hit the grass.

Sleeping on that old army cot on the porch, she used to ponder the song of the cicadas. Were the insects singing with joy at the moment they emerged from the prehistoric shells they left attached to trees? Or were they screaming with despair when their short lives ended? The young Halley didn't know the answer, but she decided to believe the cicada's call was a sound of joy. It didn't really matter if it were true or not.

It was all so simple then. She listened to the cicadas. *It is now, too. It's still simple.* As she drifted towards sleep, a small smile softened her face, and her hands gently embraced her belly.

CHAPTER 21

Halley woke early, her first thought taking her by surprise. *I'm not tired. This is the best I've felt in years.* It was still dark in the shelter, but she could see minnows of light between the edges of the leaves. Feeling drawn to witness the first holy light of dawn, she crawled outside.

It was the fragile, miraculous beginning of another day. She stared up at the sky, and realized she hadn't thought of daybreak in quite that way in a long while. It was nice to have her old self back.

A little of the night chill remained. The light was soft, the horizon a magic of deep reds and oranges, becoming more vibrant as the dark receded and life returned to the world. Dawn tickled the openness of the plain, spreading gradually, like spilled water. It burnished the yellow grass to gold. Halley watched the endlessness of the view appear; it was invigorating, open and free. The world was renewed; she was renewed. The day was abundantly clear, so clear she could see for miles. The mountains were etched with detail, high and fine. Individual trees stood out, and it became apparent how many different types of trees formed the abundant green. A thin mountain trail was also visible, a dark brown line on a grey and green background.

Then the sun shoved its way above the horizon. Its appearance was a poor climax. It was a bully. It sucked the vibrancy of color from the sky for itself, leaving behind only the usual, mundane blue. Somewhere a bird spoke, and its loud *caaa-caaa-caaa* coincided with the moment Halley's reverie broke.

The world became real again. Hard-edged.

The early sunlight already felt hot on the top of her head.

I wonder what time it is. We'd better get moving. It's going to be hot today. She lifted her arm to check her watch. But the watch was gone. There wasn't even a tan line to mark its place.

It must have fallen off days ago, maybe in the river or on the rocks in the river gully. She didn't feel any real sense of loss. The catch on that watch had never locked properly, and it was old and scuffed. That's why she'd chosen to wear it on the walk with Fernando – it didn't matter much if she lost it. *And the old-scuffed-ness fitted how I felt about me that day. That's the real reason I wore it.* She was glad it was gone.

Still, an uneasy sensation moved in Halley's stomach. It certainly wasn't because she'd lost the watch, or because she didn't know what time it was. Rather, it was because this part of her past had disappeared. It felt like it swept away with it a fraction of her. She'd worn that watch ever since she'd met Fernando. It was part of their relationship.

Suddenly her eyes felt scratchy and tired, and she closed them tightly and rubbed them hard with her fists. Maybe she hadn't slept as well as she'd thought.

When she opened her eyes, she noticed again how clear the light was. Far in front of her were the mountains – that meant the woods were somewhere behind. She felt compelled to look at them, to hold onto them like a child would a favorite security blanket. But when she looked to where the woods should have been, they weren't there.

They simply weren't there.

Her blood pulsed through her veins with force. She cocked her head to the side. *I didn't think we'd gone that far yesterday.* She tried to stay calm. Telling herself to move slowly, trying to contain the feeling that was burrowing even deeper into her belly, she looked left and then right, to the back and to the front, and then, even more disturbed, made a concentrated sweep of the view, turning in a slow full circle.

No matter which direction she looked, she couldn't see the

woods. Like the watch, they were gone; the woods too had disappeared.

For a moment, Halley felt weightless, unanchored, as if she were held to the earth only by a thin filament of anxiety. She tried to think carefully about what had happened, to reason out these twin disappearances. The watch could've just fallen off, but how could the woods just vanish? *Okay, maybe we turned a corner and I didn't notice, maybe we traveled further than I thought yesterday.*

She knew she was just making up explanations; these things were not true. The only truth she could be sure of was that the woods were gone. That meant she couldn't go back. She began to speak aloud.

"I always thought...I always thought I could return. To the woods. To my life before." True, yesterday when she'd left the woods, she'd said she wouldn't return. It was so easy to kick around the idea of irrevocable change when it wasn't real, when she still had a choice. She'd believed, if she were honest with herself at the deepest level that she could return if she *really* wanted to. But she'd been wrong.

"God..." she said.

She felt her heart strike against her ribcage like a broken thing.

I can't get back to where I started. I can never go back. That means...Fernando... I can't get back to Fernando!

The world grew blurry. She rubbed the center of her chest with the heel of her hand, as if she could rub away the sudden pain she felt there. It was as if she had split open along mid-seam.

I didn't think when I walked away that day...I didn't think it was forever. I never even said goodbye.

Her eyes moved restlessly along the horizon. If she kept looking, some part of her was sure she'd be able to find the woods, find the path back. When that didn't work, she began to pace back and forth.

Forever. Goodbye.

The words revolved around each other in her mind like herself rolling down a hillside, round and round, filling all the space. She clasped her hands together so tightly that it hurt. She stopped pacing.

She was stuck. She was pinned to the past, pinned to this place and unable to move forward, like her boots were, all of a sudden, too heavy to lift. There was still a long, thin, unbreakable thread connecting her to Fernando, stretching out from the very center of her chest. *Stuck. I don't want to be stuck anymore.* She didn't want to face the thought, but she knew. *I've got to say goodbye to Fernando.* It was the only way forward, to lift anchor, to cut the cords which bound her to the past.

One of her hands went to her mouth, and she bit her forefinger, hard. As if by causing one pain she could distract herself from another. She hated the pain. She wanted to be over it, over Fernando. She knew for that to be, she had to face it all; she had to face the love she still felt for him.

In her memory, Fernando's black eyes shone. She felt her face soften – his eyes looked as they had when they'd first met, laughing and alluring, lit with tiny points of diamond. He was tall and handsome and well-built and a tango and the color red. She felt him hold her small hand in his large one, felt him rub his thumb tenderly over her knuckles. Felt her cheek nestle into the hollow of his shoulder, in the soft pile of his grey wool sweater, where she'd always felt safe. She saw his long eyelashes resting on his cheeks as he slept. She heard the music play, in the dark, in the living room, as they danced alone together. It had begun in love. In the beginning, there had been beauty; there had been the one-ness of them. She removed her hand from her face.

It had not ended in love.

She forced herself to remember his expression just before he'd turned and walked away. He hadn't believed her, hadn't believed *in* her. Sparrow. He had always called her Sparrow. She hated it. She took a deep breath. Because of what their love had become, she had to say goodbye to all of it, even the good, even his laughing eyes on the first day they'd met. Even the tango.

For a moment, she tried to hold on – she tried to take his point of view, to forgive him. *It must have been tiring to have to lead all the time. To put up with my bad moods. I must have been hard to read, especially when I was so angry, and then I swallowed the anger back down to not speak of it.*

Halley breathed in the clear sweet morning air, and let that thought rest at the back of her throat for a moment, and then she coughed it back up.

Hell with that. I've given him too much of my thought-space, created too many explanations for his behavior that came down to saying I was at fault. She shook her head. *What we had just wasn't good for me. Even the good bits. The good bits only felt so good because it was so bad the rest of the time. I have to let it all go. I don't need to forgive him all his faults. I don't even need to assign them, or to assign blame to him or to me. I just need to leave the woods between us.*

She knew then: even if she could see a way back, she wouldn't take it.

"Goodbye, Fernando."

She said the words aloud, before she meant to. She said them looking back the way she'd come, even though she couldn't see the woods anymore. The words held a strange resonance, as if they could be heard everywhere: *Goodbye, Fernando.* As if her goodbye would reach him where he stood and he would hear it and they could simply be free of one another. The words were said without anger, without any current of harsh judgment or bite of fury. The words were said softy, with simplicity and with honor for both of their humanity. In voicing the words, the action was taken, and the past was the past. The woods were gone, and this was okay.

She felt the sadness, felt her tears draw a clear path down

her dirty cheeks for the Halley she'd been and the life she had shared with Fernando, for the watch, and the music, and the love – and beneath it, just below the sadness, she found something new, something entirely unexpected.

It was what seemed to be a tiny layer of freedom. "Ahhhh," she said. Even though it seemed tiny, this layer of freedom, she dug deeper into it, as a child digging both hands into the sand for the first time. She squeezed it and savored the sensation, wet and wild and full, and she knew it was endless. She was free! She had set herself free.

And free, she was different. She hadn't really thought about who she'd become through her journey in the woods. Now she did. Standing alone in the clear light of dawn, instead of looking back at who she'd been with Fernando, she let herself be one with the person she'd become since she'd walked away.

I didn't think I could do that, find my way through the woods alone, without a map or a compass. She saw herself again climbing up the river gully, knees bloody, expression fixed with concentration. On the steep trails, uphill and down. *Before the woods, I believed I was a sparrow. Small and incapable and unable to choose for myself – that's what sparrow meant to me. He just gave my own view of myself voice.*

That had all changed.

She looked up at the blue sky. An eagle was flying. She thought about it. An eagle would not fly two feet behind *anyone*, holding its head down in shame. It wouldn't say *thank you* for mistreatment. It would never mistrust its own judgment. *I am an eagle. I won't hide from the truth anymore. I'll make my own choices. I'll lead myself where I need to go. I won't be afraid, or, if I am, I'll simply go on.*

A sense of power flowed through her with these thoughts, and she saw it was power in both her light and her darkness. Knowing she would not return to the woods was good, she found. No, it was *great*! She was someone else, someone new, going somewhere else, somewhere important. Her body felt strong and capable and her own, and her mind felt clear.

Then, from long habit, she glanced back down to see what time it was. The watch was still gone, but this time, she noticed something else. Her stomach lurched. *My ring – I've lost my ring too!*

CHAPTER 22

The ring was gone.

She suddenly realized she'd noticed its absence once before, the day she'd entered the woods to go searching for the baby. The alarm she'd felt at the loss of the ring had been replaced by the urgency to find shelter.

I can't even remember what the ring looked like, or where I got it from. All I know is I didn't get it from Fernando. She bit her lip. *It went on this finger,* she thought, slipping the forefinger and thumb of her other hand over the ring finger on her left hand with something like reverence. *That's where a wedding ring or an engagement ring would go. But I'm not...I've never been...*

Her head began to pound. It was as if saying goodbye to Fernando had freed her to remember. *I didn't lose that ring at all – I took it off!* She breathed out hard – she could see the moment:

She was removing the ring, a gold wedding ring that shone in the sunlight, and placing it into a small red, heart-shaped box. After putting it in the box, she took it out again, as if to look at the engraved inscription. But she didn't read it.

Instead, she quickly put the ring back in its box, and stood a long moment looking at it, thinking how small and insignificant something so important could appear. Two years of marriage. Now it was over. Shaking her head, as if to shake off the hold the ring had over her, she placed the box inside a drawer, and shoved it towards the back, pulling some other boxes in front of it.

As she closed the drawer, she'd felt a presence in the room with her –

The memory made her shiver in the hot morning sun –

It was something dark and ugly, something horrible. Something that would harm her. She broke out in a sudden sweat but at the same time she felt cold all over, like she had just come down with a fever.

Frightened, she looked around, but she was alone in the room. Quite alone. Still, she was certain there had been someone there with her, hovering by her. Hating her. She left the room quickly.

The memory made Halley look around fast to make sure she was still alone. Satisfied with the yellow grass and blue sky and the aloneness, she let herself think about the rest.

For there was more. There had been someone good in the house too, hadn't there? In a different part of the house. It had been someone kind, someone waiting for her with hope and with love.

He was in the garage warming up the car for me. And then we got in the car...

Halley dropped her hand quickly, as if the movement could stop the flow of thought, but the lump in her throat did not dissolve.

Sean? SEAN??

Her breath caught and her vision blurred as the name burned through her, but she could attach no memory of a face to the name, only the image of a bright, warm smile, and a sense of utter loss, of desolation, as if she'd made a thousand wrong choices, and the relationship with Sean, whoever that was, had been destroyed by these choices before it had ever really begun. The lump remained in Halley's throat, as if to block a cry of anguish.

The watch and the woods and the ring were gone. These disappearances didn't seem coincidental anymore.

A drowning sensation overtook her; she felt herself sinking

deeper and deeper and couldn't catch her breath. She was choking and coughing and her lungs were filling and she would die soon...

Her eyes caught on the silver bracelet she had found in the forest, and she stared at it hard. She fingered the flowing pattern of waves on the bracelet, at first with desperation, and then more slowly; she found that this movement helped her to breathe again, to flail to the surface of whatever had been drowning her. The memory of first seeing the bracelet in the fallen leaves, of stooping to pick it up and closing it over her right wrist – of its familiarity – was very strong. In the memory, she was not a thirty-five-year-old woman, as she was now. She was younger, twenty-three perhaps.

As if the bracelet had come from before. But before what?

In the woods with Eden, she had placed the bracelet on her right wrist. Now, standing alone in the morning sun, it felt oddly comforting to hold the bracelet with her left hand, and at the same time hold her own right wrist that wore the bracelet. *Strange that holding my own wrist should feel good, reassuring. Like I'm making myself stronger, making my wrist thicker and straighter. The bracelet is a different sort of ring than a wedding band, but a ring still. There's comfort in that.* The bracelet grew warm from her touch. She closed her eyes and was still.

Her life dissolving. She recalled a hanging plant she once noticed, that had fallen off a balcony. It had gotten stuck on the way to the ground, its hook catching on the edge of another balcony. It hung there midair, and never fell any further. She had watched the plant over the next week, watched it wither and die from lack of care. The sight had saddened her. But the following spring, the pot still hung there, and she saw that a new plant took root. It grew robustly, with vigor the original plant had never had.

Perhaps this was what was happening with her. Maybe an old part of her needed to dissolve to make room for the new.

She looked back at the shelter, and thought to tell Eden about the disappearances, to ask her advice. She needed something firm to hold onto.

"Eden, are you awake?" she asked softly.

There was no answer.

"Eden?"

Only silence.

Halley bent down and looked into the shelter, opening her eyes wide to see in the dim light, trying to see Eden's form in the darkness. It took a moment for her eyes to adjust, but a subtle emptiness in the air told her, even before her eyes could confirm it: Eden wasn't there.

CHAPTER 23

Halley stood up straight, and looked out at the emptiness.

"Eden? Eden, where are you?" she shouted.

The sound unfurled into the space around her, and she heard the edge of desperation in her voice. It was quickly silent again. She didn't want to shout anymore.

The wind began to whistle across the low grass, which had given up its gold and was once more a pale, dead yellow. The sky was enormous and no longer invigorating.

Eden was gone.

A surge of disbelief went through her, quickly followed by the recognition that this loss was real, and absolute. The pain of it hit her like a punch.

It wasn't at all like losing Fernando. Eden hadn't held Halley's power; she was simply her friend.

Halley swallowed hard before crawling back into the shelter. The first thing she saw was her own orange windbreaker, neatly folded in the place where Eden's head would have lain. She felt around on the ground, where the pink flower blossoms lay. She touched the ones she herself had slept on – they were still slightly warm from the heat of her body. But the rest of the blossoms – the ones Eden must have slept on – these were covered with morning dew, cool and damp to the touch. Her throat constricted. Eden must have left well before dawn, must have climbed over Halley in the dark of night. *Why?*

She crawled out of the shelter, taking the orange windbreaker with her. It was impossible to believe it was the same day she had greeted with such vigor. Getting to her feet was difficult, and the vastness of the space around her humbled her when she did, and drove her back to her knees. The sun was high in the sky, and its light was harsh. There was no break in the landscape for miles, only the yellow stalks of dried-out weeds. No figure of a little girl to catch her eye. No friend to walk with.

Far in the distance, she could see the teeth of the mountains, unfriendly and unfamiliar. Standing, she turned in a slow circle, like she had when she'd looked for the woods. The view in every direction was the same. Yellow, deadening grass. Desolation.

Her eyes lit upon the white stick that Eden had given her – Halley had left it outside the shelter the night before as a kind of totem to protect them. The sight of it made her feel like she was filled with lead. It was if a dream had ended before she'd gotten to the good part. The word *loneliness* seemed too small and insignificant a word to describe the hollow she felt inside herself, the feel of ashes floating around her and alighting on her eyes.

I don't want to be alone again, not so soon. Oh GOD…

"Where are you? Won't you stay with me?" she whispered aloud, picking up and fingering the smoothness of the white branch. It felt cold to the touch. She stared at the ground, and then sank back to her knees.

From her hiding place some distance away, Eden watched closely, lying still, hardly daring to breathe. When Halley rested her head on her arms, Eden's small hand involuntarily reached out to her.

Silently, Eden weighed the options. *If I stay with you, you might think it's me who has done all the deciding and made all the choices. You've come here to find your own way, your own power. You've got to be your own hero.* She mouthed the words to herself silently: *Be your own hero.*

Eden fought the urge to go to Halley. *Maybe I can go with her, but only if I make sure she does all the deciding, even if she chooses wrong. I have to let her choose wrong sometimes.*

She sat still with this thought, waiting for Halley's next move.

Then she made a bargain with herself. If Halley turned to run back to the forest, all was lost. But…if Halley stood up and went on towards the mountains, *oh yes*, if she was as courageous as she'd once been, then Eden could join her again, and there was still hope.

"Oh please, let there be hope," Eden whispered.

It took a long time for Halley to get to her feet, and when she finally did the lack of foliage made her feel very exposed. Still she stood. *I didn't come here to hide in the weeds*, she thought, with a surge of anger at the landscape and its unclear threat. She held the white stick grimly in her hand.

"All right," she said. "I know I have to go on. You must've left for a reason. I've still got this mission, this baby to save. I'll do it, even if I have to do it alone." She wished her voice sounded more convincing.

She looked out at the mountains. It was hard to gauge how far they were. *I can't even make a guess with no landmarks to help indicate the distance. I guess it doesn't really make any difference.*

Shouldering the bamboo backpack, she started off through the yellow grass, feeling it scratch at her ankles between her socks and her combat trousers. It was strange – yesterday, the grass was gentle and kind. *It doesn't matter*, she told herself, shaking her head in dismissal. *What matters is movement, getting closer to where I'm going.*

Small clouds were scattered across the endless blue sky; they moved along fast, powered by a strong wind. Halley wished the wind would help her as well. Instead, it came from all directions at once, ruffling her hair into her eyes, taunting her, seeming bent on making her feel as uncomfortable as possible. Her footsteps in the dry grass rustled in time with the sound of the wind, and the two sounds together made for a lonely concert. It was the sound of something important, missing.

Still, the view was open and the mountains were unambiguous in the distance. This was a comfort. Halley was by herself again, but as she listened to the sound of her footsteps, she realized she was no longer afraid to be alone. On her face she wore the small sad smile of someone who was missing a good friend, but she walked on.

You're still with me, Eden, just like Mom and Dad. I know it. I can feel you in the landscape around me, in the sky and the wind. And I know I can do this by myself.

She thought of her first steps without Fernando. They seemed a lifetime ago. She stared out far into the distance as she walked, clear-eyed. *Be your own hero*, she thought.

Without landmarks or a watch, it was hard to say how far she traveled alone. However long it was, the sound of a giggle a while later made her jump. It wasn't exactly relief she felt when she heard it; it was more a settling into place of something where it belonged. She looked back quickly, and there was Eden hurrying to catch up.

"I thought you were gone for good," Halley said.

Eden smiled broadly and with innocence. "I just ran back to the woods to pick this for you. I remembered a place by a waterfall where there were all these beautiful flowers." She held one up.

Halley looked at it carefully. It was purple with six petals. Its center was a warm yellow. The colors were robust, and mirrored the emotion she felt while holding it.

"I thought it would look pretty against your hair," Eden continued, beginning to look abashed. "I'm sorry. I didn't mean to be away so long, but it took a while to find the waterfall, and then to find the perfect one."

She stepped next to Halley, and carefully placed the stem behind her ear.

The flower made Halley feel like an exotic, savage princess.

"Wow," Eden said, admiring the effect. "It makes your eyes look so… so…far away…"

Halley inhaled a deep breath, and forced herself to face the question aroused by Eden's trip to the woods and back. *How could Eden go back to the woods, when I can't see them at all?* A more jarring thought occurred to her. *Maybe Eden wasn't really here. Maybe the pressure of the journey had finally driven Halley insane.*

Reaching her hand out, Halley pressed her fingertips gently upon Eden's shoulder. She could feel the warmth of Eden's skin through her thin t-shirt. *At least she feels real. But how come she can see things I can't?* For a moment, Eden seemed to shimmer in the bright sunlight. Remembering her earlier pledge to herself about not hiding from the truth, Halley began carefully, "Eden..."

Eden's giggle interrupted Halley's question. "Of course I'm real, silly! As real as you and Trance and the baby, and the forest. I can see *lots* of things you can't, because I'm only little. I can see unicorns and fairies and monsters and magic. You're all grown now, so you hardly see anything at all!"

Halley nodded; there was truth in this. Maybe she could see the woods if she really tried – maybe she just didn't want to.

She fingered the flower. She knew where it had come from, knew the waterfall place Eden had visited. Halley had seen it at the start of her journey; she could still see it in her mind's eye as it had been that day. The desecration of the place had stopped her in her tracks: the dried up waterfall; the wildflowers chopped down and left to wilt in the sun. She contemplated the question she had asked over and over that day, *"What's happened here?"*

She hadn't understood who would want to destroy a place of beauty like that. She knew the answer now. It was Trance. The destruction of her waterfall place had been meant to shake her foundations, to help him destroy her. *I met him that very night, in the tree shelter. He must have followed me from that spot.* She felt a surge of anger. *How dare he! How dare he destroy that place!*

Eden interrupted her thoughts. "The flower looks so pretty. I wish I'd got one for me too," she said mournfully. "But I was trying to hurry."

The flower: the wonderful, living flower! Trance had failed! He hadn't been able to destroy her soul-place, because he hadn't known the truth about wildflowers. Or about her.

The wildflowers have grown back. They've self-seeded! Just like me, just like I've always come back from the edge. How could I have forgotten they do that!

Her soul-place was remade: she could see the waterfall gradually re-flowing through cracks in the dam; the scarlet ibises returning to bathe; the wildflowers abundant and colorful; the earth fertile and moist.

He couldn't destroy it. He can't destroy me.

Eden had fashioned herself a bamboo backpack just like Halley's, and from it she pulled bananas and two fresh coconuts. They had a small feast, and then moved on.

CHAPTER 24

Silence held them softly as they walked. The day was balmy, a temperature so comfortable they seemed to merge with the air, like they would the water in a perfectly warmed bathtub. Every now and then, Halley reached up to touch the flower, rubbing the petals gently between two fingers.

Between them, there was no need for words, and they simply followed their feet across the yellow landscape. The day wore on, and the serenity in which they walked was dreamlike: the grass flowing unchanging beneath their feet; their gentle breathing in and out; the warm moist air. Though they moved forward, the lack of variance in the landscape made it seem they weren't moving at all, but simply floating in space.

"Halley?" Eden said, after a long silence.

"Yes?"

"Who's Fernando?"

Halley turned to look at her.

"He was my boyfriend. How did you know his name?"

Eden looked her right in the eye.

"You were talking in your sleep last night. You said his name... you sounded sad...but angry too, all at once. You woke me up."

"I'm sorry..." Halley looked away. "I was upset. But I've made peace with it now. I've finally let go of him."

"Really?"

"Yup."

"Then why are you making fists?"

Halley looked down at her hands in surprise. "I don't know." She shook out her hands, and flexed the fingers open and closed.

"Did he make that for you?" Eden asked, pointing at Halley's bamboo backpack.

Halley's snort of laughter held no humor. "This? No. He would hate this."

"Why?"

"Not trendy enough." She rubbed one of the shoulder straps with her fingertips. *That stupid, goddamned black backpack he'd given her...*

"What are you thinking about?"

Halley looked at her. A gentle breeze stirred the hair at the back of her neck. "He did give me a backpack. A black one. I threw it away when I left him."

"That was silly. Why did you do that?"

"Let's just say I hated it."

"Why?"

"Oh, Eden...you ask too many questions!"

Eden skipped a little way in front, and looked back at Halley. "That's because you want me to."

Halley brushed the hair off her face. "Okay. He made it seem like I was an idiot for not knowing my old backpack was all wrong." Her jaw felt tight. "Every time I put on the one he gave me, I remembered that, and I felt that way. Like a complete idiot..."

"Oh. It's good you threw it away then." Eden nodded once, agreeing with herself.

Halley had stopped walking. A frown of concern appeared on her face.

"What's wrong?" Eden asked.

"Did you hear that?" Halley spun around in a circle. The plain looked very empty. "It sounded like a scream."

"It sounded a bit like a gibbon, didn't it?"

"We're not in the woods anymore – there are no gibbons here," Halley said.

"Oh."

They both listened closely.

"There it is again!"

"Maybe…maybe it's a bird – we've seen lots of those…" The sound grew in volume and Eden shivered. "It gives me the creeps. Halley, let's go back…let's just go back the way we came."

"Shhh…listen…now it sounds like laughing…like a woman, laughing…"

"It's not a very happy laugh though, is it?"

They began to walk again, Halley feeling ill at ease. The pleasure of their solitude evaporated. The tall yellow grass stood at knee height all around them. Halley towered above, and she felt very tall and very visible. It made her glad that Eden was short. It was the first time that Eden had seemed scared.

A strangely flattened area of grass appeared in front of them. Eden reached the place first, and bent down in the flattened patch. She was suddenly hidden from sight. Halley didn't like how it looked; it was like she'd been swallowed whole. Almost immediately, Eden stood up again. She looked as if she'd been struck by a viper.

"What's the matter?"

Eden didn't answer. Her face was white.

Alarmed, Halley ran to her – in a moment, they were side by side. Eden was pointing at the ground. One of Halley's hands leapt up to cover her open mouth. She tried to speak, but couldn't. They looked at each other, and then back at the object on the grass. It was a black backpack.

"That's yours, isn't it? That's the backpack that Fernando gave you."

"It is. But how did it get here? I threw it away days ago…"

The ground suddenly gave way beneath them. They were falling, uncontrolled into deep darkness.

CHAPTER 25

The fall – a tumbling, disorienting sense of being unconnected to the earth – went on and on. Halley's sense of her body disappeared. It was like becoming a droplet of sweat in a breeze, and then becoming nothing.

When she hit the ground, she hit hard. A sensation like fire shot up her spine. She cried out. They'd fallen at least fifteen feet, maybe more.

"Eden," she said, when she could speak, "Are you okay?"

Eden, lying next to her, was curled up in a fetal position. "I think so...but...ouch...I landed funny – I think I hurt my leg. What's happened? Where are we?"

"I don't know."

Halley felt around. Long bits of grass lay on top of her, and on the ground near her. From her lap, she picked up a bit of heavy earth. She stared at it. The earth was sandwiched between layers of grass, and the grass itself looked as though... no...it wasn't possible...but yes...the grass had been weaved together. The weave was broken where their weight had made it give way. Halley dropped it. Eden standing on the woven grass cover wasn't enough to break the weave. It hadn't broken until Halley got there too. It had needed their combined weight to break it. It was a trap, and it was meant for them. Trance! It had to be him!

"Say something," Eden whispered. "I'm scared."

"It's okay. We're going to be okay." Halley paused. "I think we've probably fallen into an old well or a mineshaft," she finally said. Even to her ears, it sounded like a lie.

A sound came from above them. They both looked up.

Something, some kind of cover, was being dragged over the opening of the pit.

"Stop!" Halley shouted. Pain stabbed through as she stood fast. The movement of the cover continued. "Don't close us in! We'll die down here!"

The movement didn't stop until the pit was nearly covered, leaving only a thin quarter-moon of light. It became too quiet.

Halley put her arm out to Eden and helped her sit up. In the space of the silence, the shock hit. Halley kept her arm around the young girl and felt her shaking, heard her gasping for breath that wouldn't come. Her own face was tight with tension. As her eyes grew accustomed to the light, she saw they were in a deep circular featureless pit. Its sides, when Halley reached out a hand to touch them, were sleek and slippery. The ground under them was damp and as cold as death. There was no way out.

Eden fought back tears. "I didn't know it would be like this outside the woods." She held Halley's hand tightly. "How are we going to get out?"

Rustling came from above. Looking up, Halley caught a glimpse of movement, but couldn't make out what it was. Suddenly, the scream they had heard during their walk echoed through the pit. It was terrifying, the voice of a person in such deep pain that the torment had turned to anger and the anger to fury. A hooded figure stared down at them in the pit, and then backed out of sight.

The movement of the cover resumed. In a moment, it would seal off the last sliver of light.

The person began speaking, the voice a mad whisper that made the hair rise on Halley's forearms. It was a woman's voice. "It's her. It's her! After all this time. Finally her…"

Halley and Eden stared at each other.

"She knows you," Eden whispered.

"Shhh," Halley said. "Listen…"

"Kill her...kill the one who has caused my pain," the woman continued. "I've waited so long..." The laughter came again.

The words rang in Halley's ears, and her head felt full of a twisting presence, like a creeper vine gone wild. "Who are you?" she shouted.

The cover was moving again.

"Stop, damn you! At least let Eden go – she's just a little girl! She hasn't hurt anyone." Halley pressed Eden's hand in her own.

"Eden...hahahahah...you believe in Eden! She's been gone for years!"

The woman's words made Halley's eardrums throb.

The air was becoming staler in the pit, heavy with dust.

Halley stared at Eden.

"What does she mean, 'You've been gone for years?'"

"She's crazy," Eden said. "I'm not gone – I'm right here." As if to prove it, she hit her chest with a small fist.

"Why are you doing this? Who are you?"

"Don't pretend! You know who I am! It's your fault I was left here. Your fault I'm all alone." The voice was venomous. "You were so ugly and clumsy and stupid that they all left me. Even him! I *hate* you!"

The cover closed.

CHAPTER 26

Halley and Eden sat on the cold ground, holding hands tightly. They didn't speak. Occasionally, their bodies were shaken by tremors, minor internal aftershocks, as if their flesh were processing the trauma they were undergoing.

In the darkness, it was impossible to tell the passage of time. Time became as strange as their surroundings – seconds stretched out and lengthened, became grossly engorged, misshapen, ugly. Soon, night landed on them, heavy and awful.

They remained silent. It was as if they were both afraid to voice the desperateness of their situation. When the silence seemed about to dissolve them, Eden finally spoke. In a very small voice, she said, "What are we going to do?"

Halley started; Eden's voice had come from very far away.

She breathed in, and became conscious of a slight weight on her shoulders. She was still wearing her bamboo backpack. Now, after first rubbing her vision clear with the heel of her hands, she fingered its straps, recalled its making. It brought clarity, the grainy feel of the dry bamboo. She pictured the lion-monkeys who had helped her – they would still be out there, somewhere, with their orange manes and bright, clever eyes. The eagle would be out there as well. Halley felt Eden's eyes on her.

"What are we going to do?" she repeated, as if Halley had not heard her the first time. "I'm getting so thirsty."

Halley opened her mouth to answer, but she couldn't find her tongue. Her mouth was dry, like she'd been cupping a wad of cotton balls in her cheeks. With effort, she shifted her tongue around, and then tried to use it to moisten her lips. It didn't work.

The dryness was impossible, an unbearable thirst. She couldn't speak.

Instead, she stood up. The movement felt strange, like her vertebrae had fused themselves into the bent shape of sitting, and standing straight were causing the vertebrae to break apart along thick fibrous lines. Her lower spine ached where she had hit the earth. She tried to focus on what to do. It was hard when the dark was so disorienting.

Running her hands along the smooth walls, she felt for tree roots or rocks, for anything that might give her grip and the ability to climb. She moved around the edges of the pit, touching all the sides, feeling the same wet smoothness of the walls all over. Even stretching up on her toes, it felt exactly the same. It was hopeless: they couldn't climb out. She sank down onto her haunches.

"Halley?"

"I don't know. I don't know what we're going to do…"

Eden was silent, but Halley heard her gulp and swallow a sob.

"Don't be afraid. I'll figure it out."

I have to. I'm the grown-up. I can't let Eden die down here. But what can I do?

She rubbed her forehead with both hands. Their only hope was the woman – she had to lure the woman back. Get her to help them. But how? *I don't know how.*

Halley felt the powerlessness build in her, just like it had when she was an awkward thirteen-year-old girl. She recalled herself: she'd been in love with Shaun Cassidy, had his posters scotch-taped to all the surfaces in her room. She'd liked his eyes best; they were soft and kind – puppy-dog eyes. She would stare into his eyes as if he were there with her, and feel less alone.

Eden squeezed her hand, bringing Halley back to the present.

I didn't give up then. I'm not going to give up now. I won't surrender. She bit the inside of her lip, and began to hum softly, building the melody and the words of a song she hadn't sung in years.

That song: she'd first heard it on Z100 Radio, when she was thirteen. It was a "Top 40' song, and she had spent a whole weekend listening to the radio so she could catch it playing, and tape it. Her family didn't have money for buying music, and even if they had, Halley wouldn't have wanted to ask for this particular song. This song was private. She was just beginning to build walls to protect her more sensitive feelings.

The quality of the cassette she'd made from the radio broadcast was poor; she'd missed the first few seconds of the song, only pressing "record" after she recognized the melody, and the part she had taped sounded scratchy and distant.

The poor quality didn't matter though; she had still played the tape again and again and again, until the missing seconds and the scratchiness of the recording had become part of it. It would have sounded wrong if it were any different.

When the tape was almost worn out from overuse and damage (when she was sixteen, the brown tape inside the cassette had slipped loose from its holder, and wound itself around the little dibs in her tape player, but she'd carefully managed to wind it back with a pencil eraser), she used the original tape to record a new one. The scratchiness on the second tape was worse, but it mattered even less. The words were clear and they were perfect and she knew them all by heart.

The singer, a man, sung about feeling alone, about feeling this aloneness, but still not giving up. As a young girl, she had closed her eyes and felt her body sway to the song. She had sung along – softly at first – and later more loudly, and with more conviction. Where she couldn't make out the exact words, she made them up and her words felt right. It had been comforting to know that someone else felt the same way, had felt it enough to write it into a song. Other people liked the song too, that's why it was a hit. So she wasn't really alone. Not really.

Here, in the dark of the pit, she began to recall the words. It took some time. "And nobody wants to know you now..." she sung in a hoarse whisper, "…and nobody wants to show you how…" The words came and her voice rose. "So if you're lost and on your own, you can never surrender, and if your path won't lead you home, you can never surrender. And when the night is cold and dark, you can see, you can see light, 'cause no one can take away your right to fight, and to never surrender…to never surrender…"

The words hung in the air. She closed her eyes. When she opened them, she saw a shaft of moonlight on her arms. The cover had been shifted. Fresh air stirred. Looking up, Halley could see a fine circle of night sky.

"Sing it again," Eden whispered.

Halley did.

A few moments later, a rope was thrown down. Its dangling end hit the ground with a thump. It had been knotted a few feet up to provide some purchase for climbing.

"I'll go first," Eden said quickly. "My leg feels better. And that woman isn't trying to kill *me*. She doesn't even think I'm real."

"Good point. Okay. I'll follow as soon as you get to the top." It was better this way, Halley reasoned to herself. If Halley went first, Eden would be left alone in the dark pit.

Eden jumped to her feet, grabbing the rope, climbed hand-over-hand fast like a monkey to the top of the pit.

Halley, after giving the rope a testing tug, followed. With her feet planted firmly against the wall, she began to climb, using her legs to do much of the work, stepping up one foot at a time, in time with her arm movements. It was hard work; she was a lot heavier than Eden. Her muscles burned. Warm blood pounded through her body. Its warmth felt like a returning to life.

At the top, Halley hoisted herself over the edge and stood up, breathing hard.

Eden was silent.

"Eden?"

"Look – there she goes…" Eden said, pointing.

The outline of the woman was far away, and even that was soon swallowed by the dark night.

"She gave me this," Eden said, holding up a large canteen.

"Water. Thank God!" Halley rubbed her hands together, feeling them still burning from the effort of climbing. "What was she like?"

Eden shook her head, her eyes filling with sudden tears.

Halley frowned, taking the canteen from Eden. "It's ok, she's gone now." She studied the canteen, thinking. "Listen. I know you're really thirsty, but this may be poisoned…let me go first." The cap came off easily and the water had no smell. She poured a bit on the palm of her hand, to no effect. After a brief pause, she took a small sip. "Let's give it a few minutes to make sure…"

They waited. Nothing happened.

They quickly drained the large canteen. The relief from their thirst was immeasurable. Exhausted, they lay down, Halley cradling Eden protectively against her body. She stayed awake a long time, keeping watch.

In the darkness, a horse lifted her large white head from the dew-laden grass. She didn't whinny. Turning, she nosed the rope burn that encircled her neck. Despite the woman's efforts, the rope had dug in. With a quiet grunt, she lowered her head back to the grass and began to graze.

CHAPTER 27

A bird screamed at dawn. Halley sat up fast.

A few feet away, the woman watched. She was crouched in a low squat, her arms wrapped around her knees. Her hands were white; her posture that of someone poised to attack. In the early morning light, her cloak glimmered. It concealed her entire face, but for her burning, venomous eyes.

"I should've left you to die in the pit. But I needed to see you first. I needed to see your fear!"

Like a cobra, she exploded towards Halley, murder in her eyes.

Halley leapt to her feet. *I will protect Eden. I will save the baby.* She was aware of a roaring in her ears, but she stood still, feet planted wide.

"I am not afraid of you."

The woman got so close, Halley could smell her breath.

"Not afraid," she sneered. "Of course you are. You fear everything. And you will save no one. The others who tried to save them are all dead." She pointed over her shoulder towards a distant hill.

Halley and Eden looked at the hill, and then quickly at one another.

"Are those *bones?*" Eden asked.

Halley couldn't speak.

"I didn't kill you last night, when I should have," the woman said. "You, who caused all my pain. That song you sang, it weakened me." Her body convulsed. With a grimace, she crossed her arms in front of her, as if she were burning up in her own bile. With apparent effort, she uncrossed one arm, and pointed her finger at Halley, pinning her for so long that Halley felt a growing sense of heat, as if she were being burned by the energy directed from the woman's fingertip. "Go back, or I will kill you. I will kill you, just like them," the woman said.

Eden pulled at Halley's sleeve, trying to drag her away, but Halley gently removed her hand.

"I don't think so," she replied. She stared into the woman's vacant eyes. "I don't think you've killed anyone."

The woman shook with rage. "Of course I did. I trapped them, just as I trapped you. Hope and Jordan and Eden. All trapped. All dead. Do you dare to doubt me?!"

"A killer wouldn't let us out, and certainly wouldn't leave us water. Let's sit here, together," she said, gesturing to the ground.

Halley sank to her haunches, motioning Eden to follow. Eden looked unsure, but sat down by Halley's side.

Surprisingly, the woman complied, throwing herself down several paces away.

They stayed seated in silence a long while. Morning dragged on, and the sun moved up into the sky. In time, the woman began to speak aloud, but as if to herself.

"God, I hate you. How could you let him walk away? Who am I without him? I don't even know myself. All I've ever done is follow. And now you expect me to lead. He was my life. My light. My only source of light. Now he's gone, all that's left is darkness. And you let him go! In search of what? Something better? Someone better. He might've loved me, in time. Might have come to admire me, like I admired him. That's all I ever wanted, for him to admire me, to see me. He was my hero. I don't know how to go on now. If only you hadn't been so ugly. So stupid. So disobedient. He might have stayed. At least he might have looked back. Might have said, 'Please come with me…'"

Eden and Halley sat quietly together, letting the woman talk.

"So many of them who've loved me – you drove them all away," she continued. "Once, I knew what love was. I was held by it, lifted by it. Now. Now, I'm all alone." Gradually, the sun moved directly above them, making their shadows disappear.

Finally Halley leaned forward towards her. "Who left you? And what does it have to do with me?"

The woman jumped, as if startled by the interruption of Halley's voice. "How can *you* of all people ask these things!" she said.

Halley sat up straighter, moving back from her rage.

"You know who I mean. Fernando. You know I loved him. I needed him. To lead me. To love me. And you! You had to be brave and strong and let him walk away! Freedom, you said. Liberation. I'll..."

She moved to stand, and in doing so, inadvertently threw her hood back, for the first time revealing her face.

The woman's hair hung long, curtaining her in a deep, vibrant red. Her skin was pure white, like a marble statue. Her dark brown eyes shined, gentling her appearance, softening the fire of her hair. She reminded Halley of rich, dark chocolate. Belgium chocolate. *Or maybe its kalamata olives I'm thinking of,* she thought, remembering their purple flesh and their distinguishing tang. *She looks Mediterranean. She looks like...like Fernando.*

"You may as well see it all," the woman growled, and cast her robe to the ground in disgust.

The woman's figure was slender, delicate, evenly proportioned, and long-limbed. Under the black, hooded robe, she was dressed in filmy white.

"This is why they all leave. I'm repulsive." She made a fist and thumped it hard into her chest. "Is this what you wanted to see so badly? Look then..."

She spun in a slow circle, making a mockery of herself, and then stopped and crossed her arms defensively across her chest. The sleeves of her white shirt slipped back to reveal a warm olive complexion. The contrast between her whitened hands and the olive skin just above them was strange and wonderful.

Halley stared in astonishment.

"But...but you're beautiful. Don't you see?"

"Beautiful!" She bit the word out. "If I were beautiful, I wouldn't be alone. He would never have left me." She kicked at the robe on the ground. "Even this can't hide it, not from me. I am an ugly monster."

Halley swallowed.

"What...what is your name?" she asked.

"Gail. I am Gail." The woman looked away.

"Gail," Halley said thoughtfully. "Like the wind. A typhoon wind. Strong and wild and powerful. It fits you." Halley paused. "Look at me."

Gail would no longer meet her eyes.

"Look at me," Halley repeated. "Please..."

Gail looked, and Halley almost wished she hadn't. Nonetheless, she held the gaze. "You look at me with fury," she said. "But it isn't me you're angry with."

Gail stiffened. "Don't tell *me* who I'm angry with! It was you that let him treat me as he did! You that let him abuse me and belittle me and...and lessen me! How *could* you!"

Gail slapped at Halley, aiming hard for her cheek, but Halley was too fast, and grabbed her wrist before the strike hit. She lowered Gail's arm, gently but firmly.

"I hate you! It's easy for the likes of you, with your bracelets and your eagles. What about me!" She disappeared into herself. "What about me?"

They moved away from each other. Time passed.

"I hate this," Gail said to herself. "I hate this *changing*. It's like stripping off my skin to become someone new. *She* talks about dissolving and stupid plants re-growing where others have died. But it *hurts* to be dissolved." Gail shuddered and held her stomach again. "It hurts to change. It's a hateful process, this burning up like a phoenix to be reborn. No one ever talks about how the phoenix feels when he's set alight!"

178

Gail talked to herself but she could be clearly heard. Halley and Eden held hands and listened.

Slowly, as if her thoughts were shifting with the moving sun, her tone began to change. She no longer raged against Halley. She rested her chin on folded hands and stared out across the yellow grass. She sounded puzzled. "Why would she take that from him, all of that time? The way he demeaned her…the way he rolled his eyes at her suggestions…" She lifted her chin from her hands and her eyes narrowed. "The goddamned backpack he gave her – she carried it for all those years." She shook her head. "Love…she called it love…bullshit. That wasn't love."

Their shadows, which had disappeared when the sun was directly overhead, returned, and grew long. Halley watched the woman as she spoke. She was so lovely. Though she resembled Fernando in both her complexion and her mannerisms, in Gail these things were more radiant. More authentic.

Halley listened to her speak; it was as if a slow, rich stew were cooking on the back burner of a stove top. Simmering. Its subtle aromas starting to fill the air. Finally, the stew was ready – but perhaps it was more like a hot curry – when it was ready, it had quite a bite.

Gail exploded to her feet. "It's him I hate!" she shouted. "It's him and Nick and all of them that came before them too! How *dare* they treat me that way! It was nothing to do with her – it was them! It was always them. They disrespected me from the start, every man who ever claimed to love me." Her words ran on and on. They flowed like hot lava, pouring forth with unstoppable force. "Never again. I'll never call that love again…"

Slowly the sun mellowed, and sunk low in the sky. As they watched, the sky turned first a brilliant shade of pink, then orange, and finally it fired itself an angry red. The red was mellowed by the blue of the heavens. Their shadows grew dim and then merged with the growing darkness. Gail had run out of words.

I hadn't realized it hurt so badly, Halley thought. She was about to speak when Gail held up her hand.

"Don't say it. Don't say, 'Forgive me.'"

There was a catch in her voice. Gail took a deep breath. "You were right. I'm not angry at you. I don't need to forgive you anything. I'm angry at him…at them…at the ones who hurt me."

Halley felt a lightening, as if something dark were being lifted from her, like a snake shedding its skin. Gail moved as if this lifting away hurt her, and Halley looked at her with compassion.

"Come – let's walk," Halley said, emotion choking her voice. "We've still got something to do."

The three of them moved away together through the tall grass.

CHAPTER 28

It was early evening. The terrain undulated with small hills, and the three of them walked slowly. The landscape reminded Halley of the pattern on her silver bracelet, and she twisted it around her wrist in slow circles. After some time, she began to hum.

"What's that?" Eden asked. "It sounds nice."

"I don't know what it's called. Dad used to play it on the piano, when I was a little girl. He always stopped playing if I listened openly, so I'd put my ear against the wall in my bedroom when he played." *It made me think of seagulls flying over big surf in winter.* She began to hum again.

Gail walked behind them, her silence discomforting. The moon rose as they approached the white hillock.

"Maybe we should keep away from there," Eden said. She stopped. She whispered, "I'm scared. What if those really are bones? What if she really did kill those people?" Eden looked behind her at Gail, as if assessing the distance between them. "Wouldn't it be better to just get away from her? We could run… she'd never catch us…"

From behind them, Gail's voice growled.

"I would catch you if I wished to."

Halley sensed this to be true.

Gail continued. "But she's right. It's best to leave things alone you don't understand. Leave the bones be. Go some other way." She paused, like she was searching for a threatening tone that she'd forgotten how to put into her voice. "You're putting Eden in grave danger by going there."

It was the first time Gail had acknowledged Eden's presence, and to Halley this was something of a breakthrough. She suppressed a smile. "Why do you want to keep us away? What are you hiding there? I know it's not bones."

Gail didn't answer.

"Oh stop it. If you wanted to hurt us, you'd have done it a long time ago," Halley said.

She turned away from Gail and began to walk, Eden close beside. Gail cursed under her breath. Suddenly Halley broke into a sprint. Gail made to catch her, but it was too late. Halley felt their eyes on her as she pulled away. She reached the hill and began to climb, the white objects slipping and sliding around her.

"You were right!" Eden said. She was standing at the bottom of the hill, breathing hard.

In the moonlight, it was clear that the hill was not made of bones at all. Halley picked one of the shaft-like objects to examine. It was a smoothened tree branch. The white of the branch stained her skin. Putting it down, she rubbed her hands together, but the white didn't come off. There were no trees nearby. The sticks must have been carried all the way from the woods. Their white color explained Gail's hands; she must have accidentally stained them in painting the tree limbs. The rounded objects were conch shells, carefully positioned to keep their hollows hidden. It was impossible to fathom how far it, and the others like it, had been carried, or where they'd come from. She motioned down to Eden, who, after a brief pause, scrambled up next to her.

"Listen," Halley said, holding the shell to her ear.

"I can hear the ocean. Cool! It's just like at the beach."

Halley picked up one and listened. The sound took her back many years, and she smiled.

Gail remained on the level ground below the hill. She wasn't smiling.

Halley took the shell away from her ear, and looked down at Gail's stationary figure. "What does it mean?" she asked.

Gail looked down at the ground.

"Gail, what does it mean?"

In a barely audible voice, she replied. "I built it when he left. To keep the others away." Her speech was stilted and broken. "I thought…if I frightened them away first…they couldn't hurt me…I couldn't be hurt anymore…"

In the moonlight, Halley saw her eyes glisten.

"How will I protect myself now? Who will keep me safe?"

Halley felt tears come to her eyes. She rubbed them away. "Gail, this hill wasn't protecting you. Your anger wasn't protecting you." She replaced the conch shell gently on the ground. "You're causing yourself more pain than his leaving did. Than anyone else ever could. This must be healed. We'll help."

Eden nodded.

Together, they took the hill to pieces. They listened carefully as Gail told her story; this speaking and listening was the path she needed to travel.

It took time.

The moon rose higher. They continued to work. They continued to work all night long.

The sticks were not bones. Nevertheless, they required burying to release their power. With their bare hands, Halley and Eden cleared a place in the yellow grass at the base of the hill, and dug a deep hole in the soft earth. Dirt filled the space under their fingernails, and caked on their cheeks where the sweat ran. Gail watched. It was understood she was not to help with this part. She had been enough in the earth.

When the hole was finished, Halley called to Gail. "You can help now. Climb up the hill and bring the sticks down, one by one."

And so, with the first light of dawn, with ceremony and with care, they laid the white sticks of Gail's fury side-by-side in the hollow. They placed them close together, so that they were touching, as if even this propinquity was healing.

Strange. With each stick she carries down, I feel lighter. I feel a battlement coming down that was not so much a protection, but an imprisonment. Now I'll be truly free.

When the sticks had been placed in the hole, the bare fertile essence of the earthy hill was revealed. This stood sentinel over them. On impulse, Halley removed from her belt the long white stick she had carried from the woods. She still thought of it as the unicorn stick. She placed it amongst the other sticks, where it shone with light reflected from the first light of dawn. It was right for it to be there. It restored purity to the sticks, removing the poison of Gail's fury. The three of them filled their palms with warm earth, and gently and quietly, they covered the sticks.

When the hole was full, they placed the conch shells on top of the mound they had made, positioning the mouths of the shells open to catch warm rain. Halley had a vision: wildflower seeds landing in the openings and sending up tiny green shoots. In time, this place would be a paradise of blooms and colors. In time, this compost would birth new life.

The work completed, they climbed to the top of the now earthy hill and sat in silence. The sun lit on her white clothing, and Gail finally spoke. "I thought I would never heal." Tears coursed freely down her cheeks. "I thought I needed him to return to mend me – to guide me from this place." She looked at Halley, and then at Eden, her brown eyes liquid. "But it was you I needed. The care you have given me, the time we have spent together burying these bones – how wonderful, that this could heal me. Thank you." Gail looked to the mountains in the distance. "I must go now. Farewell."

She rose to her feet, tall and beautiful and white, and walked down the hillside. Her light garments whispered around her.

"Where will she go?" Eden asked softly.

"I don't know…but somehow I'm sure she'll find her way," said Halley, watching the birds cavort overhead.

It was a warm morning. They closed their eyes to rest in the light of the sun. As they slept, long and calm, Halley dreamt she could smell the sweet scent of newly blooming wildflowers.

CHAPTER 29

She was smiling when she woke up. Her body seemed to be smiling as well, with a sense of being filled to perfection, a perfectly-stretched-brand-new-helium-balloon feel. Something heavy was gone from her, something that had been pulling her shoulders up towards her ears for a long time, making her frown with her forehead all night long. She knew what it was. The anger she had healed in Gail had also resided in her – and it was finally gone.

Still lying on her back, Halley stretched her arms overhead, lengthening her body, listening to the *crack-crack-crack* of her vertebrae releasing, arching her lower back away from the ground. When she sat up, she was facing the earthy hill they had cleared the night before, the hill which had held the "bones and skulls". It was already coated in a fine hair of grass shoots, each hair tipped by a pinhead of dew. Life came back quickly when the soil was freed of encumbrances. She longed to linger here, to let the healing sink deeper into her bones.

But she couldn't: there was more to be done. With pleasure and great relief she noted the pulse had returned to her forehead; the baby was making itself felt again. Waiting for her. Was okay. For now. But she had to get to it. The way was the mountains.

But the dawn made things very clear; it told the truth about the height of the mountains, about their granite-hardness. They would be unforgiving. Hugging her knees into her chest, Halley felt fear insert a probing finger between her seventh and eighth ribs, as if it were looking for a soft spot.

They got moving quickly, as if by hurrying Halley could contain her fear. But it was too late. It was as if she had sprung a leak, punctured by the first sight of the sharp teeth of the mountains; she was gradually deflating. Her feet became harder to lift as they approached the mountains and her stomach felt full of small, rough pebbles.

The ground too was becoming harder to navigate, rockier underfoot and stumble-provoking. The yellow grass had been supplanted by taller shrubs, and in the distance, small trees had begun to appear.

As they approached the trees, Halley's eyes were drawn to an unusual grouping of them. These looked newly-planted and they formed a straight line, perpendicular to the path, as if they had been laid out this way with a purpose in mind. The trees were all the same height, the same width. She stopped, feeling her feet throb from the distance they had already covered.

The row of trees had come into leaf. They were planted in soil from the same plain, were apparently the same age. Yet their foliage revealed marked differences in their vitality. On some, large green leaves filled the branches, exuberant with life. On others, the leaves were small and stingy. On a few there was no growth at all; these particular trees looked wasted and sad. These ones would not survive.

The differences in their growth captivated her. She stared longer, and Eden watched in silence.

Gradually, Halley saw that though they lived in much the same place, there were subtle differences in the environment of each tree. Some of the trees bore the brunt of the wind, while others were sheltered. Some stood close to their neighbors, gaining strength, while others kept their distance. There would be variations in the way water flowed from the mountains and differences in soil drainage; this would cause other divergences. There might be slight disparities in the nutrients in the surrounding soil.

Where they fell as seeds, where they had to grow makes such a difference to their lives.

The leaves on the smallest, least vital tree seemed to nod at her sadly in the light breeze, to imply, "Yes. And you're just like me".

Halley shook her head. The sorrowful tree was wrong – she was nothing like it at all. Not anymore. The trees were fixed in their positions. They couldn't move. *But me, I'm free. I'm searching for more nutritious places.*

The trees provided the inspiration Halley had needed. She no longer felt punctured; she felt ready to deal with whatever came next. The morning sun suddenly felt hot and delicious on her shoulders.

She had just begun to walk again when she heard the unmistakable sound of hoof beats. The ground trembled underfoot, making her look around in alarm. Quickly, Eden moved to Halley's side, and reached for her hand. The hoof beats became louder, almost deafening, and a moment later the animal slid to a stop near them, snorting and breathing hard. Halley eyes widened in fear and she stumbled backwards. Staring down at her was a very tall, very white, very wild-eyed horse.

CHAPTER 30

The horse stood pawing the ground with its forefoot, nostrils flaring in and out. Its warm breath blew out with force, hitting Halley on top of her head, and causing her throat to constrict.

"What's wrong? You're not afraid of horses, are you?" Eden asked. The small girl reached up to try to stroke the broad expanse of its face. At first, the horse shook its big white head, *No*, it said, *No*. Eden waited patiently until it lowered its face shyly, and gave her a well-meaning nudge in the belly that nearly knocked her off her feet. She giggled. The horse's breathing began to quiet.

"Be careful! It could kick you...or bite..." She motioned to Eden. "Keep away from it."

"Don't be silly. She looks big, but she's really a pony at heart." Eden stroked the horse's neck, scratched the always-itchy spot behind its ears. The horse turned into the scratch, rubbing into Eden's fingers, *More, More*, it said. It blew air through its nostrils in pleasure.

Halley took a reluctant step forward – she didn't want to act like a coward – but the horse threw its head high in the air and snorted.

"She knows you're scared. It makes her scared too."

Halley stayed still.

Eden smoothed the mare's mane, combing her fingers through the thick, wiry hair. "You're okay, Athena, don't be afraid." The animal calmed, dropping its head still lower to the ground. "Let's see if she'll follow us," Eden said.

They continued their walk towards the mountains. Athena

walked quietly behind them, as if tethered to them by a long, thin cord. As the day wore on, the muscles in Halley's neck grew tight. She kept flinching at nothing, imagining the horse to be darting forward to take a bite of her back.

When they grew hungry, they took time to eat, and to refill their meager stock of food from the surrounding trees. Bananas, mangoes, coconuts. The country was becoming greener as they approached the mountains, the runoff from the ice-laden peaks leaving fertility in its wake. The sound of rushing water trickled into her awareness. The first of the streams they were to ford rushed by at their feet.

Eden pulled out Gail's large canteen.

Halley looked at her in surprise.

"I thought we'd left that with Gail."

"She said we should keep it."

"What's she going to do without a canteen?"

"She said something about going home."

They looked at each other, and Eden shrugged one shoulder. They filled and drained the canteen twice each, and then left it full. Halley strapped the full canteen over her shoulder. Having water again was reassuring.

Once they were ready, they faced the stream again. The crossing would be simple; there were dry stones laid in an almost straight path. Halley and Eden were able to step across without even getting their feet wet. Athena seemed happy to cross the stream too – but only after first stopping for a long drink and then shaking the water from her muzzle. She stepped casually into the shallow water and splashed her way across.

It was a minor crossing, but like all crossings, it triggered thoughts of what was being left behind. Halley stopped and looked back, staring across the small trees and the yellow tundra. Eden scampered up to perch on a thick tree branch. Athena waited.

So much had happened since they left the woods, Halley re-flected: the final goodbye to Fernando; losing and finding Eden;

healing Gail of her burning anger; meeting Athena the horse. But – the thought struck her forcefully, because it hadn't occurred to her in a while – what had become of Trance? Halley became aware that he was back there somewhere. She could feel his presence, could *smell* him. She would have to face him again eventually.

The tall white horse stood nearby, its face hidden in the deep green grass, chewing with small grunts of pleasure. Occasionally, it lifted its head to reveal green lips covered with a foamy mixture of saliva and fresh grass, or to nip at the horseflies which teased its flanks.

Athena, that's what Eden called her.

The mare lifted its large white head and stared at Halley with a questioning look, jaw still working, lips opening and closing to reveal long yellowing teeth and bits of half-eaten grass.

The mare didn't do anything threatening. It just looked at her with those large, grey, wet eyes. *Horses don't usually have grey eyes*, Halley thought. The mare's eyes were wise, and their wisdom made Halley frown.

Something was building in Halley, and it wouldn't go away. Staring at the horse, at the way its mane curved over the edge of its neck, she could almost feel the dry coarse texture of the hair. It was as if both her hands were gripping it tightly from above, as if her face was pressed down close to it and they were at a gallop. But she was seeing a black mane in her imagining, and the horse itself was brown. She hadn't allowed herself to think about the day she was suddenly seeing in her mind in years.

Halley was young, twenty-one or twenty-two, galloping recklessly through the woods on Sampson. This had always been their path through the woods, ever since she was a little girl. They had ridden it so often that she and Sampson both knew every bump and rise, every fallen tree. He didn't need her to guide him with the reins – he knew the way. Usually, she rode there for pleasure.

Today was different. Today she was flying from the fact
that she didn't know what to do. For the first time in her life,
she didn't know what to do...

Her memory moved away from her with a darting motion like a silverfish; she couldn't remember anything else. Suddenly, her throat felt gob-stopped, like she'd swallowed something too large and it had gotten stuck in her windpipe. It hurt, this sensation, this fullness in her throat that stopped her speaking. She took a hand reflexively to her neck and massaged gently up and down the rings of cartilage, but it didn't help. Her ears felt full, like she'd been swimming underwater, making the sounds of the forest seem dull and unrelated to her. Even her eyes were glazed, seven-mile-stare-like.

From her perch in the tall tree, Eden watched Halley thoughtfully. One of her hands rested on the furry shoulder of the golden-maned lion-monkey, who watched Halley with equal attentiveness. At the end of the branch, hidden by some foliage, Halley's movements were also followed by the piercing eyes of the eagle.

Eden whispered to the lion-monkey, "I wish she weren't so afraid of poor Athena. They used to be such good friends. Halley was there when Athena was born, and Sampson was such a proud daddy, especially for a horse. I wish I knew what was wrong."

Neither Halley nor Eden could remember. But the moonlight remembered. The tree roots and their shaken leaves remembered. The hard earth held the memory too, carefully sandwiched between bits of rock and soil; even a mudslide wouldn't wash it away. The eagle had been there as well, a witness to what had happened. The eagle had seen it all, from on high.

Now, hearing Eden's wish, the eagle turned to look at her with quick yellow eyes. It glanced back at Halley and seemed to contemplate and quickly decide something, because it began to walk along the branch sideways, towards them, gripping the branch tightly with long talons. As it moved, it turned its head sharply from time to time, monitoring the woods, taking care.

While Halley stood there looking puzzled, massaging the lock in her throat, trying to grasp something just out of her reach, Eden listened carefully as the eagle, with long curved talons gripping the tree, began to tell the story.

Children are always doing things which to adults seem impossible; the fact that the eagle could whisper the story aloud, and both the lion-monkey and Eden could understand every word was not in fact overly strange. Nor was the fact that Halley couldn't hear them. It is simply the way of the world, when one is a child.

Partway through the eagle's speech, Eden stopped it by raising one hand. "I don't understand. Why didn't I know all this?" She was frowning. "I know everything else about Halley's life."

The golden lion-monkey looked at Eden, and then cleared its throat. "How could you know it, if she didn't?"

It was the first time the lion-monkey had spoken. The resonance of its voice and the certainty of its words surprised Eden. She wondered if the eagle would take offense.

But the eagle seemed to welcome the explanation. "Wise monkey," it said. "You are right. If Halley doesn't know something, you, Eden, won't know it either."

The eagle finished the story, and when it was done, Eden knew the whole truth. It made her very angry. She was furious about what had happened to Halley, but she was even madder that Halley had forgotten the truth. She clenched her small fists, and shook the tree branch in frustration. The sound of shaking leaves startled Athena and Halley, who looked up into the tree. Eden didn't want to think about the eagle's story anymore; she just wanted to move, to get away from it. She swung herself to the ground. When she was standing just beside Halley, she clapped her small hands together, hard, just once – this, she knew, would make Halley remember. It worked: the loud noise startled Halley, and cleared the way for a further memory.

Athena shuffled her feet. Halley felt her ears pop, as if she'd been descending fast in an airplane, and had finally remembered to swallow.

Sampson, her bay horse, stumbled. Halley didn't care: her mind wasn't on him, or on the ride. The woods around her might not have even existed, for all she saw of them. Her mind was stuck on this unsolvable conundrum, of how to choose between two men. The same thoughts played over and over again in her mind, like a turntable stuck on a scratch, but they didn't contain an answer. She had locked away the key to the puzzle; she had locked away the truth.

The ride through the woods was punishing, but she felt better for the pain; she deserved it for what she'd done.

A newly fallen tree blocked the path. Sampson saw it before Halley and he did his best to protect her, leaping high and clearing it with great effort. Halley knew in this moment she could have hung on; she could've stayed astride his strong, safe back. But she didn't care to. She was too angry with herself for betraying Nick, for her inability to decide which man would be the love of her life. She didn't have it in her to protect herself.

So she didn't grasp as tightly as she could, allowing herself to be flung from Sampson's back, high into air, hovering for just a second before slamming hard, first into the tree above her, and then into the unkind ground. Her breath was thrown from her body, and she couldn't get her chest to lift. She was gasping for air and panicking, and then with a start, she was breathing again. She started to sob: she hadn't realized how badly she could be hurt. And it hurt so much. Sampson prodded her gently with his soft whiskery muzzle, worry in his brown eyes.

She could remember the rest clearly now: time in the hospital; several broken vertebra; disorienting visits from both Nick and her new lover.

Her physical recovery took six months. During this time, her new lover left her, and Nick moved away to start a new job. He called often, and after she was fully healed, he began to encourage her to move to his new town, to move in with him. She put it off; he grew angry. Though she kept saying she would come to him soon, she didn't, and couldn't understand herself why she didn't. One day he told her it was over, that he couldn't wait any more. She cried for weeks.

The white horse stared Halley straight in the eye, chewing grass, watching her. The small whiskers around its muzzle moved with the movement of the horse's jaw, and made Halley uneasy. It did what horses do: it flicked its head in the air; it pawed at the grass by its feet to uncover fresh shoots; it twitched its long ears at the flies. These unthreatening things, these most natural of movements, all made Halley flinch.

She thought about riding Athena, and knew she couldn't. *I don't want to get hurt again.* She rubbed the small of her back. *Anyway, riding for me…I did that when I was innocent, before I betrayed Nick. I'm not innocent anymore.* She could still feel the devastation of losing Nick; it had remained with her always as a dull ache behind her eyes. She stared dumbly at the white horse eating grass. *I still miss him. I miss the simplicity, the innocence. I miss his kindness. I miss myself, as I was before.*

She noticed Eden. Her little friend had come down from the tree and was gently brushing the white horse's long neck with her fingertips, looking away from Halley. She ran her small hand down its right foreleg, picked up its foot, and, with a piece of stick, gently picked it free of stones and hardened dirt. She moved with confidence.

"How do I get that confidence back? How do I get me back?" she whispered, feeling silly asking this sort of question to a little girl, but knowing Eden would understand.

Eden kept her eyes focused on Athena, and shifted herself around to lift up a back foot. She spoke quietly. "You've already begun. You can take down that fortress you've built, just like Gail did. You can simply take it down." Eden looked up at Halley with big, bright, knowing eyes.

"Fortress?"

Eden didn't reply. After finishing the last of the four hooves, she stretched up high on her tip-toes, and grabbed hold of the horse's mane just above the withers. Jumping, she swung her leg over Athena's broad back. She smiled broadly, ear to ear, and made a gentle clucking sound to encourage the horse forward.

Halley walked along beside.

So, Eden thought, reflecting on the eagle's story, *that's why she's afraid of horses.* She felt the gentle rhythm of Athena's walk shift her back and forth. *That's why she never rode Sampson again. I remember – she kept working at the stable, because she didn't want to tell anyone she was scared. But the horses knew – she got bad around the horses.* Eden reached down and massaged Athena's withers. *You didn't like the jumpy way she handled you, did you? You wanted to make her go away, so you bit her and kicked her and ran at her. You were scared too, weren't you? Her fear scared you.* Eden rubbed Athena's wiry mane between her fingers.

Eden knew: Halley was going to have to face what had happened that terrible night with Nick. She was going to have to remember.

CHAPTER 31

The grass muffled the sound of their feet. Halley breathed the green scent of crushed grass stems and wildflowers, and Eden rode bareback at a gentle walk.

"Do you remember how to ride?" Eden asked, after a long while had passed.

"Of course," Halley said, feeling a chill though the day was warm. "It's just...I'm a bit scared. It's been a long time."

It hurt her neck to look up at Eden on the horse.

"Come on." Eden reached down a small hand. "I'll help you up."

Halley took a step back, crossing her arms in front of her chest. The sudden movement made Athena toss her head in fright. "No. I'd rather walk."

"Okay."

They walked in silence for some time, with much unsaid between them. Later, they came to the first of the foothills at the base of the mountains. They followed the gentle, flat path that was carved low on its flank.

"Tell me about Nick," Eden said.

"Nick? Why?"

"I just want to hear about him."

"He was everything to me," Halley said. "He was my first love."

She stopped speaking and looked at the ground.

"Was he very handsome? Did he look like Shaun?"

"Sean?"

"Shaun Cassidy! You know, silly. Da doo ron ron ron, da doo ron ronnn," Eden sang with a giggle.

Halley smiled. "No. More like Dirk Benedict from Battlestar Galactica. He had this softness around his eyes when he smiled."

"Did you love him?"

"Mm."

"Why? Why did you love him?" Eden gripped Athena's mane more tightly.

Halley thought about it. "He was very gentle. He took his time." She smiled, remembering. "There were these beautiful love poems he wrote me. He used very thin, soft paper. It was baby-blue. I scotch-taped them to the wall by my bed, and when we weren't together, I would just lie there and read them, over and over. I liked to run my finger over the paper and feel how soft it was."

"Did you...?" Eden giggled. Her pause and her lifted eyebrow filled in exactly what she was asking.

"Eden!" Halley's face reddened.

"I'm not *that* little. I've read about it."

"Well...yes...eventually." Halley's gaze shifted to the upper left as she remembered. "That was the other thing that made me love him. I was very shy. All the other guys wanted to touch me too soon. I was always having to catch their hands before they touched me somewhere I didn't want them to touch me. They wouldn't listen." She made a face. "Nick was different. He was patient. He waited a whole year for us to be together that way. I guess he taught me that love didn't have to hurt, that I didn't have to be afraid." Halley shuddered.

"What's wrong?"

"I don't know. I just felt really awful inside. Let's talk about something else."

But they didn't. They rode on in silence, and Eden kept thinking about what the eagle had told her.

CHAPTER 32

When they came to the other side of the small foot-hill, they both stopped and stared. Standing close to the edge of the path was a small wooden house, the first dwelling they had seen on their long journey.

"Wow," Eden said.

"That's an understatement."

The house was under siege. It was built on a foundation of rough-hewn grey stone blocks, giving it an air of would-be stur-diness. But in the binding concrete between the stones, small plants had taken root, turning the concrete to dust with their fine, searching roots. The planking boards, which would have been painted once, showed only scar-like patches of flaking pink paint-primer. A porch encircled the house, but its seeming welcome was negated by the thickly spider-webbed boot scraper at the base of the front steps. The garden was long overgrown, dandelions gone to seed peppering the front lawn with yellow and white. The honeysuckle had sailed beyond its lattice, and now hung over the edge of the roof, cascading wildly down the opposite side.

It must have been the mountain retreat of a small family. But they had given it up, had abandoned it to the wolves long ago.

"I'm just going to take a look," Halley said, climbing the wooden steps and crossing the weathered porch. Her eyes were fixed on the windows. With a musical crash of metal on metal on flesh, she ran right into a wind chime, hitting it smack into the center of her forehead. "Ouch! Stupid thing!"

It too was encrusted in spider webs. She pulled a few long lengths of them from her face and hair. When she tried to shake them off, they clung tightly to her hands as if unwilling to let go. Disconcerted, she rubbed her hands together briskly, balling the webs, and then plucking them off with her fingers. The wind chime continued to sing. Halley breathed out forcefully, and gave it a hard look. *I hate the webs*, she thought. It only took a moment to pull them off; the movement set the wind chime to ringing more loudly. The melody ill fit the scene. Halley reached up and quieted it with her right hand. Then she stepped around it, towards the house. With the heel of her hand, she rubbed dust from a window and peered inside. Light streamed in from several other windows. It was empty. Encouraged, she knocked gently on the door. It swung open with a gentle creak, and she smelled weathered wood and mildew.

On Athena's back, Eden shook her head. "I don't think this is a good idea," she said to herself. "In fact, it may be the worst idea ever!"

She dismounted, leaving Athena to graze, and followed Halley into the house.

CHAPTER 33

It took a moment for Halley's eyes to adjust to the change in light. When they did, she quickly held out a restraining arm to stop Eden from walking beyond her.

"I'm so sorry," she said. "I didn't think anyone was here."

The young woman she had addressed leant against the deeply mildewed wall. She didn't seem to have heard Halley; at least, she didn't answer. Alone on the uncarpeted floor, writing fast in a spiral notebook, her posture was hunched and forlorn. On the floor around her were other notebooks, pens empty of ink and pieces of paper crumpled in tight balls. The young woman was talking to herself.

"If only I could decide," she said. "Then this torture could end. But how can I decide…how can I choose, when I love them both?"

She let the notebook drop to her lap, sighing heavily. Tiny writing filled the entire page.

She looked up, first at Eden, and then at Halley, where she let her eyes rest. "What should I do?" the girl said. "You'll know – you're old. I love them both. I can't decide. It's agony."

She chopped her sentences short, as if she had forgotten how to speak to people with any grace. Her appearance validated her words: dark circles under her eyes; lusterless skin; bones sticking out through too-thin flesh. She continued speaking but Halley barely heard the words.

"I've been trying so hard to do what's right, to not hurt anyone. But I don't know what to do…" She picked up her notebook and pen, and began to write again.

It took a long while, but the young woman eventually tired,

and held the notebook out as if to re-read what she'd written. The movement revealed the white skin of her inner arms.

"What happened to you?" Eden asked.

Eden was pointing to the young woman's right arm. Halley looked where she indicated. Three deep parallel scars ran its length, from the inside of her elbow all the way to her wrist.

Halley swallowed heavily.

The young woman didn't answer.

"What are you writing?" Eden asked.

The young woman looked down at the closed notebook. "The pros and cons," she said.

"The pros and cons of *what*?" Eden said. Her voice betrayed her growing impatience.

"Of Nick and Andy, of course. It will help me choose between them. It hasn't yet, but it's got to, eventually..."

She opened the notebook again and continued to write.

Eden and Halley looked at each other, and then at the young woman sitting on the floor. Outside, the sun slipped below the horizon. Light fled the room.

Eden touched Halley's arm. "How come she doesn't ask who we are or what we're doing here?" she whispered. "That's weird." Eden looked back at the young woman, who had kept talking to herself softly the whole time.

"I don't know," Halley whispered back.

There was something in the room that filled it to the edges of the windowsills, and left no room to breathe. Halley felt overwhelmed, and sank down on her haunches near the thin young woman sitting on the floor.

"You're so young," she said, looking into the girl's downturned face. "I thought you would've been older. I remembered you older."

She started then, her own words confusing her. It wasn't possible that she remembered the girl; she'd never met her before. Suddenly she wanted to move, to get away from her. "You must be hungry," she said. "You're so thin." Halley straightened. "Come on, Eden," she said. "Let's see what there is to eat around here. We'll make her some dinner."

The girl didn't move, and didn't answer. Eden shrugged one shoulder, and followed Halley into the next room, letting the door swing shut behind her.

The sight of the kitchen made them stop short. Eden reached for Halley's hand. Like the wind-chime on the front porch, the kitchen was absolutely covered in spider webs. Some hung from the fridge, and others drooped heavily off the cupboards. Others coated the windows with frostlike patterns. The spiders sat in their webs and didn't move; their stillness in the face of strangers suggested a certain boldness. It was clear they had learned not to be afraid of disruption. There were no dishes, no evidence of recent meals. Just spider webs and silence.

"This is wrong," Eden said. "This is all wrong."

"The spider webs are awful," Halley agreed.

Eden looked at her strangely. "Not just the spider webs. It's this room – this room is wrong," Eden replied. "In winter, Dad used to put my clothes on that radiator in the corner to warm them before I got up." She pointed. "And on that shelf...the one just behind you that's all empty...that's where we kept the jars of grape jelly we made from the summer grapes." Eden ran past Halley and pulled a small tin from the counter closest to the door. The metal lid made a catching sound as she pried it off with her fingernails. She turned it upside down, and stared inside. "Empty...it was never empty..."

"What did you keep in there?"

"The bayberries..." Eden held the tin to her nose and sniffed. "I can still smell them." She looked far away, lost in memory. "We picked them from the neighbor's bushes. Dad melted them into candles for Christmas each year." Eden looked at Halley with a question in her eyes. "Don't you remember?"

"How could I remember?" Halley said. "I've never been here before."

Eden couldn't find anything more to say. She put the cover back on the tin and replaced it on the counter. She was breathing fast, like she might cry.

"Well, look…I guess we've got to fix it," Halley said. "No one else is going to." With resolve, she reached for the broom, grimacing when her hand grazed a spider web.

"Wait – let me get an empty jam jar and I'll catch the spiders first," Eden said, opening the cupboard door next to the sink. The cupboard was full of dusty jars.

"Good idea," Halley said.

Eden swept the spiders, one by one, into the empty jar. She was careful not to harm their long spindly legs. When the first jar was nearly full, Eden capped it, and took a second from the cupboard by the sink.

"You take them out and set them free," Eden said. "Make sure you do it quick – I didn't make any air holes. I'll catch the rest."

Halley opened the back door. It groaned with protest, like it hadn't been opened in years. The glass jam jar felt cool in her hand, the metal cap that read *Smuckers* in faded letters, even cooler. At the bottom of the steps, she set the jar down on the ground, and opened it with a turn of her wrist. She pulled her hands back quickly. It took a moment for the spiders to figure out where the sudden fresh air came from, but once they did, they scrambled over one another to reach the opening. Halley retreated to the top step and watched the spiders pour from the jar and then scuttle off, freed from their imprisonment. All their legs were intact.

It took five jam-jars to empty the room. After setting the final jarful of spiders free, Halley lingered outside a moment. She stared up at the full moon; its white roundness gave her courage. When she went inside, she left the back door ajar. The cool evening air stirred the dust on the counters. There was still much to do.

With the broom in hand, Halley cleared the cobwebs from all the surfaces. *I wonder how long they've been here,* she thought. She was dirty from the dust and sweat-streaked from their long day. There was only one broom, so Eden sat on the nicked wooden chair at the heavy pinewood table and watched. Every now and then they heard the girl in the next room talking softly. It was a confused mumble, solving nothing. When the spider webs were cleared, and all the surfaces had been wiped down with two damp sponges, Halley and Eden sat across from each other at the pinewood table. They were silent for some time.

"What's going on here?" Halley finally said. "You know, don't you?" She rested her hands flat on the table. "Tell me. Who is this girl? Why is she so familiar to me? And how do you know this house so well?"

Eden got to her feet.

"I'm thirsty. Real tap water will be great after drinking from rivers and canteens! I know – I'll make some cocoa." Eden flicked on the kitchen light, a bare, dim bulb that hung from the ceiling over the kitchen table. It did little to light the room, but it was better than the gathering dark. She opened a door and pulled two brown mugs from a low shelf. From another cupboard, she retrieved the cocoa powder.

Without thinking, Halley stood up, opened a drawer and picked out a silver spoon. She fingered the flower pattern on the spoon's handle, liking its feel. Being imitation silver, the spoon had not tarnished, even after all these years.

Together they stood at the kitchen sink, drinking cold water first, quickly, mug after mug, until their thirst was quenched. Then, letting the hot tap run until the water steamed, they filled the brown mugs again, and stirred a teaspoon of cocoa into each. They remained at the sink a moment, staring out the window into the back garden. Athena's white coat shone in the moonlight.

"The moonlight makes her look like a horse angel, doesn't it?" Eden said. "Like she should be up in the clouds..."

Halley let her eyes rest of the broad flat sweep of the mare's face. There was something heavenly about the horse, about the calm way it watched them through the kitchen window, as if this scene had been enacted a thousand times. "Like a guardian angel," she concurred.

"I think that girl in the other room could use one," Eden said, looking towards the kitchen door.

They sat down at the pinewood table, and drank their cocoa. There was no milk. Neither of them spoke until the mugs were drained dry. Halley set her mug on the table, and leaned back in her chair to look at Eden. Eden wasn't smiling or giggling or even looking at her. She was fingering a scratch in the surface of the table, running her forefinger over it as if to heal the scar it made.

"What's wrong?" Halley asked. "You look so sad."

"It's worse than I thought," Eden said quietly. "Halley, you've got to help her. You've got to help her see the truth." Eden got up to rinse her mug at the sink, and pointed to one of the spiders making its way in through the open door. "Look. They're coming back. They all will, unless you help her."

Halley watched the spider move. She'd never feared spiders, but the way this one lifted one leg after another, as if nothing could stop its slow progress into the kitchen, filled her with aversion. Putting her feet up on the support beam under the pinewood table, she pondered what Eden had said. "I don't understand," she said. "What truth do I have to help her see? She's very sad and very strange, but I don't see how I can help."

The spider treaded across the clean kitchen floor, and began to climb up onto the cupboard. Others were following.

"It's not just her. *You've* got to be brave enough to face the truth," Eden said. She stopped. The look on her face said she'd gone too far.

The kitchen door swung open suddenly, and the young woman stood there, a wraith, swaying slightly on thin legs. She wore a crumpled grey t-shirt and shorts, and she was carrying one of the notebooks.

"Can I come in?" Her voice was weak. "You didn't answer the question I asked. About who I should love and who I should leave…"

Eden stood up. "You can have my chair. I want to check on Athena." She slipped quickly through the back door, before Halley had the chance to say a word. Eden decided she was not going back into that room with that crazy, skinny girl, not for anything. She would make herself a camp outside, under the moonlight. It was warm, and she'd slept on this back lawn lots of times.

Through the long night, Athena stood watch over her protectively.

CHAPTER 34

Inside, the spider climbed up into a corner, and began to spin its web. The girl sat down across from Halley.

"Do you know the answer then? Surely you do, if anyone does."

Halley held her cocoa mug between both palms, wishing it were still warm. She didn't know what to say. The scratches on the pinewood table were quite deep. Taking one hand from the mug, she traced one of them with her fingertip, just as Eden had done. She looked up. Through the kitchen window, she could see the full moon. "My name is Halley," she began, taking her eyes back to the girl. "What's yours?"

"Hope." The girl said it quietly, as if she couldn't quite fathom how her parents had labeled her with such an inappropriate name. She lowered her head onto the table, resting it on her long, thin arms. "Why won't you answer me?" she asked wearily. "I've been here so, so long, waiting for your answer."

Halley fingered the silver bracelet in silence. It was hard to know what to say. No matter what she said, Hope would draw the conversation back to the same thing, the choice between two men. She folded her fingers together and rested her chin on her hands. "Tell me more about your question. Tell me about the two men."

Hope lifted her head from her arms, visibly relieved to be able to speak of this. "I can't choose between them. I love Nick. He's the only man I've ever loved. And he loves me – he wrote me poems telling me he did, on baby-blue paper...the paper was so soft..."

She stopped, as if she didn't want to continue. When she

spoke again, her voice was lower, as if she didn't want anyone to hear what she was saying. "I love Nick, but I want to be with Andy. Something about Nick…something's wrong. I know, the night I tried to kill myself, I know…he saved my life that night. But he's hurt me too, somehow…"

She got to her feet and went to stand at the kitchen window, resting her hands on the cool edge of the metal sink.

As Hope walked to the window, Halley saw that her legs seemed bowed, like her inner thighs had shrunken away. In the moonlight, she could see Hope's arms were fuzzed by soft down, giving her an animal-like appearance. Her jutting shoulder blades were visible through the back of her thin t-shirt, and were the final confirmation. *She's anorexic*, Halley thought sadly. *I know that look.*

Hope, staring out of the kitchen window at the dark, continued to speak. "Sometimes I think about those baby seals – Harp seals, I think they're called. You know, the cute furry white ones?"

She turned to glance back at Halley, who nodded uncomfortably, unsure where this was leading.

"I think how, once – a long, long time ago – they wouldn't have been afraid of people. They'd have just sat there if we walked up to them. I bet you could have picked them up, the really tiny ones, petted them." She made a motion, as if stroking a small animal. Then she shuddered, and her right hand made itself into a fist; she held it enveloped in the other hand. She turned to look out the window again. Halley could feel the tension in Hope's body.

"It all changed, didn't it? People began killing them, both the babies and the mothers, clubbing them to death. I can see their blood in my mind, red blood on white snow. I think about them a lot. I think how they must feel – now, after seeing the killings – when a boat full of people lands." Hope's hands straightened out. She laid them long and flat on the cool sink, as if she were soothing a burn. "When I'm around Nick, I think I feel the way they must do." She wrapped her arms around herself as if she were cold. "But I don't understand it. It makes no sense for me to feel that way. He saved my life..."

Halley swallowed. The image of the seals crowded her mind. She didn't want to talk about Nick anymore.

"Tell me about Andy."

"Andy?" Hope sighed heavily. "He's beautiful. He's got this long, lean athlete's body. His stomach's not just flat – I can see every individual muscle in his abs. And God, he's got beautiful shoulders..."

Halley made a face. "Is it just about his body?"

Hope shook her head. She looked inwards. "I thought it was at first, but really, it's not about his body at all. He's gentle. He makes me laugh. And he's not scary at all."

She stopped.

"Go on..."

Hope opened her mouth to speak, looked around quickly, and shut it again, covering her mouth with her fine-fingered hand. The moon shone, round and full through the window. It caught both their eyes at the same moment.

"The moonlight," Halley said. "It reminds me of a night..."

"Yes!" Hope said, looking at the moon, "Yes! Me too! But I can't remember it. Each time the moon is full, I think I'll be able to remember, but I never can. I think if I can remember the night...the night I tried to kill myself...that's the night it reminds me of...maybe it will help me...get better." She looked over her shoulder and caught eyes with Halley, and Halley saw her left eye twitch. Hope placed the pads of two fingertips against the spot to steady it. It looked like a well-practiced gesture.

"Maybe I can help," Halley said.

There was a long silence. Hope stared across the small room at Halley, as if across a treacherous mountain range. "How? I've tried to remember so many times. How can you help?"

Halley thought about it. What was it about strong memories?

What made them so vivid? She thought about the times she remembered with most clarity: the death of her parents; the first time she'd met Fernando; the first time she'd made love; the first time she'd ridden a bike. What these memories had in common was that she could sense them with her body, could see them projected in her mind. She didn't remember them in words, but in pictures. Colored pictures.

"What color do you see when you think of that night?" she said impulsively.

"Dark green," Hope answered, without a moment's pause. "I see dark green." Her brow furrowed. "I never knew I saw dark green before. Ask me something else."

"How about this? When you think of that night, what do you smell?"

"Smell? I'm not sure." Hope sniffed the air like a young wolf. "It's musty – like an old attic…or…maybe…like the woods, like old leaves? It's cold, like it's nighttime or winter." Hope crossed her arms in front of her chest. "Maybe this isn't a good idea. Maybe I shouldn't remember. Maybe there's a good reason not to remember."

"It seems like you've spent a lot of time not remembering." Halley looked around the dimly lit room. "Is this how you want your life to be, living all alone in this house, starving to death?"

Hope's face flushed. "What do you mean, '…starving to death'"? I eat, I do. I'm okay. I'm better here alone."

"Better than what?"

Hope looked away from the window, and stared at Halley with open hostility. "Better than I was when I was with Nick."

"What do you mean?" Halley leaned forward. "What was it like with Nick? You said you loved him. That he loved you. That he wrote you those nice love poems on soft, baby-blue paper."

Hope turned and walked out of the room, leaving Halley alone at the pinewood table. The kitchen door continued swinging for several seconds. Halley listened to the mournful sound it made. Moments later, Hope came back. She held a piece of paper. Sitting down in the other chair, she passed it over to Halley. In the dim light it was hard to tell the color, but it might have once been baby-blue. It was covered in fine handwriting, long cursive letters, written carefully. But there were spots on the paper, whitish spots of mildew, and when Halley held the paper between her fingers it felt damp and insubstantial.

"That was one of the love poems. He stopped writing them a long time ago. Now it's like they were written by someone else, someone long gone."

Halley breathed out hard. "That can't be all, Hope. That's not a reason to think about leaving him for this pretty boy with the great abs. A lot of people stop writing love poems when they've been together a while. It doesn't mean they've stopped loving each other." Halley thought about something Hope had said earlier. "You said you love Nick, present tense." She held the love poem out to Hope, who didn't take it. "This can't be all. This can't be the reason."

Hope looked down at the table. "It's not. It's just…the things seemed to have meaning when they happened, but I…maybe it wasn't deliberate…maybe I just imagined it all."

"What? What things?"

Hope hesitated, and looked around the kitchen, as if for evidence. Her eyes lit on the knife block. "Like that," she said, pointing at it. Nick and I would make dinner together. I'd do the vegetables and he'd do the meat. I didn't like handling meat. But when he did it, I'd actually have to leave the room. He lifted the knife this little bit too high before cutting up the meat. Like he was relishing the moment of stabbing. I didn't want to see it. It made me nervous."

Halley could not take her gaze off the knife block. "Were there other things besides that?"

"I don't know. He started picking on me, I guess. He called me names sometimes, "Hope, the Dope" or "Ugly Duckling".

He said the names like he was joking, but it wasn't funny. I was afraid to tell him to stop."

"What were you afraid of?"

Hope looked down at the old bit of blue paper on the table, and ran her fingers back and forth across the words, as if crossing them out. "I'd take him to my brother's sometimes. I have this adorable niece – Amy – she's just turned four – and Nick would play with her, throw her in the air and catch her and make her giggle. Only Amy stopped giggling after a while, and Nick didn't stop throwing her right away." Hope turned the bit of paper over and they both stared at the white spots of mildew on its back. "Amy started to hide in the closet when we came to visit. My brother and his wife thought it best if we stopped going for a while."

Hope stood up suddenly, and walked to the basement door. She checked that the door was locked. Twice. She rattled it back and forth in its frame, three times, as if to make sure it would hold. The door made a re-assuring knocking sound. Her eye twitched again when she sat back down at the table.

Halley's eyes remained on the door. The moonlight shimmered on its glossy black paint, on the mock crystal doorknob. *It's just like the door in my house with Fernando,* Halley thought, with a chill. She didn't like the door; in fact, she hated it with a sudden passion. It made her think about how often she'd checked the door at home – it was never often enough. She took her eyes from it and focused on Hope instead. "Why don't you just leave him? Go with Andy?" Halley fingered the silver bracelet.

"I don't feel like I have a good enough reason. Just impressions. He hasn't done anything bad. And like you said, I still love him…"

"You still love him," Halley said, like this fact was of little consequence. She stared hard at Hope's thin arms. "How do you know he hasn't done anything bad?"

With a startling pop, the light bulb over the kitchen table burnt out.

214

CHAPTER 35

Halley gripped the edge of the table. Through the kitchen window, the moon shone, glimmering off the glossy black paint of the basement door.

I should've checked it again. Once is never enough!

Hope had the same thought. She jumped to her feet, her eyes wide with fear. "Hurry!" she shouted. "We've got to make sure!"

Even as she was speaking, she was running across the room. Halley raced after her.

But it was too late. Light was already slipping between the edge of the door and its frame. Grabbing at the doorknob, Hope fought to hold it closed. Desperately, she tried to turn the dead-lock. But the door wouldn't lock. The lock was misaligned. Even as she turned it, it spun uselessly.

There was a pull from the other side of the door. Something was trying to get out! Hope held the knob in a death grip, her face white.

"No! No!" she screamed.

Halley was breathless with terror.

Hope lost her grip. The door yanked open. She screamed, stumbling backwards.

Halley stepped forward. She blocked the doorway, wide-stanced, arms up. Something was trying to come into the kitchen. It was featureless in the dark. Then the moonlight hit it. She could finally see. This was no monster – no dream.

It was Nick!

His height, his physique – even his clothing – was just the same. But his face! It was heavy, weighty with rage. His eyes were strangely translucent, staring. They were the eyes of a madman.

She couldn't let him in! There were knives there. She stepped forward, hitting him hard in the chest, shoving him backwards. It was like punching ice. He stumbled on the stairs, falling backwards a few steps. Her knuckles throbbed.

But he came back quickly.

She wanted to flee. But she stayed where she was. She watched. He climbed the stairs. His smell was rank, unwashed. His hair tangled, filthy. His empty eyes held her. His arms reached for her. For a moment, his eyes seemed tender. Then the look vanished, replaced by a look of murderous intent.

Quickly, she struck, a back-fist snapped hard into his forehead. The blow stunned him. Her front kick slammed hard into his stomach. He fell, tumbling to the bottom of the staircase. She took a breath. But he was up quickly. He took the stairs two at a time.

"Stop!"

He just kept coming.

"I said stop!"

Nick climbed the stairs and she felt a sharp pain in her right arm that made her flinch. He came faster.

She took a step backwards.

Hope cried "No!"

The man stormed into the kitchen, into the cold moonlight. His eyes found the knife block.

Halley swung her leg in a sweeping kick. She hit him just above his knees. The force threw him against the wall of the stairwell. His head snapped to the side. He slid to the bottom of the stairs.

Quickly, Halley slammed the door. The lock caught on the first turn. Sliding the extra bolts across the top and the bottom of the door, relief flooded through her. She checked the door one more time, shaking it back and forth in the doorframe, and then looked behind her. Hope had sunk to the floor.

Halley moved to her. She took her in her arms. "It's okay… it's okay…it's okay." She gently rocked Hope in rhythm with the words. Slowly, calm filled the kitchen. She held Hope gently, trying to send her strength through the warmth of her body.

When Hope finally spoke, it was with the voice of someone broken. "It's not okay. It will never be okay. That man...that Nick-that's-not-Nick...he keeps coming back," she said. "I can't fight him anymore. I just can't..."

Holding Hope, Halley felt her knuckles throb.

From the basement, all was quiet.

CHAPTER 36

Eden watched through the kitchen window. She'd seen the whole thing. Now Halley and Hope were sitting on the floor in the dark, Halley holding Hope in her arms. The moonlight glistened on Halley's wide-open eyes. They weren't speaking.

"It's like they're waiting for something," Eden said.

The horse lifted its head and neck, and looked over at the house. A sudden beating of wings made the horse snort. Eden watched as the eagle landed in the maple tree, on the branch just above the kitchen window.

"What should we do?" Eden asked it, staring upwards.

"Leave them a while longer," the eagle replied. "Halley will find the answer."

"But that man from the basement! What if he comes back?"

"Did you see him too?"

Eden nodded. "Of course – it was that man you told me about, the one in the red shirt. Halley fought him."

"Ah, moonlight is strange," the eagle replied. It held the branch tightly with sharp talons.

Eden wondered why the eagle sounded sad.

After a pause, it continued. "Halley was fighting. But there was no one else there. She was fighting all by herself."

Eden went quiet. This would take some time to understand.

Halley drew in a deep breath. She got up and switched on a small lamp that stood in the corner then sat down again.

"Okay. Let's try some more. You said could see dark green and you could smell the woods. That it was cold, like night or winter. What else can you feel?"

"Do you think it's a good idea, to try for more? I mean…"

"You mean the man from the basement."

Hope nodded.

"He'll come back anyway, won't he?" Halley said. Her voice betrayed no emotion.

Hope didn't answer.

"Won't he?" Halley repeated.

Hope nodded and wrung her hands.

"So…what else can you feel?"

"You mean with my body?" Hope said.

"Yes."

"I feel…I think…the ground. Like I'm sitting on the ground, and it's hard underneath me." Hope shifted on the kitchen floor. "Hard…but soft. I've got something in my hand, crinkly sort of – I think maybe leaves. Wait…I'm…we're under a…tree…under the canopy of a gigantic tree." Hope's chin tilted up and she looked at a place on the ceiling, off to the left. "I can see the stars. There are thousands of them out tonight. And Nick's here – he has his arm around me. It's heavy, his arm, but I like it. It feels reassuring."

"What else is happening?"

"He's talking. Oh, I love the sound of his voice. Its like a soft summer rain in the treetops." Halley felt Hope relax in her arms for a moment, and then suddenly tense again. "Wait…it…his voice…it sounds different tonight. It has an edge to it. I don't like it…"

Halley was breathing faster. "The moonlight? Is it fading? I think it's fading," she said.

"Yes, you're right." Hope paused. She turned around to look at Halley, the gap between her eyebrows narrowed. "How did you know?"

Halley didn't answer.

Hope turned back. "There's a cloud over the moon. I can see it. It's just a little one. Oh…it's getting more solid, it's blocking the moonlight." Her hand covered her mouth.

"What?"

"Nick. He's talking very quietly. He's talking about having trouble. Something about enemies and pressure and…"

Hope pushed Halley's arms from around her and stood up quickly. She faced Halley, breathing fast. 'But I know every angle of his face, every curve," she said. "I know the texture of his eyebrows." She ran a forefinger along her own, as if to demonstrate. "I know that curlicue in his inner ear like I was born to know it." Her face crumpled in on itself. "How can this be? How can I feel the way I do?"

Halley got to her feet.

"Forget about what you feel. Go on with what you remember. What do you hear?" She tried to keep her voice calm, but was aware of the tightness in her throat – it made the words feel like a huge wave channeled between jetties onto too small a beach. "What do you hear?" she repeated.

"His words…they're like a floodwater, drowning our love… drowning me…" Hope's voice cracked. "His eyes…they're so…"

Hope stepped quickly to the basement door. She took hold of the doorknob, and rattled the door back and forth in its frame, making sure it was still locked. "His arm is too heavy now. I can't bear the weight of it. I've got to get out from under him. The moon…"

"The moon is gone."

CHAPTER 37

Outside, all was calm. Eden had crept back to Athena, and she slept again in the hollow made by the horse's legs, curled up tightly.

The eagle kept watch from the maple tree, watching Hope rub her arms as she leaned her back against the basement door. *She has never processed this*, the eagle thought. *She feels the same sensations and emotions that she felt that night with Nick. By now, the memory should be a picture, far removed, not something that can stir her body this way.* The eagle gripped the tree with thick talons. It fought its instinctive urge to screech. *If only I could have been there that night. I might have saved her.*

Inside the kitchen, Halley sat down at the pinewood table, keeping her eyes on Hope.

Hope crossed her arms in front on her chest. "I can't remember anything else," she said. "It's too dark. I can't see."

"You mean you won't," Halley said flatly.

She thought about Eden, about what she'd said just before she left the house: You've got to be brave enough to face the truth, she'd said. What did that mean? What truth was Halley avoiding?

She thought about what had been recalled so far: moonlight; dark green; a tree's canopy; Nick; floodwater. The series of words felt frozen and impenetrable; they yielded nothing. Halley shifted in the chair – her closed pocketknife was digging into her leg. She stretched out the leg and reached into her pocket, but she couldn't get to the knife. She stood up, undoing the buttons that held the pocketknife in place. Shifting the knife slightly to the right, she sat down again. Hope was watching her closely.

"What? What's the matter?" she said.

"What's that in your pocket?" Hope rose to her feet, her whole body tense.

"In my pocket?" Halley was perplexed. "It's just my knife."

Hope covered her face with her hands. A dim light began to emanate from the gaps around the basement door, and Hope began to pound repetitively on the glossy black door with her fists. "I don't want to remember. I don't want to remember. I don't want to remember." The pounding made the door shake.

"What is it?" Halley said. Her heart felt like it was beating in time with the pounding on the door. "What don't you want to remember? Hope, what's the matter? Stop it...Answer me..."

Hope wasn't listening. She was pounding harder and faster; she'd break the door if she didn't stop.

"Did Nick have a knife that night?"

Hope shuddered. The pounding stopped.

"No. It was me. I did it. With my knife...I tried to kill myself."

But something in Hope broke just then. She sank to the floor. "God...no..."

"What?"

"You're right. He did have a knife." Hope rubbed her hand back and forth on the kitchen floor, as if trying to erase the memory. "He kept going on and on about these 'enemies' of his. About what he was going to do to them..."

Halley's hands were white, holding the empty mug. "Maybe he was just venting, just getting it out of his system..."

"No...No." Hope looked up at Halley. "There was too much detail for just venting. He was talking about knifes and stabbing and blood. Even about how he'd planned to get rid of the bodies..." Hope breathed out hard and wrung her hands together. "I could tell he'd been thinking about it for a long time. He said he was afraid he was going crazy, but the way he said it...he had this glee in his voice..."

"What happened?"

Hope's body closed up. "He reached across my lap and pushed some leaves aside. He uncovered something," she said flatly. "The moon came out again, just for a second, and the thing Nick was holding *glinted*..."

"The knife."

"Yes. The knife. It was a hunting knife." She shivered. "He opened and closed it, really smoothly, like he'd been practicing with it. Its edge...I couldn't take my eyes away from it...it was so jagged and awful."

"What did you do?"

"Nothing. I couldn't move. Only I stopped leaning against him. He played with the knife for ages without saying a word. I didn't know what to do."

Halley pulled the other chair beside her, and patted it softly. "Come sit here."

Hope shook her head.

"What happened?"

"When Nick finally spoke, his lips had gone all thin and white. I started to shake – he must've felt it. He whispered. He asked me if I was afraid of him. I couldn't answer. He said it again, "Are you afraid of me?" It was louder this time. Each word seemed so long, like he was speaking in slow motion."

"God."

Hope's fist clenched. "I didn't know what to say. Of course I was afraid. But I couldn't say that."

She looked down.

"Why not?"

"If I admitted I was afraid of him...that would mean there was something to be afraid of. If I believed it, he'd believe it."

"And there you were, alone with him in the dark. And he had a knife."

"Yes." Hope looked up, pleading in her eyes. "But he never said he'd hurt *me*. He was talking about those other people. He's a good man." Hope rubbed her hands on her arms, as if to warm herself. "I did it to myself. I hurt myself."

Halley noticed again how little there was left of her flesh. The memory was eating Hope up from the inside out. "You were afraid if you told the truth – that you *were* afraid of him – that he'd kill you," Halley said.

"That's right."

"So you lied," Halley said flatly.

Hope looked startled, and took a moment before answering. "I guess so. Yes. I did lie. I told him I wasn't afraid. That I was just cold…that I was shaking because I was cold. It started to rain harder. The raindrops were huge – they exploded when they hit the ground. I just wanted to get out of there. He stared at me for so long I thought my heart was going to burst. He didn't believe me. He couldn't have believed me."

"Did he hurt you?" Halley asked quietly.

Hope shook her head. "No." She shook her head again. "No. He just reached across me and put the knife back, without saying a word. The rain stopped, and we walked home and we never talked about that night again."

Halley stared at her, and then shifted her gaze to the glossy blackness of the basement door.

"So, when did you try to kill yourself?" she asked.

CHAPTER 38

Hope sat on the floor in front of the basement door, her head in her hands. Halley sat across from her at the pinewood table, turning her empty brown mug around and around, looking at the patterns in the glaze, at the slight indentations and uprisings around the edges, at the tiny air bubbles that had not burst when it had been fired. She put the mug to one side, and rested both hands on the tabletop, palms down. She sat upright and looked at Hope. "The lie you told him," she said, finally. "You believed it, didn't you?"

Hope looked up sharply.

"What? What did you say?"

"When you said you weren't afraid of him." Halley pressed her palms into the tabletop. "You didn't believe it that night. That night, you knew you were afraid – you just said so. You knew something was wrong with him. But you had to convince yourself your lie was true. You had to convince yourself that you weren't scared of him."

"I don't understand. Why would I do that?"

Halley leaned forward. She spoke gently. "You couldn't love him *and* think he was a monster. You had to rub out that night from your mind. You had to convince yourself all those other frightening moments were just 'coincidence'."

"I don't know what you mean. He didn't actually do anything, hurt anyone. He's not a monster. It was all talk."

"Come on, Hope. You're lying to me now. He hurt you. I know."

"He didn't. I hurt myself."

Hope stood up.

"I don't want to talk to you anymore. You're confusing me."

She moved towards the kitchen door.

Halley stood too.

"Finish the story. Tell me what else happened that night. It's the only way out."

Hope's body tensed. "I already told you. He put the knife away. We got up. We went home."

The basement door began to bang behind her, *bang bang bang*. Hope didn't even look.

"We went home," she repeated, more loudly.

"No. That's not what happened."

Halley sat down at the table and held her own wrist tightly, wrapping her fingers around the silver bracelet; the bracelet dug into the palm of her hand. "Tell me how it ended. Tell me about trying to kill yourself."

Hope stood a little straighter. "Nick moved away after my riding accident," she said. "I didn't see him much. I met Andy and slept with him. I betrayed Nick. That's all. That's it."

"That's not it. Tell me how the night under the tree ended. Stay with what happened that night."

"I can't. I won't," Hope sobbed, and ran out of the kitchen, leaving the door swinging behind her.

CHAPTER 39

Halley let her go. She wouldn't go far, not until this was over. Staring down at the pinewood table, Halley's eyes moved restlessly over the worn-out love-poem, the empty brown mug, and the notebook Hope had left behind. If only there was a clue. If only it didn't depend on Hope having to remember this way.

The notebook!

Halley quickly pulled it towards her. It was spiral-bound, just like ones she'd used for taking notes during college. She stared at the cover a moment before flipping it open. Notes from Biochemistry; Psychology 101; Animal Science. Each in their own section, and all neatly written with different color pens. Each section of notes ended abruptly – the last lectures were dated early November. But that didn't make sense – the term didn't end till mid-December.

Halley flipped to the last section of the notebook. This section hadn't been used for class notes; this was personal. It began with love letters to Nick, which must have been written during some of the duller lectures, but the later writing seemed to be more self-reflective. Lists and lists of pros and cons of each man. This must have been what Hope was writing here in this house, about choosing between Andy and Nick. Halley read a bit of it, but it was too repetitive to stay with for long.

She flipped the pages, and something caught her eye – it was a bold sketch, slammed in among all the tiny writing. She flipped through the pages more slowly. Hope hadn't drawn the sketch just once. She'd drawn it ten, twenty, maybe thirty times. Halley flattened the notebook open on the pinewood table with both hands, as if it would get away. She looked closely at one of the more detailed sketches. It made her head hurt.

It was a drawing of a nightmare forest of tangled trees, their branches crossing one another in thick wavy pencil lines. At the very center of the forest, Hope had drawn a fortress, shading its thick, grey stone darkly with the side of the pencil. She'd drawn winding paths through the woods – they all led to the fortress, but on each path, she had drawn a black, snarling dog. She was a good artist; the picture made Halley look up quickly to make sure she was still alone.

Halley placed her finger on one of the paths, and moved it towards the fortress. Her finger was shaking. There were doors on the fortress; Hope had drawn them as if they were open. Inside the fortress, right at the center, Hope had drawn a box. It could be a tomb. There was something written on it, not words, but a symbol. Three parallel lines. Like bars in a prison window.

Halley flipped through the notebook again, taking care to bookmark the detailed drawing with one finger. This time she noticed the three parallel lines everywhere. Small etchings and larger ones. Some horizontal to the page and others vertical. She went back to the bookmarked drawing and looked again.

CHAPTER 40

Halley opened the kitchen door, and saw Hope slumped on the floor of the living room. She held the notebook out towards Hope, opened to the most detailed image of the fortress. "Did you draw this?"

Hope looked up. "What?"

Halley walked over to her and extended a hand, helping Hope to her feet. "This…"

"No…I don't…but who could have…it's my notebook…"

Halley led her slowly back into the kitchen and helped her into a chair.

"Oh, Halley…" Hope said. She rested her head in her hands.

"Something's hidden there, isn't it?" Halley pointed to the place on the sketch with her forefinger. Behind those bars. What is it Hope? Is it the truth?"

Hope looked at the sketch, and quickly looked away. "I…" Her hands had fallen to the table. Halley was mesmerized by what she did. Hope spread the fingers wide, keeping three fingers slightly closer together. She pressed hard on these fingers, so they lifted off the table at the second knuckle, flattening the fingertip and first knuckle onto the table. Then she drew the hand towards herself on the pinewood table. The movement looked awkward and painful.

"Stop that," Halley said.

"What?"

"What you're doing with your hand. Stop it."

It bothered Halley in a way she didn't understand.

Hope folded her hands tightly together, as if this were the only way she could control them.

Halley stared at Hope's folded hands. It had become difficult to speak. "Try this. Something bad happened that night. Something you couldn't face. You can't face. But you didn't do it. It's okay, Hope. Stay. Please...sit back down." Halley reached out and placed a gentle hand on Hope's arm. "It's over now. I'm here." She breathed in deeply and waited until Hope resumed her seat. "We can take off the bars; we can open the tomb. Together. Nick can't hurt you anymore." Halley took her hand. It was cold. She placed her other hand over it, to try to warm her. "Did you draw this?" she asked again.

Hope placed her thin finger on the sketch, on the tomb that lay in the center of the fortress. "Yes." She sighed heavily. "I built it...I mean drew it. Years ago. I drew it so well that it took on a life of its own. Even when I wanted to open it, when I needed to remember what I'd put in that tomb, I couldn't. I can't."

"I guess you did build it. In your mind."

"I guess so."

"Can we open it now?"

There was a long silence. Hope stared down at the drawing. When she looked up at Halley, her face was ashen. She took a quick glance at the basement door, then drew in a deep breath and sat up straight.

"Okay. But stay with me...please, stay with me."

"I'm right here."

Hope breathed in like it hurt.

"What really happened that night?" Halley said. She pressed Hope's hand between her own.

Hope looked down at her sketch. She swallowed. With one fingertip, she pressed hard on the sketch, on the tomb. The tip of her finger turned red from the pressure. "What I told you before was all true. All up to the last bit, where he put the knife back under the leaves." Her eyes filled with tears. "He didn't put the knife back, Halley, he didn't."

Halley felt her own hands grow cold. Together, they looked down at the sketch.

"I couldn't move, like I said. He had his arm around me. He pulled me in tight, like he used to when we were first dating and he couldn't get me close enough. But he still had the knife." She stopped speaking and removed her finger from the drawing. "I was wearing this lovely filmy shirt. It had long, white sleeves. I remember the sleeves. They flared out at the ends by my wrists. It was something like a princess might wear. It made me feel pretty, feminine." She hit the table with her fist suddenly, making Halley's empty mug jump. "He ruined my beautiful shirt."

"Ruined the shirt? What a strange thing to care about," Halley said.

"You think so? Dad gave me that shirt," Hope said with real anger. "I thought of it like armor, like he'd magicked some special powers onto the shirt to protect me when he wasn't there. But it didn't, did it? It didn't protect me at all." She looked up into Halley's eyes, her pupils enormous in the dark room. "Nick grabbed my wrist. Tight. It hurt. I tried to pull away – I could feel the fabric of my shirt digging into my wrist. He wouldn't let go, even when I cried out. He wouldn't let go."

Halley looked at Hope's thin, down-covered arms. "What did he do?"

"He put the knife between his teeth. I can still see the white of his teeth on the knife." Hope closed her eyes. "He rolled back my sleeve. I looked down, and my skin was so white. I remember being surprised that even in the dark my skin could look pale. It made it feel like it wasn't even my arm. But it had to be, because I could see it had my bracelet on it, the silver bracelet I won riding Sampson over fences."

Halley looked down at her wrist. The silver bracelet encircled it accusingly.

"He took it off, my bracelet. I remember the sound of it, the little click the catch made. The sound seemed significant." Hope's words came from far away, like she was talking underwater. "He threw it into the dark. I didn't see it fall. It just disappeared. I remember wondering how I'd ever find it again."

A long silence followed, and Halley realized Hope was waiting for her to say something. She didn't want to. She wanted to get up and run away. She bit the inside of her cheek, and tried to think of something to say. "Did you fight him?"

Hope looked immediately ashamed. "I didn't know what he was doing. I kept thinking maybe I was wrong. He was moving so slow, in almost…a…loving way…But when he started to move the knife towards my arm… God…I panicked…" Hope's hands began to shake, and Halley held them tighter. She was shaking her head back and forth quickly, her face flushed. "I began to scream. But there was no one there to hear."

She was talking faster now, as if she couldn't stop the torrent of words. "But I kept screaming – I couldn't help myself. Then I hit him – I hit him as hard as I could, but we were sitting too close for it to work. I tried to get my arm away. But he was too strong…" Hope's eyes darted back and forth, as if she were seeing the scene all over again. Her breath came fast.

Halley didn't say a word.

"I heard another sound. I heard his knife click – he'd closed it – he'd put the blade away. For a second, I thought it was okay, that I'd just over-reacted. Then I heard it click again. Open."

Halley tasted bile in the back of her throat.

Hope's voice flattened. It was like she was telling a story that had happened to someone else. "He lifted the knife. He placed the blade against my arm, up by that little hollow on the inside of my elbow."

A tear ran down Halley's cheek.

"He slid it down my arm, very slowly. It was almost gentle. I didn't really feel it – he did it so softly, it didn't hurt. But I saw the blood. A thin line of it. When I saw it, I heard myself scream again and my hand tried to pull itself away…it was wet with blood, so it nearly got away." She paused. "I nearly got away…"

Halley couldn't bring herself to ask what happened next, but it didn't matter, as Hope continued anyway, without further prompting.

"He shoved me over. He pinned my arm down with his knees. Really fast, he ran the knife down my arm twice more, with more pressure than the first time. Maybe it was because I couldn't keep still, but that's when it really started to bleed, these three lines he'd carved in my arm." Hope looked at her with hollow eyes. "It was like a brand. Like he was saying I was his property, and no one else could ever touch me. No one...no one...kind."

This time Halley got the question out. "What happened next?"

"Everything turned black. I must have passed out."

CHAPTER 41

It was nearly dawn. Eden and Athena were asleep on the back lawn. The eagle kept its vigilant watch.

To Halley, it felt like they'd been sitting at the pinewood table forever. Her eyes felt scratchy and her body felt like it had been pummeled by rocks. "Let's go outside," she said, breaking their long silence. "Let's sit on the front porch and watch the sunrise."

She pushed her chair back. Hope stood as well.

Together, they walked through the kitchen door, which swung back and forth behind them, until settling closed. Opening the front door made the wind chime stir, and it sounded its inappropriately cheerful greeting. Halley reached up to still it.

Carefully, as if wounded, they sat down on the porch steps. The stars were visible, but the moon had set. On the furthest horizon was the slightest hint of dawn. The story wasn't finished. "What happened when you woke up?" she said. She turned to look at Hope, who was also looking out at the sunrise.

Hope's gaze moved from the horizon to the dandelions. "Dad was always so careful about this place. He would've hated those dandelions."

Halley nodded. "Remember how mad he'd get when you blew them after they'd gone to seed? You couldn't help it – 'angel parachutes', you called them – that's why you did it. You thought you were helping the angels get to earth. But you never told him that..."

"Mm. Angel parachutes. But just look what a mess I've made of things," Hope said, gesturing to the lawn.

A long silence sat heavily between them, a massive black

rock. Halley put her hand on top of Hope's. "You don't think… Hope? You've got to know that nothing that happened was your fault. It wasn't your fault."

Hope shrugged her off. "Maybe if I'd fought back sooner…"

"He might've killed you. You did what you had to do."

Hope didn't respond.

"You didn't answer my question," Halley prompted. "What happened when you woke up?"

Hope reached over and pulled a stray piece of honeysuckle towards her. "I don't think I ever *have* woken up," she said quietly. "The next day, I couldn't remember how I got hurt. I didn't remember what he had done."

"You didn't remember? How is that possible?"

"I don't know. All I know is what Nick told me."

"Which was?"

"He told me that I'd tried to kill myself." Her fingers played with a loose strand of honeysuckle, tying it into small knots. "That he'd saved my life." Without warning, she kicked hard at the porch railing. "I feel so fucking stupid!" There was a cracking sound as a bit of the old wood began to splinter.

Halley stood. The anger was good. She began to kick at the porch railing too.

Hope looked perplexed for a moment, like she'd been expecting Halley to scold her. Then she kicked harder, slamming into the wood again and again. With a crash, a section of the porch railing broke off, falling to the ground below.

Halley put a gentle arm around her and led her back to the steps. She waited until Hope's breathing had become quiet.

"Tell me…

Hope bit her first finger, then balled her hand into a tight fist. Her voice sounded controlled, but barely. "When I woke up, I had a bandage on my arm. It hurt so much. I didn't know what had happened. Nick was sitting next to me on the bed, wiping my forehead with a damp washcloth." She took a deep breath. "It was a lovely navy blue, that washcloth. So soft. It was so comforting to wake with it being swept across my skin." Hope touched her forehead with her fingertips, as if in remembrance of the feeling.

Halley didn't speak.

"Like I said, I didn't know what had happened. I saw the bandage on my arm, all clean and white, but I couldn't remember how I'd hurt myself. Isn't that ridiculous?" She looked up at Halley. "Stupid weak mind! If only I'd remembered then, I could've…"

Halley shook her head. "Your mind couldn't handle what had happened. It did what it had to do, so you would survive."

"I guess."

Hope had picked up the honeysuckle vine again. She dug her fingernails through its stem, cutting off several inches at the end. She threw it down the steps.

"So you didn't know what had happened. But Nick knew. He knew he'd done it."

Hope rubbed her face with her hands, as if wiping something away she couldn't bear. She lifted her gaze to the lightening area of the dawn sky. "He told me I'd done it to myself," she repeated. She got up and began to pace again. "But I've told you that part already. There's no point in talking about it anymore." She looked like she might kick down the rest of the porch railing, but she didn't. Instead, she rubbed at the scars on her right arm, hard, as if she could erase them.

"Maybe there is."

Hope shook her head, but spoke just the same. "He said…he said I'd brought my pocketknife with me, the one I always carry."

Halley put her hand into her pocket and fingered the knife.

"He said I told him…I told him I thought he was going to break up with me. That I was crying, saying I couldn't live without him, kept repeating it, like I was in a trance or something. I scared him, he said. The bastard!" She kicked the porch railing again and another piece of splintered wood flew into the air. "He tried to stop me, he said, but it happened too fast. I cut myself with my knife. I tried to kill myself."

"It wasn't true. You didn't try to kill yourself."

Hope's face showed her doubt. "How do you know? For sure? Maybe I just invented that story about Nick doing it, to make me feel better." She'd stopped kicking at the railing and stood very still. "I don't know what's true anymore. I don't know what to believe." She closed her eyes.

Halley drew her hand from her pocket. She was holding the pocketknife. With a practiced motion, she flipped it open and held up the blade.

Hope opened her eyes at the sound of the click, and took a quick step backwards.

"Don't be afraid. I just want to show you…" Halley held out the knife, but Hope didn't move closer. "Look. This blade is smooth – it would never make those scars you have on your arm…" To demonstrate, she drew the blade along one of the flooring boards of the porch.

Hope stepped forward cautiously, and looked at the fine straight line the blade had made, and, turning her arm over, compared it to her own serpentine scars. Bending down, she ran her finger along the straight line – her hand was shaking. "You're right," Hope said. She sat down heavily and let her arm fall into her lap. "But…"

"But what?"

"I believed him. Halley, I truly believed him…until just now… until you came and helped me remember the truth. Until you proved it to me. Oh my God. Believing him has shaped every moment of my life since that day. I thought…I thought I had decided I was worthless, that my life wasn't worth living."

"Why did you believe him?" Halley asked.

Hope sat absolutely still, and closed her eyes. When she spoke, it was like someone in the confessional asking for forgiveness.

"What he said made sense. Things weren't right between us – I kept thinking we were going to break up, that I'd done something to make him stop loving me. It was easy to believe what he said. That I'd hurt myself." Hope was silent for a long time, just rubbing the honeysuckle flower between her fingertips, looking down at the porch steps as if there were something of great interest lying at her feet.

"Why was it easy to believe you'd hurt yourself?"

"I'd tried once before...when things were bad between us. We'd had this huge fight...he said it was my fault, that if only I could behave better...then he could love me..." She swallowed. "He went out, slammed the door. There was this black hole right here, right in the center of my chest. I just wanted it to stop. For the pain to stop. I got my knife out. It looked dull. I didn't know if it would be sharp enough. I meant to...I planned to cut myself...but I didn't...I thought if I just waited...eventually, I just went to bed." Hope's eyes filled with tears and she held her fist to her mouth.

Halley put a hand on top of hers.

"You thought about it. But you didn't do it."

"No...so..."

"So that's what's important."

Hope looked at her.

"What do you mean?" Hope sat up straighter.

"You didn't do it. You never tried to kill yourself."

"You know, you're right. I never did. That is what's important. I never tried to kill myself."

"And even if you had, you are alive now. You have chosen life." Halley paused. "So...what did Nick do next?"

"He was kind to me, from that morning on. He took care of me." Hope placed her foot on the discarded flower and ground it into the porch. "He said he'd never tell anyone what I'd done."

"No one noticed the bandages? What about Dad? Surely he'd have noticed?"

Hope deflated. "It happened six months after Dad died."

Halley's eyes moved back and forth: she knew this.

Hope continued. "We didn't see any of our friends until the bandages came off. After that, I always wore long sleeves. That was his idea. By then, he had stopped being so nice – he told me our friends would think I was nuts if they knew. He said we should keep it 'our secret'."

"Son of a bitch."

"Yes."

They sat in silence as the sky lightened.

Halley shook her head, and slid the bracelet back and forth on her arm. "Son of a bitch," she repeated. She took a deep breath. "When did you meet Andy?"

Hope smiled. "A few months later. My cuts had healed. It was my best friend's birthday – it was the first time I went out with her in ages. I remember we were dancing on this picnic table – it was an outdoor party – Andy just scooped me off and started dancing with me. I was so drawn to him. He seemed so... so light. I didn't mean to kiss him. I really didn't. Especially not after Nick..."

"After Nick had saved your life," Halley finished flatly.

Hope nodded. "I'd never felt so guilty. I still loved Nick. But I couldn't give up Andy. I kept reading Nick's love poems, but I couldn't feel anything at all. I cried all the time. I didn't know what to do. It was the first time in my life I couldn't hear the voice inside me. You know, the voice that always knew the right thing to do."

"You couldn't talk to your friends about it. So you took Sampson out." Halley shifted her seat on the porch step; the boards were hard underneath her.

"I thought a ride would clear my head, help me think. Help me decide what to do." Hope picked up the discarded honeysuckle vine.

"But you couldn't get clear, because your mind had built that thing, that 'fortress' you drew in the notebook, to hide the truth. To keep the lie safe. To keep you sane."

"That's right," Hope said, as if finally making the connection between her indecision and the repressed memory of Nick's actions. "I couldn't figure out *why* I couldn't make up my mind. I just kept hearing the same thoughts over and over and over again, and it made me feel so weak, and so stupid. *I love Nick; I want Andy; I love Nick; I want Andy.* I was disgusted with myself. When that tree appeared out of nowhere in the middle of the path, it was like it'd been put there on purpose to punish me, for my stupidity, for not being able to make up my mind, for betraying Nick. For everything. When Sampson jumped, I could've stayed on – of course I could have. I was a great rider. But I just let go. I let myself fall off. I didn't know how badly I'd get hurt."

Halley rubbed the small of her back. "And you didn't think there was much left to lose. When did you start checking the doors and windows?"

Hope was surprised. "Just recently. I've never told anyone about it. I was sure if I did, something dreadful would happen. Like it would make it not work. Isn't that funny?"

Halley shook her head. "I do it too."

"You do? But why?"

Halley didn't answer.

Hope continued. "That man from the basement…at first, I just had nightmares about him. But now he's started coming up the stairs, even when I'm awake. I can really see him. I must be crazy."

"I saw him too," Halley reminded her.

"I know."

They looked at each other.

"Maybe Nick hurt you too."

Halley turned to stare at Hope. Her eyes moved to Hope's thin, white arms; her own were muscular, possessing life and vitality. She wore them like armor. Her gaze ran to her forearm, the back of her hand. The silver bracelet: Halley stared at it, and in that moment she could see it on the wrist of her own much younger self. She was once again riding Sampson, flying through the woods, innocent and free. She remembered the taste of freedom, the smell of dirt and leaves, the ringing of hooves on gravel.

It was the time before; she could finally remember the time before.

Without looking up, Halley turned her palm to face the sky, and rested her arm in her lap. She gently pushed the bracelet higher up her arm, and stared at the long red scars. They were identical to Hope's. She ran two fingers up her arm, between the lengths of the scars.

Then she dropped her head into her hands and cried as if the world was ending.

Hope put her arms around Halley and held her tightly.

* * *

When the tears were finished, Halley looked up. The sun was high in the sky; the day was light.

"The man in the basement…the man that looked like Nick…" Halley's voice was thick and heavy.

"Yes?" Hope said.

"He wasn't Nick."

Hope looked startled.

"I think he was you. And me. Us…"

"That makes no sense at all."

"He was a part of us that knew, that was warning us. The same part that made you draw the sketch of the fortress, that made you leave the notebook out for me to see. That man in the basement was your intuition, telling you to beware. He had to keep coming back, until you faced the truth. Until you decided to leave Nick."

Hope was silent for some time, rocking forward and backward. She turned to stare uneasily at the house. Suddenly, she stood up.

"Come with me," she said.

Together, they walked across the porch, and through the front door. The living room was light now. They walked into the kitchen, letting the door swing freely behind them. Hope went straight to the glossy black basement door. She opened the door wide. Nothing happened. Hope's body relaxed and she sighed. It was a full, lifting sigh. Halley had a sense that this was to be the last sigh. Hope's careworn face lightened and she said, "You're right. I know the truth. I'm leaving Nick."

"What about Andy?"

"It never had anything to do with Andy."

* * *

Halley walked out of the back door. It was still cool on this side of the house. Athena watched her with big grey wet eyes.

"What happened?" Eden said, running up to Halley at once. "Where's Hope? Did you fix her, or is she still crazy?"

Halley smiled. "She was never crazy, and yes, I think I fixed her."

The back door opened a second time, and Hope stepped out. She must have showered; her hair was still damp, and she had pushed it back behind her ears, which gave her an elfish appearance. "Do you two have anything to eat?" she asked. "I'm starving!" She jumped down the back steps and landed on two feet. "Don't look so surprised, Eden – I bet you're hungry too."

Halley reached into her bamboo backpack, and pulled out three ripe bananas. "Eat these. They'll give you strength."

Halley and Eden watched as Hope devoured all three bananas without pause.

"It's funny. I forgot how good it was to eat." She looked thoughtful. "Hey… I've got something better than bananas. Give me a minute…"

Eden and Halley watched Hope enter a small shed at the back of the garden. "The freezer!" they said in unison.

"Peters Monkey Bars!" Halley added. "I'd forgotten all about Dad's secret recipe. Didn't he say they'd last for years in the freezer?"

Eden nodded.

Hope came back with an armful. They were individually wrapped in aluminum foil, and sealed inside zip-lock bags. Condensation had already begun to form on the plastic. Hope dropped them to the ground. "God, they're cold!"

Eden giggled, and picked one up from the pile. "We used to eat these on those long hiking trips. They taste awful! But if I had one, I'd be full all morning." She turned it over in her hands and studied the handmade wrapper. Halley and Hope grimaced as she tore one open, and sniffed it. "Smells just like it used to – terrible!" She took a big bite, and spoke through a full mouth. "Yuk! It tastes just like it used to, too!"

Hope and Halley opened their own bars and tasted.

Hope made a face.

"But the second bite's better, right?" Halley said.

"No!" Hope and Eden shouted in unison.

They began to laugh.

They ate the bars quickly. Halley felt a surge of energy flow through her. Hope helped them fill the two bamboo backpacks with enough Peters Monkey Bars to keep them going for a week.

They were silent for a moment, each lost in their own thoughts.

Hope was the first to speak. "Thank you," she said. "Thank you for everything."

Her voice reminded Halley of freely flowing water. Halley opened her arms wide and Hope stepped in for a hug.

Hope soaked up the embrace and then stepped free, gazing

out at the mountains. "It's a beautiful morning." She stretched her arms wide, as if to take it up with her body. "I think I'll take a walk."

With a smile that held within it both thankfulness and farewell, she turned and walked around the house and towards the front garden. Halley and Eden followed her to the front of the house, where she stopped for a moment and then bent down. When she stood up, she was holding a ripe dandelion. She blew hard, and white dandelion seeds suddenly filled the air.

"Angel parachutes," Eden said.

"Yes." Halley smiled.

Hope turned to wave goodbye. In time, she became small in the distance, and finally disappeared from view entirely.

CHAPTER 42

Tired from the sleepless night, Halley slept for hours. Upon waking, she spoke decisively.

"I have to see the basement."

Eden looked at her in disbelief. "But he's down there!"

"No, I think he's gone. But I need to be sure." She stood and dusted grass from her clothing. "I know you're frightened. It's ok. You can wait here. I won't be long."

Slowly, she made her way inside. A familiar coldness washed over her as she crossed the kitchen and approached the basement door. The dark stairwell gaped.

"It's just a basement. I'm not a child anymore." With a shaking hand, she reached for the doorframe.

Eden's voice startled her. "I'm coming too," she said.

Halley turned. "You sure?"

She nodded.

"Ok." Halley hesitated. "But listen, stay close. I'm pretty sure I'm right about that man but..."

Eden swallowed and didn't answer.

Quickly, Halley reached into the stairwell, and flicked on the light. The small click was unnaturally loud. Tentatively, she stepped forward, resting one foot on the top stair, the other leg lifted as if it hesitated to follow. "It's been years since I've gone down this staircase. When I was a child, that thing used to climb the stairs in the middle of the night..."

Eden shivered.

"It came into my room. I believed that if I closed my eyes, I would be invisible. If I was absolutely still, it couldn't get me."

"I remember," Eden said.

The light from the bare bulb was cold and lifeless, not bright enough to illuminate the darker shadows. Halley took a few steps down the stairs, and then forced herself to take a few more. The descent felt endless. The back of her knees were sweating, her pulse racing. By the time she'd reached the bottom, she was half-blind with panic.

Taking a deep breath, she stepped off the stairs, and turned the corner. There, she stopped in her tracks. It was completely dark. She felt around on the closest wall, but there was no central light switch. This had not changed. Despair filled her. The lights were the very worst thing. To turn them on meant venturing into the dark. Four bare bulbs, turned on and off by pulling long hanging cords. Turning them on was bad. Turning them off was worse. Pulling one cord, leaving a dark space where anything could lurk, and then another, the darkness growing like a shadow, and then the third, so the whole basement was nearly dark but for a small, safe circle of light. To turn off the last light was terror. She would flee the darkness, racing up the stairwell, pursued, desperate to lock the door behind her. Sometimes, the lock wouldn't catch.

When she was little, the basement had terrified her. It wasn't just the darkness or the junk. It was the dark spaces behind it. Anything could hide behind those discarded sofas; inside her grandfather's old war chests; between warped bookshelves. The empty armchairs, stuffing overflowing, were often peopled by figures she would see from the corner of her eye.

Biting her lip, she took two paces forward, reached up, and pulled a cord hanging from the ceiling. The single bulb lit. She pulled on the remaining three bulbs. Then she stood still, stunned. The basement was empty. It was all gone. The cement floor radiated cold through her shoes. The scary things were gone.

But the good things were gone too. The bookshelves with all their childhood toys; the photo albums that went back to her grandparents' time; the barnyard of plastic horses; Dad's collection of old bits of strangely shaped wood from the forest; the broken old typewriters. Even her father's old oil paintings were gone. Halley felt hollow; she understood now why her parents had saved things. The objects had held their memories.

One object remained. Hung on a rusty nail, on a metal hanger, was an old raincoat. She reached out to touch it. A memory came to her. She was young, perhaps three or four, waiting for Daddy to come home. Every night was the same; he was home by exactly six-thirty. She would watch the clock in anticipation, knowing the angle the hands made when it was time for him. In her memory, it was a cold winter's night. Daddy would get home, and she'd run across the living room, jump up and be hugged tightly in his arms. She could still smell the cold of his raincoat, that outdoor smell; the sense that he had been somewhere else, but now he was come home to her. This was his raincoat.

Halley looked over at Eden.

"Dad wasn't always so nice," Eden said.

"Yes, he was."

Out of long habit, she went through the pockets of the raincoat. It was empty, but for a small object wrapped in a handkerchief in the inner pocket. She opened it. It was a small brown ceramic horse. Its fourth leg had been reattached with Elmer's Glue, and bore a lump from the childish paste that had been used in her time to mend the precious objects of children.

Halley ran her finger along the lump of dried glue. *It's held all these years.* With her smallest finger, she stroked along the back of the figure. It was a bay horse. Like Sampson. It was just an inch tall, fine-boned and delicate. She closed her eyes, and felt a flush of warmth before tucking it safely in her pocket.

It was time to go. Halley was no longer frightened, and there was nothing more to find. The basement was empty; there was no man with terrible eyes haunting the place. She'd been right.

"Let's go," she said.

They climbed the stairs, hand in hand. At the top, Halley was surprised to see that the basement door was closed. *I've never noticed the back of this door. I've always been in too much of a hurry to get out of the basement and lock it behind me.* The stairwell light shimmered in the glossy black door. She was now the one in the basement, opening the door into the kitchen, into the light. She had become one with the thing that had climbed these stairs in her nightmares. But she was no longer angry, no longer a monster at all. Maybe she never had been.

They left the basement, left the house, closing the back door behind them. The basement door they left wide open.

CHAPTER 43

He arrived at the abandoned house shortly after they'd left. "Monsters and nightmares. So you think it is that simple, do you? You think you can forget all of this, wish it all away? I don't think so, my dear, I really don't think so."

He left the house. It didn't matter that they were far ahead. They were easy to track.

They were no longer afraid. So they were making far more mistakes.

He smiled, and strode on.

Athena was waiting patiently, nibbling grass. Halley patted her on the shoulder, and Athena swung her big white head up and looked at Halley with wet eyes. *Yes, yes,* those eyes said.

Using the back steps of the house as a mounting block, she grabbed hold of Athena's mane just above the withers, and swung herself lightly onto the horse's back. "Give me your hand," Halley said, looking down at Eden, helping her up behind herself with a big tug. When they were both settled, Athena began to walk slowly. Feeling the horse move under her, Halley felt the long-familiar sense of height and poise that came with riding.

As Athena clomp-clomped down the stony path, Halley felt Eden's arms around her mid-section. After a while, her hold loosened a bit, and Halley guessed she'd dozed off to the gentle swaying of the horse's stride. This swaying allowed Halley's thoughts to quiet in a way the action-embedded last few days had not. As the events of those days played through her mind, she focused upon her breath moving in and out, letting her thoughts of the experiences slide by as if they were simply words on a screen:

escaping Trance up the steep hillside trail; sliding downhill and traversing the tundra; losing Eden, and finding her again; falling into and escaping from Gail's pit; helping heal Gail by taking down the hill of 'bones'; finding and healing Hope.

And myself, healing myself too.

Her mind came back into the now. A sense of change was upon her. Through her encounters with these others, she herself was evolving. *I'm recovering parts of me. Parts I'd forgotten even existed.* At this thought, the distance from the top of her head to the base of her spine lengthened. Her chest lifted.

The path forward was clear today, straight and obvious and long. Wide-open. Up in the sky – high above, riding the air currents – an eagle soared in a wide circle. Its enormous wingspan made it look powerful and unearthly.

Eden stirred, and lifted her head.

"What do you see?" she asked.

Halley pointed upwards in answer, watching the eagle. The speed and power of the bird's movement woke something in her; she wanted to move fast too. "Let's do some running," she said.

Eden tightened her grip around Halley's mid-section. "Hooray! I thought we were going to walk this slow forever!"

Halley nudged the horse with her heels, and Athena broke obligingly into a slow jog, and with a little more encouragement, a fast trot. Each bounce at the trot was jarring, so she urged the horse on until they had moved into a smooth cantor and from there to the sweetness of a full gallop. Halley grasped Athena's wiry mane, and Eden held tight to Halley.

They flowed over the landscape, melded to the horse's back like they were born to be there. Hooves *kerchunked* against hardened earth. Athena stretched long through her forelegs, and there were moments when, for an instant, all four of her hooves were free of the earth. They were airborne, creatures of the sky. The wind was in Halley's hair, her blood pulsing wildly through her body. It was the essence of liberation, distilled from the air, movement, and breath.

They galloped for miles, letting Athena decide when she was tired. Finally, she slowed to a walk, blowing hard. Her neck was flecked with white foamy sweat.

Eden burst into laughter. "That was so much fun!"

Halley was lost for words. She swung to the ground. The air was sweet with freedom. The blood was still pounding through her body. "I can't remember the last time I felt so alive."

After Eden slid from Athena's back, the horse lay down in the grass on the side of the trail, rolling back and forth, her legs stretched high. She had enjoyed the run as much as they. When the horse had recovered, she rolled back to her feet and shook herself heartily, dirt and foamy sweat flying from her white coat. Satisfied, she took a few paces around a clump of trees. Halley listened to the sucking sound of her drinking: Athena had found water.

Following, Halley and Eden found themselves facing a wide river. The swiftly flowing water was grayish-white and looked cold. Athena finished drinking, and shook the drops from her muzzle; they hit Halley's arm and made her shiver.

"It's too wide to cross here," she said, frowning as she looked up and then downstream, searching for a narrower crossing.

Athena pawed at the ground. She tossed her head, and snorted appraisingly while staring at the water, as if issuing a challenge. Her grey eyes shone.

"I'll just bet you could, Athena. You could swim it, even if we can't." Halley stroked the flat of the horse's face, who answered by bumping Halley gently in the chest with her large white head. "I guess we've got to try."

"Before we do, let's have some food," Eden said.

"Good idea – I'm starved!"

They choked down several of the 'Peters Monkey Bars'.

"Feel better?" Halley asked.

"Well…less hungry."

They had four bars left. Halley zipped them inside the

zip-lock bag from her earlier food supplies to keep them dry during the river crossing.

"Ready?"

"Ready! But can I sit in front this time? Please?" Eden said. Her eyes asked as well.

"Of course. I'll give you a leg up…"

Eden bent her left leg and Halley took her knee in her hands.

"Ready – on three…one, two, three!"

Eden jumped with her right leg, pressing into Halley's hand with her left knee and she was up.

"You want a hand up?"

"Yes, thanks."

The river mud made a sucking sound as Athena entered the water. As the river deepened, Athena began to swim, her muscular white legs pulling against the water, carrying them across. She swam effortlessly, with her neck stretched long.

Halley, however, was no longer smiling. The river was colder than she'd imagined, and far swifter. Without warning, a heavy branch, swept along by the strong current, smashed into her leg. Her leg blazed with pain. *I didn't even see that coming!* Holding onto the horse's mane with one hand, her other pressing against the hurting leg, she felt her thighs begin to slip. She was losing her balance. She tried to grip tighter but her injured leg wouldn't work properly. Sharp-edged fear was upon her, worse because she was responsible now for both Athena and Eden.

It was then that she looked upriver, and saw the boat.

It was bearing down on them from upstream. It came fast. Faster than the current. It was steering directly for them. There was only one oarsman. He was cloaked in a familiar grey-green jacket.

CHAPTER 44

Eden's arms were wrapped around Athena's neck, her face tucked down. She was humming softly. Athena looked straight ahead, her neck stretched long as she swam. Halley opened her mouth but could make no sound.

The boat was close. Trance's thin, dangerous smile made her jaw clench. He plied the oars. The boat surged forward.

Halley drove her right heel hard into Athena's side. It took the horse by surprise. She immediately curved around the pressure, shifting direction to swim downriver.

Halley glanced over her shoulder and saw Trance working the oars furiously. They were nearly abreast. He lifted one of the oars from the water. He held it like a baseball bat, ready to swing. Halley could see it all happening, in an instant, an irretrievable moment: he would aim for Athena, a deadly blow to the horse's smooth beautiful head. Smash her, as he'd smashed the carp by the river. They would be pulled under by the weight of the dead horse. They'd drown.

Trance cocked his body back. He would destroy everything!

The boat swept up next to them. Eden kept her head low. Athena swam. Trance began the swing.

The world stopped.

But Halley was fast, and unpredictable. Trance believed her a sparrow; he was unprepared for an eagle.

From Athena's back, she launched herself, pushing off with her legs. She slammed into him, knocking him off balance. His smell – fetid, damp, dead – was upon her. But only for a moment. Her jump propelled her into him, and then beyond. She landed in the river with a tremendous splash.

The cold stunned her.

Seizing the moment, Trance reached out to grab for her. "Here, take my hand. I'll help you aboard the boat...you could drown..." His expression was terrible to behold.

"No way!" she shouted.

Before he could react, she dove and pulled herself deep underwater. She held her breath and pulled forward with long strokes. The water tasted like the first rain of spring. Once her hands moved within the reeds at the edge of the river bank, she cautiously raised her lips above water to take a breath. Slowly, she rose up out of the water, keeping her knees bent, careful to stay hidden. She looked downstream, and felt a strong pulse of dread. Trance was pursuing Eden and Athena.

Underwater, something slid slowly across her calves, something warm and heavy. She froze. The water near the reeds was murky. She couldn't see through it. She kept absolutely still. A long thin ripple disturbed the river's smooth skin. It was moving away from her. Her relief was short-lived. It circled and moved back towards her. Fast.

A *fish, let it be a fish,* she willed.

But the head that emerged from the water was not that of a fish. It was a snake! It flicked its tongue, and then fixed her with its yellow staring eyes. It reared higher, twelve inches of the snake defying gravity, the rest flattened along the water's surface. It widened, became suddenly and ominously hooded. It opened its mouth and hissed from deep inside its throat. Its long white hollow fangs became visible, its forked tongue tasting the air. It was not just a snake. It was a cobra!

Godlike, it swayed above the surface, as if enchanted by some gypsy snake charmer, before sinking and disappearing into the murky water. Halley swallowed. The ripples reappeared on the surface – they were moving towards her!

Suddenly, a scream split the air. At the same time, a forceful wind struck Halley in the face. The surface of the water was broken. A moment later, an eagle arose. It was gripping the cobra tightly in its talons. It flew away, its thick legs extended backwards, holding the snake by its mid-section. The snake whipped about, but it could not get to the eagle.

Halley scrambled to shore. She looked downriver. Trance's boat was closing in on the others. He plied the oars. Halley pursued them along the riverbank.

CHAPTER 45

Eden kept her eyes fixed upon Trance. He was more frightening than anything she had ever seen. He was the man from the basement and Bad Dad and her brother when he beat her up; he was her nightmares that never went away. She wanted to cry out for Mommy, but Mommy was gone. Biting her lip, she forced herself to remember about heroes. The Lone Ranger. Superman. The Incredible Hulk. Batman. Heroes were the good guys. And the good guys always won.

She took a deep breath. She was the Good Guy. Even though she was terrified, she would be brave.

Carefully, she lifted herself onto one foot, and then pushed up with the other leg, until she was standing on both feet, wide-stanced on the horse's broad back. Athena's back was slippery. She gripped with her toes and the balls of her feet, reassured by the feeling of height. A moment later, Trance caught up, and made a lunge for her. She simply leaned forward, held on, and swung herself around Athena's neck to hang below her, her legs dangling in the cold water.

Athena sensed what she must do: she turned parallel to the river's current, and resumed her course across the river. Trance couldn't turn as fast. He was unable to follow, and his boat was quickly swept away.

Athena and Eden climbed the river bank.

Halley watched the boat slip away, eventually turning a bend in the river and moving out of sight. Her leg ached where the stray branch had hit her; her hair dripped coldly down her back and made her shiver. Even so, she felt strangely elated. Eden and

Athena had crossed a few hundred meters further downstream. Halley ran to join them. Athena lifted her nose in the air and whinnied.

Halley looked at Eden with wonder. "Are you all right?"

Eden nodded, her eyes wide. They sat down to dry off in the sun, back to back, to gaze at the river. They were quiet for some time.

Looking towards the mountains, Halley felt the familiar pulse return to her forehead. "The baby," she said aloud.

"You haven't mentioned the baby in a really long time."

"I just felt her again, stronger than ever before."

"Do you know where?"

"The mountains."

"What about Trance?" Eden said.

"He won't be back today. But soon, I'll have to face him. I'm nearly strong enough. Let's focus on the mountains."

A clearly visible ridgeline would make for easy climbing, and she pointed it out to Eden, tracing the way with her finger across the range. "There. We'll start the climb just there." It looked challenging and would require skill as well as strength. The thought made her very tired. Lying on her back, she let the sun warm her, soaking up its golden light.

The sun shifted overhead, and the shadows began to lengthen. It was too late to travel further, so they decided to spend the night where they were, by the river.

With a sense of calm unexpected after the battle with Trance, they slept. The *hussssh* of rushing water over rocks was a soothing lullaby.

CHAPTER 46

The next morning at sunrise, Halley and Eden gathered themselves, ate the last of the Peters Monkey Bars, drained and refilled the canteen at the river, and began to walk. Athena followed just behind, nibbling at undergrowth.

They had not been walking long when Halley sensed a change in the air. Athena had stopped, her head and neck turned to observe something in the far distance. A sudden cool breeze from the West made the horse lift her head higher as she sucked in the air. She was suddenly lithe and light-footed, a coiled spring awaiting release.

Halley gazed at her with a mixture of sorrow and joy. With slow steps, she approached the horse, following the direction of her gaze. A herd of horses was just visible in the distance. They had stopped and were watching the little group. A loud whinny split the air as the lead stallion summoned her; Athena's answer resonated with an echo of the wild. She turned to face Halley, as if seeking permission, her nostrils flaring in and out. Reaching out, Halley gently stroked the flat of her palm down Athena's nose, around the curve of her jaw, along the bold sweep of her neck.

"Thank you," she whispered. She patted the horse gently on the shoulder, and then took her hand away. It was a farewell.

Athena paused a moment and nudged Halley in the belly, as if saying, *Sure? Are you sure?*

Halley nodded. "Go."

In a moment, she was off. Her tail flicked at the air as she galloped lightly towards the herd. Halley watched the puffs of dust arise from each foot fall, watched the sunlight play on her white coat, and in the sound of her movement heard the echo of the horse's freedom.

"I love to see her run like that," Eden said.

"Now we're both free."

They watched as she rejoined the herd, as she touched noses with the lead stallion. Halley felt another piece of herself, long missing, slide back into place. Eden stepped away and appeared to be fascinated by the frogs at the edge of a small stream.

"Ahem."

Halley started and turned: a very old gentlemen was standing next to her, also watching the horses run in the distance. Halley's mouth went dry. What was he doing here! Where had he come from! Her eyes sprinted over him. He was familiar. In a moment, she took him in, and knew he was wrong.

Though old, the man's posture was upright – he stood as if he could stand for hours without discomfort, as if his joints bore him well. His skin was the deep, weathered brown of an old sailor. Like Halley, he was lean, with a similar strength to his build. His calves in particular were still thick and powerful. He was dressed simply: tan shorts held up by a brown leather belt; a blue crewneck t-shirt; old, dusty sandals. Between his teeth, he held a brown pipe, and he sucked at it as he watched the horses.

The pipe was okay. It belonged. It was the only thing that belonged. The smell of the smoke was sharp, that of an inexpensive tobacco, but was appealing in the way familiar scents often are. His hair was white, fine, old man's hair. It would be soft to touch. His blue eyes peered mischievously from a nest of wrinkles. They were the marks of a person who'd spent a lifetime smiling. These smile lines were wrong too, like almost everything else about him. Smile lines? They were not what she'd expect.

Halley consciously drew her mouth closed, and stood staring, looking as though she were trying to process some impossible algebraic equation.

The old gentleman simply watched the horses run. Finally,

he looked at Halley, and removed the pipe from between his teeth with one hand. "Ahem," he said, clearing his throat again. "Hello, Halley."

Tears came to her eyes.

"Dad?"

Her voice was a whisper.

It couldn't be. He'd been dead for fourteen years. And Dad had dressed like a country gentleman. This fact seemed, oddly, more important than the fact of his death. Her father would have been in his tailored tan raincoat. He'd be wearing his fine woolen slacks and a long-sleeved shirt with a collar. He wore this every time they went to see the horses. He didn't believe in slovenliness. *My father in shorts and sandals? Impossible.*

Still, he *was* her father. Halley's legs were trembling. The old gentleman reached out a hand and touched her shoulder. She stared at the hand, at the thick, straight, strong fingers. The smell of pipe smoke drifted around them.

"Even your hand is wrong."

"You will be all right," the old gentleman replied.

The words made her ears ring; the crow, the one she had met at the very beginning of her journey. *He had brought a note.* It had said exactly that: "You will be all right".

The world shifted under Halley's feet. The old gentleman left his hand on her shoulder, and placed the pipe back between his teeth. He puffed, and she stood trembling in the cloud of familiar smoke. In time, the trembling ceased. A little while later, she could speak again.

"But..." she said, not meeting his eyes, "but, you are dead." The word 'dead' felt slippery on her tongue. "I remember. When you died. A part of you was with me on the train when I was trying to get to you. A part that wasn't in the hospital. I knew you had a choice and I held you and said *No, don't go* but you chose to leave. I... I felt you go."

The words held the dry, brittle kernel of anger she had carried all these years. As she spoke, she felt the hard kernel swell and burst open. "You had a choice. I know you did…"

She bit the inside of her cheek. He had left before she was ready; he had left her unprepared, and unprotected.

He took the pipe from between his teeth and held it between two fingers. "I know, love. That day. That horrible day." He looked away from her, out to where the horses ran. He rubbed his chest, as if, even now, it still pained him. "I'm sorry, love…I just couldn't stay," he finally said, shaking his head. "My heart would never have worked properly again. I know it was sudden…" He pressed on her shoulder, his fingers strong.

"Sudden…" Halley said bitterly. "It wasn't sudden – it was impossible." Her eyes overflowed.

The memories had never faded. Memories were supposed to fade. The grey of his hands on the clean white sheet; the knuckles that had been deformed by arthritis; the strangely over-white half-moons on his fingernails; the down-turned lips; the thinned hair that was not quite white anymore but an inexplicable yellow. Pulling the strip of ECG paper off and rolling it into a tiny tube and tucking the tube silently into her pocket because it had recorded his last heart beat, and telling no one about it ever; it was something he would have done himself. His heart had stopped beating and they'd never known why.

He puffed at the pipe. "I couldn't face being incapacitated, being dependent. I would have been in your way. And you were all that ever mattered. Love, you were what made my life worthwhile."

She took a deep breath and rubbed her hand across her face. "You wouldn't have been in my way. You might have saved me."

"Ah, but Halley…I knew you would save yourself."

Halley was silent, overcome. It helped explain his leaving. *You believed in me.*

She thought about what else he'd said, about not wanting to be dependent. That had been his way. He'd been strong and silent in the face of tremendous pain.

She stared at the man. The words were important. But more important was the fact that he was dressed wrong. It made her doubt him. There was something funny about the way he spoke too. She pondered what he could have said that made her think that, as he watched the horses. She played his words over in her head. It was the nickname. He had called her "Love". Her father had always called her "Sweet".

The elderly gentleman spoke. "You're right. I am not the father you knew." He said it as if reluctant to explain. He met her eyes. "I am who your father would have become. Had he lived. Had he had time enough…to become…" The old gentleman stopped. "I am who your father has become. In you."

With that, he let the pipe fall to the earth and pulled Halley into a close embrace.

Halley didn't hug him back.

The old gentleman held her away.

"I have watched you since I left. It taught me what I'd never seen in life, that you needed me to tell you the things I took for granted that you knew. Like the fact that I love you." Before he spoke again, he glanced around quickly, as if he sensed danger. "Listen carefully. I must tell you something." He held her an arm's length away, his long straight fingers placed gently on her upper arms. "When you were very little, I frightened you."

"What?" Her body tensed.

"I frightened you. I'm sorry. I thought it wouldn't matter. Not if I loved you well the rest of your life. But it did. I'm sorry."

"I don't know what you're talking about."

"Yes, you do. One day, you will face it. Then you will hug me back."

She tried to relax her body, but couldn't. "At least you loved me well for the rest of my life." She tried to smile; the old gentleman did not smile back.

"I never could tell you how I treasured you. Not in words. It wasn't my way. But I did, Halley, I treasured you. By God, I did."

He squeezed her upper arms gently. The palms of his hands felt warm as he looked her full in the face.

He drew a deep breath; what he was about to say was very important.

"You must see all of who I was," he said. "You must let me step down from this pedestal you have placed me upon. I was only a man. A father. I made mistakes. You must see all of me now. You have no need to fear my anger any more."

Halley swallowed. "Angel parachutes," she said impulsively.

"What, love?"

"Angel parachutes. That's why I blew the seeds off the dandelions – I was helping the angels get to earth," Halley said. It was odd to feel like a child again in his presence.

The old gentleman smiled. "By God, you're right! I didn't know that then – it made me so furious that you were purposely ruining our lawn – but I can see now. That's exactly what you were doing!" He looked into the distance. "The world can always use a few more angels on the ground."

The horses were galloping in the distance and the white form of Athena caught Halley's eye. Her father followed her gaze.

"Athena," he said. "I gave her that name when she was born. Do you remember?"

Halley nodded.

"I never told you why," he said. His eyes disappeared into their nest of wrinkles. "Athena was a Greek goddess – the goddess of wisdom and war. She was grey-eyed too, just like your Athena. Not as hairy though, I'm sure. And she certainly didn't have a tail."

He laughed and this made Halley laugh too.

"Athena," he continued, "was a protector of heroes. That was the reason I named your horse Athena. I thought it a fitting name for a horse that would carry you."

"That explains my name too."

"Yes. Do you remember? I told you when you were very small. Halley means *hero*."

CHAPTER 47

Hero! An ill-fitting name if ever he had heard one. If there were a name that meant "coward", then, that would be fitting. His lips curled in a sneer.

Yes, she had escaped him a few times. That didn't bother him so much.

Her time was running out. Soon the car, inert under the deep river, would be full to the roof with water. Soon, none of this would matter. One way or another, he would have her. But this way would be more fun.

He swung his canteen back over his shoulder, and rubbed his hands together. Unaccountably cold on this warm day, he decided to increase his pace.

As suddenly as he appeared, her father was gone. Halley's shoulder tingled where his hand had lain. She placed her own hand there and spread her fingers wide. She wanted to soak up his essence; to draw inside what had been outside, to become one with her father who was so long gone. Her hand fell back to her side, and she heard the sudden sound of the horses thundering as one who had recovered a lost sense of hearing.

"You okay?" Eden asked.

"Did you see him?"

"Of course I did, silly! Dad. He's always showing up!"

"He is?"

"You've just got to know how to look," Eden said. She picked up the discarded pipe – it had burnt out – and played at holding it between her teeth. "I like how he dresses now much better – silly old thing, with his pipe – it was time he let go of that too!"

She giggled and let the pipe fall back to the earth. "Why do you look so surprised? I told you he was real!"

Halley didn't reply. She was thinking about what her father had said, about facing all of who he had been. It seemed like Eden thought he was perfect too.

Eden began to trot forward like a horse. "We'll have to do the trotting ourselves now. Come on, let's pretend we're mustangs!"

Eden didn't trot for long: the weather changed and trotting became less fun. First, the sky dulled. Then the clouds slid off the mountains, dropping heavily upon them, forming a thick fog. The world became opaque, the air thick with mist and yet uncomfortably hot. Halley sweated heavily and the sweat didn't dry – it lingered on her skin, and she ran her hands down her bare arms and flung it off. "With this fog, I can't even tell if we're headed in the right direction. I don't understand – it was so clear this morning. Now I can't see two feet in front of me."

"I like the fog," Eden said. "It makes it easier to play hide and seek!" With that, Eden darted a few feet away, giggling.

"Where are you? Come on, I don't want to play right now."

Eden jumped out of the fog, tapped Halley on the back, and then darted back into the whiteness, shouting, "Right here," and then laughing.

"Oh – I see!" Halley spun around; she could only see fog. "Okay – where?"

"Right..." Eden tapped her on her kneecap, "...here!" And jumped back. "No..." Eden jumped and touched the top of Halley's head, "...here!"

Halley finally laughed. "Okay, okay, you win! I won't be so grumpy about the fog. Come on, come back."

With a little skip and a hop, Eden reappeared.

They walked on. The fog thickened, swathing them in a blanket of white. Thus cocooned, their conversation felt both secret and safe.

"What were you like when you were little?" Eden asked, without preamble.

"Hmmm?"

Halley's eyes were smarting from the effort it took to see through the fog.

"When you were little...what were you like?"

"Little? You mean, like your age?"

"*I'm* not little," Eden giggled. "No – little...you know...like four or five."

"I'd rather not talk about it."

"Why?"

Halley bit the inside of her cheek and looked away.

Eden waited.

Halley sighed heavily.

"Scared," she said.

As if she hadn't had enough to worry about before. Dad – *the man who watched the horses with her,* she corrected herself – had to remind her of the way he'd scared her when she was little, had to speak his futile, 'I'm sorry'. She hadn't thought about it in years, and his 'sorry' was a long time too late.

"Are you mad at me?" Eden asked.

"No...it's just..."

Eden looked at her appraisingly and Halley looked down, and unclenched her fist.

"Why were you scared? You had Mom and Dad to keep you safe. That's what parents do..."

"That's what parents should do," Halley corrected. "And Dad did, very well...before, and after. Just not when I was five."

"What happened then?"

"Mom died."

The words seemed to clump, like sticky rice.

"When I was five. She died. Left me. No more ribbons in my hair. No more little dresses. Dead."

"Oh."

Eden crossed her arms across her chest; it was a defensive movement and Halley noticed it and was surprised.

"What is it?"

Eden shook her head, and looked away.

Halley looked at Eden's hands – they were small and soft, still the hands of a child.

"Tell me," Halley said.

The fog was so thick, they had stopped walking.

"It was my fault."

"Your fault?"

"That she died. It was my fault."

Eden spoke as a child who had learned the rules, and was well aware that she'd broken the most important one of all. It was black and white, and she was black.

"Mom died of cancer. That can't be your fault."

It was becoming hard to see Eden in the fog.

"It *was* my fault. She got it when I started school. That's what caused it."

"But..."

How could Halley explain that what Eden believed so absolutely made no sense? It was the theory of a five-year old, who had put two unconnected events together – her mother's death and her own starting school – and glued them solid with cement made increasingly impregnable with each passing year. The theory had never been disproved. Halley knew this for sure, because there was a place inside her grown-up mind – somewhere hard, just left of center – that believed exactly as Eden did: Mom's death *was* her fault.

"Anyway..." Eden was saying, drawing the conversation backward, onto safer ground, "It doesn't mean you weren't safe, just because Mom died." Her words were rehearsed, like she was parroting something she'd been made to read in a book. "Lots of people die – it's the ones who are still alive that keep the children safe..."

Halley looked at her in dismay; she knew what Eden said wasn't true. Not this time.

Eden continued, as if speaking to herself, but dawning awareness made her sentence break into small bits, like a favorite toy, smashed.

"But. But I didn't *feel* that way. Not safe. Not when I was five."

She looked at Halley with wide eyes, like she'd like to run into the fog and hide away.

Halley reached out a hand but Eden didn't seem to see it. "The basement?" she prompted.

"The basement," Eden agreed.

How awful to shine light on dark truths. Far easier to think about how good her father had been, how smart and kind and gentle. Why did they have to talk about how everything had changed? Why even think about it? They should stay in the time before her mother's death. Not after. Not then. *Not the basement.*

Halley tried to walk again, but in the thick fog she tripped on a rock and nearly fell. "Ouch," she said.

"You know I'm a good listener…"

Now Eden was shining the light; they kept trading places, one probing and then backing off, and then the other.

The fog made Halley's head pound; if only she could see her way through. "After Mom died…" she began. She stopped. "I haven't thought of it in years. It doesn't matter. It's ancient history."

"No, it's not."

"What do you mean, 'No, it's not?'"

"Ancient history is about *ancient* stuff – like the Greeks and the Romans," Eden said. "This is like…well, more like…modern history…"

Halley had to smile. "I guess you're right."

"Tell me like it's a story about someone else. That makes telling stuff easier."

"Don't be silly."

Eden just looked at her.

"Okay...Once upon a time, there was a little girl whose mother died...God, this is ridiculous!"

"What happened when her mother died?"

"It was all different. Her dad would get home from work, like usual, just like before. He'd kiss her and she'd hug him and he'd be 'Nice Dad'. Then he'd go to the basement..."

"Bad Dad," Eden said, in a quiet voice. "That's when he became Bad Dad."

Halley gave up on the bedtime story idea. "It was terrifying, the noise he made down there," she said. "He must have been throwing things around. I don't know what..." There was a tremor in her voice, like she was still little and still afraid. "He'd come up some time later – I couldn't tell time yet, so I don't know how long he stayed down there. But when he came up, he'd be 'Bad Dad'. It was dinnertime. Not the same dinnertime as when Mom was alive – it must've been much later, because I was very hungry."

"Very hungry," Eden echoed.

"He'd crash around in the kitchen, just like he had in the basement," Halley continued. "Bang crash bang smash. The noise was closer to where I was playing then, much closer. It sounded like war, like I'd see on TV when I wasn't meant to be looking. Like people were battling in the kitchen, throwing things at each other. I couldn't believe one person could make all that noise. It made my ears hurt."

Eden looked thoughtful. "It was because you made him mad. You made Mom get cancer and die." Eden's voice held all the authority of a five-year-old, even though she was ten and should've lost this way of thinking by now. "That's why he did it, made all that noise, why he was so angry. He was mad at you."

Halley didn't respond.

Eden rubbed her small arms. "The noise in the kitchen. It wasn't just the plates..."

"No." Halley began to breathe faster, like there wasn't enough air. "He shouted to himself in there too. His voice was like a tightrope. I felt like I was walking on it. Like I could fall off at any moment. All the other sounds in the house got quieter...until there was just his voice and the crashes..." She stopped and looked at Eden. "I kept thinking...I kept thinking he'd come out of the kitchen one day and hit me...throw me around, instead of the pots and pans."

"Did he ever come out?" Eden said. "Did he ever come out of the kitchen when he was 'Bad Dad'?"

"A few times. That's when he hit my brother."

They fell silent.

Halley saw the scene: the thin wooden stick slicing the air, connecting with her brother's flesh. *Smack smack smack.* The beatings had happened three times. The fourth time, she'd got between the two of them and the thin stick. She could still see the stick lifted above her and her brother, could see it hesitate, stop, shiver in the sudden silence. When her father had dropped it, the stick had bounced twice, making an unforgettable sound of wood on wood.

"He was a good man," Halley said firmly. "He told me I was the most important thing, all the rest of my life. Both of us, me and my brother. He was wise, and gentle, and..."

Eden's brow furrowed. "That was later. He was nice later. But what about when you were five? What about then?"

Halley stared at Eden. "What are you asking?"

"Did he ever hit you?"

Halley released the breath she'd been holding. "I never gave him the chance. I disappeared, hid in my room, just in case. Closed the door. Leaned my back against it. I put my stuffed bear against the door too. As if that would've stopped him."

Eden smiled. "Fluffy. He was a warrior bear."

"Sometimes, hiding in my room wasn't enough," Halley mused. On those really bad days, I'd pretend there was a secret room I could get to through the inside of my closet. I imagined making a hole in the back wall that only I could fit through – not grown ups."

"Like in Narnia!"

"That's what gave me the idea. But it wasn't just there to begin with, like in Narnia. I made it. Dug it out myself. It took a long time. But it was small and cozy and not a bit scary. I made sure of that."

"That sounds even better than Narnia."

Halley kept speaking, as if she hadn't heard Eden's reply. "I'd go into the closet through the door, and then I'd magic the hole in the back wall open, and crawl through to the secret room. I'd take Fluffy with me to be on guard. When I was in, I'd pull the hole closed behind me."

"Weren't you scared to be alone in there?"

"I wasn't alone. There was always someone waiting for me there, someone warm and soft, with a belly I could snuggle into. She'd protect me. Keep me company. Brush my hair."

"I bet she smelled like bayberries." Eden smiled through her tears. "So you were always safe, and always loved."

"As long as I stayed in the secret room I was."

Eden nodded.

They both fell silent. With tacit agreement, they began to walk again, though the fog still obscured much of the path.

* * *

Some time later, the fog thinned.

"Hey – look at that…"

In front of them was a large mass of green ferns, punctuated by one tall tree.

"That's strange," Halley said. There had been no other ferns for a long time, and certainly no trees to speak of.

"I bet it's an underground river! Maybe there's even a cave! With treasure…"

276

Halley put her arm out to stop Eden.

"Remember the trap Gail set with the backpack? Let's take it slow."

She stepped forward cautiously, testing the ground with each step. When she reached the ferns, she gently pried them apart. In doing so, she uncovered the narrow entrance to a cave. The white light of the fog penetrated only a few feet inside. Beyond that was absolute darkness. She heard the sound of dripping water, and then another sound.

It was the sound of a child, crying.

CHAPTER 48

*I*t's not the baby. The cry lacked the confident urgency of an infant. This person had no expectation of being helped. In fact, it sounded like they were trying hard not to be overheard.

"You'd better wait here," Halley said. "I don't like the sound of that."

Cautiously, Halley entered the cave, thumping each foot down hard to give any snakes plenty of warning to slide off.

"But I want to come," Eden said softly.

Halley looked over her shoulder. The glare of the fog made her eyes hurt; it was already difficult to see Eden. "I know...but... look, I'll be right back. You...you keep watch."

"For what?"

But Halley didn't answer. A few feet into the cave, she came to a fork. *It might be the first of many. If I get lost down here...*

A chill ran through her. Wary in the half-light, she raised her left hand to the wall. It was cold and damp. Feeling around, she noticed the cave's walls had no support beams – it was formed from solid stone. Halley fought the urge to remove her hand and turn back.

The child cried again. Halley stared down the tunnel. It was too dark to see. *Okay, I'll keep my left hand here, and take all the left-going branches first...*" She stretched her right arm in front to make sure she didn't run headfirst into any dead-ends.

After the first fork, it was completely dark. As she walked, she tried to draw a mental map of the cave's layout, but it was impossible. There were too many turns and tunnels, and the lack of light was disorienting. For a moment, she shut her eyes to try to concentrate. Even though it was no darker with her eyes shut, it was so disconcerting to walk that way that she opened her eyes again immediately. She could see nothing.

Keeping her left hand on the wall was troubling. Each new thing she felt was a shock: the slippery patches she had to fight not to pull away from; the webs that wound their way around her arm. Once, she brushed against a small, furry creature which skittered away in alarm; she did pull her hand away that time, and she stood breathless and absolutely still for several moments. When she was certain the thing had moved off, she reached for the wall again, and was relieved to find it smooth to her touch.

The sound of the crying child echoed down the tunnel, large in the dark. Halley tried to hurry and was grateful the floor of the tunnel was flat.

Unexpectedly, she bumped rock with the fingers of her stretched-out right arm, sending a jolt of alarm through her. She was motionless for a moment, and then moved her left hand from the cave wall and placed it next to her right hand. Stepping sideways, she felt along the front wall with the fingertips of both hands, until she had reached the cave wall on the right. There was no way through. She'd come to a dead-end.

The crying continued, but it was muffled. *That doesn't make sense. Where's it coming from?* Halley leant her ear against the wall. The crying became louder.

"Where are you?" she said urgently.

There was a sharp intake of breath.

"Who's there?" It was a child's voice, pretending courage. "Dad…is that you?" There was a pause, and then the child asked more quietly, "Are you still mad at me?"

"It's not Dad. It's Halley. Where are you?"

"I'm behind the wall."

Halley heard relief in the child's voice, coupled with something bitter. It was the sound of violated trust. "Why are you there?" she asked, knowing the answer as soon as she voiced the question.

"It's where you put me."

Halley felt a sudden hollow in her stomach. The truth of the words spurred her into urgency. Scrabbling at the wall with her fingernails, she tried to find ingress. It surprised her how quickly she was able to pull out the first stone, and then stone after stone after stone. "Wait for me," she shouted into the darkness. "I'll be right there!" Her voice sounded stricken; it made the blackness of the dark feel infinitely more engulfing.

The little voice didn't answer.

Halley pulled out stones from the cave wall until there was a small opening, and then dragged herself through face-down, head and shoulders first. She opened her eyes wide, but could see nothing. In the dark, it was her fingertips that noticed a change in the floor. The space she was entering no longer felt like rock. It felt like wood.

Like floorboards.

The smoothly varnished wood made her fingertips slip. She pushed herself forward into the space with her feet. She had only moved a little way when the top of her head bumped against a wall. The space was only a few feet wide. She pulled her knees in close to her chest, and climbed her hands up the cool back wall. She moved slowly, getting one leg at a time underneath her, and straightening cautiously to stand. It was a very small space, but it extended quite high. She explored the dark with her fingertips, feeling first along the walls. On the right-most wall, her fingers lit upon a small patch of rect-angular smoothness. She knew the feel of it: it had once been a sticker of Shaun Cassidy, gleaned from Teen Magazine. She remembered placing it there when she was thirteen, remem-bered the slight lift in the left corner where the adhesive had not held. She ran a fingernail under the edge, not enough to pry it loose, but enough to feel the familiarity of the sensation.

Even without vision, she knew where she was: she was back in her house, inside her own childhood closet.

She was strangely unsurprised.

CHAPTER 49

The closet had been emptied. In the dark, Halley went through an inventory of what was gone: her clothing; her shoes; her box full of diaries with their tiny childish locks; her riding boots and helmet. The two clothing poles were still there, one at a height of three feet, the other at five – she must've sensed where she was before actually knowing, because she'd subconsciously avoided them when she stood up.

Halley crouched down below the lower of the two poles, and moved her right hand as if drawing a circle on the back closet wall. Immediately, a round opening appeared. The dark closet flooded with warm yellow light. Halley turned quickly to reassure herself that the way back to the cave was still there. Then, in a movement smoothed by habit, she squeezed herself through the hole in the rear wall she had opened.

She was inside the small secret room that she'd created inside her closet, in her five-year-old imagination. The stuffed bear sat between her and the small child, who was no longer crying, who, instead leant with her back against the wall, watching Halley with startled eyes.

Halley looked at the bear. *Fluffy. He does look like a warrior bear.* Halley patted the bear on the head, picked it up, and held it out to the child.

She didn't take it. Instead, she shivered and hugged her bent knees tightly into her chest, as if she would make herself smaller and smaller, until she disappeared. Her cheeks were marked by dirt, streaked in lines where tears had run.

"Where's Bad Dad?" she said. "You didn't let him follow you

here, did you?" She shifted her body, as if to try to see behind Halley. "Close the hole! Quick! Close the hole!"

Halley looked behind her. *No, I'll leave the way back open.* She turned to the child again, and saw that she had resumed crying, but silently this time. Halley dropped the stuffed bear to the floor, and held out her arms. For a moment, the child hesitated. Then, she threw herself into Halley's arms and held on tight. Halley ran her hand over the child's fine, smooth hair, soothing her. She waited until the shaking had subsided before asking, in a gentle voice, "I know how you got here, but why are you still here?"

The child pulled away from the embrace and looked at Halley in confusion.

"Because you...you said...you said I should stay. You said it was safer here."

She wore green jeans, rolled up at the ankle, and a dirty blue t-shirt. Her feet were bare. She would be cold at night.

"But why are you all alone? I didn't leave you all alone..."

The little girl's lip trembled. "I didn't used to be," she said. "For the longest time, there were others. Eden, and Hope and Gail...even Mom was here." A wistful expression flickered across her face. "One by one, they all left." The little girl waved her hand towards the opening Halley had made. "Through there. Then there was just me." She picked up the discarded bear and hugged it tightly. "And Fluffy. Fluffy didn't go."

Halley closed her eyes. *What have I done? A new place to begin? Oh no.* "Oh, little one, I'm so sorry...I didn't know that would happen." She gathered herself. She was the grown-up. "I'm here now. I've come to get you out."

"But...it isn't safe, not out there. Mom's dead. Gone. Who'll protect me from Bad Dad?" Her eyes caught on Halley's red t-shirt. She reached out and touched the sequined crown, and then slowly ran one of the edges of the sequin under her small fingernail. "I like this..."

284

"Like a Queen, right?"

"Mmmm…" She touched the tiny pearls. "If you're a Queen, does that make me a Princess?"

Halley smiled. "Of course."

The little girl kept playing with the sequins and pearls. "How come I don't have Princess clothes then?" she mused aloud.

"Princesses don't always have to wear dresses. Cool Princesses wear jeans. It makes it easier to play."

"Like this, you mean?" The child jumped up from Halley's knee, leaving the bear in her place, and skipped around the small round chamber, bouncing, lifting her skinny legs high off the ground. When she was breathless, she threw herself again on Halley's lap.

"Just like that. That's great," Halley said. "Maybe you'll be a gymnast one day." Halley hugged her tightly for a moment.

The girl sat back and her eyes shone.

"I don't want to be a gymnast. I want to be an adventurer!" She sobered suddenly. "But I can't – I can't leave here."

Halley held her gently away. "Yes, you can." She stroked the child's soft hair. "I was wrong. You don't have to hide here to be safe."

The little girl frowned. "But Dad – you said he might hurt me, with Mom dead. Like he hurt my brother. Bad Dad, Always Mad. At me. You said I had to hide here."

"Dad wasn't really bad," Halley said. "He was the same good dad when he was in the basement banging things around, when he was in the kitchen shouting, when he hit your brother, *and* when he was hugging you."

"No, he wasn't."

"Yes, he was. He was very sad, and because it hurt so much to be that sad, it made him angry. But angry isn't bad. It's just angry. Just a feeling. He won't always be so sad." Halley lifted the little girl's chin so their eyes met. "And he won't ever, ever hurt you."

"I don't understand."

It was hard to explain to a child, but she had to try. "It broke his heart when Mom died…"

"Like when I broke my arm?"

"Sort of. Do you remember how much that hurt?"

The little girl nodded, big-eyed. "I felled off the Monkey's bars. It hurt lots…"

"It hurt him like that when Mom died, but even worse."

The little girl rubbed her arm. "Ow." She looked thoughtful. "What?"

"Is that why he took away my dresses? Because he was so sad?"

"You outgrew the dresses," Halley said. "Mom made them for you…and…well…she wasn't there to make any more." Halley looked at the little girl's green jeans. To her, they had become imbued with the same love her mother's dresses had contained, a love born of her father's providing for her the best he could, trying in his way to move her some distance from the pain of her mother's death. He couldn't clothe her in the past; he had tried to dress her for the future. If he couldn't help her be a little girl in dresses, maybe he could help her be a warrior. That's what he'd tried to prepare her for. As if he'd known what was coming.

Halley swallowed. "He loved you, little one. That's why he went to the basement to be angry. That's why he stayed in the kitchen. He couldn't stop being upset at Mom dying, but he tried to protect you."

"He hit my brother."

"He did. That was wrong." Halley paused – it was important for the little girl to really hear her, to have time to think about what she was saying. "Dad was human and he made some really bad mistakes. But he tried to protect both of you, the best he could. He loved you."

"I…I hated him. Sometimes…" The little girl looked ashamed. "When he was Bad Dad. But Mom told me it bad to hate. So I bad too…"

Halley hugged her tightly. "You're only little. It's okay. It's okay to be angry at him. Even to hate him sometimes."

"Really?"

"Um hmm. He loved you. No matter what."

"I think I love him too. And hate him too. Is that okay?"

"Yes...that's okay," she said. Halley looked in the little girl's sad eyes. "He was much better at loving you later, you know. There'll be a horse named Athena and wildflowers, and..." She took a deep breath. "Come on. Let's get you out of here."

The little girl looked down.

"I can't go. And you can't go either."

CHAPTER 50

The warm yellow light of the secret room had dimmed. "Why? Why can't we go?" Halley asked, perplexed. "I've told you – you'll be safe."

The little girl looked away. "I don't want to. Because it was my fault. When Mom died. My fault." The child's lip trembled again, but she didn't cry.

My fault, my fault, my fault.

Halley wished she could turn off the echo of the words in her brain, where it resonated and filled all the available space.

The little girl looked at Halley's expression closely, and drew away. "It's true then. It *was* my fault."

Halley was seeing her mother, stretched out in her coffin. Of course, she'd never really seen it – she'd been far too young to take to a funeral. In her mind, though, she'd seen the scene scores of times. Her mother: cold, with wide-open, staring, accusing eyes. Too thin. Thin as a bone.

It had happened so fast, the cancer eating her, and they made Halley keep going to school, even after she began wetting herself. She'd lied the first time it happened, had said she'd landed in a puddle at the end of a slide, but they could smell the urine, and they knew. *My fault.*

Halley shook her head to clear it. "It was cancer," she said. She had learned the right words to say many years ago.

"Can..." The little girl tried to say the word. "Can...cer? I don't know that word. What does it mean?"

"It means she got..."

Halley struggled to force the words out. It was like pushing bubble gum through thin wire mesh – some got stuck, and the bits that got through were deformed into unintended shapes. "…sick," she finished lamely. The word seemed round, and all-encompassing.

"Like when I got fever," the little girl said.

"What?"

"Like when I got fever. I stay in bed, all day," the little girl said. "Sick people must stay in bed. Mom stayed in bed after I go school, all the time. My fault."

Halley looked around the small secret room. She'd been so focused on the little girl she hadn't taken time to examine it before. It was larger than she'd remembered, and brighter. Its walls were rounded, and edged with vibrant cushions. It was like they were sitting in a genie's jar. *Like in "I Dream of Genie"*, she thought suddenly. She'd fashioned the room after the show that she and her brother watched every Saturday at noon. "It's not so bad in here, is it?" she said, as if to herself. She picked up Fluffy and rubbed his worn brown paw between two fingers. "I could stay here with you." *My fault, my fault, my fault.*

The little girl looked suddenly very frightened.

"Halley?" The voice called from back in the cave.

Halley didn't answer.

"Who's there?" the little girl asked. Fear made her voice tremble.

"Halley? Are you in there?" Eden's voice sounded distant.

Halley remained silent. She was mouthing the words to herself: *my fault, my fault, my fault. Stay here. Hide here.*

Eden popped through the small round hole from the closet into the secret room. "Oh, wowww! It's still here. I can't believe this place is still here." She crossed her arms in front of her chest and hummed the refrain from "I Dream of Genie", just like the actress in the show used to do.

"Who are you?" the little girl said, also crossing her arms across her chest, but in a defensive way. "And…Hey! Why are you wearing my clothes?"

"I'm Eden." She looked down at the little girl and giggled. "I guess I am wearing your clothes. They sure fit me better than you – you're tiny!" The little girl scowled. Eden looked at her more closely and added, "And you need a bath." She addressed Halley, who still hadn't spoken. "What's the matter?"

Halley didn't look up. She continued to massage the bear's brown paw. *My fault, my fault, my fault.*

"Halley? Halley!" Eden grabbed the bear and pulled it away. "What are you doing?"

"Stay here. Hide here," Halley said, in a strange, child-like voice.

"What!?"

"My fault."

Eden and the little girl looked at each other.

"Did you tell her that?" Eden said.

"No, you did."

"I think we both did. Come on."

Eden got the two of them to stand up, and helped them to join hands with her. They stood in a circle in the center of the genie room.

Halley moved as if mesmerized. She lifted her chin and stared up at the conical roof. It was like the photos of the Pantheon; she'd always wanted to go there. It was lovely here in this safe place, it really was.

"I've read about cancer," Eden said.

"Can-cer," the little girl said.

"It's no one's fault. It just happens."

There were the words from the books again.

"Just happens," Halley parroted. The others' hands felt cold and almost bloodless.

Eden squeezed Halley's hand so hard it hurt. "It wasn't your fault. You've got to let it go."

"If I let it go, I let her go."

"No!" the little girl shouted. "No! Don't let her go!"

The light in the cave shimmered. The air was suddenly permeated with the pungent seaside smell of bayberries.

The little girl gasped. "Mom…" She breathed in deeply, lifting her chin, savoring the scent. "You've come back…"

"Not my fault," Halley said.

"That's what *she* said," Eden replied, gesturing towards the empty space in the center of the circle.

"Who?" Halley asked.

"Mom. Didn't you see her? She was there, but just for a moment." Eden looked perplexed. "She said the same thing you did – that it wasn't my fault."

"She's never said *that* before," the little child said.

Halley lifted her chin and stared up at the roof. "The three of us have never been here together before," she said. She looked down at their joined hands, at the way their fingers overlapped. Her hands were the largest by far, the most grown. She had to be the one to decide.

"It was cancer," she said firmly. "No one was to blame." The words were no longer simply words from a book; they were the truth.

"No one was to blame," Eden repeated.

"Dat's right," the smallest girl confirmed.

The smell of bayberries settled into them, scenting their clothes and their skin. The spell that had fallen over Halley was broken. Eden quickly and quietly left.

When Eden was out of sight, the child said, "Can we go outside now? I'd like to go too…"

"You bet!" Halley replied immediately.

The child bounded to her feet. "I'll go first!"

She slid easily through the round opening into the closet. Halley followed closely behind. When they stood side by side in the closet, the child swept her hand over the hole in the back wall and it vanished. The way to the secret genie room was closed forever.

With the genie hole closed, the closet was dark again, and the air immediately began to feel close. There wasn't much space to move. A slight variation in the darkness of the closet wall was the only indication of the hole that led back into the cave.

We're going to go from the inside of a closet into a cave, Halley reflected. *I almost wish we'd end up back in the house instead.*

"Halley?"

"Hm?"

"It didn't look like this in here before..."

"What do you mean?" *Her five-year-old eyes must be able to see better than mine.*

"That hole in the other wall...that wasn't there before."

"That's the way we have to go."

"I always just walked out through the closet door. Can't we go that way?"

"I don't think so."

The little girl reached up impulsively and turned the knob. Halley felt a chill run down her spine. The little girl peeked through the crack. "Water..." she said.

"Water?"

"Not my bedroom. I just see lots of water and..."

Halley grabbed the doorknob and pulled the door firmly shut. "This is the way." She indicated the hole she'd made that led to the cave.

"Oh, okay."

God, what would have happened if we went through that door? The idea of being underwater made her feel suffocated.

They slid through the rocky hole back into the cave. It felt so good to feel the earth under her feet again.

"Cool!" the little girl said, looking around. "A real cave!"

"Haven't you been here before?"

"Never!"

Taking the child's hand, she reversed the process she'd used to find her way. "Don't be afraid. I know the way out."

"I'm not afraid. I'm with you."

The walk through the tunnel was shorter this time and much less frightening. When they exited the cave, still holding hands, the fog had cleared and the sky was a remarkable blue. Eden giggled from somewhere above them, and they looked up to find her waiting for them up in the tall tree. With a swinging somersault, she jumped down, landing solidly on both feet.

"Yippee!" she shouted. "She's free!"

"We all are," Halley replied.

With a laugh, the little girl darted off into the grass.

CHAPTER 51

It was a short walk from the cave to the foothills at the base of the mountains. The last of the long grass disappeared, and the trail started to slant gently uphill.

It was good to have to focus on small things, on the slight incline, on the extra effort in heart and muscles that it took to walk uphill. The trail was littered with large rocks buried deeply in the earth, ideal for climbing, making the initial foothills easy to traverse. They soon left the tundra and the rivers far behind, and the colors became subdued and hypnotic: tans; beiges; light browns.

Later, dark green tree ferns appeared, abundant with fronds uncurling from the center of their crowns. When a frond broke off at full maturity, it left behind a circular pattern on the tree trunk, as if to say, "I was here: this is my mark." Halley herself was now unfurled, stretched out to a full and glorious length. She was ready to make her mark.

The sun was hot on her back, and sweat dripped off her elbows. She slipped off her orange windbreaker and tied it loosely around her waist, and walked in her long sleeved t-shirt, sweeping her hand across her forehead now and then to prevent the sweat from dripping into her eyes. Eden was singing, bounding from rock to rock.

The foothills came to an abrupt end at the base of the first tall mountain. They had finally arrived at a real climb. Halley took a deep breath, and tilted her head all the way back to look up the steep ascent. Doing so made her mouth drop open. Even with her head back, she couldn't see the top. *Just take the first step, and then the next one, and then the next one.* She began.

As they climbed, the gradient became steeper, and the green tree ferns disappeared. Weeds replaced them – dusty, dry and stringy, hued in grey and olive tones. These were hardier things not crafted for beauty, but for survival.

Soon, the terrain became so steep that the only way up was via hundreds of rough steps carved into the solid bedrock. It was a switchback trail, just two feet wide, its camel-colored steps shallow and dry, and just that bit too small to allow a full foot-length. Before long, they were hundreds of feet up with nothing to prevent a fall. The wind, which occasionally gusted with unexpected force, made her feel like they were being tracked by some malevolent being.

She began to hurry. In her haste, she jammed the toe of her boot on the edge of a step, and stumbled. Struggling for balance, her arms flailed the empty air, the silver bracelet banging back and forth against her wrist bone. With great effort, she regained her balance, and then stood still, breathing fast. In her mind's eye, she saw herself plummeting to her death, what had once been her living body dead, smashed into pieces on the hard grey rocks far below. It had nearly happened; it still could.

No, this won't do. I need a different picture than this in my mind if we're going to make it.

Eyes closed, swaying slightly with the force of the wind, she visualized herself tall, strong, confident. She was making her way up the steep climb, not stumbling. In her imagination, she was actually smiling at the challenge. With this image fixed in her mind, she opened her eyes. She found she *was* smiling. Her belly expanded with her breath and new energy blossomed in her. She liked this new image. *I'm really not afraid – that's amazing!* She couldn't wait to begin climbing again.

It was his fetid smell that warned her. She spun quickly on the spot and nearly lost her footing. Fifty feet below, Trance was climbing, with cold, swift arrogance. His eyes met hers; they were ice-blue with disdain.

"You silly, stupid, little girl," he said. As if you could get away from me."

Laughing, he devoured four more steps with his long stride. His laughter was humorless and harsh, a grating sound like rock on rock. The white braided snake of hair swung side to side. His arms looked thick, his torso muscular.

Halley stood firm. "Who are you calling 'little girl?'"

"You, Sparrow." He kept coming. "I want you. I want you and the baby." He paused. "I want you dead."

"Never," she said. She cocked her head like a bird of prey.

"You say never. Yet I've nearly had it, many times. The knife on your arm...cutting...cutting. Three long lines..."

His feet looked enormous on the steps. Halley forced her eyes from them.

"Nearly doesn't count. I didn't do it. And it wasn't me cutting my arm with that knife. It was Nick. You said it was me. You've been lying."

Trance's stride faltered.

"Nick?" he said.

She rubbed her right arm as if it pained her. "That's right. Nick."

Trance's eyes moved quickly back and forth. "It doesn't matter," he said, climbing fast again. "The other time with the knife – that was all you. You wanted to die."

"I didn't do it. That's what matters," she said. "I chose life. I choose life."

"You don't get to make that choice!" he snarled, through gritted teeth.

"You've tried to kill me many times," she said, softening her voice in response to him raising his. "But you've never succeeded." She spoke a bit louder. "Why do you think that is?"

"I've just been biding my time, Sparrow."

Bullshit, she thought.

"Let me take you down the mountain." The sun was behind

him now, making his expression harder to read. He had injected a note of kindness into the words. "It isn't safe to climb any further."

Take me down. Yes, you've taken me down many times. His words penetrated at a point just below her heart. *I was going to do this,* she thought, suddenly weakening, *climb this mountain, save the baby...*

He went for the jugular. "No, Halley. You weren't. You were never going to *do this.* Save the baby! You've just been running from me. You, on some great quest..." He laughed his mirthless laugh, and took a step closer. "Look at you," he said, like a patronizing teacher to a rather dim student. "So messy, so dirty. How could you look after a baby when you can't even keep yourself clean?"

Who will save the baby if I give up?

"The baby will not be saved!" Trance roared. "You are not strong enough! You will never be strong enough!" He quieted his voice. There was no need to shout. "I'll show you the way down. Forget about the baby. Trust me. I won't hurt you. Follow me..."

"Save the baby, save the baby, save the baby," Eden chanted from a few steps above Halley.

Halley only heard the buzzing in her ears.

They might have stood there an eternity, Trance and Halley and Eden, the wind swirling around them, the gritty dust biting at their ankles.

Halley thought of Gail, of Hope, of the small child she had saved. Their energy was whirling inside her, pulsing through her bloodstream, pounding from her heart to her extremities and back. There was life there. They had imbued her with life, where before there had been death. The warmth of life; old life; new life; her face grew hot with it. Suddenly, her voice shattered the silence between them like breaking glass.

"No. I won't follow you. Never again will I follow you."

"You will do as I say!"

"I will not."

He smiled mirthlessly. "You're a big talker for someone who's scared to death."

"I'm not scared."

"Look around. Look down. Feel the wind? It's pushing at you. You'd better hold on." He jerked towards her, as if to strike, to throw her off balance. "Better come down with me. You're not competent to do this."

"That's funny. I feel competent. I've *been* competent. I think you're wrong."

"Ah, but you're the one who's been wrong before, aren't you? Wrong so many times. Why should you be right this time?"

"Who are you?" It was the question she'd never asked.

"I think you know."

"You're insane."

He laughed. "You looked down! I saw you! You're scared now, aren't you? It's time to turn around, Sparrow. Time to let me lead again. I'll lead you right." He took a step towards her.

"No."

"Yes." Another step.

"NO! I'll kill you first."

"Go ahead." He stopped. "Kill me." He might have been made of ice. "What's the matter? Do something. Kill me." His teeth glowed. "I'm waiting."

Halley looked down, deflated; she couldn't even kill a spider.

"No. You couldn't," he said, mocking in his voice. "You can't."

The wind swirled. Halley's bracelet banged again on the sore spot on her wrist bone. The painful sensation reminded her once more of the people she'd met on her journey, of their anger and powerlessness, of their fear. She stilled the movement of the bracelet with her other hand. How useful it would have been to inject the others with some of Trance's power, some of his absolute conviction. How useful, to have access to those hyena teeth when needed.

"Come here," she said. She couldn't believe she was saying it.

"What?" He was incredulous as well.

"Come here."

"You've never invited me close before."

"I never understood before." She held out her arms. "It's just a few steps."

He didn't move.

"You're right – I can't kill you," she said. "I need you too much. Let us now work together. Let us both live."

"I don't want you to live." He drew out each word for emphasis.

"You are not in charge of that."

He began to walk up the stone staircase as if mesmerized. The sun glowed on his white hair and thick torso. He began to look less solid, almost transparent. The wind swirled the dust in the air; it seemed to blow it right through him. He stopped three steps away.

"Closer," she said.

When he finally reached the step on which she stood, he shimmered like vapor, a white, gaseous cloud.

She breathed the vapor in. It reminded her of the dawn mist rising from a wintertime river. "Yes. That's where you belong," she whispered. "With me. In me." It was like inhaling a mixture of menthol, eucalyptus and pine: refreshing; clearing; powerful. With her breath, she guided him to the ancient, primordial place in her brain stem where the wild things were kept.

"You are mine. You are me," she said.

She felt him pushing at her, trying to shove his way higher into her consciousness, up her brainstem. "No. I am in charge this time," she said firmly.

"Sure, Sparrow, sure," he whispered back. "You're in charge."

She shoved him back where he belonged.

"My name is Eagle."

* * *

His essence remained. It resided within Halley, where its rage and craftiness could be put to good work.

"You succeeded," Halley said. "You killed some of me. But it was a part that had to die, a part whose work was done."

CHAPTER 52

Eden ran down the steps to embrace Halley, clapping her small hands. "You won! That was so cool!"

Halley smiled, but it was not a smile of conquest. "I didn't win. I just put him back where he belonged."

"You mean..."

Halley nodded and massaged the small hollow near the base of her skull. "It's not over. The battle between Trance and I will never be over." She gazed out into the distance.

"But...what will you do?"

"I'll be vigilant. I'll have to be conscious he's there, stay stronger than him." Halley looked back at her. "I guess I mean I'll have to keep my eyes open."

Eden glanced around at their unsafe position on the stone staircase. "Halley?" she said.

"Yes?"

"It's just that..."

"What?"

"Speaking of keeping eyes open...it's just...I'm a little scared. That's all," Eden finished, gesturing at the drop.

Halley felt tension flow back into her tired muscles as she re-awoke to precariousness of their position. They were at least five-hundred feet up, on a narrow stone staircase, with no shelter and no ropes. To slip meant death, or worse, impossible injury. It was hard to force her body to relax, to soften her joints, but it was essential. She took a deep breath and focused her mind.

"Okay. Listen," she said, forcing her shoulders down. "Here's what we have to do..."

Eden frowned with her eyes but paid close attention.

"Keep the weight on the balls of your feet, and keep your knees bent, see, like this." Halley demonstrated. "Now lean your body just a little in towards the solid rock, so you're angled away from the drop. That's it – that's the way! That will make you more secure. Okay? Let's go…"

They climbed for the best part of the afternoon. The sun was warm, and the gentle breeze was just enough to wick away their sweat. They reached the top of the camel-colored steps, and Halley sighed with relief, moving out onto a wide ledge that was sheltered on both sides by large outcroppings. They were safer than they'd been on the stairs, and this was a huge comfort. Still, Halley instinctively bent her knees, lowering her center of gravity towards the wide ledge, towards safety. Only then did she look outwards and down.

"Wow," Eden said, entering the ledge and looking out as well.

The view was tremendous. The river was a thin serpent winding its way across the landscape. It nestled between the foothills which marched towards the mountain range. Beyond lay the immensity of the yellow grass plain. Just visible was the edge of the woods (*I can see it again*, Halley noted, with some surprise), though most was hidden by heavy cloud cover. Perhaps it was raining in the forest; the thought was restful, mist on trees.

Halley lifted her eyes. The sky, with its gradations of deep blue, aqua, and light blue, was awe-inspiring: thin white clouds; circling eagles; an immensity of nothingness.

"Wow," Eden said again. "Hey…look at that tiny bird…"

The bird was being tossed about in the wind, its small brown wings flapping furiously. The eagles were keeping it in the center of their wide circles. On one wheeling spin, however, the small bird was tossed free of its shelter. It spun about wildly at the mercy of air currents, until it careened onto the ledge.

It was a sparrow.

It's just a bird. It is no longer my namesake. It is simply a perfect, beautiful little bird. A small wonder.

"You're a long way from home, brave bird," she said.

The sparrow looked at her with black eyes and sang a greeting. *So are you*, it said, *so are you*.

The eagles floating on air currents heard the exchange, and screamed for joy. Halley laughed aloud. *It's just a bird – I haven't thought that about a sparrow in years.* She looked upwards; her chest swelled with gratitude for simply being alive on this high ledge.

The sparrow took flight. It fluttered in the air, dancing along the rock wall like it was trapped inside a house and trying to find its way out. Its wings stirred the air as it hovered, and a small clinking sound echoed off the rock face. Halley searched for the source of the sound.

"Is that...? It's a rope!" she said. Addressing the sparrow, she added, "Thanks, my friend."

It dropped back down to the ledge, and began to hop two-footed down the staircase.

Halley took her gaze back up the rock wall, evaluating the rope. Its placement looked good, and better yet, it looked new. The carabiners holding it in place were not rusty. She pulled on both ends of the rope at once and was reassured by the answering tension of its anchor-point. A gentle pull on a single end told her that the rope would move freely if not tied off.

"The rope looks good. And the climb doesn't look too technical. I think we can do this!"

"Looks like fun to me!"

Something in her voice made Halley turn. She looked from Eden to the precipitous drop. Kicking at a small pebble, she watched it bounce away. It moved slowly at first, but with each bounce it gathered momentum, height, and speed, until it careened out of sight, swallowed up by the vastness of space. Halley was adult enough to climb the wall, to take the risk, but she couldn't let Eden. Eden was just a child. "It isn't safe. We'll have to turn back."

"What? We can't turn back! Not after coming all this way!"

Eden didn't see the danger. Halley tried again.

"We've got to turn back. We can't climb that wall without gear."

"Did you hear that?" Eden asked, looking up.

Halley heard a repeat of the plaintive cry she'd taken to be a birdcall. But it wasn't a bird, she realized.

"It's the baby!" they shouted in unison.

CHAPTER 53

The cry came from above. It was slightly muffled, suggesting the baby was still some distance away. But it was definitely up.

"Well?"

"We've got no choice. We've got to go." Halley paced back and forth. "But there must be some way to make it safer…"

Her voice trailed off as her eyes fixed on a brightly-colored object hidden in a small gap in the ledge. She walked across carefully, edging aside a flat rock. Hidden in a small cache were two climbing harnesses, a number of locking carabiners, and a Figure-8 descending device. Halley picked up one of the harnesses, turning it over in her hands.

How did these get here? Right where we needed them?

A sudden impulse to drop the harness came over her. It could be a trap! Then she saw the initials, sewn in blue thread: PW. She closed her eyes.

Eden came to stand by her side, and placed a small hand on her arm.

Halley looked at her.

"This was Dad's. This must have been the place he used to tell me about, in his bedtime stories." She handed one of the harnesses to Eden, who held it cupped in two palms.

"But I thought that place was just make-believe."

Halley ran her finger over the initials on the harness she held. "It was real. This is the place."

"But why would the harnesses be here? He wouldn't have just left them…"

"Maybe he'd planned on coming back and didn't want to carry it all up again..."

Halley stopped speaking suddenly. Her hand went to her mouth.

Eden's face reddened. She looked like she might cry. "And then he died..." she said, looking at the ground. "He never made it back."

Halley turned the harness over and over in her hands. "We'll climb it for him," she said finally. "He'll make it back, through us."

"You think?"

"Yes."

"I miss him."

"Me too."

They sat down together for a while, each holding one of the climbing harnesses, lost in their own memories.

"The baby's stopped crying," Eden said, after a time.

"You're right," Halley replied. "We'd better get moving."

She got to her feet, and examined the rope. Its newness suddenly worried her. Unlike the other gear that had been sheltered, the rope had been exposed to the elements. If it had been hanging there since her father's time, it should be more weathered. It must have been put up later. But by who? And where were they? Were they at the top, or – the thought chilled her – had they fallen? She forced herself to dismiss the thoughts.

"We've got what we need," she said.

The harness slipped loosely over Eden's thin legs, and Halley tightened the straps, making sure it was snug around her legs as well as over her belly. Locking the straps by tucking them back upon themselves, she gave them a hard tug to test them for slippage.

"You sure know what you're doing."

Halley didn't answer. She did up her own harness, and attached carabiners to the middle loops of both harnesses.

"Can you check my harness now, like I did yours?"

"You trust me?"

"Of course."

Eden made sure Halley's harness was secure, and then the two of them approached the wall.

"Look – can you see the handholds and footholds?" Halley asked. "That's the line we have to climb…"

Eden shook her head no.

Halley pointed up to a series of rock outcroppings that looked solid enough to bear weight. "There, and then there, and then there."

"Oh…I see…" Eden said.

Halley could tell she didn't. "Don't worry. I'm going to climb first to test the rope. You belay me, I'll make sure it's all safe, and then I'll come back down, and belay you up. Once you're safe on top, I'll join you."

A cool gust of wind whipped the hair across Halley's eyes and she brushed it aside impatiently.

"This is really scary." Eden frowned with her forehead. "And I don't get it. When one of us is here on the ledge, we can belay the other. If the climber falls, we stop the rope, and that way we stop the fall. I protect you. You protect me. But what happens later, when I'm at the top waiting for you, and you've got to climb up alone? What if you fall then?" Her eyes widened. "You'd die if you fell then!" She clenched her fists. "You weren't going to tell me, were you?"

There it was – in black and white; Halley would die if she fell with no one to belay her. But there was no choice, no other way; they had to get to the baby.

"Come on – let's get you ready."

Eden breathed out hard.

After attaching both their climbing harnesses to the rope, Halley got herself ready for the test climb. She checked the knots, flexed her fingers open and closed. "Okay. You're on belay. Take your feet wide and then take one in front of the other. Bend your knees a bit. That'll make you more stable." She looked at Eden. "Don't forget to breathe, okay?"

Eden gave a tight nod.

"I'm ready to climb," Halley said. "You ready to belay?"

Eden hesitated, grasping the rope tightly. "I've only ever belayed on a climbing wall, never for real like this."

"I know. But you'll do great." Halley touched her shoulder. Remember, I trust you."

She turned to face the wall, trying not to think about the hundreds of feet of empty space between her and the earth. "Here goes," she said, reaching a bare hand up towards the rock face. Her heart was in her throat, pounding a rapid pulse. The rock felt cool and slightly damp. This close, she could smell its mineral make-up, the iron and quartz and the streaks of amber.

Quickly driving down with her elbow, she used her back muscles to pull up, immediately reached for a second hand-hold with her free arm, and footholds for her dangling feet. In a moment, she was five feet above the ledge, with the whole world at her feet. Her face was inches from the rock. Staring upwards for a moment, she studied the line she would climb, and reached for the next handhold. The rest of the world slipped into insignificance.

The muscles in her back were powerful. Her fingers instinctively found grips. The rope gave her a sense of security as Eden pulled up the slack. After several minutes of breathless ascent, she stopped. The line up the rock face had ended abruptly. From the ledge, it had appeared to go all the way to the top. She was stuck, hung high above the earth.

"You okay? Why've you stopped? You're only halfway!"

Halley's body was trembling. She felt nauseous. Her fingers throbbed. The rock face blurred. She failed to convince her body to move. Then, without warning, the rock under her right hand shifted. She tried to take her weight off it. It moved a little more. Suddenly, it broke loose, falling, plummeting towards the ledge below.

"Below!" she screamed, trying to warn Eden.

Then she too plunged downwards, in free fall.

CHAPTER 54

On the ledge, the heavy rock whizzed by. Eden had heard the shout, knew the sparse jargon used by climbers to warn of falling rocks. With a quick movement of her arm, she braked the rope.

Halley felt a sharp jerk on the middle of her harness. Her free fall stopped abruptly. She swung on the rope, back and forth, praying she wouldn't smash into the rock face, praying that the rock anchors would hold. Reaching out with shaking arms, she was able to stop the swinging motion, finding a grip with her hands, her feet scrabbling to find purchase. Finally motionless, her heart pounding like it would explode, she began to breathe again.

She had not fallen. She had survived the moment, and the moment was over.

Glancing downwards, she called out, "Thanks." She was breathing hard.

"You're welcome!"

Several minutes later, Halley had calmed enough to try to find a new line to the top. She leaned her body back against the harness, releasing her hand grips, and took the weight on her feet. Now she was sticking out from the slope, horizontally, as if the world had turned sideways on its axis, and she was standing up straight on solid ground. It was a dizzying position; she was staring straight up into the blue sky, but it was the only way to find the line to the top. She studied the rock face, looking right and then left, and then right again with a longer gaze. *There it is.*

With a few bounces on her feet, she moved under the new line. The wind blew, and she hugged her body tight back into the rock face, gripping with hands and feet. Instead of minerals, she now smelled her own sweat. It reminded her of rusted metal, tinged with fear.

I'm okay. I've found the line again. I've just got to climb.

Her stomach moved nervously. She spoke aloud: "Come on. That slip is over now – leave it behind." She imagined wiping one hand on her thigh, parking the fall there to examine later. "Do what you've got to do. The longer you wait the worse it'll be."

She reached up; it felt like pulling the rock wall towards her rather than climbing. She was aware of each second, each tiny finger grip.

Rock after rock, moment after moment, finally, she reached the top of the face, and could look over the edge to the expanse of land on the peak. She leaned her whole body into the rock face. This close, she could feel the rock radiating warmth, as if it were alive, breathing, gripping her as tightly as she gripped it. Carefully, she released her handholds, first one and then the other, testing, taking some of her weight onto her firmly-planted feet and the rest through the rope and harness. Her placement remained stable. With her palms over the top of the cliff, her fingers digging in to grasp tiny edges of rock, she shoved her body upwards. She rose above the cliff-edge. Smiling, she tipped forward and scrambled onto flat ground.

Up here the air was sweet. She stood and stretched up her arms in a "V" of triumph, her fingers wide, as if in thanks to some higher deity. It was pure joy: she had surpassed who she was, become someone new in getting to the top of this mountain.

After taking a moment to catch her breath, she glanced around. The plateau was bare. She had climbed the most difficult of the mountain peaks. From here, there were slow descents and minor ascents, but most of the mountain range was of lower elevation.

I've made it.

Eden's voice came from below. "You okay?"

Halley smiled. "I'm great," she shouted back. Her voice was full with emotion. "I'm just going to check the anchor and then I'll come back down."

CHAPTER 55

W hen she was certain the anchor would hold, she got the descending device in place, and she stepped toward the edge of the cliff. The first step off the edge was the hardest – she had to have absolute faith in her preparations.

"Here I come," she shouted. "Pull the rope tight."

"Climb!" Eden shouted back.

The tug of the rope came against her harness and she leant her weight first gingerly and then fully against it. Carefully, she stepped from the horizontal ground of the plateau, to the vertical drop of the cliff face. Now her back faced the ground, as if she were lying on the air. She stared up at the blue sky. It was a slightly different shade from the last time she'd looked. The day was beginning to wane. Her right hand held the rope tightly, locked against the descending device.

She moved the rope slightly towards her body and felt it slide slowly through. Slowly, very slowly, she walked her way down the rock face. When the pace became too fast, she simply opened her arm to the side and slowed her progress. Each individual inch of the rock face was important. There was no time to think of fear; the task at hand took all her concentration. She was fully immersed.

When she saw the top of Eden's head, she knew she'd made it. The last few feet down were almost fun. She made it to the ledge. The ground felt wobbly. It took a moment to realize it was just her legs shaking.

"You did it!" Eden cheered. "Now it's my turn!"

Halley nodded. "Just let me catch my breath, and you can go."

A few minutes later, Eden was off. She scrambled up, following the line Halley had taken. In no time, she stood at the top of the mountain, waving and smiling.

Now to solve the real problem: how to get herself up to the plateau again safely, with no one on belay? Free climb it without a rope? She shook her head: if she slipped just once, she was dead. Maybe she could tie the rope off.

"Eden, can you undo the rope from your harness and throw it down?"

Eden quickly did as she asked. The two lengths of rope now hung side by side, as they had when Halley had first found the rope.

I don't know if it will work, but it's the only chance. She selected the first carabiner, which was still attached to the solid rock face. Taking great care, she tied the loose end of the rope to it, ensuring that its gate was facing the correct direction so the rope could not accidentally pull it open. She used a Figure-8 knot, re-threading it to make sure it couldn't work loose. It was a basic knot, but she checked it carefully. The other end of the rope was still attached to her harness. She flexed her fingers: they didn't have an ascending device. She would simply have to hold on and pull herself up the rope. Any fall would be limited by the length of the rope. The higher she climbed, the riskier a fall would become. If any of the anchors pulled loose…No, she couldn't let herself think of the consequences. She would make it.

Her hands gripped the rope, and she pulled hard with her back and her arms, willing herself up the steep face. She climbed with her feet up against the wall. Sweat poured into her eyes, and her arms burned with effort. This time, she climbed steadily and with precision, knowing that too fast or too slow would wear her muscles out before she reached the top; she knew the line she had to climb and her feet found their placements by instinct. When she got to the point where the rock had broken free, where she'd free-fallen, for just an instant the world went black. *Just fear. Breathe through it.* She forced herself to stay still and waited until the wall came back into focus. Cautiously, she bounced across to the second half of the line and continued up.

When she reached the top, she simply kept climbing with her feet and arms until she was standing vertically on the solid, wonderful plateau. She sunk first to her knees, and then fell onto her back. Her whole body was shaking.

"I'm okay," she said, to reassure both herself and Eden. *Just for a minute, need to rest.* She let her eyes shut. Eden watched her: Halley slept immediately and soundlessly.

She dreamed of Trance:

He was standing on the shallow camel-colored steps, where she had last seen him. He was alone. A moment passed, and then the eagles came in convocations. There were dozens of them, then hundreds. Trance shut his eyes and raised his arms. With talon and beak, the eagles dismantled him, swallowed him, and in time, returned him to the landscape.

In her sleep, the thin skin below Halley's left eye twitched. A melodic voice soothed her, speaking in the dream.

"Ah, recall: the eagle is, first and foremost, a bird of prey. It lives according to its nature. What the eagles have done is good. Because of their right action, Trance, in time, will too make the wildflowers bloom…"

CHAPTER 56

When Halley awoke, she slowly sat up. Eden, sitting beside her, was quietly humming.

Upright, Halley started at what she saw: sitting close by was a tall woman wearing a bright orange climbing harness and outdoor clothes. For a moment, Halley was frightened, but she quickly relaxed: there was a familiarity about the woman that was both immediate and reassuring. Whoever she was, the woman belonged here up on this windswept summit, Queen of nothing, yet Queen of all.

The woman was sitting in profile, cross-legged, staring out over the expansive view. The sound of Halley's sitting up had not stirred her, nor had Eden's humming. The woman sat as if she could sit for years, needing nothing, being troubled by nothing. Her head was positioned directly over her spine, her chin slightly lifted. Even in stillness, there was a visible elasticity about her body. It was reflected in her hands, which rested palms down on her knees. Halley imagined she could see the energy flow from the woman's hands into her body and out again, bathing her in an infinite pool of warm blue light.

The woman's skin was dark, burnished by the sun perhaps, or maybe she was just naturally this deep, lovely chocolate color. Her age was difficult to discern – the light shimmered off her skin so brightly it dazzled Halley's eyes.

Drawn by her glow, Halley and Eden exchanged a look, and without a word, they approached the woman.

She did not shift her posture or her head, and she did not speak, but her hands beckoned to them, directing them by means of a gesture to sit by her side. It seemed appropriate to sit cross-legged as well; they positioned themselves one on either side of her. Even though the woman was tall, Halley did not feel small sitting beside her. It was as if her height augmented rather than diminished her.

"Ah, I am glad you have finally woken," the woman said. "Look – the eagles too are dancing for joy." Her voice was rich, reminding Halley of the full sound of a river after heavy rain. Its melodious tone lacked all self-consciousness.

The woman stretched her right arm long and straight, her palm lifted heavenwards, her fingers spread wide. She was offering the vista to Halley as a gift. Halley looked away from the woman's profile, and out to the view, but not before noticing the three parallel scars that were etched upon the woman's arm.

While she had slept, the blue of the sky had softened, becoming the light blue of a baby's blanket. Thin clouds were lit from below by the afternoon sun. The eagles were soaring in the air, swooping and diving, riding the winds. There was a sense of jubilance about their movements that Halley had not seen before, and she was mesmerized.

"Yes. It is good to look on beauty such as this," the woman said, echoing Halley's thoughts.

She let her right hand fall gently onto her knee, this time resting it with her palm upwards. Her left hand was still palm downwards on her knee; she shifted it just slightly so that the fingertips of this hand now also grazed the earth. Her silence held the three of them as they gazed outwards, and it was several moments before she spoke again.

"You know, Akilina," she finally said. "Yes, you know." Her eyes followed the large birds in their swooping games. "This is your way: the way of the eagle."

Halley felt the words as a swooooosh, as a soaring sensation in her chest. "What did you call me?" she asked, knowing the answer, but wanting to hear it spoken again in the woman's river-voice.

"Akilina. The beautiful Latin word for Eagle. Much lovelier, said that way, don't you think?" she replied.

It was as if Halley were being pulled taller by a golden thread that linked the crown of her head with the base of her spine. Her chin tilted slightly upwards. "I had forgotten that name," she answered slowly. Her posture became a mirror image of the woman's. Eden looked at her and smiled; Eden had always known she was of the eagle. She had never lost her way.

"Akilina, you have undertaken a tremendous journey," the woman said. "You have learned what you came here to learn, that you are powerful beyond any of your imaginings. You have recalled your true nature, recognized for the first time your beauty. You have done this through the leaving of Fernando, the healing of Gail, and Hope, and Little One. It has come also through your courage in recalling your true history with Nick, and the releasing of your parents to their truth, so that they may rest in peace."

Halley sat immensely still: she was seeing her long journey play out before her.

"The losses of your life, you have grieved for and accepted," the woman continued. "From your errors, you have gained wisdom. You have found the courage to inhale your darkness, and, perhaps more difficult, to bathe in your light." She stopped. She turned to look directly at Halley for the first time. "This is your reward; this is your birthright."

The woman's gesture offered Halley the view again and though Halley wanted to look, she couldn't yet; she couldn't bear to break contact with the woman's candid gaze. In her eyes was an absolute transparency, allowing Halley to see all the way down to her depths. Her eyes were fathomless, infinite, the deepest of wide-open spaces. Yet they did not pull or drown or threaten; instead, her eyes opened Halley and this opening was good. Halley had the impression of brown and cinnamon, gold and air, of limitless compassion.

The woman reached out and rested a warm hand on Halley's shoulder, and Halley felt an aching at her touch, a sense of absolute fullness. She had never been touched with such acceptance before, as if the very universe were flowing through the warm palm of the woman's hand. The woman left her hand there, and Halley felt benevolence infuse the air.

Looking back towards the vista, the woman continued, "You have had the courage to find this place. Now feel the space around you. Now see."

The air, which had been dotted with eagles before, now became rich with them. Their wings did not flail or flutter. They rode the wind with no apparent effort, shifting with the air currents, circling and rising and falling. There was wonder in the effortlessness of their flight, in the inherent stillness in their movement. Their black lines against the white of the clouds brought to Halley's mind the music of celebration.

Without thinking, Halley said, "Come with me. Come with me on the rest of this journey."

She had not analyzed her reasons and she really didn't even know where she was going next: she simply wished to remain near the woman, who was the essence of kindness, personified.

"Ah, yes, I will certainly accompany you," the woman replied. "But for now, simply be here."

They sat in silence as the sun set. It took time. Halley felt the colors immerse her. Finally, the sun began to sink below the horizon, dropping like a flat rock in deep water. The woman turned to look at Halley again, and it was as if the sunset had been absorbed into her eyes, and had speckled them with gold.

"It is good you stated your desire immediately, your wish for me to journey with you. There is great power in knowing what you want, and in speaking it aloud. We will go. But first, if you choose, you and Eden may stay with me here tonight, before we travel on. I have much to speak of with you."

"I feel as if I've known you a long time," Halley said.

"Her name's Jordan," Eden whispered in Halley's ear, breaking her long silence. "She's the one who put up the rope..."

Jordan placed a hand on Eden's shoulder as well.

Halley looked back and forth between the two, with dawning understanding. "You know each other?"

Eden nodded solemnly. "I've known Jordan all my life," she said.

The skin between Halley's eyes creased. "Have I?" she asked Jordan. "Have I known you all my life as well?"

Jordan kept her eyes focused on Halley and did not answer the question immediately; she was comfortable with long silences.

Halley shut her eyes and swallowed. It was the time of immensity, just between the setting of the sun and the onset of night. Halley felt as if she were floating just above the earth; she had a sense of connection to something far larger than herself, pulling her upwards. She opened her eyes to stare at the vista, which was turning from colored to various shades of gray, black and white, and found she knew the answer to her question. "I have known you all my life. I know you, because you are me."

Jordan's eyes twinkled.

Eden leant back behind Jordan to whisper again in Halley's ear, "Can we stay, please? Have you noticed? She's got the kindest eyes."

Halley nodded, a very small, quiet nod. She felt the ground under her once again.

When the sun had fully set, the stars poked white pinholes in the black fabric of the sky, and the three of them stood. Halley and Eden shook their legs, which had cramped from the long time of stillness. Jordan, however, simply arose, and was immediately at ease.

There was a low grumble from somewhere.

Eden giggled. "Was that your stomach?"

Halley looked embarrassed to have broken the mood. "I'm famished," she admitted.

"Ah, that is good," Jordan said. "You will need strength for the rest of your journey, for your return. To assist you, you will also require great warmth tonight. Eden, perhaps you can help?"

Eden giggled. "Sure! I'll get us some food *and* build us a fire."

Turning her back to them, she tossed a small pile of sticks together. She blew on her hands, and the space was filled with the warming light of a fire. Some time later, she presented them with a dinner of root vegetables and rice, served upon huge flat leaves.

The aroma of the simple food made Halley's mouth fill with saliva. The sensation was almost painful.

CHAPTER 57

They began the meal under starlight, sitting in a circle around the fire. Tall flames licked at the bits of broken tree branch, swaying orange, white and red. At the very edges of wood, the flames were a hot blue. The blue drew Halley's gaze, marking, as it did, the line between what was and what was to be.

Jordan interrupted her thoughts. "It is right to ask all your questions."

Halley hesitated, chewed an unfamiliar vegetable, and swallowed. Eating with her fingers was a strangely pleasant sensation. She pinched some rice between two fingers, and placed it in her mouth. Its taste was fresh and cleansing. Licking the stickiness from her fingers, she let her hand rest in her lap. The first question she wanted to ask sounded crazy: *Is all this real?* How could she ask that, when she could feel the earth solid beneath her, could taste the food?

"You must ask the questions."

Halley hesitated. Did she want to know the answers? What would it mean to her, if this weren't real? Would it mean she was crazy? Or, perhaps, dead? She ate another mouthful of rice. She'd spent much of her life avoiding the truth. Not knowing had its costs too. She placed the broad leaf-plate on the ground, and sat up straighter.

"You don't have to stop eating," Eden giggled. "It's not as serious as all that."

Halley didn't smile. Depending on the answer to her question, her whole world could collapse.

Eden picked up the leaf-plate and placed it back on Halley's lap.

The edge of the leaf felt good between her fingertips, real and substantial. She gripped it tightly.

"You must trust. Believe you are strong enough to know the answers to your questions."

"Like a leap of faith?" Halley said.

"Even eagles must take one, the first time they fly."

The words made Halley's ears buzz. She took a drink of water from her canteen, and swallowed hard. "Since I left Fernando at the crossroads-that-was-not-a-crossroads, my journey has been... these people I've met, who knew me, who seemed somehow to *be* me..." Halley stopped. "I knew the waterfall, and the house on the plains. I knew the forest and the wildflowers. And the secret room..." She ran her fingers through her hair, mussing it.

"And..." Jordan prompted her.

Halley let her hands fall to her lap.

Jordan looked at her through clear eyes. The silence held.

"Was it real? Were those people real? Jordan...are you...are you real?"

Jordan held her hands up to the fire to warm them. "Ah, Aki-lina, who is to say what is real? Was your life while you lived with Fernando real, authentic? I think not. How could it have been, when you were not living the truth?"

"Yes, but..."

That wasn't an answer; it was an evasion.

"But you need to know," Jordan said. "This question of real or not is very important to you."

How could it not be? Halley wondered.

"Look at the stars," Jordan said, gesturing with one hand.

Halley looked up. In the towns, the stars were masked by ground light; in the city, they disappeared completely. On this mountain-top, the multitude of stars made the night more light than dark. She had never seen so many at once. This was authentic; this was spectacular. Halley bit the inside of her lip.

"It looks real."

"Then let it be real," Jordan said. "Let it be." She continued to eat, slowly and thoughtfully. "What we imagine as real is only one of a multitude of ways the universe may present itself."

"So..."

"So it is real. I am real."

Halley breathed out a great sigh of relief.

"Thank God," she said. "I couldn't have borne it otherwise."

"Yes, you could have," Jordan said. "You can bear all."

She placed her leaf-plate into the fire and they watched the fire flare up, transforming it into green and gold light.

"But, I...it sounds stupid...but...I need you...it's like, you're my..."

"Be your own hero," Eden interrupted. "You don't need Jordan to be your hero, or anyone else."

Jordan laughed. "Ah, the young – they are close still to the infinite wisdom. If only we could hold onto that as we age, and not have to go through a whole lifetime before remembering such truths."

"I'm not *that* young," Eden protested.

Halley wasn't listening. She wanted to ask a different question, one that mattered deeply, all of a sudden. She rubbed her ring finger, and felt a burning pain in the very center of her chest. "I had a ring. Once. I took it off."

"Do you wish now that you had not?"

Halley looked away; she immediately missed the connection with Jordan's eyes. "I don't know. I can't remember anything about it, except the name Sean and a warm feeling inside when I think of that name."

"You cannot remember, but still, you must decide."

"Decide? What do you mean, 'decide'? Decide what?"

"Whether to wear the ring. Whether to choose to live the life that goes with it. Whether to stay within the circle of the ring."

Halley rubbed her throat, as if to free a voice that had been silent too long. "Yes, I will. I will wear the ring."

The stars glittered.

"You answer too quickly, without thought." Jordan placed her hands on her knees. "First, you must face the reason you took the ring off. Why did you remove it?"

Halley looked into the fire. The answer made the food lose its flavor.

Jordan rested a warm hand on her shoulder.

"You cannot speak the words. Would it help if I were to speak them for you?"

Halley shut her eyes.

"Sean loved you. He treated you well. To him, you were a Queen. But not to yourself. To yourself, you were no Queen."

Halley wrapped her arms around herself, cold in the warmth of the fire.

"You could not allow his love. In your heart, you belonged with one more familiar. More cruel. To a Fernando or a Nick or a Trance. Someone who would hurt you, who would validate for you the way you saw yourself." Jordan paused. "The way you thought your father viewed you – at fault for your mother's death, and deserving of great pain."

Halley opened her eyes. The sky, which had been so full of light just moments ago, was infinite and empty.

Jordan's voice was full of compassion. "You came here to save yourself. Not to save your marriage with Sean." She waited until Halley had again met her eyes. "Love for another does not make you whole. Understand this: you are already whole."

"Then why does the ring seem so vitally important? Why does my chest hurt the way it does?"

Jordan rubbed her hands together, generating heat. "Love does not make you whole. This is true. But it is also true that to accept another's love – to accept that you carry light within you that can be seen and recognized and loved – that, Akilina – that allows you to soar."

Halley placed her hand over her mouth.

"If you believe yourself worthy of great love, yes, you will wear the ring again…"

Eden interrupted in frustration. "But this whole thing wasn't just about some stupid man," she said. "That would be so dumb, to go through all this for a man."

"Ah, Eden, of course not," Jordan said. "It was for Halley, and the horses, and the baby. You – small-girl-soon-to-be-woman – are also wise to ask your questions." She placed a gentle hand on Eden's arm. "You know you are worthy just because you are. It is a fact of your creation. This, you have always known."

"Well, of course…" Eden said.

"Halley had forgotten this worthiness. She had to discover it once more. First, we must love ourselves. When we do, loving another is possible, and right."

"So the stupid man…"

Jordan smiled. "Loving is simply recognizing the spark of light in another, and re-uniting it with that in ourselves. We are already whole; when we love we become holy. We become more connected to the infinite."

"Like, more deeply rooted?" Eden said.

"That is right."

"So…" Eden said, turning to Halley, wanting to get back to basics, "Are you going to put the ring back on?"

Halley looked back and forth between the two of them. "I don't have it."

"Ah, this does not matter. Do you know what it means, to wear it?" Jordan asked.

How can it not matter? She looked inwards anyway. "Wearing the ring means I must tell the truth. I must open myself. I must tell others of what I have learned of myself here."

"This is right, but there is more. Wearing the ring also means you let go forever of unloving lovers who do not satiate your soul."

"You mean Fernando." Halley said. "I let him go."

"That jerk!" said Eden.

"Fernando, and the others that came before, and nearly came after," Jordan clarified. "Do you understand why you were able, finally, to free yourself? Why it was so hard to let go?"

Halley didn't answer.

"It is because you have learned that the light you saw in him – and the others – was your own. You have re-swallowed it: it shines from your very pores. When you look into the smoothness of a river you will see it in the glow of your eyes. It is a beacon to all beings, that light. It was always there, even when you could not see it. It is what drew Sean to you. It is what will make him stay."

"And Nick? Is it what drew Nick?"

"Yes. It drew him as well. The light draws both good and evil – you must be wise, and alert enough to tell which is which."

"Is the light you speak of…is it what I see, when I look at you?"

"Yes. It is your light. Reflected back."

Halley's eyes filled with tears; all that beauty resided in her, and now she knew.

They were all silent for a time.

"What about…" Halley began, and then stopped. Maybe it was too much to ask.

"The baby?" Jordan finished. "Your question is of the baby?"

"It's just…I thought I would find the baby when I got here. When I got to the top of this mountain. But I haven't. And he's not crying anymore…"

"And you want to know…"

"Is it real too?"

"Ah, that is up to you."

"I don't understand."

"Do you still feel the pulse?"

Halley placed a finger to her forehead, where she had felt the pulse of the baby since she had first heard its cry. "Yes," she said, "I still feel it. But why do I feel its pulse there?"

"You feel its pulse here…" Jordan said, placing two warm

fingertips on the center of Halley's forehead, "…because here is your inner eye. It is your physical body's connection to the universal."

"I don't understand. My inner eye?"

"You will understand all, soon, Akilina," Jordan said gently. "You will understand."

That night, Halley and Eden slept a golden sleep, not waking once. All around them was benevolence. Jordan watched them, breathing in and out, breathing life.

PART 4:
DEEP WATER

Her feet were cold. The covers on the bed must have slipped sideways and left her bare feet exposed to the night air. Or maybe they'd left the window open too wide. She moved to get back under the covers, but it was no good – the covers must have slipped all the way off the bed. She shivered. In vain, she tried to snuggle into Sean for warmth. Something was in the way. What was it? It was hard. It was uncomfortable. She wanted to turn on her side, but couldn't. Now her feet weren't just cold – they were freezing. The ceiling of the house was leaking and ice-water was dripping on them – drip, drip, drip. With a muted growl, she tried to stir Sean, to make him give the covers back from his side of the bed. He was always stealing them, and the extra weight on his side made them slip off. But he wouldn't move, not even when she shoved him with her elbow. He was cold too. Why didn't he wake up?

The cold became so intense that it began to feel warm. No, it wasn't warm. It was hot. It was like fire. The fire swept up her Achilles tendons, up her calves and shins. It leapt onto her knee-caps and burnt off her skin. Up and up it went, over her hipbones and across her belly. But it wasn't until it kissed her throat with cold, thin lips that Halley began to rise into consciousness.

Her body felt peculiarly buoyant. *Like floating in bed, how strange…* She sucked in a breath and coughed out furiously – it wasn't air she was breathing, it was water! She tried to breathe again, with the same result. *Drowning, I'm drowning! But… how…I was sleeping, we were in bed…*

But she wasn't sleeping, she wasn't lying down in bed, she was sitting up. *Jesus!* She couldn't move. She was tied down, a rope around her waist. And she was pinned – some dark round object sat heavily on her lap. Wildly, she struggled. The taste of the water was in her mouth, grit and bile and fear, and she couldn't spit it out. She held her breath and instinctively fought to move upwards, shoving her numb hands against what she sat upon. Her head rose above the water line, into the remaining slice of air. She breathed in greedily, like it was the first time she'd ever done so. As she did, she became fully and terribly conscious.

"Oh my God," she whispered.

She was staring through the windscreen of the car, which was criss-crossed with fine lines – it had broken, but not shattered. Instantly, she remembered: the suspension bridge and the truck swerving into her lane; the moment of collision; the sensation of flying, bird-like, through the air.

She looked over at Sean – his chin was slumped onto his chest, but his height had kept his face clear of the water. "Sean!" *Oh Jesus, oh Sean…oh no!*

There was blood on his face. She reached for him but when she took her hands from the seat, her head slid back under water. She shoved herself back up, coughing hard.

"Sean! Sean!" she shouted, trying to wake him.

He wasn't moving, except for the blood that ran down his face through a gash in his forehead. He must have hit the windscreen. His eyes were shut, his skin, where it wasn't bloody, was grey. *I can't tell if he's alive.*

Using one hand to keep her head above water, she put the other to his chest, slipping it between the buttons of his shirt. He was so cold. But her hand rose slightly – he was still breathing. And the cut on his forehead was still bleeding – that meant he wasn't dead, didn't it? In the muffled silence of the car, she heard him take a slim labored breath. *Thank God.* The breath shuddered, stopped. Her hand on his chest lay still. An awful silence filled the car.

"I don't know what to do," she said.

Something inside her squirmed in delight. *Trance!* She pressed her hand down through the water onto the car seat, hard.

"Shut up," she said, "just shut up." A shudder passed through the base of her skull. Even underwater, even in the doomed car, with death fluttering its cold wings about her, she remembered to stay vigilant: he still must be contained.

"We will be all right," she said. Her words held the aura of gold about them; the tone of her voice was rich and melodic, a river-voice.

Taking her hand from Sean's chest, she searched underwater for her seatbelt latch and clicked it open. It made no sound. *Hurry, got to hurry.* She checked Sean again; there was no sign of breathing. *In six minutes, he'll be brain-damaged. Or dead! Get the door open! Get him out!* The door handle slipped in her grasp. She got hold of it and pulled it hard upwards. The door wouldn't open. *The pressure! The water pressure is too much. Got to let more water in, even it out.* She cranked the window open a slit. *Not too much water – not to the roof or he'll drown.*

She turned to Sean – he had begun to breathe again, with a thin whistling sound. He didn't move. The breath came at irregular intervals, and was too shallow.

The water flowed into the car through the window, raising the level slowly. *Too slowly. He could stop breathing again.* Sucking in a full breath, she stopped her throat like she did when swimming underwater. Then she quickly opened the window the rest of the way. Water flooded the car furiously. The car filled to the roof, the air bubble sliding out through the window like a fat round fish.

Sean's lungs would, even now, be filling with water. *No,* she thought, remembering her First Aid, *his throat will spasm and shut his airway, but only for a short while. Got to get him up. Not much time.* Instinctively, she pressed the timer button on her bright orange sportswatch – she had to know how much time was slipping by. The watch face lit up in the murky darkness.

Moving out from under the steering wheel, she quickly dragged herself through the water, over Sean's immobile form.

His seatbelt wouldn't open. Anger gave her power. With a fast move, she unbuttoned the small knife from her pocket and cut the seat belt in half. She checked her watch: twenty seconds had passed.

The manual lock on his door lifted with reassuring ease. The door handle, though, wouldn't budge. Growing desperate, she jerked it upwards. It snapped off. *What next!* She swung back to her side of the car but that door too was stuck fast. Forcing her movement to be slow, she gentled the handle upwards, as she would a reluctant horse into a horsebox. With huge relief, she felt a click. The door was going to open. She pushed at it, but it still wouldn't budge. *Hell with gentle!* Flipping her body around, she slammed at the door with both feet, once, twice, three times. The door sprung open, swirling dirt from the river bed around in the water. A surprisingly pleasant sensation of shadow and darkness slid down her spine.

Grabbing at the collar of Sean's shirt, she dragged him out. The buoyancy of the water made him surprisingly light. Once free of the vehicle, she quickly looped her arm around his body under the arm pits, hugging him tightly to her. She checked her watch: forty-five seconds gone.

At the depths of the river bed, the water was black, too dark to see. She shoved her feet against the roof of the car, and followed the bubbles of her breath upwards, kicking her way toward the surface.

It was so very far to travel.

After a few seconds, the water began to change color. It became a dirty green, then aqua, and then almost clear. And then she was looking up, holding tightly to Sean, not letting him go, and she could see the light of a circular yellow object. It was surrounded by an aura of thin lines, shining through the topmost layer of water. *The sun!* With a powerful final kick, she burst through the surface, gasping deeply.

What relief she felt was short-lived – Sean was unconscious.

His head lolled to one side. Without the underwater buoyancy, he trebled in weight. Keeping her grip, she dragged him, cursing aloud at the difficulty, towards the shore. "Hold on! You're going to make it. I *won't* let you go!" She spoke as if he could hear her.

The current had moved her close to the bank, and in only a few moments she was feeling the weedy river bed under her feet. The seconds raced by as she slipped on the weeds and loose mud, her boots sliding and Sean dropping back into the water. He was so heavy. *Help me...someone help me!* The urgency of her need gave her strength. With a final heave, she moved Sean onto the hard, slanting river bed. His head and chest rested above the water.

Quickly, she turned him on his side. She opened his airway, clearing his mouth. The grit of river water ran over her hand, and he reflexively vomited the contents of his stomach. She swept out his mouth again, fighting back her own vomit. His tongue felt lifeless. With a shove, she returned him to his back. Tilting his head back, she confirmed that his airway was clear. *Stay calm,* she told herself, as her heart pounded. Holding her ear near his nose, she listened for breath. No sound. She watched his chest – it didn't rise. *Five breaths, then check for a pulse. No pulse!* "You are *not* leaving me!" she said. She checked her watch: two long minutes had gone by already.

Halley began the resuscitation, forcing Sean's heart to pump, forcing her breath into his lungs. *One, two, three, four.* The silver bracelet banged back and forth against her wrist bone. *Breathe, please breathe.* She used the timer on her watch to time the chest compressions.

She worked, and while she did, she had a vision of a mountaintop, of eagles, of the color orange, and she focused her mind on it, was there, as her body pumped life back into Sean. "Come... come see it with me..." she whispered.

Halley sat up quickly to see whether Sean had begun breathing. She put her ear next to his nose and listened. *Nothing.* Her desire to see him awaken was overpowering. She looked at the thin skin of his eyelids. There was a quick darting movement of his eyes under the lids, like he was dreaming.

"Yes! Come back! Come back!"

A moment later, he was conscious, sitting halfway up, gagging and coughing. With a violent wrenching of his upper body, he vomited the rest of the river water, and coughed his lungs clear. It took several minutes. Halley supported him at his shoulders, sitting on her knees beside him. Through his cold wet shirt, she could feel the warmth of life returning. She took one hand to her mouth, and fought back her tears. He sat with his head between his knees for several minutes, half in and half out of the river.

"Thank God," she whispered, looking upwards. "Thank God, you're alive..."

"Thank *you*," he said.

Gently, she helped rinse his face and upper chest. It was like a baptism. When they were done, they moved from the water onto the dry grass, Halley supporting him on her arm. They collapsed down on their backs next to one another, exhausted.

In a little while, Halley leaned up on one elbow and looked at Sean. His eyes were closed and he was breathing slowly. She ran a finger tenderly over the late-afternoon stubble on his cheeks. His reflexive smile made small apples in his cheeks, and she kissed each one. Unexpectedly, she began to giggle. The sound surprised her as much as the thought that had triggered it: *kicking open the car door was kind of fun.* She surrendered to the giggle, and felt it expand in her belly to a full-blown laugh.

Sean's eyes opened. He looked at her in wonderment. Then he kissed her hard on the lips, and joined her in laughter.

The air took on a clearer quality, and for a moment, Halley let herself think of all the things that, together, they still would do.

"I knew you would do it. I knew you would save us."

They heard a rustle of leaves. In the forest nearby, Halley saw a little girl watching them, dressed in the greens and browns of the woods. On one shoulder, the girl carried a tiny golden monkey, and on the other, an eagle. The monkey made a sound, *ch ch ch ch ch*, and the little girl giggled, as if they were sharing a great joke. The eagle screamed, as if in triumph, and the little girl covered her ears with a laugh, as she moved into the woods.

"Eden," Halley said.

"It's a bit like that, isn't it?" Sean replied.

Halley looked at him quizzically. "Oh. Oh, yes. Like the Garden of Eden. That's right." Her hand brushed the edge of something soft. It was a horse blanket, monogrammed with the letter A.

"That's lucky."

"What?"

"I guess she forgot her blanket."

They were wet and it was getting cold. They wrapped up in the blanket, their combined body heat quickly warming them.

PART 5:
EPILOGUE

SIX MONTHS LATER

Early on a winter's evening, Halley and Sean were sitting at the pinewood table in the newly renovated house, drinking strong coffee. Outside, snow was falling.

"I can't believe you never told me about this house before," Sean said. "It's fantastic. And once I get the extension built..." His green eyes looked towards the future.

"Underfloor heating and a fireplace, right?"

He nodded.

"It'll be cozy as a dream," Halley said, rubbing her swelling belly.

"Much better than our old place in the city," he continued. "Plenty of room for kids."

Halley looked up and laughed. "Kids, plural? Hmm. Let's get this one out first, hey?"

He put his hand on hers. "We are so very lucky. We could have lost him in the accident."

Halley placed a fingertip in the center of her forehead, feeling the pulse there again, strong and sure. "It still seems so strange. I felt it the moment we got back to shore. Somehow, I knew it meant I was pregnant."

"Good thing the paramedics got there so fast."

Halley changed the subject. "You know, this house is a lot closer to my work than our old place. I've got lots of ideas for new wilderness hikes."

Sean didn't answer. He smoothed the creases from the paper, removed the classified sections, and spread the rest of the sections out on the pinewood table. When he looked up, his eyes were serious. "Those hikes are part of what makes you who you are. I'm glad you're going to do them again, especially after all that's happened."

"Me too."

The Sunday paper was thick with promise. Halley focused on the book section and then on the comics. Her giggling kept interrupting Sean's more serious perusal of the news.

Time passed, and evening fell. The lamp above the pine-wood table encircled them in an intimate pool of yellow light.

"What are you reading?" Halley said.

Sean looked up. Wordlessly, he passed the paper over to her.

She rested both hands flat on the paper and leaned forward. In the photo, Nick was ten years older than she remembered him, but there was no mistaking him. He still wore the red-checked shirt, but it was stained and torn in several places. His eyes held madness.

Sean got up and wrapped his arms around her. She held onto him like she would a life preserver in deep water.

They stared at the headline together. "Nick the Knifer Gets Life for Brutal Murder of Three, and Attempted Murder of Star Witness."

The details of the trial, kept from the media until a final verdict was reached, were finally revealed. The murders had been easy for the police to link, it said. In each case, the victim had been strangely mutilated, her right arm carved with three parallel lines. A friend of one of the victims was quoted in the article: "Shirley said he called them 'love lines', told her to think of them as a love tattoo." Shirley disappeared shortly after the friend noticed the mutilation. Three weeks later, she was found murdered. The story was the same for the other two women. All had been in their early twenties.

Halley held her mug of coffee tightly. A small paragraph at the end of the story told the rest. Nick had confessed, with some pride, at nearly killing the Prosecution's best witness, Halley.

But you didn't. That's what matters. She turned her arm to face upwards, pushed up her sleeve, and looked at the scars. *I was one of the lucky ones. I got away.* She took a deep breath, and turned the paper over.

346

"Your testimony is what got him put away," Sean said. "You know, you are the bravest person I've ever known."

Halley smiled as he held her close.

TWO YEARS LATER

Late on a warm summer afternoon, Halley, Sean, and little Jake drove into town.

"Let's split up – I want to get back in time to see the sunset," Halley said.

"Great idea. I'll get the fencing planks from *Sam's*. You get the groceries. Meet you back here in, say, twenty minutes?" He smiled a challenge. "Bet I beat you!"

Halley laughed. "Come on, Jake, it's a race!"

The two of them darted away, reaching *Annie's* in moments.

Annie's was the local grocery. The shop was, of course, named after Annie herself. The small town of Westwood had an *Annie's* and a *Lennie's* and a *Sam's*; in fact, the bank – The National Bank – was the only business in the whole town without a living namesake. It made the locals slightly doubtful about placing their money there.

Halley opened the door, the metal bell tingling invitingly. Entering *Annie's* was like stepping back to a simpler time. Here, she could still sit on a red stool at an old-fashioned counter and have a real egg-cream-soda in a tall cold metal cup, legs dangling. *Annie's* was always cool inside, even on the hottest days, even without air conditioning. The floor was, as always, dusty from hiking boots, but the goods and counters were spotless, just like Annie in her clean white apron. They walked the short distance to the front counter. "Hey you," Halley said, seeing Annie.

"Halley and Jake!" Annie bent down and held out her arms. "Come here and let me give you a kiss, you little angel…"

Jake held back, wrapped his little arms all the way around Halley's leg and tucked his face into the denim of her jeans.

"Sorry," Halley said. "He won't have anything to do with anyone but me and Sean lately." She looked down at Jake and tousled his fine brown hair which was still warm from the sun. "It's pretty nice, really…"

Annie laughed. "Why don't you go look around the aisles so poor Jake can relax – I'll clean you up some fish for dinner. It's fresh today." She shooed them with her hands.

"Fish fish fish," Jake chanted.

"That's right, Jake, fish," Halley said. "Good talking, my love."

Annie bent down to the fish display and disappeared from view. Slowly, Jake peeled himself from Halley's legs, taking a careful look to make sure Annie was gone. "Candy?" he said softly, pointing up at the counter.

Halley handed him a bite-sized piece from the complimentary plate Annie left on the counter for just such small customers. It was gone in seconds.

"T'ank you," Jake said with a broad grin, highlighting his tiny teeth that were now liberally covered in chocolate. He pointed away from Annie's counter, and said, "Go." Halley held both his small hands and they toddled their way down the wide aisle.

The metal doorbell clanged harshly, as if the door had been opened too fast. A hot blast of air overtook them.

"Halley?"

The voice sent a shock through her. Her face grew warm. Even after all these years, she would've known the sound of him anywhere. She recalled the familiar litany she hadn't thought of in years: the tango; the color red; the taste of mangoes. She rolled the words around on her tongue and was surprised – they tasted sour, like a green apple. Like ancient history. *Modern history*, she corrected herself. She squeezed Jake's tiny hands to bring herself back to the present.

"Halley!" the voice called again. It was more insistent this time.

Halley stopped walking, and leaned down to Jake.

"Want to be carried?" she said.

"Up, mama, up!"

Jake stretched himself to his full height, both arms reaching towards the ceiling.

His enthusiasm brought back her smile. When she had him in her arms, she turned around. She wore her son like a security blanket. Jake, in turn, hugged Halley tightly, facing away so as not to have to see this other stranger.

"Hello, Fernando." The name felt unfamiliar on her lips. Jake hugged her tighter, and Halley could feel his small arms wrap uncomfortably around the back of her neck. "What are you doing here?"

"I thought it was you! You look gorgeous," Fernando said. His black eyes shone. "Your clothes and your hair and your eyes… It's been what, three years?" He paused, searching her face. "You don't look very happy to see me…"

"What are you doing here?" she repeated.

"I'm leading a group into the woods for an overnighter," he said, as if it were the most natural thing in the world.

Why here? Their home had been hours away, and there was nothing unique about this spot. *Why did he have to show up here?*

Fernando took a step forward. Halley whispered into Jake's ear; he shook his head sharply and hung on tight. Halley whispered again and kissed the top of his head; he nodded, and let himself be put down. She stood a little taller, while Jake made immediately for Halley's offer – the lowest shelf of goods, full of individually wrapped toilet paper rolls. "Tower," he said to himself. "Build tower."

Halley swallowed hard and glanced up at the ceiling. She wanted to ignore Fernando, to walk out of the store and never have to speak to him again. But that would be wrong.

"It's great to see you again," Fernando said, talking fast, as if he sensed she might just turn and walk away. "We've got lots to catch up on. How about a coffee? Can we get a good espresso here?" He looked around the shop, and then his eyes fixed on Jake. "Or...?"

Jake looked up at him suddenly. "Jerk," he said.

Fernando's mouth dropped open.

Halley bit her lip to keep from laughing. "He's just starting to talk," she said. "He doesn't really know what he's saying."

Fernando held her eyes; he wasn't listening to her explanation.

The mirth left her. She crossed her arms in front of her chest. 'It's good to see you too," she began. "No. That's not what I want to say."

She was silent for a moment, looking down at Jake, who had very carefully emptied the bottom shelf nearest her. He'd lost all interest in Fernando – sometimes it happened this way too, instead of being anxious about strangers, he just grew bored of them. "Big tower," he said reflectively. She looked back at Fernando. "I don't know what to say. It's been so long." For the first time, she looked Fernando over carefully, as if with a searchlight. He soaked up the attention.

"What is it?" he finally said. He was frowning.

"Nothing. Just..."

As hard as she looked, she couldn't find what she was looking for. Although he was as handsome as ever, the brilliance that had stunned her into hero-worship was gone. *It's mine again, the brilliance – the light. It's mine again.* She was smiling. Fernando had become nothing more than a good-looking man. *A fellow human being who deserves compassion,* she corrected herself. "Sorry," she said, shaking her head. "You're right. It has been a long time."

"So...about that coffee?" His tone was suggestive, and she sensed he was certain that she would say yes.

Halley breathed deeply. "No, I can't do that. I'm married now. Besides, I'm not who...I'm not what you're looking for." She paused, and her eyes rested on her silver bracelet, before she looked back up at him. "But know this. I forgive you."

Something broke in Fernando's face, and he shut his eyes. "I've waited a long time to hear you say that." They were silent. When he opened his eyes again, all the swagger had left him. He swallowed. "Is this..." He gestured towards Jake, who had built his tower to a height of four toilet rolls and was just about to kick them over.

"This is the baby from the woods."

A shadow passed across his face, as if he were calculating when he had seen her last, and whether this baby could be his.

"My husband's son," she clarified. "My son."

Fernando nodded.

"You look sad," Halley said.

"I messed up, big-time."

"You didn't mess up."

"Aren't you angry?" He was incredulous. "You should be furious at the way I left you...on a trail you didn't know, deep in the woods." He shook his head. "I was so angry at you for acting crazy, for going on and on about hearing that baby crying...for everything..." He looked down at Jake. "I didn't remember I'd taken the map out of your backpack until I got home. I went back to find you, I swear I did. But...you'd gone...I couldn't even find your tracks..." A shattered look came into his eyes. "You never came home..."

"I was angry when you left," she said. "I was furious. For a while. But when you left me, I found myself." She paused, and then gestured to Jake. "And him. I found him." Tears of joy filled her eyes. "How can I be angry, when I'm so very blessed?"

Their eyes held for a moment, until Halley very gently took hers away.

"Don't...don't go," Fernando said.

Halley heard the pain in his voice, and touched him gently on the arm. "You don't need me." She took a step back. "What you see in me, you'll see, one day, in yourself. Goodbye Fernando."

Fernando couldn't find anything else to say.

"Come on, Jake," Halley said, bending down and kissing his soft baby cheek. "Time to get back to Da Da." She helped him put the toilet paper rolls back on the shelf.

The little boy held her fingers tightly, as if she were his whole world. "Da Da," he repeated.

"That's right," she said with a broad smile. "The best Da Da in the whole world."

Still holding fingers, they walked four-legged down the aisle, completely in synch, looping back up the next aisle to pick up the fish and say goodbye to Annie.

"Friend of yours?" Annie asked, gesturing to Fernando, who was still standing where she'd left him, as if mesmerized.

Halley gave her a half-smile. "A very old friend. Be kind."

Just before the door swung shut, Halley heard Annie say, "Get you something, Sir?" in that tone she used with dubious strangers.

* * *

"It's all about choices, Jake," Halley said, as they moved through the nearly-empty parking lot. "It's all about choosing well, and then sticking with your good choices."

"Ma Ma," Jake said, and squeezed her hands tightly.

"Jake and Sean," she replied, looking down at his tiny hands and her gold wedding band. "My best choices."

With a walk that felt to her like floating on air currents, they made their way to the car. Sean was waiting for them, leaning against the car door with a lazy smile. He'd won the race! He leaned inside the car, and turned up the radio so she could hear. He was playing her favorite song.

THE END

APPENDIX

Symbols and Archetypes in *Akilina*

Carp: there is a legendary saying that if the carp can swim up the fast-flowing Hwang Ho River in China, it can become a dragon. Thus, the carp is symbolic of strength. When Trance kills the carp by the river, it is a direct threat to Halley's strength and regenerative powers.

Cicada: an ancient Chinese symbol for perseverance, immortality and life-after-death. It is an appropriate creature to intrigue Halley, who, through most of the novel, is living in the nether-world between life and death.

Crow and Crow's feather: while a negative symbol in many Western cultures, the crow is intended to be a positive harbinger here. In China and Japan, the crow shows love and filial gratitude, while in ancient Greece, the crow was worshipped for its oracular powers. In this novel, the crow brings Halley the message "You will be all right", which is indeed prophetic. When the crow's feather disappears, it is a potent symbol of danger.

Eagle: Halley's true nature or totemic animal is the eagle. The eagle is renowned for its courage, ferocity and strength. In some cultures the eagle symbolizes resurrection and rebirth.

Horse (**Athena**): the horse is often an emblem of speed and perseverance. Here, it is also symbolic of Halley's lost intuitive powers. Athena was named by Halley's father after Athena, the Greek goddess of wisdom and war. The name means "protector of heroes".

Lion-monkeys: based upon the Golden Lion Tamarin, one of the most endangered species in the world, and native to Brazil. They are symbolic of the help of wild things in the forest.

Red: the color red symbolizes happiness, and is a lucky color.

Shadow: a Jungian concept, the shadow has been defined as an unconscious complex that is the exact opposite of the conscious self. It is what we don't want to acknowledge about ourselves and everything that we are not. It is often uncivilized, and conceals those things we are ashamed of and don't want to know about ourselves. Trance is Halley's shadow, brought to life. His most enduring characteristic is his desire to kill Halley, because he cannot bear her light. She must integrate her shadow within her psyche to have the full power of which she is capable.

Silver bracelet: the wave pattern on the bracelet is symbolic of the life-death-life nature of the world (e.g., spring vs. autumn, light vs. dark, day vs. night, waves vs. troughs). It was thrown away by Nick in "the time before" when Halley was innocent. She discovers it on her journey, and it stirs her first memory of that time.

Snakes: snakes, while often feared, can represent transformation, knowledge and wisdom. They are also thought to be indicative of self-renewal and positive changes. Here, though Halley is frightened by the snakes she encounters, they are a sign of her awakening, and, indeed, becoming awake is often terrifying at first.

Sparrow: the nickname for Halley during a powerless phase of her life. She has to let go of the emotional connection to this creature and just let it be what it is, a small miracle of perfection.

Unicorn horn: it is said that a unicorn can restore purity to a poisoned stream by simply dipping in its horn. The unicorn horn here is used to help neutralize Gail's fury. It represents purity and innocence.

Characters in *Akilina*

Elements of Halley:
- Halley: the heroine. Age 35
- Hope: Halley at age 22. Part of Halley became stuck at this point in her development because of a suppressed memory of abuse. Only by recovering this memory can she recover her powers of intuition and decisiveness.
- Eden: Halley at age 10. Eden possesses all of Halley's knowledge, with the exception of the things Halley herself has suppressed. Her giggle is symbolic of the joy of youth.
- Little One: Halley at age 5. Halley is stuck at this point because she never let go of guilt over her mother's death (cancer), and fear of her father's fury.
- Trance: Halley's Shadow or dark side, as well as her power. Ageless.
- Gail: Halley's fury. Garnered across an entire life of abuse, but her appearance here centers around Halley's leaving Fernando. Ageless.
- Monster in basement: Halley's intuition warning her of severe danger.
- Jordan: Halley's higher self, closest to God and infinitely wise and kind.

Other characters:
- Sean: Halley's husband of two years, her passenger in the car crash.
- Fernando: Halley's lover before Sean, when she was 29. Her journey into the nether-world begins when he leaves her, and she chooses not to follow because she has heard a

baby cry, and feels compelled to find it. He is the last in a series of abusive lovers.

- Nick: Halley's lover when she was 22. Psychotic and source of suppressed memory of abuse.
- Jake: Sean and Halley's son, and the baby from the woods.
- Dad: Halley's real father and also the archetype of the ideal father in Halley, after her real father has died. In the nether-world, he is a guide and authority figure.
- Annie: proprietor of *Annie's*, the local grocery store.

www.ingramcontent.com/pod-product-compliance
Lightning Source LLC
Chambersburg PA
CBHW051226260626
47162CB00002B/298